a legends of lobe den herr

fourth
Point
of
Contact

the warden and the general
book One

aj sherwood

This is a work of fiction. Names, characters, places and incidents either are the product of the author's imagination or are used fictitiously, and any resemblance to actual persons, living or dead, business establishments, events or locales is entirely coincidental.

FOURTH POINT OF CONTACT
The Warden and the General Book One
A Legends of Lobe Den Herren Novel

PRINTING HISTORY
October 2018

Copyright © 2018 by AJ Sherwood
Cover by Katie Griffin

All rights reserved.

No part of this book may be reproduced,scanned, or distributed in any printed or electronic form without permission. Please do not participate in or encourage electronic piracy of copyrighted materials in violation of the author's rights.

Purchase only authorized editions.

www.ajsherwood.com

Books by AJ Sherwood

Legends of Lobe Den Herren

<u>The Warden and the General</u>
Fourth Point of Contact

Jon's Mysteries

Jon's Downright Ridiculous Shooting Case*

A Sorcerer's Grimoire

A Non-Comprehensive Guide to Sea Serpents*

*Coming soon

prologue

The nightlife in Hashilin City didn't match up with Ren's memories anymore. It used to be lively with a throng of people coming and going, foreigners mixed into the crowd; geishas strolling slowly along advertising for their brothels; rich and spicy scents pouring out of doorways, luring hungry customers into the restaurants.

Now the streets seemed dead in comparison. Hardly anyone walked down them, and while he still saw foreigners, they were all in military uniform of some sort. Perhaps the rapidly cooling weather could be blamed for it, as fall threatened to turn into winter, but Ren didn't think it that cold. He felt perfectly warm in his coat. They passed a few geishas, but Ren had no interest in them, his nose hunting for the elusive scent of food. Someone had scrounged up enough paper lanterns to illuminate the main street, so there was light to navigate by, but half the stores still bore war-ravaged destruction. Ren felt a little bad about it—of the opinion they somehow should have fully protected at least this city—but in truth, they'd pulled off miracles just preserving half of it. This section near the docks had been hit the hardest, the buildings bearing testimony with their scorched walls, boarded up windows, and half-collapsed frames.

A shoulder bumped into his and he glanced up at his companion with a smile that strained at the seams. "I know, I know, we won the war. I should be happy. And I am happy it's over, but it basically destroyed my country, and I can't be happy about that."

Brahms listened to him patiently, as he always did, not condemning Ren for his somber mood. The man was an exceptionally good listener. Well, to put it more frankly, he was a terrible communicator.

General Arman Brahms didn't care to use more than twenty words at any given time, no matter how important or vital the reason, and Ren was convinced that if Brahms said more than five hundred words in a day, the man would collapse on the spot.

Thinking back to their first meeting, Ren felt his smile go more natural. "You know, when the war first started and you and I were assigned to the northern front together, I really didn't know what to do with you. Don't give me that look, you know very well what I'm talking about. I thought at first you didn't really talk because you didn't understand the language, which is why I went through all the time and effort to learn *your* language—which turned out to be completely unnecessary. You still wouldn't say more than two words to me."

Amused, Brahms gave him a slight shrug. "Didn't need to talk."

"No, you really did, you just didn't want to. And yes, I learned how to read those facial twitches that you deem expressions, but I had to learn how to read you or we would have lost the damn war," Ren informed him in exasperation. "Seriously, even when you were explaining some tactic or strategy to me, I had to guess half of what you meant!"

Brahms patted his shoulder in a consoling way, the glint in his eyes making it clear he was mocking him. "You did fine."

"I have no idea why we are friends," Ren retorted to the open air, as clearly he wasn't going to get any sympathy from the other general. "Aside from fighting, we have absolutely nothing in common. I like men, you like women. I like spicy food, you can't tolerate it at all. Oh no, you can't feign otherwise, I'm onto you. The last time we ate together, that meal gave you serious indigestion. You went even more expressionless than usual trying to hide it—which scared me, by the way, I thought I had lost my ability to read you overnight. Speaking of which, will you please tell me what you want to eat? Our options, as always, are limited to noodles, dons, or soups."

With a shrug, Brahms gestured toward him with a small wave of the hand.

"No. No, I am not picking where to eat tonight, I have picked the last three times. It is your turn. I'm tired, I don't want to make any decisions, and this is quite possibly our last meal together." That last sentence hurt a little, as Ren honestly wasn't looking forward to their parting. As much as this man sometimes aggravated him, he could honestly say he'd never had a truer friend. It would feel like losing a part of himself when Brahms left.

A stubborn look morphed over Brahms' face, a set to the jaw that he knew well. "Not the last."

Ren's attention sharpened on him. They were in-between lanterns at the moment, the light soft and dim, which naturally made his hard-to-read friend even more enigmatic. Ren resisted the urge to pull him into stronger lighting. "What do you mean? You ship out in three days, you shouldn't even be taking two hours away from your troops right now to eat with me; you can't possibly think you can pull this off again."

Frustrated, Brahms grabbed Ren by the arm and towed him into the nearest restaurant, which turned out to be a noodle shop half-crammed with customers. Absolutely no stools remained empty near the bar, but fortunately Brahms ignored that half of the room and went to the tables on the right, sitting them both on the waiting flat cushions.

Ren folded his legs comfortably up underneath him, used to the low tables and cushions, although Brahms had to put his back to the wall and stretch his legs out. He was too tall to possibly fit, even if he could cross his legs comfortably. Ren thought himself to be a tall man, but Brahms topped him by another hand's span, which made maneuvering about in Shiirei challenging for someone of his height. When settled, he faced Ren square on, that strong jaw of his still set in a stubborn jut. Uncharacteristically, he spoke in Ren's native tongue, as if he wished to make sure Ren properly understood him. The words sounded a little strange and stilted in his mouth, a catch in his deep voice betraying his emotions. "I want you to come with me."

"You want me to come with you," Ren repeated, trying to make sense of those words. Granted, he'd been discharged from the Shiirei Royal Army last week, so he was certainly free to do whatever he wished. Brahms knew this, just as he knew that Ren had lingered here in the city because he didn't know what to do. His hometown had burnt to cinders during the war, and his pay wouldn't last him long enough to afford a career change, as they hadn't been given full pay. And what was a discharged general supposed to do for work? Ren knew precious little except fighting and strategy.

He could understand Brahms' unease in leaving Ren here. Ren felt it himself. But still.... "You want me to come with you as what? A male war bride? Don't give me that 'you're being obtuse look,' you are in fact being more cryptic than normal. Use your words."

A little agitated, Brahms ran a hand roughshod through his wavy hair, eyes tight at the corners. He opened the top button of his green coat, releasing the high collar enough that he could comfortably breathe and finally opened his mouth. "Ren, you can't stay here. There's no place for you. Come home with me, become a citizen of my country."

Beyond touched, Ren lost his irritation, feeling his heart warm. "You'd sponsor me?"

He got that 'you're being obtuse' look again.

Ren had called this man a brother-in-arms before, and meant it, but he'd never quite known what Brahms had thought of him in return until this moment. He saw concern and determination in those clear blue eyes mixed with a healthy dose of affection. He resisted the urge to hug the stuffing out of him. There were enough rumors about them already; Brahms didn't need Ren to further muddy the waters. "I'm beyond touched, really, that you want to keep me with you. But I refuse to be dependent on you forever, you know that, right? Good, glad you do. So I assume that you have some thought of what I can do in your country. Let's hear it."

"My country wasn't impacted directly by the war," Brahms pointed out, "except in loss of manpower."

"You think if you sponsor me I can join the Aart Royal Army?" Certainly the idea held considerable appeal. Aart was one of the wealthier countries, and also one of the few whose location was far enough removed from the battles that it had suffered no direct damage. If its economy didn't hinge on the spice trade, it wouldn't have gotten involved in the war at all. "Aren't you taking that a little on faith? I know you lost a lot of men over here, but Aart's a big country; it can draw more troops out of the rising generation. They're not necessarily going to need a former Shiirein general."

"Backup plan: I hire you. Remember where my home sits."

Ah yes. He'd never seen it with his own eyes, of course, but he'd been told about it one rainy afternoon as they whiled away the time. Brahms descended from a long line of soldiers out of necessity. His land sat on the very eastern border against an antsy neighbor. Brahms Fortress was the first line of defense, and those defenses were tested regularly—whenever their Zaytsevian neighbors got bored or desperate enough to give invasion another try. Considering his location, and the potential for trouble, his friend could certainly justify hiring a castle warden.

Ren leaned both elbows on the table, propping his chin on folded hands, and considered the matter carefully. He saw no downsides to this—well no, there was one. Aart's culture didn't have same-sex relationships. Not that it was forbidden, or illegal, it was just unheard of. When Ren and Brahms had first met, he'd had to explain the concept, and even now Brahms didn't really get it. He didn't treat Ren any differently for his sexual orientation, but that was probably because he didn't understand it and chose to just accept it. If Ren went home with him, it would probably mean being celibate for the rest of his life, or at least for as long as he lived in Aart. That was not at all enticing. Ren was a people person, always had been, and the idea of not having any chance of companionship did not make his libido happy.

Then again, if he stayed, the situation would be much grimmer. He tugged absently on his ponytail, pondering the main problem. Shiirei had little in the way of crops, as they'd been fighting all year, and what crops had been planted were destroyed in the war. Some of their allied countries were shipping food in, but that would take months to arrive and likely inadequate to feed a whole country. Food was scarce, money scarcer, and work nearly impossible to find. If he stayed, he'd likely end up living on his brother's charity, and Takahiro didn't have enough money to feed his own family at the moment. The question really boiled down to this: which was more important to him, sex or food?

It didn't take much of a debate.

Brahms probably hadn't thought of that wrinkle, and Ren wasn't about to bring it up, as his sex life (or lack thereof) was his own business. Celibacy wouldn't kill him, and Brahms' offer was more than generous—definitely the best he'd ever get. Ren would be a fool to pass it up; his pride just smarted a little from accepting this kind of help from a friend. He dropped his hands to the table, a sigh escaping him. Not that he didn't need it at the moment, but still, that pride was strong, and kept him from readily agreeing.

"Renjimantoro."

Ren's head snapped up, as Brahms only used his full name when being completely serious.

Those dark blue eyes met his levelly, penetratingly, as if he could see every thought going through Ren's head. And he likely could. The man was exceptionally good at seeing through people. "Come with me."

Oh hell. He really had no defenses against that plea. Brahms rarely asked anything of him, and every time he had, it turned out to be for Ren's own good. "You realize that if I go, your reputation is never going to recover. People assume I've seduced you over to my side as it is."

Brahms just stared at him.

"Right, you don't care. Of course you don't, silly me, why am I worrying about it?" Relief filled him, making him a little giddy with it, and he had the strangest urge to giggle. Which wasn't manly, he stamped that out immediately, but still a grin took over his face. "Alright, alright, I'll go home with you."

For the first time in the year that they'd known each other, a true smile broke out over Brahms' face, lighting up his entire expression and wiping five years away, making him look twenty again. Ren swallowed hard seeing it, amazed that it meant so much to him for Ren to go. He would never be Ren's lover, but that didn't mean there was no love there, just a different type. A strong bond forged in fire, conflict, and a true desire to understand each other.

Really, he couldn't ask for any more than this.

The smile faded into a look of supreme contentment. Brahms gave him a satisfied nod. "Good. Pack up tomorrow. I'll arrange ship's passage."

"I will." Realizing that they didn't have the luxury of just sitting here waiting on a waitress, Ren lifted up onto his knees and signaled a very harried looking teenage girl, clearly one of his countrymen. Odds were she wouldn't speak anything but her native tongue, and Brahms' accent was thick enough to give people trouble, so Ren took on the job of ordering for both of them.

She gave them a slight bow and asked, "What would you like?"

"A bowl of noodles for my friend—"

"Shirachi soup," Brahms cut in firmly.

Rolling his eyes, Ren asked in exasperation, "Seriously? We're doing this? There is nothing wrong with being spice intolerant, everyone has different tastes; just because I like it—do not glare at me like that. I am trying to save you from indigestion. I hate it when you get stubborn like this; it's always over the stupidest things. Fine, fine, be up all night with an upset stomach. It's not my stomach, I don't care. Waitress, two bowls of shirachi soup, please."

Hiding a smile, she ducked her head and scurried off toward the back, putting their order in.

Ren shook his head, wondering again, how they were friends. They couldn't be more different. Brahms fit the archetype of his people to a T—big as a mountain, bulky with muscle, and a chiseled bone structure that could be hewn from granite. Ren almost felt small next to him sometimes, as he stood a half-head shorter, was lean with compact muscle, and could be carried without any real effort on Brahms' part. (He knew that for a fact because of the one time he'd been shot in the leg.) With Ren's slanted, dark eyes, long jet-black hair pulled into a high pony tail, and fair skin, they were polar opposites in looks. Even their personalities lay on different ends of the spectrum, with Ren being a chatterbox and Brahms the strong, silent type.

Everyone wondered how they got along, why they were so close, and assumed Ren had seduced Brahms. Because if they weren't lovers, how could they read each other so well? Ren didn't understand it either, but he'd come to realize that sometimes the best things in life defied explanation.

Their shirachi soups arrived. Without a flicker of his expression changing, Brahms dipped a spoon in and took his first bite.

"See?" Ren challenged, shaking his spoon at him. "It's too spicy for you. Will you please let me order you something else?"

Eyes locked on Ren's, Brahms put another spoonful in his mouth.

"Not everything is a competition, you know," Ren growled, torn between exasperation and amusement. "Why are you so competitive? Does it have something to do with how you were raised?"

"Maybe."

"Maybe meaning not at all. I'm on to your tricks, Arman Brahms, don't think I'm ignorant of what you mean when you say that. It might have taken me a full year, but I have learned how to translate you."

"See?" Brahms said smugly. "I don't need to talk. I have you."

"That is not at all how this works," Ren denied, amusement winning. "You lazy bastard, you're only taking me home with you so I can do all of the talking for you, aren't you?"

Brahms' lips curled ever so slightly at the edges, as smug as a feline with the canary in his paws.

"Argh, I knew it! I should have known you had an ulterior motive. I am not talking for you for the rest of our lives, do you understand me?

Hey. Listen to me. And seriously, stop eating the soup, your stomach lining is going to dissolve, you're not used to this level of spice."

Of course, Brahms kept eating it, and, of course, Ren kept talking enough for both of them, because that was just how they'd always been. Ren laughed through dinner, feeling lighter than he had in a long time, anticipation curling through him at the thought of starting over in a new country. He wouldn't be able to have a lover, but he'd have Brahms, and surely that would be enough.

1

Five years later

Ren always felt that the name 'Zonhoven Palace' fit the place perfectly. Or, at least, he'd come to that conclusion once someone had explained it meant 'enclosed garden.' The palace seemed made of gardens, with the rich, vibrant colors of plant beds weaving their way in and out of the building. When Ren first saw it five years ago, he'd thought it a gem of architecture, with white spires so sleek and tall they threatened to touch the sky. His opinion of it hadn't changed in all his years of being Castle Warden. Even during the winter months, the palace grounds still displayed a wealth of colors due to the evergreens and winter flowers.

Shiirei had winters, but not like the ones here, with snows that reached several feet deep. Ren liked spring best, though, with its warmth and gentle breezes. He walked along the outer courtyard, enjoying the sun on his face and the delicate murmurs of the fountains. Truly, the place still looked stunning to his eyes, each curve of the flower beds and the mosaic tilework under his feet a masterpiece. Aart liked bold, contrasting colors, and this hallway had a red theme weaving through it. Red, black, and white tiles, red flowers, even red marble columns in a stark contrast against the white marble of the building. Fall touched the trees outside, turning the leaves golden orange mixed in with the reds. His first few months here, the color coding of the hallways guided him, preventing him from being completely lost. Now he could just appreciate the beauty of it as he did his patrol. Ren breathed it all in with a smile on his face and hoped he never got used to it.

Funny, how he ended up here instead of at Brahms Fortress. Brahms had had every intention of Ren either joining him in the army or making him warden at his own home, but neither had happened. Upon meeting Queen Eloise, she'd taken a shine to Ren and instead made him the warden at Zonhoven Palace in Castel-de-Haut. It wasn't what Ren had planned, back then, but he didn't regret his choice. It was a good place, with good people, and he enjoyed his work here. The only downside was that he only saw the Brahms family irregularly; which was a shame, as he adored the whole family.

It was just as well he'd found work here, anyway. Since the war, the countries of the world had entered an era of peace and had little use for a discharged general. The Mongs and Zaytsevians up north still rattled about promising trouble, but they'd been doing that for centuries. Ren didn't pay it too much attention.

Ren had worked with the Bhodhsans, Scovians, De Contis, and Tu'is during the war, as they had all come to help protect Shiirei. He'd found the Bhodhsans to be large, dominating warriors who could cheerfully drink anyone under the table. Aart shared its eastern border with Bhodhsa, and Ren was very thankful for it, as they were a staunch ally who had no humor where either the Zaytsevians or the Mongs were concerned. The De Contis were closer to Shiirei and leaned toward the finer arts over warfare, but could be dependable in a tight spot. The Tu'is possessed the size of two men and ate like three, but the island people were cheerful and outgoing on a regular basis. And, of course, the Scovians were ambitious and ruthless. Scovians were inclined to react with commendable speed and force against any attack. Then again, they shared a direct border with the Mongs and Zaytsevians, so it was no wonder.

Ren felt rather thankful for his experience in the war, working with all of those countries' soldiers, as it had prepared him for his job now. A great deal of politics went into the job of warden. He had a deputy warden, of course, but he and Hartmann divvied up the duties for their mutual sanity. Hartmann dealt with change of shift, general security on the grounds, and staff problems. Ren dealt with everything else, which included insuring that his foreign guests didn't run afoul of trouble or start any.

Technically, walking patrol of the main buildings was more along Hartmann's line, but Ren found it beneficial to do at least one patrol a day. It gave him a chance to spot any possible problems, for one thing. And bending another set of eyes to the general security of the palace grounds was never a bad idea, as Hartmann could only oversee so much. As Ren walked, he continued his inspection, making sure the right doors were locked as they were supposed to be, and that the lantern sconces had enough oil in them. He saw a few that were low and made note to have them filled later. Well-lit buildings were the first step to discourage intruders or petty trouble.

"Warden!"

Turning, he spied one of his young guardsmen sprinting toward him, flushed in the face and panting for breath. All of his guardsmen were in good shape, Ren made sure of it, so if he were this out of breath then he had been hunting for Ren for a while. "Chaz, what is it?"

Chaz stumbled to a halt, hands on knees, and lifted a palm to wipe away sweat before it could drip into his grey eyes, making his fair hair slick into weird spikes. "Sir. The queen urgently requests your help. A magpie flew down and grabbed her signet ring."

That did not sound good at all, although Ren wasn't entirely sure what he could do about it. "Where?"

"Formal Gardens, sir."

Ren took off running, legs stretching out as he left the current garden and raced for the one centrally located inside the palace grounds. He didn't bother with the stairs. Leaping up and grabbing the window sills, he hauled himself through the opening, then crossed the hallway in two bounds before exiting out the window on the other side. He repeated it twice until he'd reached the second level, bypassing multiple staircases before exiting out another window, lightly leaping onto rooftops and skidding down the sleek tiles to land on the ground again. Doing this, he shaved off ten minutes of running through packed hallways and reached the back gate to the Formal Gardens in five minutes flat.

The queen stood facing the opposite direction, obviously agitated as she shifted from foot to foot. In front of her, two stories up and perched on the climbing vine that crawled up the exterior wall, was a magpie curiously pecking at something it grasped in its claws.

Ren breathed out a sigh of relief. So the bird was still here. Good, that gave them a chance to do something. Not wanting to startle the bird into taking off, he slowed his pace to a normal stride. "My Queen."

Turning, Queen Eloise spotted him and lit up hopefully, wringing a delicate handkerchief with both hands. "Oh, Ren. You came so quickly, good. Please, the magpie has my signet ring. We tried to catch it, only it evaded us and landed up there."

"I will do all I can," he assured her, sizing up the situation.

Catching the bird was out of the question—it would take off as soon as he got too close. It only left one option. Turning, he spotted one of his guardsmen and directed, "Wilkes, I need a bow."

"Had a feeling, sir," Wilkes answered, greying mustache tweaking up into a grin. "I sent young Fillmore for one a few minutes ago. None of us wanted to attempt it; you're the best shot here."

Ren could, in all honesty, say that Wilkes was perfectly correct. "Good thinking. My Queen, how did this happen?"

"I was eating pastries on the bench," she answered, staring at the bird in distress, her voluminous skirts swishing as she shifted her weight back and forth, "and got a bit of jam filling smeared on it. Ada took the ring from me to clean it, and the bird swooped down and snagged it right out of her hand. It was the most alarming thing; I thought he'd scratch her head as he came in, his angle was so steep. I've never seen a bird so bold."

"Your ring is just that pretty, My Queen," Ren responded, teasing a little, as he could tell she was truly worried about it. "Even the birds can see its beauty."

She cast him a glance, her upturned nose scrunching in aggravation. "I can do without their praise, if this is the form it takes. Oh, there's Fillmore. Slowly, man, don't scare the bird off."

Ren met the guardsman halfway, as he knew you didn't arm yourself openly while pointing a weapon at your prey. Birds were smart enough to recognize a bow and arrow and they would fly off if it looked like imminent danger. He had already memorized the position of the bird; he didn't need to look. Taking bow and arrow, he kept his back to the bird and nocked the arrow. "Thank you, Fillmore. Step back, please."

Fillmore immediately did so.

Taking in a deep breath, Ren cleared his head of all thoughts, all distractions. He'd only have one shot at this. Everyone else went perfectly still as well, holding their breaths. With a quick spin, he faced the bird, lifting the bow high and drawing the arrow back so the fletching kissed his cheek. The bird realized the silence was odd, something must be happening, and spread its wings to take flight.

The arrow whistled through the air, striking it dead in the chest.

Wilkes immediately trotted over to where the bird landed.

Queen Eloise clapped, bouncing up and down in place, which looked a little odd considering she was over forty years old and had two children. She beamed at him. "Good shot!"

"Thank you, My Queen," he acknowledged with a small bow. Queen Eloise had welcomed him warmly in this country, so he was relieved, for her sake, to get such an important keepsake back. It was one of the few things she had left from her father. "Wilkes, is the ring down as well? I didn't hear it hit the ground."

"That's because it didn't, sir," Wilkes reported in aggravation. "The bird let go of it before it fell, I think. It's still up there in the branches somewhere."

Queen Eloise growled, staring upwards. "Of course it wasn't that easy."

"Nothing ever is," Ren commented idly, already taking off his coat. The fall weather had some remaining heat to it, and after running frantically here, Ren wanted to doff the garment and cool down a little. "Fillmore, hold this please. Thank you. Don't fret, My Queen, I can fetch it back again."

"I have no doubt, assuming it's still up there and not fallen somewhere out of sight," Queen Eloise responded with full confidence. "Tell me, is there anything you can't climb?"

"I'm sure there is," he responded, testing the vines that clung to the wall. They had a sturdy grip in the masonry; he felt reasonably sure they would hold his weight. "I just haven't found it yet."

Queen Eloise snorted, blue eyes sparkling in amusement. "So humble."

"Now what use is false humility?" he asked her. Grabbing a branch, he hauled himself up and paused for a moment. Not even a creak in the vine. Good, it was safe to climb. He passed hand-over-hand steadily, using foot holds if he could find one, trusting in his upper body strength if he couldn't. He hadn't yet done a training session this morning, and this workout warmed his muscles quickly, making him doubly glad he'd shirked his jacket.

Two stories took him a minute to climb, cautiously testing the vine's attachment to the stone as he went, as it looked a little flimsy to hold an adult man's weight. It proved sturdy enough, however, allowing him to scale up to the same area the bird had perched on. Carefully, he rummaged around through the thick green leaves, not wanting to carelessly knock the ring off. Surely it was in here somewhere. He shifted a little more to the right, and by doing so, the sunlight previously blocked by his head shone through. From the corner of his eye, he spotted a gleam of metal. He had to nearly flatten his head against the vines to see it neatly tucked away underneath the leaves. "Got it!"

"Excellent! Oh good job, my Warden."

Placing it in his front breast pocket, he climbed carefully down, dropping the last six feet, his knees bending to absorb the impact. Then he fished the ring out again and presented it to her on a flat palm. "At your service, My Queen."

"This is one of those times that I bless General Brahms for bringing you to us," Queen Eloise informed him, replacing the signet ring on her middle finger. "Although I don't think he expected me to keep you."

Ren laughed because it was completely true.

"Here, come sit and take some refreshment. You certainly earned it. Guardsman Wilkes, Fillmore, thank you for your assistance. And please thank Guardsman Chaz for me."

"It was our pleasure, My Queen," Wilkes assured her before resuming his post near the side door once more.

Ren took his jacket back from Fillmore with thanks, shrugging into it before joining Queen Eloise on the bench. The maid, Ada, served him a cup of cool ginger tea, which he appreciated, along with an orange scone. Queen Eloise feeding him some treat was nothing new. She seemed determined to put extra flesh on him somewhere, as by this country's standards he remained too thin. But with all of the training, patrolling, and running around he did, her efforts were thwarted. It didn't keep her from trying, however.

The scone dissolved in his mouth with a burst of flavors and he hummed his appreciation.

"Divine, aren't they?" Queen Eloise said knowingly. "Norman has a niece he brought in as an apprentice last week, and she is gifted with pastries. She's a lovely girl, you know. Very pretty and with a great deal of charm."

Knowing very well what she drove at, Ren finished the bite in his mouth and eyed her wearily. "My Queen."

"Don't start," she responded, full mouth thinning into a line. "I know you keep saying you have no interest in women, not in that way, but have you even tried? What if you just haven't met the right woman yet?"

"My Queen." Ren kept his patience, although he struggled to do so. It wasn't her fault, this persistence, and he understood the root of it, why she kept trying. Queen Eloise thought of him as a nephew or a cousin—someone precious to her. She wanted him happy, hated seeing him alone, and kept encouraging him to date. But she had no concept of what same-gender attraction meant, what it was like, and couldn't understand his refusals. Every attempt to explain it had failed, but Ren gamely tried again. "My Queen, let me ask you something. Are you attracted to cats?"

Queen Eloise blinked, expression blank, then a little horrified. "Heavens, no!"

"How can you be so sure? Perhaps you haven't met the right cat yet." He didn't say another word, just waited.

With her own words turned neatly against her, Queen Eloise sat for a moment, speechless, then she grew perturbed. "Is it really the same for you? The idea of being in a woman's embrace is that odd?"

"I'm afraid so. It's not that I don't enjoy your company—in fact most of the women in the palace are perfectly delightful people. But being intimate with them is unfathomable to me." Had he finally gotten this across? She wasn't blithely moving on, for once, but seriously pondering his words.

Queen Eloise looked away, toward the far corner of the garden, a frown bunching her brows together. "I see. Well, no, I don't completely understand. I suppose I never will. When I first heard of your inclinations, I thought it strange, and likely a phase of some sort. I thought you'd pass through it. I hoped so, at least. You're such a lovely young man, Ren. I do want to see you happy."

"I know you do." He decided to leave it at that.

Worrying at her bottom lip, she pondered it another moment. "Perhaps when General Brahms returns from the border he can take over your duties here for a month or two. If we send you temporarily back to your country, do you think you can find someone?"

Ren spluttered, grateful he hadn't taken a sip of tea. "Are you seriously suggesting sending me back to Shiirei for an omijei?"

"An omijei?"

He didn't quite know how to link it to something in Aart. As far as he knew, the tradition didn't exist in this culture. "It's something like a marriage meeting. Parents on both sides introduce their children with the hopes that they might be attracted to each other."

Queen Eloise clapped her hands together, perking up. "Splendid!

So your country does have a way of introducing you to someone."

"Wait, wait." Ren put up a staying hand, torn between groaning and wincing. "It's not that easy. You do remember that my parents died during the war? I don't have anyone to make the introductions for me. Also, doing introductions for a same-sex couple is unheard of. Shiirei barely tolerates men with my orientation and marriage is illegal. That's something for couples who can produce offspring."

It was a funny sight, seeing the Queen of Aart openly pout. "That won't do at all. Shame on you, Ren, you got my hopes up for a moment. But surely even without this omijei thing, you can find someone for yourself?"

"Do you really think I can find someone in two months who would be willing to abandon everything in Shiirei to follow me here?" he asked her dryly.

"You're charming," Queen Eloise responded tartly. "You'll manage."

Perhaps because Prince Charles was on the verge of being engaged, his mother had weddings on the brain. Ren decided it high time to change the subject. "If it's all the same to you, My Queen, I'd prefer to spend time with my friend once he's home. I haven't seen him in over a year, after all. Did you say he's returning soon?"

"In the next couple of months, they're just about finished up there," she confirmed. "And I suppose I can't blame you, I know how close the two of you are. He was very disappointed when I wouldn't give you leave to serve with him."

This was news to Ren. Surprised, he asked, "He requested I be deployed with him?"

"He did, quite earnestly. And I knew why—the two of you are practically inseparable—but I really can't do without you here. You're the best warden we've ever had, and with all of these preparations for Charles' upcoming engagement, I really cannot afford any mistakes. They'd have international repercussions." Mouth downturned, she admitted in a lower tone, "Although I did feel awful about refusing the request. He didn't look it—you know how straight-faced he always is—but I gained the distinct impression he felt vastly disappointed."

And likely pouting. Ren seemed to be one of the few who could see past the ever-present stone-faced expression Brahms wore. Queen Eloise's mothering instincts had probably given her a hint to what her lead general really felt. "I'm sure he understood, though."

"I'm sure he did," she agreed. "Still, I think I'll feel better about the matter when he's home again, as I know you dearly miss each other. Does he write?"

"To the absolute surprise of no one, our dear general is as verbose on paper as he is in person," Ren drawled, finishing off the last of the scone. "That is to say, I get regular letters from his batman, with one or two lines from the man himself. If not for Robert, I wouldn't have the faintest idea what he's doing."

"That doesn't surprise me," Queen Eloise admitted with a giggle. "His formal reports are about the same. Truly, we should probably send you along on the next deployment so that we at least know what he's doing. Well, Ren, I won't keep you. I know you do your rounds at this time. Thank you for the help. You were splendid."

"My pleasure, My Queen," he assured her, standing and giving her a proper bow.

With her dismissal, he turned and left the garden, picking back up where he had left off. A couple months, eh? Brahms would be home again in a couple of months. Ren prayed the time would fly by.

2

Ren made it a point to stop at the training grounds and spar for two hours before lunch. Partially he did it to keep his own skills sharp, as he certainly couldn't afford for them to slip, but also to keep everyone else sharp. It was understood that after he had warmed up, he'd welcome anyone as a sparring partner. The other guardsmen regularly took him up on the offer, but sometimes the other lords in Aart, or even visiting foreign dignitaries, did so as well.

He probably couldn't linger for long, as Princess Alexandria and her people would arrive sometime in the next two days, which meant preparations on Ren's part. He'd already worked out a different schedule of guards to be her protection while she stayed in Zonhoven Palace, but he wanted to go over that one more time, with substitutes lined up, just in case. Ren had heard war stories about assassins taking advantage of nobility being in foreign lands and picking them off. He absolutely refused to have such a scenario occur on his watch.

"Ren!" Hartmann hailed as he entered the yard. His Deputy Warden had about eight years on Ren, but he looked older with random gray hairs in his curly dark hair and lines around his eyes. He took the steps leading down into the training yard two at a time, hair flopping about on his forehead as he moved.

Ren paused in his handstand, but even upside down, he knew that expression and dreaded it. Hartmann had the most easy-going nature to ever grace a man, with a permanent smile on his face. When he lost that smile, something serious had happened. Immediately, Ren came out of the handstand, regaining his feet. "Is the castle falling in on our heads?"

"I might actually prefer that," Hartmann responded, agitation pouring off of him in visible waves. His baritone voice resonated a pitch higher than normal, although he tried to keep it low to avoid alerting the rest of the yard about his news. "We just received word that Princess Alexandria and her escort were attacked."

Swearing, Ren snatched up his red uniform jacket and sword, not bothering to put on either. "Where are the king and queen?"

"King's study, and they requested I brief you on the way." Hartmann had to lengthen his stride to keep up, despite being taller than Ren, and he puffed a little for breath as he spoke.

Leaving the training yard behind him, Ren shrugged on his jacket as they hit the main hallway. "Please do. Is she hurt? Anyone injured?"

"Some injuries, although Princess Alexandria is thankfully not one of them. They're in Brahms Fortress now, as they took shelter there after the attack."

Ren said a prayer of thankfulness for small blessings. At least she would be safe there, as absolutely nothing got past Brahms Fortress. The first time Ren had seen it, the word 'impenetrable' came to mind. Lord Anthony Brahms, his friend Arman Brahms' father, was a veteran soldier who wouldn't let a fly past his defenses. "I'm relieved to hear it. Who's behind the attack?"

"Not sure." Hartmann made a face as he answered, the words unpleasant in his mouth. "We have little in the way of details. The message came by pigeon."

Which meant it was, by necessity, slim on words, as the bird couldn't carry a full-length letter. Dammit. Ren took a right turn, headed upstairs to the second level as fast as he could ascend the stairs, and then strode directly into the king's study. Fortunately, the doors leading in stood wide open, everyone clearly expecting him. Queen Eloise, Prince Charles, and King Gerhard all looked up at his entrance. The king sat behind his massive desk, half of his face hidden by his cupped hands, his crown resting on the desk's surface. He only removed the crown when fighting off a headache, and Ren couldn't blame him for having one now.

Queen Eloise and Charles, so alike in looks and expressions, sat in wing-backed chairs in front of the desk, facing the door. Queen Eloise kept her poise, although she had her hands clasped tightly in her lap. Charles sat on the edge of his chair, hands on the arms of it in a white-knuckled grip, blue eyes coldly furious. The twenty-year-old looked worried, too, his blond hair not immaculately combed back as usual, but standing up on end, as he if he'd run his hands repeatedly through it.

But then, who could blame him? His relationship with Princess Alexandria was not solely for the sake of politics. It was actually a love match, one obvious to anyone who saw them together. In his place, Ren would be vibrating out of his own skin, dying to go to her.

Reading the situation very well, Ren had a good idea of why he'd been called, and immediately assured Charles, "Of course I'll go with you."

Half of the tension riding in Charles relaxed in one breath. "Thank you, Ren. See?"

King Gerhard regarded his son with considerable asperity. "Charles, the question was never 'Will Ren go with you' but 'Can Ren go with you.' Ren, I assume that Hartmann briefed you on the way? Excellent, thank you, Hartmann. Ren, considering what has happened, I am loath to send any of my children out of the palace right now, although I understand Charles' desire to see Alexandria."

Considering that Princess Alexandria had been attacked while traveling through an allied country, Ren could certainly appreciate the king's concern. "We have absolutely no idea who attacked her?"

"Lord Brahms' note to me only said: 'Princess at my fortress. Attacked on road, enemy unknown.' You now know as much as I do."

If Anthony had known more than that, he certainly would have said. Unlike his son, the man was good at giving information. "Then I do appreciate your worry, My King. However, I think I can leave the palace for a few days without repercussions. We already have everything planned for Princess Alexandria's arrival, Hartmann knows them as well as I do, and the staff is just as clear on their instructions. Barring an emergency situation, I foresee no problems."

Queen Eloise shared a speaking, worried glance with her husband before stating, "The only way I'm comfortable with Charles leaving the palace is if Ren goes with him."

King Gerhard didn't exactly disagree, but he did say in some exasperation, "I'm still of two minds about Charles going. And we do have other, highly trained and qualified soldiers who can be entrusted with our son's safety."

"And I'm sure Ren will choose some of them as a guard," Queen Eloise agreed with a pointed smile.

Ren had to bite the inside of his lip to keep from smiling. Years ago, when Brahms had first brought him to the palace and introduced him, he'd arranged for a martial arts display to showcase Ren's skills.

No one here had seen the Rising Sun style before. Aartans felt that the bigger and stronger a man, the more invincible he must be, so watching the slimmer and shorter Ren repeatedly put those burly warriors on the ground had been shocking. Queen Eloise especially became entranced with him, so much so she had offered him the position as castle warden on the spot. To this day, she believed Ren could do anything he put his mind to, and couldn't fathom the possibility that he could be defeated.

Knowing all of this, and perhaps sharing his wife's opinion to some degree, King Gerhard splayed open a hand in acceptance. "Fine. Charles, you have permission to go, but take at least a complement of twenty guards with you. I don't think we'll have anyone dare attack their own prince inside his own country, but then I never entertained the idea that Alexandria would be attacked while traveling through Bhodhsa either."

Had she still been in that country or had she just hit Aart's borders when attacked? It had to be somewhere along the border if Brahms Fortress was her nearest haven. Either way, that wasn't good.

Charles, relieved, gave his father a tight smile. "Thank you, Father. Ren, how much time do you need before we can leave?"

"An hour?" Ren offered. Thinking fast, he tried to work out the journey logistics even as he spoke. It took two days to reach Brahms Fortress, even riding hard, which meant they would have to stop somewhere. "At least that. Meet me at the stables in an hour, I'll try to get a guard put together in that time. My Prince, if you could send a message to Lord Linden, request hospitality for a night's stay? He'd make the best halfway-point for our journey to Brahms."

"I'm sure my cousin would be glad to host us in our time of need," Charles responded, his tone saying 'he'd better be.'

Ren decided to leave that alone and not comment. "Then I'll see you in an hour."

The trip to Brahms Fortress strung out, taut with tension and silence, the thunderous repetition of horse shoes against the stone highway the only sound. Ren spent the entire trip thinking hard about various scenarios, but with no information, he could only speculate. Two different countries stayed in constant conflict with the rest of the world, and Ren could handily blame either of them for this attack. Zaytsev made more sense than Mong, being the bordering country with Aart and Bhodhsa, but he couldn't discount Mong just because it lay further east. Mong and Zaytsev often allied together, trying to break through the iron guard of Scovia, Bhodhsa and Aart.

And it could be that they, for once, were innocent in the matter. Perhaps some other person had a political agenda to push, or wished to thwart Scovia's and Aart's marriage alliance. Who that might be, Ren didn't know, as international espionage was not his specialty.

He just hoped, for Charles' sake, that they'd be able to get to the bottom of it and resolve the matter before Alexandria was hurt. His young prince would not take the loss of his princess well.

They arrived at Brahms in a day and a half, something of a record, and Ren's sore arse protested in silent testament of how they'd made it so quickly. Charles had acted like a possessed man getting here. When the solid grey stone of Brahms Fortress panned into view around the mountain's slope, Ren breathed out in relief. Finally, they'd made it.

He scrutinized the fortress as they galloped over the drawbridge. Nothing about it indicated a state of emergency, although he saw a few signs that they were in a heightened state of security. The yellow flags flying from the top of the battlements indicated a higher level of defense than normal. The fortress had been built directly inside a mountain pass, its sides flush against the rock faces. Four stories tall, it loomed over them with a slightly menacing air, promising blood to anyone who dared lay siege to it. The weight and power of it always sent a shiver down Ren's spine.

He loved Brahms Fortress. It was sort of a shame he'd been snapped up to be warden of Zonhoven Palace instead of getting to live here. Ah, well, such was life.

A horn sounded at their approach, alerting the rest of the fortress, and Ren signaled the rider behind him to raise their banner. He did not want to be shot at because someone confused them as an enemy. Someone quickly recognized the prince's colors, as the main gate immediately opened, the gears cranking with loud clinks of metal to slowly lift the portcullis.

Standing square in the inner courtyard, arms crossed over his chest, waited Lord Anthony Brahms. Aside from the size, he and his son Arman looked little alike. Anthony Brahms was as fair as his eldest son was dark, hair mostly silver, eyes green, and a slightly ruddy complexion from constant exposure to the sun. In fact, come to think of it, most of Brahms' family had lighter hair coloring and green eyes. Ren had to wonder where his friend's dark hair and blue eyes came from.

Charles skidded to a halt in front of Anthony Brahms and threw himself off the horse, demanding as he moved, "She's alright?"

"She's fine, princeling," Anthony informed him, his normal brusque tone softened a little in sympathy. Pointing a finger to an open door, he encouraged the man, "She's through there."

"Thank you," Charles stated before sprinting that direction.

Both men watched him go for a moment before Anthony turned to Ren with a smile crinkling up the corners of his eyes. "Well, Ren, looks like you had an interesting trip up here."

"I could barely get him to sit still or eat," Ren complained, half in jest as he gratefully dismounted. Extending a hand, he greeted, "Father, how are you?"

Anthony accepted the hand in a firm grip. "Well, boy, I'm well." It always tickled Anthony when Ren addressed him as 'Father.' Of course, for Aart, that wasn't the correct mode of address for a friend's parent, but Shiirei looked at the matter differently. A friend's parent was your parent as well, their uncle your uncle, and so on. Unless instructed differently, you called them as you would a family member. "Here, come in, rest for a while and catch your breath. Eida and I had an idea you'd be coming along with the prince, and she's got your room ready for you."

"I'd be very glad to," Ren responded as he handed his reins over to one of the stable hands. "Thanks, Sam. Rub him down good, give him an apple for me. He was a jewel on the trip despite me being so demanding."

"You got it, Master Ren," Sam assured him with a quick smile, before leading the horse toward the stables.

Ren turned around and found that Miss Lavonne, the head housekeeper, had already taken his guards in hand and was drawing them into the house. No doubt she'd make them comfortable and ensure someone fed them soon. Satisfied, he waved them off, indicating they were free to relax.

Following Anthony's lead, Ren trailed after him into the house, asking questions as he went. "What exactly happened?"

"Not much, fortunately. The ones that attacked Princess

Alexandria's party didn't send enough men to do the job. They didn't count on that bodyguard of hers. The man could give even Arman a run for his money," Anthony said with a faint hint of praise. It wasn't just a father's prejudice, as Arman was one of the best fighters in Aart. "Enough were injured they couldn't readily move, not quickly, and they sent a courier ahead to me. I went out to fetch them, hauled them all here. We've been patching people up and nursing them ever since."

"I bet Mother is delighted," Ren commented, entering the main hall of the fortress. No one was in the large, vaulted foyer, but the curved staircase at the far end carried the sounds of multiple voices from the second story. "All of those people to look after."

"She really should have been a doctor," Anthony agreed. "She's been scurrying about with a smile on her face for two days now. Anyway, no one's seriously injured, which is a blessing, and the princess herself is more mad than anything. A good woman, that. I'm glad we got to meet her. Charles did well, picking that one."

"Oh?" Ren hadn't had a chance to meet her yet, only hear about her, as Charles had done their courtship in Alexandria's country. "Charles raves about how beautiful she is, how kind, how intelligent, and so forth, but we haven't known how much of that to believe. A man in love sees a woman very differently."

"I can attest that she's beautiful, kind, and intelligent, at least." Anthony led the way into the kitchen, calling to the cook as he went, "Get Ren a snack and some ale."

Bertie waved at Ren with a grin, showing gapped teeth. "Good to see you, Master Ren. Starving or hungry?"

As his appetite was legendary in this place, having out-eaten all three of the Brahms sons, Bertie had developed this question solely for his benefit. It was the difference between serving him two plates or four. "Starving."

"Coming up," she assured him, waving him toward the roughhewn kitchen table.

The air smelled of roasted chicken, fried vegetables, and baked bread. Ren's stomach gave a petulant rumble as breakfast had been quick and light, and lunch skipped altogether. "Father, going back to the attack, they really have no idea?"

"Attackers were in all black, heads swathed in cloth; no one was able to get any distinguishing features. And they were quick to retreat when they failed, taking their injured with them." Anthony leaned on the table's surface a little, ankle crossed over his knee, and confided, "My money's on the Zaytsevians. Damn Z's have been restless lately. Their last attempt was climbing the mountain and then trying to rappel down the cliffs onto the battlements."

Ren winced. "But that rock is all limestone; it's too powdery to hold an anchor for more than a few minutes."

"I know it. They now know it too, the hard way. They keep trying to get through or attack the highway. I've had to patrol it more often to keep people safe as they're traveling. We've put up many a traveler the past two months, offering safe haven to people before escorting them down to Hill's Borough."

"It's the first time we've seen them attack in a while, isn't it?"

"Near on two years," Anthony confirmed darkly. "There's been so much in-fighting in the country, they haven't tried to borrow trouble by attacking us. Means someone over there gained more power than the rest, although we'll have to see how long he can hold onto it."

"So it's possible that this is just a random attack? That she wasn't specifically targeted?" Ren didn't know if he bought that theory.

Anthony splayed his free hand in an open shrug. "I'm saying it's a possibility, although I don't put much stock in it. She was too well guarded to invite random thieves. I'll investigate more on this end as I can, but I've written up two formal reports already. I sent one to Bhodhsa, as it technically happened on their soil, and I have another copy for you to give our king."

"I know he'd appreciate that; he was dying to have more information. So she was attacked on the highway crossing out of Bhodhsa? That's not good. Bhodhsa is not going to be happy about this. They pride themselves on being good allies and keeping tight security on their borders."

"They're going to be livid and might start a war over it when they figure out which idiot dared to attack our new princess," Anthony corrected. "You're friends with their lead general, aren't you?"

"General O' Broín? Certainly; we served together in the war. A good man, very steady. Why do you ask?"

"I'm sure they're going to send someone out my direction to investigate this. I thought it would help if I requested someone you knew. Maybe if we put all three of our heads together, we'll get to the bottom of it."

Ren nodded agreeably. "I think that's a wonderful idea. I'll suggest the same."

"Good, good. I assume you'll stay a day, get rested, then return? Charles is surely anxious to get her back to Zonhoven Palace."

"That and they've got an engagement party to be ready for in a little over three weeks," Ren acknowledged. "We're all half-crazy with the preparations; I don't think we have much time to dawdle here, unfortunately."

Anthony looked slightly disappointed by this. "I don't get to see either you or Arman much, what with duty pulling you both different directions. Eida and I both miss you two. Now that Lance and Marshall have moved out to the auxiliary fortresses, it's far too quiet in this place."

"How are they doing, anyway? I haven't been up here since Marshall's wedding last year."

"Can you believe that we're already expecting a grandchild? I don't think those two have left a bed since exchanging vows." The words could be taken as a complaint, but a wide smile graced Anthony's face. "Lance is on his second child as well, praise to the gods. I now have enough grandchildren to carry this place on, at least."

"Even if they're girls?" Ren teased.

"Bah! My mother ran this place after my father died and did a better job at it, to boot. As long as she can keep her head in a crisis and react quickly to an attack, any woman can be a warden. I'm not worried. But tell me, have you heard anything from Arman?"

"Just a brief letter—and by brief, I mean two lines—last week."

Bertie plopped plates of food and ale on the table, the smell enticing enough to get a petulant rumble from Ren's stomach. He beamed at the matron and dug in.

They fell into sharing information, eating, and enjoying each other's company with ease. Ren soaked up the peace and safety that resonated in Brahms Fortress, and prayed that whatever had happened, it wouldn't keep them from returning to Zonhoven Palace safely.

3

The trip home went smoothly, praise be to any god listening. Ren didn't get to interact much with either the princess or bodyguard, unfortunately, despite spending two days on the road with them. By unanimous agreement, no one wanted to stay outside of Zonhoven Palace any longer than necessary, so they kept up a very good clip. Moving at a trot, conversation became impossible, and Ren didn't even attempt it. At night, people ate quietly and immediately went to bed, so while he saw the Scovian visitors, he barely got more than their names.

There was something fishy about that, really. Ren didn't understand why, but the Scovian party seemed to be avoiding him on some level. Was it because their princess had been attacked on foreign soil? Although, Ren understood there was some unrest in Scovia as well about the marriage. Or was it something else entirely? He had no chance to put a finger on the problem during the trip, as haste was their priority, and the thundering hooves drowned out any chance for conversation.

Arriving home again, he gave all of his formal reports, passed along Anthony Brahms' report and suggestions, then immediately went back to his duties. Hartmann had done his usual excellent job in Ren's absence, despite covering for two people, and Ren took him off palace grounds, to one of their favorite haunts, to buy him dinner and a round of drinks as thanks.

While the mystery of who attacked the princess's party hung unsolved, it was temporarily put aside, as the engagement party's preparations demanded their attention. Ren fell back into his usual routine at the palace, making sure he still trained for two hours every morning. If he didn't, he was convinced he'd go crazy. Beating things up (or people, whatever might be at hand) remained his only outlet for stress relief.

This morning, as Ren stepped into the training yard, he found it to be more crowded than normal. All of the practice dummies normally stored in the far right awning had been moved to make way for benches, and several blond-haired men and women all gathered there, chattering to each other—lords, ladies, maids, a few retainers, and their guards. Looking left, Ren saw that it was the same on that side, the only shaded part of the training yard being crowded with onlookers, although there was nothing to look at. The training yard held nothing more than hard packed dirt and targets along the back wall for archery.

Upon his arrival, the chattering increased, with many a side glance aimed his direction. The tone of it reminded him of heckling crows upon spying something they wanted to peck at. It was not a friendly sound—at least not from the Scovians in the crowd. The Aartans seemed more defensive, a low grade anger buzzing in their words. Ren took in this reaction with growing unease. Why did he have this feeling they'd all been waiting for him?

Charles popped out of one group, spied him, and waved. He turned to his companions and said something before disengaging, striding quickly Ren's direction.

Hoping that perhaps the prince possessed some knowledge of why they were all here, Ren stopped just on the edge of the training yard and waited.

Lifting a hand, Charles wore a smile that looked eerily similar to his mother's when she'd done something she wasn't supposed to, but would use charm to get around it somehow. Granted, he looked more like his mother than his father, with the same wavy blond hair and blue eyes, although fortunately he'd gotten his father's height. Still, after five years of being the castle warden, Ren knew the royal family very well and he especially knew that smile.

"My Prince," Ren greeted with all due suspicion, "what did you do this time?"

"I can't even get a word in before I'm being accused of things," Charles complained. "How do you always know?"

"You have the easiest expression to read out of anyone I've ever met, that's how. Now, what did you do?"

"I blame the wine," Charles responded promptly, innocently.

Ren rolled his eyes. He'd heard that line before.

"What happened is—wait, are you aware that the people of Scovia are prejudiced against same-sex relationships?"

"Unfortunately, I am." Ren did not like this opening one bit. "Why?"

"I was talking with Alexandria, and she was very surprised when she learned of your inclinations. I didn't think much of it, but apparently it was quite shocking to her, as she passed it down to someone else, and then it spread further, and you know how rumors go."

"The point, My Prince," Ren growled.

"I'm getting there, I'm getting there," Charles defended himself, a hand lifted to ward Ren off. "Anyway, so last night after dinner, several of us gathered for a game of cards and a drink, and I got numerous questions. Actually, it was more like accusations. Not one of them seemed to believe you have the skills to be a warden or a general because you like men, which doesn't make any sense to me. What does sex have to do with fighting skills?"

"I've been asking that question my entire life," Ren sighed, resigned. His shoulders slumped a little as he had a feeling he knew where this was going. "Continue, please."

"Anyway, they adamantly wouldn't believe it. I got quite upset after a while, and said if they couldn't believe me, then I'd show them. And somehow that turned into their best fighter sparring with you today." Charles eyed his expression cautiously, like a man would an upset tiger. "How mad are you?"

Ren was actually proud of him. Charles had stood up for him, and while he really should have checked with Ren first, it wasn't a bad way to prove his point. The prince had done stupider things. "Not at all. You might have done me a favor, actually. This will shut their mouths and perhaps change their very stupid opinions."

"So I don't need to blame the wine?"

"Not this time."

"Oh good, 'cause it was my idea." Charles beamed at him, as carefree as a puppy, then bounded off, calling as he went, "He's agreed!"

Ren had the distinct feeling he'd just been played.

Well, this should be interesting, at least. Shrugging out of his jacket, he took a moment to redo his hair into a high topknot, making it less of a target. Then he moved toward the center of the training yard, starting his warm-ups. The princess's bodyguard stepped out to join him. Ren had met the man before this moment, of course, but hadn't the chance to do much else. He looked to be about Brahms' size, a half head taller than himself, with the muscle mass of a blacksmith and the stride of a soldier. Indeed, a formidable opponent, and that warhammer on his back explained the massive upper body strength.

Stopping in front of Ren, he gave a slight nod. "Warden."

"Galvath," Ren returned amicably.

Galvath took the hand extended to him in an iron grip, but didn't try to do anything petty like crushing Ren's hand, just evaluated the strength in it. Galvath's eyebrows quirked a little, dark eyes narrowing thoughtfully as he felt sword calluses and a firm grip.

Much could be told by a man's hand. Ren smiled at him and didn't say a word, letting him reach his own conclusions. He certainly drew a few of his own from Galvath's grip. "I understand we are to spar to prove a point. I'd prefer it not be weapons. We increase the risk of injury that way and we both have jobs to return to after this is over."

"I agree. Hand-to-hand, then?"

"If you're willing," Ren answered steadily.

The watching crowd murmured openly at this, thinking Ren a fool for agreeing, as Galvath obviously was stronger. Ren shared the opinion about his opponent's strength, but being stronger didn't necessarily mean you'd automatically win. Brahms had learned that lesson the hard way.

Even Galvath thought this foolish, but shrugged. "Then let's do that. Best two out of three?"

"Certainly." Ren unbuckled his sword belt and gestured for Chaz to come and take it. The guardsman took Galvath's warhammer as well, then scurried back to the sidelines with a grin of anticipation on his face. He, at least, knew how this was going to end.

"Let me finish stretching," Ren requested.

"Wise of you," Galvath approved. "I'll do the same."

Never being one to be falsely modest, Ren decided to play with people's minds a little, and he did the more extreme stretches that showed off his flexibility. He couldn't quite do the splits, but he could come close, and when standing he could put his hands flat on the ground. People thought this funny, that a man with the flexibility of a dancer would claim to be a fighter who could best Galvath.

Galvath watched this unfold with a growing frown. "By any chance, are you from Shiirei?"

"Hadn't you already heard?"

"No, Prince Charles didn't say where you were from exactly. But your name and looks reminds me of a fighter I met from that country. Are you trained in the Rising Sun style?"

"Oh, you've heard of it?" Ren smiled sweetly at him.

Galvath's whole countenance did an abrupt turnabout from confident to troubled. He threw back his head and groaned. "I'm in trouble."

"Ah, so you have crossed paths with my martial arts style before," Ren smirked, delighted over Galvath's reaction.

"Only once, when I was a teenager. I thought I was the best. He taught me better." Galvath flicked his arms out, limbering up. "Alright, let's get this humiliation over with."

Laughing, Ren came out of the last stretch. "Galvath, I think I might like you. I'll buy you a drink after this."

"After this, I'll need one," Galvath ruefully acknowledged.

Charles, standing nearby, thought this exchange entertaining, judging by his grin. He lifted a hand in signal. "Fighters ready? Three, two, one, begin!"

Ren came in low and smooth, not giving the larger man an easy target, spinning in and around him as lithely as a shadow. Galvath tried to turn and keep up with him, but all of that impressive bulk did not make him fast enough to manage it. He was a hair behind, enough for Ren to get up behind him and grab his wrist, using his other hand to lock Galvath's elbow at an awkward angle, and force him sharply to his knees. In three seconds, he had the man down, with his arm twisted up awkwardly behind him and the spectators froze in disbelief.

With his face in the dirt, Galvath let out a resigned sigh. "Yield, let me up. And thank you for not dislocating my shoulder. I appreciate that."

"Not at all," Ren responded, carefully letting go, as he really could do damage in that hold. Then he offered Galvath a hand up and hauled him easily up to his feet.

A hand slammed against the railing and Princess Alexandria sharply came to her feet. "Galvath! What are you doing?"

"I'm not going to win against this man, Princess," Galvath

informed her bluntly. "I've run across this fighting style before. The warden is actually a better fighter than the other man I'd fought with, curse my luck."

"But, but he's—" she abruptly cut herself off, staring at Ren in consternation.

Ren gave her a feral smile, feeling his adrenaline kick in a little. The expression alarmed her, so he brought it down a few notches. This was a beautiful opportunity to cut the legs out from underneath a few cultural prejudices. "Strangely enough, Princess, my desire to kiss handsome men senseless has no impact on my fighting ability."

She stared at him like she couldn't believe him, like her own eyes were betraying her.

Right, another round was needed, then. "Galvath, one more time?"

Galvath's shoulders slumped, a great sigh billowing out from the man. "As humiliating as it's going to be, I think she needs to see it. Alright, once more."

Clapping the man on the shoulder, Ren grinned at him before resuming their former positions. He was a good man, this one. Probably, unfortunately, straight as an arrow, which was a pity. He was rather handsome, in his own way, even with that hawk of a nose.

Charles couldn't keep his grin contained as he lifted his hand in signal once more. "Fighters ready? Three, two, one, begin!"

This time Ren didn't try to trap Galvath. That wouldn't necessarily prove anything if strength was what he needed to showcase. Instead he went toe-to-toe with the man, catching or blocking the punches thrown his direction, dodging the ones he couldn't conveniently grab, then when he thought he'd made the point, he stopped defending and went on the attack. He dropped low once more, leg sweeping out and around, knocking Galvath's knees out from under him. Galvath was still going down when Ren came up and around in a flip, putting his leg directly under the man's chin and holding it there steadily.

"Yield," Galvath groaned. "Ow."

Laughing, Ren withdrew his leg before giving the man a hand up again. "I didn't hit you that hard."

"The ground is not exactly soft, thank you very much," Galvath grumbled to him even as he was hauled up to his feet. "There, Princess, you see? Nothing about this man is weak. I daresay that's why he got the position he did, despite being from Shiirei."

"That, and General Brahms highly recommended him," Charles confirmed loudly, making sure everyone could hear. "I know that Scovia has some very definite opinions about men like Ren, but we in Aart do not share them. A man is judged here by what he does, not by who he loves."

And that was why Ren loved this country. Not only because it was ruled by a family who accepted him, quirks and all, but they really did judge him based on what he could do. "Well said, My Prince. Is there anyone else you want me to fight?"

"I think you proved the point admirably, Ren," Charles denied. With a sly grin, he added, "Unless Bodyguard Galvath isn't satisfied?"

"Respectfully, Your Highness, shut it," Galvath hissed at him, making Charles laugh. "Although I would love to train with you, Warden, if that's alright."

"Please do," Ren invited, meaning every word. "And don't forget, I'll buy you that drink later."

Bemused at the outturn, the crowd broke up and filtered out of the training yard. Princess Alexandria, Ren was pleased to note, looked very pensive as she went. Hopefully she would seriously think about what she'd seen today and get rid of some silly notions. Galvath gave him a casual salute before moving off after her, Prince Charles following along.

Ren hardly felt warmed up, so he lingered and spent some time putting arrows into a few moving wooden pegs. When he felt he'd done enough for the day, he put the equipment away, heading for the main door back into the palace. Somewhat to his surprise, one of the lords lingered there, clearly watching him. He'd known someone was over there, but thought it a guardsman, as the man hadn't said anything.

It took him a minute to connect name to face, as he rarely saw this lordling. Wasn't he the younger son of Councilman Giles? The high nose, grey eyes, and heart-shaped face made him think of the man, at least. "Lord Deidrick, isn't it?"

"Exactly so, Warden. I'm surprised you remember me; I think we've only passed each other in the halls." Deidrick had a pleasant baritone, easy and smooth on the ear.

"You bear a strong resemblance to your father, that's why," Ren explained easily. "Can I do something for you, my lord?"

"I find myself avidly curious," Deidrick admitted hesitantly, "although I do realize it's quite uncouth of me to ask questions about it."

His body language and tone filled in the gaps of what he didn't say. "You're dying to ask me questions about gay sex, aren't you? It's quite alright, I'm very open about it, and you certainly aren't the first Aartan to ask me questions."

"Really? Oh, of course, how stupid of me. General Brahms certainly would have."

Actually, Brahms hadn't. He certainly listened in on Ren's other conversations, though. "So? What are your questions?"

"Where did these prejudices come from, do you know?" Deidrick waved a hand to indicate the training field and what had just happened on it. "There obviously isn't any truth to them."

"I'm not quite certain myself," Ren admitted honestly, relaxing his back against a nearby post and settling into the conversation. "I have a working theory, however, if you care to hear that. Well, at one time in my country's history, men of my orientation weren't allowed to occupy any position that required strength. Careers in the army, government, and such were out of the question. They usually were hairdressers, actors, things of that ilk. I think they were forced into the reputation of being 'weaker' than other men."

Deidrick took this in with a contemplative nod. "I see. What changed?"

"The Mongs started invading us on a regular basis and every man was drafted, 'able' or not," Ren responded dryly. "Fortunately this change happened eighty years ago, decades before I was born; otherwise I would have been forced into a similar role. I shudder just thinking about it. It's fine if that's where your talent and interests lie, but I'd be lousy in those careers. All of them. Forcing a dog to play the role of a cat does no one any favors."

"I don't blame you. It would be difficult to live a life you weren't suited to." Deidrick canted his head, a slightly sly look tugging at his mouth. "You said you don't mind questions about sex? Truly? Then I must ask, how does it compare with making love to a woman?"

Ren snorted, amused. "I haven't the foggiest. I've never been with a woman."

"Truly?" Deidrick blurted, astonished. "You're so good looking and exotic, and I know that every woman in this castle adores you. I would have thought someone would try to seduce you by now."

"They tried, certainly," Ren conceded.

This flabbergasted Deidrick completely. Ren took in his reactions, his looks, and tried to guess his age. Early twenties, perhaps? Six years or so younger than himself. Had he ever been that naïve in his early twenties? Ren felt like he'd lost that sort of innocence before leaving his teens. But then, Aart was more sheltered than Shiirei in some ways.

Shaking the thought off, Ren decided to tease him a little. "Sorry, I can't tell you, only offer a demonstration."

"Oh? A kiss, perhaps?" Deidrick perked up, and if he'd had a tail, he would have been wagging it.

Not at all expecting this response, Ren stared at him, jaw dropping a little. "I was joking."

Deidrick's face fell. "Oh."

"But if you're really that curious…" Ren trailed off, not at all sure where he himself headed with this.

"It's my one true vice," Deidrick admitted, head coming back up as he sensed the tide might turn yet again. "Once I become curious about something, I absolutely cannot leave it be until I have an answer. I got into a ridiculous amount of trouble growing up because of it. But I don't see how a kiss could hurt anything."

"Neither do I." Ren felt the situation more than a little surreal. Was he really about to kiss a straight man at the other's invitation? "Well, alright, if you're sure?"

Deidrick didn't answer with words, instead sliding a hand onto Ren's waist and leaning in, his head angling just so. Ren felt it odd, but approached as well, angling his head to meet slightly-parted lips in a gentle caress. Not wanting to push past the point of Deidrick's comfort zone, wherever that might lie, he only did that before retreating a half step.

Blinking, Deidrick studied him for a moment, lifting a finger to touch his lips lightly. "Odd. I think I liked that."

Ren's eyebrows shot into his hairline. "You did?"

"I believe so. Once more, please?"

Perhaps this was an illusion. Perhaps Ren was the one on the ground with a ringing head and not Galvath. That would explain this situation, surely. Still feeling dazed, he hesitantly placed his hands on the man's waist as he leaned back in, and this time he lingered, lips working on the other's as he dared to use a bit of tongue to swipe at the bottom of Deidrick's mouth.

It had been so long—five years since he touched a man—that it felt blissful to kiss like this. He'd forgotten how much he liked kissing.

With real effort, he drew himself back, breath coming a little quickly. He looked at his companion, no longer sure where this led, or how Deidrick would respond.

A stormy cloud hovered in those grey eyes, a look of desire that wasn't there before. "Oh yes," Deidrick purred at him, "I quite liked that indeed. It's different from kissing the court women—you demand a response and take your own pleasure as well."

"I'm quite astounded you're enjoying it so much, but happy you are." Was there something in the water? And if so, how could Ren assure it stayed in there?

"Do you have time, Warden?" Deidrick asked, leaning in a little, the words more a whisper against his cheek than anything. "I have an empty apartment here in the palace, not a stone's throw from here. I would dearly like to continue this…conversation."

Ren swallowed hard. It might have been five years, but he knew an invitation when he heard it. So help him, though, if this turned out to be a practical joke, he'd murder everyone involved. Taking a chance, he murmured, "I have another hour before I need to return to duty."

"Then please, do come up."

4

That invitation turned out to be a standing invitation, with Ren seeing Deidrick six times in two weeks, and sex being part of it every time. Happily confused at this turn of events, Ren tried not to look a gift horse in the mouth and just enjoy the companionship offered. He made no demands on Deidrick, and neither spoke of where things led, but eventually that wore thin. Ren was not the type to like casual sex—he wanted the true intimacy of a dedicated partner, which meant it was time to ask questions. No matter the answers.

But that didn't mean he knew how to approach the matter.

There was one person in the palace who had become a drinking buddy and confidant: Chaplain Bertwin, the army priest. Ren dearly needed his advice and an outside perspective, so as soon as his shift was done for the day, he swung by the small chapel in the back of the palace's grounds. His luck held fair, as Chaplain Bertwin stood replacing some of the burnt-out prayer candles along the side wall.

The little chapel saw irregular use due to the wave of military personnel coming in and out. It could comfortably seat a hundred people but not a soul more, the pews lined in perfect order near the front doors and ending at the altar at the end of the single room. People had come in at some point, as prayer candles were sporadically lit along the walls. It smelled strongly of beeswax, the floors gleaming dimly in the candlelight. Cleaning done for the day, then? Good. His odds of dragging the man out for a drink were excellent if that were the case.

Stepping inside, he hailed, "Bertwin."

"Ah, Ren, good to see you. I heard all about that show you put on at Prince Charles' urging," Bertwin stated, putting the box of candles down on an open bench. Candlelight caught his greying hair and the fine wrinkles of his face, aging him in an unflattering way. Or perhaps he'd had a trying day, which made him look older than his fifty years. "I hoped to get the story straight from you at some point. Are you here for something?"

Ren hesitated a moment, not willing to burden him if the man had already had a long day, but...in the end, selfishness won out. "To invite you out for a drink, perhaps get a little advice. I'll be happy to retell the tale."

Bertwin gave him a happy nod and smile as he shed the chaplain robes, revealing his street clothes and the slight paunch of his middle. "I'll be happy for the drink and glad for a conversation that doesn't include confessing sexual sins."

Ren winced. "Well, actually...."

Doing a double take, Bertwin demanded, "*You?*"

"I know, I know, last thing you'd expect from me. It's... complicated. And I'm honestly still not sure how it happened."

"Who's your partner?" Bertwin spluttered, incredulous. "Surely not one of the Scovians."

"No, not at all. Um, are you acquainted with Lord Deidrick Giles?"

"Giles. Deidrick Giles." Bertwin's tone indicated he tried to use that name in some sort of equation and failed. Miserably. "Yes, I can say I am acquainted with the young man. I have not found him to have a steadfast nature."

"If by that you mean he leaps from interest to interest every three days, then yes, we are definitely talking about the same man." Ren felt better hearing this, as it helped Bertwin give him good advice if he knew the other party.

Bertwin chose his words carefully. "And how long have the two of you been...interacting?"

"Two weeks," Ren supplied with a shrug. "Which gives me a little hope."

"Two weeks. I see." Bertwin firmly put the box back under the table, smoothing the tablecloth back over it. The robe, he threw over the back of a pew to hang. "The candles can wait. I need that drink."

Ren couldn't help but agree and led the way as they left the chapel and walked to their favorite haunt, a local pub just outside the palace gates that served decent food and excellent beer. At this time of the evening, it had the usual crowd packed around the bar, but no one sat at the outdoor tables in the front. Ren chose to sit there, away from the door, as he felt like some privacy would be needed for this conversation.

Bertwin stuck his head in to call for two drafts and two plates of the night's special, then joined Ren at the table. Planting both forearms on the metal surface, he demanded, "How?"

"Here's the thing. Deidrick was curious." Ren related the tale and chose to spare his friend's sensibilities by not describing just how far into intimacy they'd ventured. Being hyper-aware that Deidrick was not naturally inclined towards men, Ren had not asked for anything more than handjobs and the occasional fellatio. Most of the time they didn't even fully remove their clothes. But Bertwin didn't need to know any of that to follow the stream of events. "Which leads us to today, when I realized that while it's quite fun having an intimate partner, we're not truly *intimate*, not in the full meaning of the word."

"Emotional intimacy," Bertwin stated knowingly. "Of course, that would be your sticking point. You are not one for casual friendships, Ren."

"I know it," Ren sighed. "But I'm a little scared."

"Scared to ask? You think you won't like the answer?"

Ren looked out into the deepening sunset, trying to find the way to explain just what held him back. "I had a lover before, when I was barely out of my teens. I'd just joined the army, so had he, and we connected with each other in a way that was lighthearted and fun. When we learned about each other's orientation—quite by accident—we thought, why not give each other a chance? We liked each other well enough, after all, why not try? And so we did. But he couldn't stand the thought that someone else might know about us. We hid the relationship although it grated at me to do so. Within six months, the secrets and the lies tore us apart. I swore to myself I would never do it again."

Bertwin followed this story, eyes narrowing. "Has Deidrick asked you to keep it quiet?"

"That's the thing. He hasn't. Which makes me ridiculously happy. He even reaches out for me in public. Today he held my hand as we went up to his apartment, not caring in the slightest who saw. Which, of course, raised my hopes even more." Ren rubbed at his face with both hands, not able to put his finger on the problem, just knowing there was one. "I have a gut feeling that the course I'm on will not be smooth sailing, but I can't figure out why. Is it because we haven't spoken to each other properly about our relationship and where it's heading?"

"That could very well be it," Bertwin acknowledged. "That would trouble anyone, male or female. I think you need to discuss the matter before it goes any further."

Ren blew out a breath, rubbing at his face again. "I agree."

"Don't give me the details; I don't want to know them, as people often tell me far too much of their sex lives. But are you two physically compatible? He doesn't find that part of it strange or awkward?"

"I keep waiting for him to, but it hasn't happened so far. Granted, I've tried very hard to ask only basic things from him in that regard," Ren admitted. "Nothing that would give even a teenager pause."

"Ah. Wise of you, I expect. But he still enjoys his time with you? How often have you met up these past two weeks?"

"Six times."

Bertwin's bushy eyebrows rose sharply. "I think I can see why you're growing nervous, then. He's acting like you two are courting or in a relationship. This doesn't sound casual to me at all."

Ren felt a little better hearing that. "Nor I. So, a proper talk, then. We've made plans to meet tomorrow for dinner, I'll try for it then."

"Please, for all our sakes, do. I hope you realize, Ren, that we all wish for your happiness in the most fervent way. You've been a guardian, friend, and brother to most of this city since your arrival. The royal family has made no secret that they hold you very dear to their hearts, and they're certainly not alone in that. If you've found someone that can be a partner to you, we'll all celebrate. But do take it in stages. I would hate to see this backfire."

"Thank you, Bertwin. And trust me, I'm trying not to rush things, as sometimes pushing too hard can break it. Still, I hope. I can't seem to help that." Ren shook his head and smiled, feeling the need to move to a lighter topic. "So you heard about my sparring match with the Scovian bodyguard?"

"You know how rumors go in the palace. They can make a round by lunch and two rounds by dinner," Bertwin joked. "Of course after two weeks I've heard about it. Tell me, was it really Prince Charles' idea?"

"That's what he confessed to me. Here's how it started…."

Ren ducked his head out of an open window to glance at the city clock across the street. An hour until the end of his shift, and then he'd have to hurry to his apartment to change out of his uniform in order to make his dinner date. Dinner and the sex that would likely follow it didn't make him nervous, but the looming conversation with Deidrick certainly did. How did he even start it without sounding like a lovelorn fool? Or one of those damsels-in-distress found in the novels, the ones who fainted and screamed all the time?

Pulling his hair over one shoulder, he tugged on it absently, a habitual tic. What to say, what to say? Magically hoping that Deidrick would develop the ability to read minds overnight was implausible at best, curse the luck. Despite the fact that Brahms used him to do the talking all of the time, Ren didn't consider himself to be a particularly gifted orator. In fact, he spoke three languages, and still he had no idea how to talk about this.

"Warden!"

Turning sharply at the hail, as that tone didn't indicate something good, he found one of the young palace runners sprinting for him. "Nixie, what's wrong?"

"Fire in the kitchen, sir," she panted, sweat beading around the child's forehead. She must have sprinted the entire distance, as it would take crossing the palace grounds to get her this out of breath.

If she were fetching him, then Hartmann was neck deep in some other trouble. Normally this was his domain. Either that or Ren was just the first person she'd found to report the trouble.

Swearing, Ren took off running, vaguely aware that she chased after him. Nixie was one of their fastest runners, but with her out of breath, he was able to stay well ahead of her. He practically flew, taking all of his shortcuts through open air hallways, windows, and over the lower roofs, until he dropped in the baking courtyard outside of the kitchen's doors. Even from here, his nose caught the acrid scent of smoke and saw the sooty, black trails of it along the white walls. It didn't appear to have impacted the main structure, however, so he held some hope that they'd contained it.

Skidding to a halt just inside the main door, he surveyed the scene with a sinking feeling. The kitchen supplied food to everyone in the main palace, so by necessity it was a very large room. Counters and cabinets lined three sides, several large stoves and ovens dominated the back wall, and work tables sat in rows down the middle. Half of the room still worked steadily—they couldn't afford for everything to grind to a halt—the cooks chopping and preparing ingredients as fast as their hands could move. The trouble came from one of the stoves in back right corner, the damage clear from the crackled plaster, singed beam overhead, and soot everywhere.

Ren dodged around people, slipping in and around them, calling for the head cook as he moved. "Chef Norman!"

Norman turned, ponderous belly moving people out of the way like a ship's prow, his hands and face lined with traces of soot and a scowl darker than the traces of fire. "Warden. Don't worry, fire's out."

"So I see, and I'm relieved. Good work. How did this happen?"

"This young fool—" Norman pointed to one of his apprentices, who ducked under the appendage, looking very hangdog, "—wasn't careful with the pot and splashed some oil over the surface. It caught fire, and in a panic, he grabbed one of the water pitchers and doused it."

Ren winced. He knew precisely what had happened after that. Cold water over burning oil would cause quite the explosion, the flames temporarily reaching several feet in the air. No wonder the beam on the ceiling looked scorched. "Anyone injured?"

"Praise all the gods, no injuries. I wet a towel and threw it over the fire, so it went out quickly after that. My deepest apologies, Warden, I know this isn't the best of times to have a kitchen fire."

"My dear chef," Ren drawled, his humor kicking in now that he knew it wasn't too serious, "is there ever a good time for a kitchen fire?"

Snorting, Norman's usual good humor surfaced for a moment. "Not that I know of. I take your point. Still, this is quite possibly one of the worst times to happen. My apologies. I assure you that the rest of the kitchen can work around being one stove short."

"While I'm relieved to hear that, let's get some workmen in here quickly and get this cleaned up. You can't continue to work with one stove short for tomorrow, not with this many people in the palace."

Nodding, Norman agreed, "It will make it very difficult."

"I'll take care of the workmen, you worry about dinner," Ren advised, internally resigning himself to a missed date in the process. He couldn't ask Hartmann to cover for him, though. Shift change was in an hour, and considering their troubles with security recently, he wanted Hartmann on hand to supervise that over babysitting a work crew. Ren had a bad feeling this would take several hours to fix. It might be midnight before everything finished.

"Thank you, Warden, that will help," Norman acknowledged.

Ren stepped back out, a little disappointed that duty called for him to stay, but also a little relieved to put off what would undoubtedly be an awkward conversation. He found Nixie waiting just outside and requested, "Can you run a message for me? Three, actually. Tell Chamberlain Frei that we've had a small kitchen fire and I need some workmen in tonight for repairs. Find Hartmann, tell him to focus on shift change, that I can manage supervising here. Then run down to the east side of the palace and tell Lord Deidrick Giles that I can't make dinner tonight. Give him my apologies, explain that the fire here demands my attention, and I'll make it up to him another night."

"Yes, sir," she responded promptly. She repeated it back to him to make sure she had it all straight, then stopped and really looked at him. Nixie, at nine, did not possess a fully-developed women's intuition yet, but it apparently was strong enough to sense something. "Sir, you look very disappointed for missing dinner."

Since she was one of his favorites, Ren leaned in and confided, "It's actually a date."

"Ooooh," she responded, eyebrows waggling. "First date?"

"No, you scamp, it is not the first. Off with you, he'll wonder where I am soon."

Giggling, she turned and ran back up the stairs, hopefully heading for Chamberlain Frei first, as Ren needed that work crew sooner rather than later.

Ren turned back to the kitchen and glared at it. What rotten timing. As much as he wished he could just leave it in other people's hands, he didn't dare. Ren didn't suspect for a moment that the apprentice had set the fire deliberately—the boy risked doing himself serious injury after all. But he also didn't put it past the criminal mind to take advantage of the situation to get past palace security and inside. If an assassin wanted in, posing as a workman would be a marvelously simple way to get his hands on a gate pass. As they still didn't know who had attacked Princess Alexandria, or if she had been deliberately targeted, it made the situation even more potentially dangerous. She might have enemies waiting in the city for just such an opportunity.

No, Ren had best stay and supervise, make sure everything was done right and the work crew didn't go anywhere they weren't supposed to. He'd just have to reschedule the date and The Talk with Deidrick for tomorrow night instead.

Dammit, he couldn't; tomorrow night was the engagement party for Prince Charles and Princess Alexandria. Fine, the night *after*, then.

Sometimes he hated being a responsible adult.

"Another date?" Galvath came into view with an empty plate balanced in one hand. His eyes caught the sight through the open kitchen door and he emitted a low whistle. "Damn. What happened?"

"Small kitchen fire that turned into a serious one due to an overzealous kitchen hand," Ren explain succinctly. "It's fine, no one's hurt."

"I came for another helping of that amazing flaky whatever-it-was," Galvath stated absently, neck craning to get a better look. "But I think I'm out of luck on that."

"Probably. Their major baking stove is now out of operation as it's right next to the damaged one." Ren often ran into Galvath near the kitchen, considering how much the man liked to eat. Seeing him here didn't surprise Ren much.

Galvath ducked inside long enough put the plate into a kitchen sink, then retreated to stand next to Ren. "So, another date?"

After their bout, Galvath had become a drinking buddy, so Ren felt comfortable enough to confide, "Yes. Same man."

"I thought Aart didn't do same sex attraction." Galvath cupped an elbow with one hand while tapping a finger to his lips with the other. "Isn't this whole situation strange?"

"Believe me, I find it strange, but happily so." Ren shrugged, hands splayed, as he didn't know how to explain this. "I'm sure anywhere else in the world, people would look at Deidrick sideways for this, but in Aart? Even if he's just experimenting and curious, no one's going to say much to him."

"Huh." Galvath pondered that for a moment. "Well, hopefully he's not pissy at a cancelled date. Even if he breaks things off with you, it'll be fine."

Ren didn't trust that twinkle of mischief in Galvath's eyes. "And why is that?"

"Because I'll be your date," Galvath informed him cheerfully.

Knowing very well the man was pulling his leg, Ren snorted. "Is that right."

"Hey now, I'm an excellent date," Galvath goaded him, eyebrows waggling outrageously. "I have many ladies who can testify to this."

"My dear friend," Ren drawled, enjoying the teasing, "I am not a woman. Taking me on a date is very different experience, I can assure you."

"I sure hope so. Otherwise there's something wrong with the world."

Chuckling, Ren decided he wished he could keep Galvath long-term. He wasn't sure if Galvath would stay with Princess Alexandria after the marriage. "I'll keep you company," Galvath offered, the mischief fading as his eyes took in the area, attention sharp and alert. "Better to make sure no one takes advantage and slips someone in with the workmen."

"My thought exactly." Ren clapped him on the back, glad to have the company.

5

The workmen were all ones Frei had used in the past, and they greeted some of the people in the kitchen by name, which set most of Ren's fears at ease. Still, he stayed and supervised, as he'd rather be safe than sorry. The kitchen staff took pity and fed him and Galvath, including a midnight snack when the hour ran late, bless them. Somewhere around one, the repairs were finished and everyone thankfully left for home. With it being so late, Galvath offered to take him drinking a different day, and Ren agreed it was for the best. The man still stayed until the bitter end, when the last workmen were escorted out, though, which he appreciated. They headed their separate ways afterwards, and Ren staggered into bed only to wake up at first light with sleep gluing his eyes together.

Today, Prince Charles and Princess Alexandria became officially engaged. As much as he would prefer sleep, his plate held far too much to afford even another half hour.

Ren pried himself out of bed—he suspected his covers were in league with demons or some such, they kept tripping him—washed up, ate a quick breakfast, and forced himself out the door. After that, he ran around like a chicken with its head cut off until the very last minute. Then he rushed to the formal chapel inside the palace, watching as Prince Charles and Princess Alexandria stood on either side of the altar with a marriage contract in front of them. Everyone that was anyone gathered inside, cramming to fit in, packed in like sardines. Ren estimated they had the entire noble court and half the city inside, and the chapel was only designed to fit about two hundred people. With great ceremony, the prince and princess read the terms aloud and then each signed a copy. Ren only stood at the doors long enough for the ceremony to proceed, and the moment it ended, he rushed off again to make sure that nothing calamitous happened.

Which, of course, nothing did. Not on his watch.

He found no time to socialize until the ball was well underway. The maids and Chamberlain Frei had outdone themselves decorating the place. Gauzy material in snow white swung down from the main chandelier in a soft arc and tied to the marble columns on both sides of the ballroom. Large bouquets of flowers perfumed the air in every conceivable corner, every gilded edge in the trim work shone dully by candlelight, and a buffet table full of delectables stood alongside the back wall. Breaching the main doors, Ren took in the sight of people dressed in the very finest of silks and velvets, dancing, chatting, laughing, all with a background of excellent music. He smiled at the sight, as truly, it was a beautiful one.

Entering properly, he searched for Deidrick, but had trouble finding him in the crowd. Ren knew he was present; he'd seen him during the ceremony and exchanged a wink and smile with him. Surely he was here as well. Deidrick adored social events.

"Ren!" a high voice scolded.

Turning to his right, he spotted the youngest child of the royal family, decked out from head to toe in her favorite blue, the delicate silver crown on her head ensconced in blond ringlets. "Princess Roslyn. You look quite cross."

"I want to dance. You took *ages* to get here," she informed him.

The two of them were dedicated dance partners, granted, but still, he found this demand amusing. At fifteen, Roslyn possessed the budding beauty of a woman who would slay men in the near future. If she wanted, with a snap of her fingers, any man in the room would oblige her. "I believe there are other men present?"

"They step on my feet," she sniffed, nose upturning.

Snorting, he couldn't refute that. The men in this country were not always graceful. Extending his hand, he asked, "Would you do me the honor?"

She promptly put her hand in his, informing him as she did so, "Lots of spins."

"Your wish is my command, my spoiled princess." Winking at her, he got her to giggle, then assumed the proper position. She'd finally grown enough that he no longer had to bend nearly in half to reach her, thankfully. Roslyn gave every sign of still being in her growth spurt, as her body grew straight up like a tree, her womanly curves struggling to keep up. Ren idly wondered just when she'd stop, or if she'd outgrow him at some point. The top of her head already hit his collarbone. Shaking the thought off, he turned his ear to the music. Their timing was good—a new song had just started, a quick paced folk dance. He stepped out strongly with his right foot, fearlessly joining the crowd circling about the room, and spun the princess as often as he dared.

Roslyn giggled and twirled, skirts billowing out as she moved, confident in her beauty and flaunting it to the world as only a teenage girl could. Ren indulged her, thoroughly entertained with this front-side seat of the show. He saw more than one young lord glare at them, no doubt miffed that the princess had turned him down only to dance with the warden. Some of them were quite good looking, if young, so he leaned in to confidentially ask, "Do none of them catch your eye? I find some of them quite handsome."

"They're boring," Roslyn answered, nose scrunching up. "All they want to talk about is hunting and how they bagged such-and-such and how dangerous it was. Boys are idiots."

"My dear friend, that does not improve with age. I'm afraid to tell you that we remain idiots for most of our lives."

"*You're* not an idiot," Roslyn refuted. "If you didn't like men so much, I'd seduce you."

Ren choked, nearly missing the beat.

"Although Mama said I shouldn't tell you that, I decided to tell you anyway," Roslyn continued, as if oblivious she had just landed a whopper on him. "She's quite determined to marry you off, you know. I told her that I'd marry you, I wouldn't mind, and she was actually tempted for a minute until Charles ruined it by pointing out that you are literally twice my age. Why does he do things like that?"

"Because he's your brother and it's his job to ruin things," Ren responded promptly. "I have a brother, trust me, I know."

"It's very inconvenient to have a brother," Roslyn concluded, still a little cross. "Do you think after they're married, I can convince Alexandria to take him home with her? Then I wouldn't have to deal with him."

"Sadly, Princess, he will likely remain here. Being the Crown Prince and all." Part of the reason why he adored Roslyn stemmed from the fact that he always knew exactly what was on her mind. She said everything that occurred to her. He also never knew what she would say next.

Roslyn's perfect bow mouth scrunched up into a pout. "Damn. You're likely right."

"Please don't curse at a formal ball," Ren pleaded with her lowly.

"You're the one that taught me all the curse words," she reminded him smugly.

Ren really couldn't refute that. "You caught me when I was drunk, I take no responsibility for that."

"I don't think you were that drunk," Roslyn refuted thoughtfully. "And you always give me frank answers when I ask you questions. You're the only one that ever does. Are you quite certain you won't marry me, Ren?"

"Quite certain, Princess. Sorry." Ren absolutely had to tell Brahms about this conversation later. His friend would get a good chuckle out of it.

"Damn," she repeated with a very heartfelt sigh. "If you change your mind, let me know."

"I promise," he responded, having to bite the inside of his cheek to keep from laughing. "Are the boys really bothering you that much? I tend to get proposed to when they're plaguing you."

If she weren't dancing, Roslyn would have stamped her foot. Her blue eyes flashed fire as she growled, "They're just such idiots. Even when I say no, they try to drag me anyway. But don't worry, I punched them in the stomach like you showed me."

"That's my girl," he approved. He made a mental note to investigate just who was being that persistent later and have a little talk with the young man.

The music ended and he delivered her safely into her parent's hands, bowing as he reached the front dais. "My King, My Queen, congratulations on a successful engagement."

"Thank you, Ren," King Gerhard responded with a weary eye on his youngest. "Roslyn, you *can* dance with people other than our warden."

Turning her nose up, she looked away, pointedly ignoring this.

"Thank you, Ren," Queen Eloise repeated, then gestured him to come in a little closer to whisper, "I heard a rumor that you're seeing someone. Please tell me that's true!"

Ren hesitated, not at all sure what to tell her. "Ah, well, it's true in a fashion. We haven't properly decided if we're courting each other yet or not."

Smacking him on the arm with a fan, Queen Eloise hissed in a low whisper. "Ren! Tell me these things when they happen! Who is it?"

"Ah. Actually it's—"

"Warden Ren?"

Turning, he found Princess Alexandria directly behind him, her hands clasped directly over her stomach. She did indeed look the part of a newly engaged woman, with a glow in her fair cheeks, her dainty figure wrapped in an elaborate gown of white velvet. Even Ren could see why Charles had taken one look at her and promptly asked for the right to court her. "Warden Ren," she continued in that lilted, charming accent, "I wonder if you'd do me the honor of a dance."

Ren's eyebrows rose, as he hadn't expected this. It was the first time she had spoken to him directly aside from a polite greeting. "I'd be pleased to, Your Highness."

Queen Eloise shooed him on, indicating they'd talk later, and he promptly stepped down from the dais with a feeling of relief. He really didn't know how to answer her questions.

They clasped hands lightly before stepping onto the dance floor, this time to a slow three beat tempo, the music encouraging people to lightly sway and twirl around the floor. He didn't dare spin her as enthusiastically as he did Roslyn, as he had the sense she wouldn't appreciate it in that heavy gown. She might also be trying to find a moment to speak with him. Her body language indicated something weighed on her mind, at any rate.

"Warden Ren," she said, chin up, her eyes on his. "I feel that I owe you an apology. Without realizing it, I have done you quite the disservice."

Well. How unexpected. "Your Highness, it is not many that can own up to a fault. I accept the apology and thank you for it."

"I'm sure you're aware of the prejudices among my people, but I shouldn't have followed so blindly along with them, or ignored the obvious," she continued, still a little troubled. "Charles esteems you highly, everyone in my family-to-be adores you, and it's obvious you run a tight ship in the palace. There is nothing that goes on here that you are not aware of. After your fight with Galvath, he told me many things about your countrymen, and the fighting style you use. I think I would like to sit and have tea with you tomorrow. I want to understand you better. I feel that I must."

"And now I understand why Charles loves you." Ren smiled as she blushed, slowing their pace a little so that they could talk more easily. "I would be pleased to, Your Highness. I think it would make life easier all around if we were on good terms with each other."

"Yes, precisely. And Roslyn tells me that you've trained her in self-defense, something that even a woman can use against an armed man. I want to learn that as well."

"That is entirely prudent and I'll gladly teach you." Galvath might join in on the lessons, for that matter. The man thought highly of the Rising Sun style. The music trailed off as the band ended the song, and Ren released her hand to give her a slight bow. "Thank you for the dance."

"Thank you for being understanding," she responded with a brilliant smile. "I do believe a young lord behind you is trying to get your attention?"

Turning, Ren saw Deidrick right on the outskirts of the dance floor, his eyes warm. "I certainly hope he is, Your Highness."

Perhaps woman's intuition told her something, or Ren had a very obvious look on his face that told the story. Either way, she lifted a fan to her face, hiding a smile behind the white lace. "I see. Go, then. We'll chat more later."

"Thank you." He bowed again, then lost no time in going to Deidrick's side.

Deidrick caught his hand, stepping in close enough to be well within Ren's personal space. "I thought you'd never join us."

"Duty," Ren shrugged, not caring about that at the moment. He was not oblivious to the many stares and whispers they garnered, but he chose to be blind to it. Let them say what they wished.

"Ren, I didn't know you could dance so well. It makes me want to dance with you. Do you know how to follow?"

As it was Brahms who'd taught him how to dance Aart's dances in the first place, at least the basic ones, Ren had by default learned the women's steps first. "Yes, I do."

Drawing him out onto the floor, Deidrick gave him a devilish smile. "Then dance with me."

Was it his imagination, or had the air grown noticeably warmer all of a sudden? Ren swallowed hard, but gamely followed his—lover?—something, anyway, onto the dance floor. Deidrick brought him confidently into the dance position. Ren gripped his shoulder, hand in hand, and moved with him as the song started, another slow ballad that encouraged close dancing. Butterflies swarmed in his stomach.

"You're nervous," Deidrick observed, bemused.

"Believe it or not, I've never danced with another man at a formal event like this. And you've surprised me. You've been surprising me since our meeting, really, I never know what you're going to do next."

"Like this?" Deidrick darted in for a quick kiss.

A titter went through the watching crowd but Ren ignored that, too. "Like that. The queen asked me earlier about you, you know. I wasn't sure what to say."

"Well, now, you don't need to say anything," Deidrick told him, bringing him in a little closer so that their lips almost grazed each other. The heat was definitely rising in the room, no question about it. "They can see for themselves."

A grin of unholy delight spread over Ren's face. "That's good enough for me."

6

A permanent smile lived on Ren's face for three straight days after that night. Not that he and Deidrick had seen much of each other, the duties of the castle demanding most of Ren's time, but it pleased him enormously that Deidrick would so obviously claim him in front of a crowd. They had plans to meet up tonight, and Ren had secretly bought a few things with the fervent hope they would finally get into a proper bed with all clothes off.

Most of the visiting dignitaries who had come for the engagement left, freeing Ren's time up and allowing him to return to his usual schedule. He went to the training yard before lunch and stretched to limber up, taking his time, as he hadn't been able to train in three days and felt stiff because of it.

Not many people trained at the moment; just a few guards and one lord practicing archery off in the corner. Ren enjoyed the relative peace, stretching flat on his back with his legs held over his head. Ahhh, that was better. That helped the knot in his lower back unwind.

Now if he could just solve the problem that had cropped up yesterday, of how a young maid gained entrance to the west wing of the palace without proper authorization, his life would be set. She seemed completely innocent of any wrongdoing, and very apologetic for being in the wrong place, but *how* had she gotten that far without someone checking her movements? Ren didn't think his guards complacent—in fact, they knew better than to let anything go, so how? How did an unfamiliar woman wander that far past his security?

He'd have to investigate this. If an enemy caught on to this and figured out her route, he could be in serious trouble.

"Ren."

Rolling up, he greeted with a smile, "Deidrick! I thought you were out with your family today."

"I was," Deidrick responded, making a face. Putting his back to the railing, he leaned against it, his expression strangely reminiscent of a sulking child. "My father blistered my ears this morning. Apparently, Harriet is up in arms about my conduct at the ball—"

Ren got up to his feet, stalling him with a hand. He'd learned that Deidrick would just roll with a story and not give him all the details if he didn't stop him. "Wait, who's Harriet?"

"Oh, my fiancée. Supposed to be fiancée, at least. We haven't done the proper announcement yet. It's just an understanding that's been in my family forever," Deidrick blithely responded.

The words hit like a slap in the face. Through numb lips, Ren croaked, "You're engaged?"

"Not officially, like I said. But Harriet acts as if we were already, which can be troublesome, like now. Anyway, she went whining to my father, and he's always doted on her, so now he's mad at me for making it obvious that we're together in front of everyone. Ridiculous, really; as if the man didn't have multiple lovers himself. I ask you, how is that fair?"

Ren owed an apology to his instincts for not listening. They'd tried to warn him something was wrong, but he'd overrode the feeling, convincing himself that it was alright now. That Deidrick wouldn't kiss him in front of the reigning monarchs if he wasn't serious. Ren's fists clenched into a white-knuckled grip, bile rising in his throat. For the past two and a half weeks, he'd been involved with someone else's fiancé?

Blithely unaware of Ren's growing anger, Deidrick continued, his voice growing louder. "I find it unfair, anyway, but he's threatened to cut me off financially if I don't at least appease Harriet. So I can't meet up with you tonight, sorry; we'll have to reschedule for tomorrow. I'm supposed to take her to some musical event to make up for my behavior. But it's fine, she's easily distracted. I'm sure we can be with each other on the weekend. Just not at my apartment, she'll be watching that; maybe yours?"

"You arrogant, unfeeling bastard," Ren breathed, appalled. Was this the true nature of the man he'd developed a liking for?

Deidrick had the gall to look surprised. "Why are you cursing at me?"

"*BECAUSE YOU'RE AN ASSHOLE!*" Ren roared. Never one to be quiet when mad, his voice echoed around the training yard, bouncing off stone and repeating itself. All sounds of training behind him abruptly ceased. "Do you really think that if I had known about your engagement, I would have casually started a love affair with you? And now you tell me that you're ignoring a sweet woman who was appalled at your conduct, that you'll put her neatly in her place, and go right back to pursuing me? Have you no shame or conscience whatsoever?"

"Ren," Deidrick responded with a roll of the eyes, impatience sending him off his casual sprawl against the rail. "This marriage is mostly a political one, alright? It doesn't really mean anything to me or her. She was just embarrassed that I was obviously with someone else. She felt like she lost face over it or something. Calm down. It's not like our affair is going to break any hearts."

The lack of any empathy shocked Ren into a spluttering silence. How did he argue with a person who didn't see anything wrong with their conduct?

"And it's not like we have to stop seeing each other when the engagement becomes official," Deidrick assured him. "Is that what you're worried about? Don't be. My father is married and keeps two mistresses in town; it's not uncommon, you know."

Ren's heart clenched unbearably, constricting to the point of pain. Those casual words, putting him on the same level as a mistress, were akin to taking a punch to the balls. Without thinking, Ren cocked a fist back and hit that smug mouth with full strength.

Deidrick spun with the force of it, and fell hard onto the ground. Gasping in pain, he lifted a hand to his bleeding mouth, staring up at Ren with bewildered astonishment and growing anger.

"Fuck you, Giles," Ren snarled at him. "I'm not your bloody mistress. Be thankful that I don't leave you half-dead for the wrong you've done both me and her. Her name."

"What?" Deidrick mumbled past the blood in his mouth. "What are you doing, you're taking this too far—"

"GIVE ME HER NAME," Ren yelled at him, grabbing him by the collar and shaking Deidrick like a dirty dishrag. No, even a dirty dishrag would have some use. This young lordling wasn't even comparable to that.

Not understanding any of the situation, but angry just the same, Deidrick glared back at him. "Unhand me! Seriously, what are you doing?"

"Deidrick Giles, men like you are pigs and should be neutered before you do even more damage to the world. At the very least, that young woman deserves a heartfelt apology, and since it's very obvious it won't come from you, it falls to me. Give. Me. Her. Name."

"Harriet Eberhardt."

Ren promptly dropped him. "If you come near me again, I'll break every major bone in your body. You are rank, a general offense to both men and women, and any further conversation with you would infect my brain. I pity the poor woman who's forced to marry you, as you're unfit for any place but hell."

Spluttering, Deidrick put his feet back under him. "That's uncalled for!"

Too angry to rein in the impulse, Ren gave him one more hard punch, this time landing it solidly in the gut, forcing Deidrick to bend sharply over. After that, though, the idea of touching Deidrick again sickened Ren thoroughly. Nauseous with loathing, shaking in anger, he snatched up sword and jacket and left the training yard in a half-run before he could give into impulse and really neuter the rutting hog.

He went straight to his apartment, filled the pitcher bowl with water, and dunked his head into it. Partially to wipe away the growing tears, partially to cool his head, as he felt enraged enough to do something stupid. Shaking, he pulled his head out after a good minute and stayed there, hunched over and dripping.

Never before had he missed Brahms so desperately. He needed his friend's cool head and even temper right now more than anything. Well, no, come to think of it, Brahms would hear about this and probably tear Deidrick's head right off. Maybe it was better he lived on the opposite end of the country at the moment.

It took a long time for him to calm down. When he felt like he wouldn't burst into either a murder spree or tears, he changed his clothes, redid his hair into a tight ponytail, then left the apartment again.

Perhaps Deidrick was right on one point. Perhaps Harriet really didn't love the boy and wanted only to save face in their political marriage. It wasn't uncommon for this sort of alliance to be made among the nobility. But Ren didn't really care if that were the truth in this case. His honor demanded an apology be given at the very least, and if there was something he could do to make amends for this, he would immediately do so.

While he wasn't acquainted with the Eberhardt family directly, he did know the name and was aware they had a house in town. But he didn't know where it was located, so he hunted up the one person who knew everything.

Chamberlain Frei was ancient as the hills, with the energy of a sixty-year-old, and the stooped posture of a man in his hundreds. He'd been chamberlain in the palace since King Gerhard's grandfather reigned, and consequently knew every scandal, secret, and history amongst the nobility for the past century. He'd taken Ren under his wing when Ren had first assumed position as warden here and saved him in the process, giving him the time to really learn the job without blundering into embarrassing mistakes.

Because of his age and limited mobility, Frei lived behind a desk on the main floor with dedicated teams of runners to deliver all messages for him. It looked more like a war room, with a table covered in correspondence and lists, timetables pinned to the walls, and sketches for event decoration layouts. Ren stepped in and around the runners with practiced ease as they scampered out the door, and came directly to the desk.

Frei glanced up, took one look at Ren's face, and immediately dropped the list in his hands. "Ren. Have you been crying?"

"That obvious, eh?" Ren dropped into the overstuffed chair near the desk, feeling a decade older. "I just discovered that Deidrick Giles is a base whoreson who should have been drowned at birth."

"Ah. I'd wondered at your connection with him. His father is not, shall we say, the best of men. I've seen little of Deidrick, being raised in the country as he was, so I thought perhaps he did not take after his father."

"Unfortunately, the apple fell right on the tree's roots in this case. He just informed me in an oh-so-casual manner that his fiancée was upset with his conduct, that we'd need to be more discreet in seeing each other, but not to worry, his father had two mistresses so there shouldn't be a problem with him having me." Ren was proud of himself for reporting factually, even though he felt another surge of rage wash through his system.

Frei's eyes closed in fatalistic understanding. "Ren, my dear friend, I'm so sorry. If I had known his true character, I would have warned you."

"I know you would have, Frei, I don't lay a lick of blame at your door."

"He's truly engaged? Why haven't I heard of it?"

"It's apparently not official, just an understanding between families, although the way he said it made me think that they're going to make it official soon."

"They're likely trying to time it to not impinge on Prince Charles' and Princess Alexandria's announcement," Frei commented. "Which is smart of them, truly. It wouldn't do to steal the spotlight. Unfortunately, the effort to be shrewd has backfired immensely in this case. Did not that young fool understand you are a favorite of the royal family? That they will not take news of this well?"

Oh hell. Ren had not thought that far yet, but Queen Eloise and Roslyn especially would be very vocal in their displeasure. "I can't say the thought disturbs me overmuch."

"Nor I. It would do well, I think, for someone to teach that young whelp a lesson since his parents failed to instill any moral principle in him." Frei leaned toward him, eyes sympathetic. "Ren. What can I do to help you?"

"I need information," Ren responded, dearly wishing he had Brahms' shoulder to cry on. Or get drunk with. Gods above, he needed a drink. "The fiancée is Harriet Eberhardt. Do you know where she lives?"

"You wish to visit her? Why?"

"Because that poor girl deserves a heartfelt apology, and I'm the only one who can give it to her."

"Ren, if there's any blameless party in this mess, it's certainly you."

Shaking his head, Ren repeated, "Please tell me where she lives."

Frei's thin lips pressed together. The man clearly didn't agree with Ren's thought process but bent enough to answer, "She's in Garden Square, Three Shields Manor."

"Thank you." Ren marveled once more at Frei's memory. Was there anything the man didn't retain? "Can you ask Hartmann to cover for me for the next two hours?"

"I will ask Hartmann to cover for you for the rest of the day," Frei corrected sternly. "You take the rest of the day and sort out your emotions."

Probably for the best. Nodding, he agreed and stood. "Thank you. Ask him to look into the matter of that young maid in the west wing, would you? I want that answered."

"I promise we'll look into it. Go, my friend, and let me know if you need anything else from me."

Not knowing what else to say, Ren nodded and left.

Ren didn't go directly to Garden Square, deviating long enough to stop by a flower shop and have a small bouquet of purple hyacinths made up. He didn't know what else to do to relay his contrition without speaking to the woman herself. Odds were good that Lady Harriet wouldn't want to see him. The flowers might be the best option to get his apology across, as the women in Aart were very well versed in the language of flowers. If all else failed, hopefully the bouquet would help relay his sincerity.

The florist put the bouquet together with a sympathetic look to him, which he really didn't need, and he paid quickly. Leaving, he made his way with a hasty stride, as he wanted nothing more than to get this over with.

He found the house easily—not because of its unique architecture, but because of the metal name plate near the front gate. Every house on the square was made from white limestone, with circular front porches and grand three-story buildings. This one looked no different, aside from a selection of flowers in the front courtyard instead of the usual grass and bushes. Stepping through the gate, he raised his hand to knock on the door, then paused as his courage faltered. Strange, how this scared him more than fighting in a war had.

No. He had to do this.

Squaring his chin, he raised the wolf head knocker and gave it a solid thump.

It took only a moment for the door to open, and judging by the livery, it was the butler of the house. He appraised Ren with a doubletake of surprise, especially the flowers, before training shut his expression down into one of polite disinterest. "Can I help you, Warden?"

"I'd like to see Lady Harriet Eberhardt if she's in."

"She is, sir, although I'm not sure if she is entertaining visitors. Regardless, if you'll step into the front parlor, I'll inform her that you're here."

"I appreciate that, thank you. If nothing else, would you convey these to her?" Ren wouldn't blame her for not wanting to see him, but he hoped the flowers would help.

The butler took them with a doubtful frown, then gestured for Ren to go right, through a pair of open sliding doors. He did so, then stopped, as he didn't know if he should sit or not. The room was small, with only four chairs and a fireplace, furnished with a thick rug and a tasteful landscape on the wall and nothing else. Clearly, it was meant only for waiting visitors.

Too agitated to sit, he chose instead to stand at parade rest, hands clasped behind his back. Time passed by with unbearable slowness, the ticking of the mantel clock loud in the silence. Gradually, however, he heard the smart clip-clop of heels against tile. Looking up, he saw a young woman coming his direction with the bouquet of flowers in her arms.

So this was Harriet Eberhardt. She looked lovely—not a stunning beauty, but a pretty girl nonetheless. Her hair was curly and rambunctious, put up in a high bun, but dark tendrils escaped, framing an oval face and red-rimmed eyes. Ren took one look at her expression and knew that this was not a formal alliance, not on her end. She'd been just as upset and betrayed as he.

Damn that fool for being such an odious codpiece.

"Warden." She paused in the doorway and greeted him with a small curtsey. "I don't believe we've formally been introduced. I'm Harriet Eberhardt."

Ren swept into a low bow, feeling even worse, if possible. Despite everything, she still greeted him civilly. If their roles were reversed, he wasn't sure he'd be able to do the same. "My lady."

"I've received your flowers, but I'm afraid they confuse me. Did you choose this bouquet knowing its meaning?"

"I did." Ren took his sword in one hand, maneuvering it back and out of the way so that he could kneel, then fold himself completely down so that his forehead touched the floor, hands forming a triangle on the ground in front of him.

"Warden!" she protested, coming fully into the room.

"Lady Harriet, please accept a heartfelt apology and plea for forgiveness," he said thickly without looking up. "I have no excuse except that I honestly didn't know until this morning about the engagement."

She stopped abruptly. "You didn't know? Did he not even mention me to you?"

"Not a word."

There was a choked sound above him, a cry cut off. When she spoke again, her words shook with restrained emotion. "Warden, please do rise. You of all people do not owe me an apology."

Ren gracefully got back on his feet, not sure how she took this, but glad at least she didn't seem to blame him for any of this disaster. "Perhaps, but is not an apology owed?"

"Yes, certainly, and I thank you for it." She clutched the flowers a little tighter to her, eyes bright with unshed tears. "I am quite at a loss, you see. Deidrick didn't think anything about his behavior deserved a scolding. I knew him to be somewhat fickle, but we grew up together; at the very least I thought he would not trample over my heart like his father routinely does with his mother."

"I'm afraid that he instead grew immune to such heartbreak instead, as he blithely assured me that—" Ren abruptly realized that was probably not the right thing to say, and snapped his mouth shut.

"That it would be perfectly fine to continue seeing each other, just more discreetly?" she finished sadly. "Yes, I expect he did."

"If it makes you feel any better, I punched him for saying that," Ren informed her. "Twice."

Startled, she blinked at him, then gave a watery chuckle. "Actually, that does. Thank you. Hopefully that helps him understand that his behavior is not acceptable. Words certainly haven't made any impression on him."

"One can hope." Gently, he asked her, "What can I do to make amends?"

"Oh, Warden." Taking his hand, she squeezed it softly, trying her best to smile at him, although it wavered badly. "I feel that you have been just as hurt by this affair as I have. I'll make no demands on you. In fact, I will make it clear to anyone who asks that you are solely blameless in this. Your conduct has been beyond reproach to me, which is more than I can say about everyone else. Answer only one question for me? Deidrick wouldn't tell me."

"Ask," Ren encouraged and prayed she didn't ask him about any intimate details. He'd tell her, but she'd likely faint at the answer. Everything about Harriet screamed she was a sheltered, properly brought up young woman.

"Who approached whom, initially?"

Oh good. Well, not good, actually. "Deidrick approached me. He was, ah, curious."

"The illicit and unknown has forever drawn his attention," Harriet commented sadly. "Thank you, Warden, for answering me so truthfully."

Sensing that he shouldn't linger any longer, he directed, "Please, if at any point you need either a sympathetic ear, or for me to punch that young louse again, send word. I'll immediately come to you."

"Thank you," she repeated, her smile briefly genuine. "And please, feel free to ask the same of me. Not that I can punch as well as you, but I'm quite angry enough to stab him with my fan."

And do damage, likely. The ladies' court fans were made from either hard wood or metal. "I encourage you do it regardless. And—I'm sorry if this is out of line—but I hope you don't marry him. I feel that you'll be in for a lifetime of heartbreak if you do."

Harriet studied him for a moment, brown eyes clear and unreadable. "Until this moment, I thought I might be able to forgive him for this. But seeing your conduct, I realize that what he has done to us both truly is unforgiveable. Rest at ease, Warden. I won't marry him."

Relieved, for her sake, Ren gave her a smile. "Good. Then I'll take my leave, my lady. Truly, let me know if you need my assistance."

"I will, Warden, thank you. And I know the odds are stacked against you here, but please don't let this disastrous affair close you off to future possibilities of happiness. You deserve that as much as I."

Ren smiled, gave her another bow, and left. He couldn't tell her that this whole affair had hammered in the lesson that anyone who approached him here would be like Deidrick—satisfying a curiosity. He wouldn't be fooled again.

"He said *what* to you?" Queen Eloise demanded, high spots of color on her cheeks, her motherly frame nearly shaking with outrage.

Ren sighed, weary now with the whole affair. He'd barely stepped foot in the castle when Chaz snagged him and dragged him directly to the Queen's Garden. It was a lovely garden, filled with babbling fountains, beautiful flower beds and a maple tree gone red and gold in the fall air. The mood, however, was so dark in the garden that it threatened to wilt everything in the tranquil space.

Clearly the whole family had heard something about that morning, and they all sat tensely on the padded benches, waiting for his return. King Gerhard appeared the calmest, but even he paced back and forth, a troubled and unhappy frown pulling his face into long lines. Somewhat to Ren's surprise, Alexandria sat next to her future husband, biting on her bottom lip and looking at everyone else in worry.

"I can't believe the audacity of the man," Charles said to no one in particular. "Did he really think he could just have a dalliance with you without any repercussions?"

"Well, he thought wrong," Queen Eloise snarled, eyes snapping. Ren had seen kinder eyes on an assassin. "No one messes with *my* Ren and just waltzes off afterwards. He's banned from the castle for life."

"Now wait, dearest," King Gerhard protested, his head coming up sharply. "We can't do that."

"And whyever not?" his wife snapped back.

"Because he is Lord Giles' only heir," the king responded in exasperation. "He has to sit on the Council of Lords when his father retires, which means he needs to learn how to do all of that now. I agree he needs to be punished. I don't want that kind of moral degradation in my lords, but we can't banish him forever."

"How about a public apology to everyone wronged and he's banished for six months?" Charles suggested.

Ren felt that was more reasonable. "I like that suggestion. Don't glare at me so, My Queen, I got my revenge this morning."

Grinning, Roslyn demanded, "Did you punch him?"

"Twice. He's not going to be eating comfortably for a while." Winking at her, he ignored the evil cackles this got, and tried to be more adult about the whole thing. "My Queen, as angry as I am about the whole affair, I do not want to be a stumbling block for any of you. He's a lord, he's accountable for many people, and he is their advocate. He must be able to speak with you on their behalf."

Queen Eloise's jaw set in an angry and stubborn way. She clearly didn't appreciate him being reasonable about this. Right now, she wanted blood and this milder sentence did not appease her.

"If anything, there is only one favor I can ask," he continued, hoping to set her on a different path and redirect the anger a little. "His family has set great store in the marriage. I'm not sure why, but I have no doubt it's because of land or prestige, something along those lines. If you deny them the right of that marriage and take Lady Harriet in hand, finding her a better husband, I feel like that would be the best revenge."

"I'm for that," Roslyn voted, putting a hand in the air. "I only met her once, but Lady Harriet is a sweet person, Mama. She doesn't deserve that—"

"Language, Roslyn," Queen Eloise corrected.

"I didn't even say anything yet," Roslyn grumbled, rolling her eyes.

"No, but we knew what you were thinking," Ren assured her. He really shouldn't have taught her all of those insults. He'd turned her into a swearing princess. "Not that you're wrong, he certainly is."

"Listen to Charles and Ren," King Gerhard pleaded with his wife. "They speak sense. And the public apology will be especially humiliating; you know Lord Giles hates embarrassment more than anything else."

Outmaneuvered on all sides, Queen Eloise grumpily subsided. "Oh, very well. I'll speak with Lady Harriet myself and make sure that she's better situated with a husband who won't dream of cheating on her. Ren, we'll do the same with you."

"Now wait a minute." Ren put up both hands, trying to halt this idea before she got the bit between her teeth and ran with it. "We've already had this discussion and I told you how impossible it is."

"One step at a time, dearest," King Gerhard advised. "Let's tackle the easily attainable things first and consider Ren later. Besides, I think he needs some time to heal from all of this. We shouldn't try to force the matter."

Ren mouthed to him a fervent 'thank you' behind the queen's head, to which the king gave him a barely perceptible wink.

"I do wish that General Brahms was here," Roslyn sighed. "He would be the right person to cheer Ren up."

Not able to disagree with that, Ren chose to skirt around it. "It's just as well he isn't here, as he would be perfectly willing to serve as the queen's assassin in this matter."

Queen Eloise lit up. "Excellent, we'll recall him at once."

"Eloise," King Gerhard growled in exasperation. "You can't have the idiot murdered."

His wife glared daggers at him and pointedly didn't agree.

Knowing very well that Queen Eloise was like a lioness when one of hers was harmed, Ren chose to take her attitude in the spirit it was meant.

Clapping a hand on his shoulder, Charles invited him, "There's only one way to deal properly with heartbreak. Let's get smashing drunk."

"Best offer I've heard all day," Ren admitted, readily standing.

"Me too," Alexandria surprised him by saying. "I will drink with you. The more people to share your sorrows, the quicker they pass."

Charles leaned in and whispered, "Don't be fooled, she can drink you under the table."

Ren and Alexandria still didn't know each other all that well yet, so it touched him that she would be sympathetic and make this offer to join in. Smiling, he agreed, "Please join us. And don't worry, all of you. This isn't the first time I've been disappointed in love."

"Hopefully it's the last?" Roslyn offered. "And remember, I'll marry you, if you can't find a man to appreciate you."

Crossing to her, he kissed her on the cheek. "I wouldn't dare, your papa would murder me."

Giggling, she didn't disagree. King Gerhard gave his daughter a weary look, so accustomed to her proposing that he couldn't bring himself to scold her for it again.

"Come." Charles caught him with an arm around the shoulders and guided him off toward the palace's wine cellars. "Let's bury all sorrow in alcohol, wake up with splitting headaches in the morning, and not give this idiot any more of our time. He's claimed too much of it already."

Ah, really, with friends like this, what else could he possibly wish for? Ren gave a firm nod. "On that, I heartily agree."

Arman Brahms glared at the relic of a castle as if it had personally insulted not only his mother, but every woman in his ancestral line. He could feel his already irritable mood darken another notch as he took in the site.

Supposedly, when he'd first gotten his orders, he'd been tasked with simply coming up here for six months while they fixed Kassmeyer Fortress along the northern border. It was old and crumbling, parts of it needed to be either shored up or knocked down and replaced completely. As a Brahms, Arman knew precisely what to do, as every Brahms child basically cut their teeth on swords and masonry. He'd first laid eyes on the problem months ago, determined they might be able to fix it in six months, and felt a little relieved that he could get back to Ren quickly.

And then the damn Z's had attacked this morning and burned half of the fortress down.

They'd been repelled quickly enough, but the fire had spread fast in this dry spell, and they'd not had enough water or shovels to put it out before it had done damage. Arman had had to order half of the supports they'd built be removed, as they were nothing more than charcoal now.

He'd wanted, before his deployment orders landed in his lap, to talk to Ren. To change their relationship from what they had now. Arman had petitioned Queen Eloise, fruitlessly, to release Ren to go with him. He'd expected her to deny the request, but even still, it'd stung. He wanted Ren with him. And despite his best efforts, apparently his unhappiness had hung over him like a dark cloud, as no one up here was at all pleased to be stuck with their irritable general for another year.

Sighing in resignation, he tromped back to his tent. Technically, he could commandeer a room inside the fortress, but he was so mad at the building he couldn't even contemplate staying inside of it.

No, to be honest, it wasn't the fortress he was mad at. It was the idea that he would be stuck up here another year fixing this mess. He didn't dare take his troops back down or call this a lost cause, either. Kassmeyer was here for a reason. It and Brahms Fortress protected two of the roads coming into Aart. It had to stand. It had to protect their northern border. It was in no condition to do either at the moment, hence why he had three hundred men to augment the garrison already stationed here.

Before he could reach his tent, his batman Robert hailed him. "Sir! We have a courier."

Eager for news, Arman switched paths and went down to the open command tent instead. A fresh-faced courier—he must have been in the army a whole three months, as he looked barely sixteen—

immediately stood at his entrance and saluted him, which Arman returned. He looked moderately dusty from the road, but Robert had already fetched him a drink, being the considerate man he was. Robert was good at seeing to other's needs; hence his position as Arman's batman.

"General, I've a bundle of letters for you," the courier informed him, handing over a thick stack held together by cheap twine.

Hoping a letter from Ren was in there somewhere, Arman took them and gave the lad a nod and gestured for him to take one of the stools next to the table. He sank into one opposite as he asked, "What news?"

"Precious little good, sir," the courier confessed with a sour face. "Princess Alexandria was attacked on the way in to visit us, did you hear of that?"

"No," Arman responded in alarm. "Anyone hurt?"

"Most of her guards, sir. They were attacked in Bhodhsa, actually, nearly in Aart. The *who* is still in question, or so I heard. They're investigating, but the men who attacked her were careful to cover their tracks. As to *why*, there's all sorts of reasons flying about. There's a group that says there's some sort of financial gain to be had from the marriage, some monopoly that will be formed, and they want no part of it."

Arman snorted. Nonsense, that was.

The courier apparently agreed, as he shrugged wryly and continued, "Not that anyone's paying attention to the screaming. But the main people who are unhappy are another group. They say it isn't done, that people shouldn't mix blood, which don't make sense to me either, although not many are saying that one too loudly. Have you heard of that, sir?"

"No, but don't put much stock in it," Robert advised the young man. "People are always leaping to conclusions they shouldn't. So they still don't know for sure who attacked her...that bodes ill."

So it did. Protecting against an unknown enemy was the hardest thing to do. Arman didn't imagine Ren was very happy about the situation right now considering it would be his responsibility to protect Princess Alexandria while she stayed in Aart.

Because Robert knew that Arman wouldn't ask, he did it for him. The middle-aged veteran gave Arman a pointed look as he did so, one saying Arman should really start speaking for himself at some point.

"And how is Warden Ren?"

"Not happy, sir," the courier answered frankly. For some reason, he cast Arman a nervous look as he answered, his body leaning back as if expecting an explosion soon. "He, ah, had a love affair go very wrong on him."

Breath, thought, motion—everything ceased for a moment. Nothing but pitched blackness and silence resounded in his head for a split second, as his world came crashing to a halt. Arman focused on the courier, sure he'd heard that wrong, praying he had, alarm rising and twisting his chest. "What?"

"A young lord, Deidrick Giles, he was courting Warden Ren a month back," the courier explained, drops of sweat dewing on his skin. His eyes skittered nervously about, not settling on Arman. "But no one knew Giles was engaged already, not until they'd been courting a few weeks. The warden thrashed him right in the training yard when he found out, but…the fallout hasn't been pretty."

An internal scream resonated in his head. Arman's breath rasped in his throat, his emotions torn between anger and pain. Ren.

His Ren, in other man's arms.

Understanding struck as the full depth of his emotions blazed across all of his nerves, making all his previous wishes fall flat in comparison.

Dammit.

No, not his Ren; not *his* Ren at all because Arman, like a stupid fool, hadn't asked. Hadn't said anything before he'd left. He'd wanted their relationship to change, but Arman had assumed it would be safe to wait until after he came home again before broaching the subject to Ren. After all, no one in Aart had come out with same-sex inclinations in the past five years; who would be Arman's rival?

The fact the relationship had barely lasted a few weeks only gave him a small measure of peace. His Ren never went halfway on anything, so if he'd been involved with this man, his heart had likely taken a bruising from it when the relationship turned poorly. Arman hated that Ren was in pain without Arman being there to comfort him. His fists clenched until his nails bit into his palms, the knuckles white under his strain.

He heard the courier hastily get up, Robert hustling him away before Arman's temper exploded. Of course, Robert understood exactly why Arman was ready to murder someone. He'd confided everything to the man before they'd even left Castle-de-Haut.

With the cool, cold logic that had served him well in the war, Arman's mind clicked over double-time, thinking of logistics, timelines, supplies, all in an effort to find the most efficient way for him to get back to Ren. He had to return to Ren as quickly as he could. Time was clearly not on his side, nor fate. He'd be wise to not give either a second chance of screwing with them.

When Robert re-entered the tent, he did so with the air of a man facing down a half-starved wolf. "Sir?"

"Seven months," Arman rasped, already standing. He needed to take one of the workmen's spots, tear into the half-ruined castle himself, or he'd go mad. "We get this done in seven months."

"Sir?" Robert swallowed, nervous for the first time in their acquaintance. Then again, he'd never seen Arman in a pitch-black rage before. "Is that possible?"

"Seven months," Arman maintained, his tone brooking no argument. He'd make it possible.

And damn anyone that tried to stand in his way.

7

Seven months later

The deck of the boat bobbed gently on the water as it floated ever closer to Castel-de-Haut, Aart's capital. Arman had been away for nearly two long years, and he'd cursed every second of it. Guarding the northern border until the new fortress could be finished had been vital, he understood that, and he'd done his duty. But he also hadn't waited for the mortar to completely set on the last stone before ordering his men to pack up and start for home.

Enough was enough.

Zonhoven Palace came in sight, the early evening sun gleaming on its white stone walls and copper roofs, sitting high up on the hill. Its towers and spires reached high into the sky, arches formed between them, framing the heart of the structure's main wings. The windows sometimes caught the setting sun, gleaming in the light like a magical flare. People sometimes referred to it as the fairytale castle. Arman wasn't the type to be given to fancy, but even he could see it. In this moment, a sharp pang tugged at his heart as he took in the sight, and he swallowed hard to keep his emotions in check.

"General Brahms."

Turning his head to the nth degree, Arman looked toward his batman.

Robert, not deterred by the lack of a verbal greeting, spoke anyway. "Our ship captain assures me we'll dock with the hour. Might I ask as to your plans, sir?"

"I'll report directly to the king." Arman thought that obvious enough, then realized that Robert would need more instructions than that. "Take everything to the general's quarters."

"Of course, sir." With a glance about, Robert checked everyone's positions on the narrow river boat, but most of the officers traveling with them were well aft, out of hearing. Still, he stepped in a little closer and lowered his tone. "Sir, about your plans...."

Arman knew Robert worried about his plans for Ren. And the batman wasn't alone in that—Arman felt half-convinced Ren would not go along with them. The other half desperately hoped he would.

A fine knife edge to balance on, emotionally speaking. Arman kept his emotions to himself most of the time, too private of a man to comfortably share them. Robert had been with him for years, though, ever since Arman made officer. He trusted the man completely, and had needed help arranging preparations, so he'd taken him in confidence. Only to Robert could he confide, "He might not agree. I know."

Robert's round face creased in worry as he looked up at his employer. "Sir, everything I know about Ren encourages me to think he'll look very favorably on your offer. But I want to impress upon you, he might not be in a suitable mindset right now to receive it."

Biting back a sigh of impatience, Arman reiterated, "I know, Robert."

"I'm not talking about just that unpleasantness of seven months ago, sir. I'm talking about right now. Ren is likely up to his ears in worries, trying to safeguard everyone in the palace while enemies are scrabbling at his defenses, trying to break through. You might have to wait until this trouble is settled before he is ready to hear you properly."

That was something else the rumors had brought to him, news of strange events happening in Zonhoven Palace. People getting in that shouldn't, or being in areas they weren't authorized to enter. The rumors contained an ugly twist to them, laying the blame at Ren's feet, but Arman knew him too well. Something else was at play here, something he hadn't heard through those deliberately damning rumors.

It seemed like he returned to Ren at precisely the time he needed him most. Laying a hand on his batman's shoulder, Arman tried to impress on him that he didn't need to say any of this. "I know, Robert. I'll help him first."

Robert gave a nod, accepting this, greying brows drawn together briefly in a frown. "Sir, are you sure about not going home yet? Your family will be quite cross that you won't even try to see them."

"I can't leave Ren's back undefended." Just hearing the news of what his friend had already endured without him made Arman's skin crawl. A part of him still wondered if he had confided more in Queen

Eloise, explained to her what he truly wanted, would she have granted his request for Ren to go with him?

Too late to speculate on it now. Two years and one heartbreak too late.

His mind taunted him again with images of Ren embraced by a shadowy figure of a lover. Arman's subconscious liked to do that and torment him. He dug his nails into the palms of his hands and forcefully returned his attention back to the here and now. To his worried batman, he added grudgingly, "I'll send a note to my parents explaining. They'll understand."

"They likely will," Robert allowed, frown easing. "Alright, then, sir. I'll take care of the luggage. What about the, ah, other matter?"

Arman appreciated his batman's tactful question, as he didn't want his intentions noised about just yet, and sounds sometimes carried out here on the water when they shouldn't. "File the necessary notice immediately."

"I will, of course, but it might have to be in the morning." Robert frowned at the slowly descending sun. "I doubt I'll be able to get to the general's quarters and unearth all of the necessary paperwork before the city office closes."

Arman bit back a sigh of impatience. It wouldn't matter if Robert could go immediately to the city office upon their landing, he hadn't even asked Ren yet or gotten a yes from the man. "That's fine. Remember, not a word to anyone, not even a hint. I don't want Ren harmed by anymore rumors."

"Not a word, sir," Robert promised faithfully.

Grunting thanks, he gave his batman a nod and then moved past him to find his second-in-command. Konrad did not stand out immediately from the crowd, not being a particularly tall man in stature, but Arman could hear him readily enough. Konrad possessed a naturally loud voice, such that he could calmly state an order on a battlefield, and the enemy commander would hear it clearly. Reaching the crowd of men at the aft, he signaled for Konrad to come in closer.

"General," Konrad greeted, popping up from his makeshift seat on the coils of rope. "I know you planned to report directly to the king once we landed. Shall I take charge of the men, dismiss them for home?"

Part of the reason why Arman liked Konrad, aside from his excellent leadership skills, was that he often thought aloud. It saved

Arman from making tedious explanations. "Yes. After that, go home yourself."

"I will, sir, no worries." Konrad beamed, smile revealing slightly crooked teeth and highlighting the crow's feet at his eyes. At thirty, he shouldn't have them, but his early life had been far rougher than Arman's, aging him a little prematurely. "In case I need to find you, I assume that if you're not with the king, you'll be with Ren?"

Arman almost smiled. Was he really that predictable? Perhaps he was. "Yes."

"I thought as much, sir." Leaning in, he confided, "I'm right relieved you're finally going to be reunited with him, if you pardon my bluntness. And sir, I have to tell you, I hope that I never deploy with you again without Ren."

Snorting, Arman asked him dryly, "Was I really that bad?"

"I didn't say that, sir," Konrad denied blandly, expression confirmation enough.

Arman knew good and well he had been a bear to live with. Bad enough he'd had to go up without Ren, which had felt like leaving without all of his limbs attached. That alone had put him in a foul humor. But then he'd arrived and discovered his six-month timeline wouldn't be enough to get the job done. And then the damn rebuilding. If Arman had possessed a handy target to blame all of his troubles on, he would have killed it without mercy.

Feeling a little bad for being so difficult, he reached into his pocket and drew out his wallet, counting out a hefty stack of bills into Konrad's hand.

His colonel tried to withdraw his hands, protesting. "Wait, sir, I'm teasing!"

"You're not," Arman denied easily, not at all bothered by Konrad telling him the truth. It was the other part of the reason why he liked the man. "Take all of the officers; first round's on me."

Konrad's attitude did an abrupt flip and he promptly folded the bills and stashed them into a pocket. "Well, if that's how it is…"

Shaking his head a little in amusement, he gave one final order. "Listen carefully. My last communication from the palace indicated that there's serious trouble brewing."

"About Prince Charles and Princess Alexandria's upcoming wedding, sir?" Konrad's mobile face went hard, lips drawn back in a feral grimace. "We heard. We don't like the sounds of it, sir, not one bit. Don't you worry. We've all talked about it, and we'll keep our eyes and ears open for any sign of trouble. If it gets bad, you tell Ren for us that we'll happily step in and help safeguard everyone. I've only heard about Princess Alexandria, but that's a good woman, and I don't want any heartbreak for our prince. You can count on us, sir, if it comes to that."

Arman looked about, checking with the majors and captains standing around him, seeing the same anger and determination in their faces. He'd served with most of these men for years, some of them longer than he'd known Ren, and knew them to be both loyal and good at heart. Knowing they would do everything in their power to protect the people of this country gave him courage, and he felt a little tug at the heart strings. "I know you would. You all would. Thank you, gentlemen. For tonight, though, be with your families."

"We will, sir," Captain Marcin promised him. "And give our greetings to Ren. We sorely missed him on this trip, and not just for your sake. His counsel on fortifications would have been helpful."

"Mmn." Arman didn't take that last statement as a criticism, as he knew what Marcin meant. Having grown up in a fortress, Arman knew the design and strengths of stone walls very well, but Ren's experience lay in wooden structures that could be quickly and easily erected, even readily removed to create moving barriers. It would have been very handy to have that expertise up north.

"Ho, land!" the ship's captain called out as a warning to his passengers. They all turned expectantly toward the docks, moving aside so the crew could cast their lines ashore. Once they were firmly tied off to the pier, Arman wasted no time in bidding the officers a brief farewell before putting his boots to the docks. It felt strange, having something solid to stand on after a week of a moving deck. It took him more than a few strides to lose his sea legs.

As soon as he left the docks, he hailed a buggy and climbed in, directing the driver to the palace. He might not look entirely presentable after a full day's travel, but close enough, and he knew King Gerhard wouldn't care. His king did not put much stock in frivolous appearances.

They arrived at the palace's main gate in short order. Normally he'd need to show his pass, but Arman's face was enough for the guard, one who he knew by name. "Chaz."

"General!" The guard hopped up a little to stand at the coach's open window, a bright smile on his face. "Warden Ren will be ever so glad you're back, sir. He's been antsy for days expecting you."

Pleasure spread through Arman. "Don't tell him. I want to surprise him."

"Wouldn't dream of it, sir," Chaz assured him, smile going impish. "You're here to report to the king, aren't you? I thought so. Go on through."

Hopping down, Chaz waved the driver onwards. Arman sat on the edge of his seat, studying the positioning of the guards and taking in the general ambience of the palace. On the surface, all looked as it should. It took an experienced eye to see that the people moved a little too quickly, a touch too furtively, with many a glance over their shoulders, as if afraid trouble might appear at any moment. More guards were stationed along the walls than normal; as he descended from the coach, he saw guards on both the outside and inside of the main doors as well.

That did not bode well at all.

Arman cursed that thrice-begotten fortress all over again. If only it hadn't been so much trouble, he could have been here when Ren needed him, when his monarchs needed him. Damn thing. If it wouldn't cause more trouble, Arman would go immediately back up and torch it to ease his frustrations.

Shaking off the fancy, he strode through the main hallways, going to Chamberlain Frei's office first, as only he would know where to find the king at this time of the evening and get him an immediate audience. He found the man in his overly-plush chair behind the desk, as usual, with a dozen runners swarming about him, also as usual.

Frei saw his approach and lit up in a smile, spreading his arms wide in welcome. "General! Excellent, excellent, you're finally here. Does Ren know?"

It pleased him infinitely that everyone automatically linked him to Ren. Perhaps that's why he smiled a little at the man. "Not yet. Don't ruin my surprise. I want to report to King Gerhard first."

"Ah, of course. That way Ren won't have to wait on you to give the report. I'll send a runner immediately announcing your return and ask for an audience." Snapping his fingers at one of the girls, he scribbled out a note and sent her on with instructions where to find the king. With her dispatched, he waved to a chair. "Here, sit. I need to warn you of a few things before you go."

Arman sat, worried, as Frei didn't pass along useless gossip. "Mm?"

Leaning forward, the Chamberlain asked seriously, "Did you hear that Ren was briefly involved with a young lord, some months ago?"

Just the reminder brought bile to the back of his throat. He nodded curtly, a low growl escaping with the motion.

"I can see from the look in your eye you want to pound the young fool. Between me and you, he needs it, but I promise you he has been punished for the matter." Frei sat back, a year's worth of sighs leaving him. "It hurt Ren dreadfully. Not the affair itself, I think. He was already a little concerned by the young man's…flighty nature, shall we say. But I think he saw it differently than just a love affair gone wrong. He seems to have lost all hope that he'll be able to find a partner. That is the correct term, is it not?"

"It is." Arman's heart raced hearing this, and not in a good way. Had Ren closed his heart off to all potential possibilities? "Why?"

"Why would he do so? I'm not certain, he hasn't confided in me. I just know that Queen Eloise has made some noise about sending him home for a few months after the prince's marriage is finalized, give him a chance to find a lover, but so far he's been evading her. At first, I thought the wound was too new, he couldn't bear to even think about it, but now I suspect he's given up on the idea altogether. General, I mention this only to you because I want you to talk sense into him. Our Ren is a wonderful man, and if he weren't so, er, inclined toward his own gender, I could present a dozen suitable ladies to him with a snap of my fingers. Alas, he is as he is. And our country has no men who share his inclinations."

Queen Eloise wanted to send him home? To find a lover? Terror raced through him. He didn't know which to be more worried about—the queen's kind but misguided intentions, or Ren evading all possibility of searching for a partner. "I'll talk with him."

"Please do. I hope you can get through to him; you're the only one who can, at this rate."

The runner returned, not even out of breath, which meant the king couldn't be too far. She verbally reported to Frei, "The king wishes to see General Brahms in his study immediately, Chamberlain."

"I suspected he would." Frei forestalled Arman from rising with a hand. "Before you go, one word of caution. You've heard about the attack on Princess Alexandria? I thought you would have, if you knew of Ren's matter. I'm afraid that wasn't the only attempt, and we're experiencing some trouble here. You might not have much time with Ren, not with the near-constant emergencies we're managing these days. I know that you've only just arrived, but if you could see to staying for a few days, perhaps ease his burdens?"

This, Arman knew how to answer, his tone firm as a mountain. "I won't leave his back unguarded."

Ren loped through the main floor of the castle, double checking that the changing of the guards went smoothly, relieved when they did. He'd had enough emergencies over the winter months, what with strange people somehow coming inside and bizarre attacks, that he didn't take anything for granted. Not even a simple changing of the guards.

Some part of him kept anxious track of the date, and Queen Eloise was kind enough to give him regular updates, as they all anticipated the return of Arman Brahms and the three hundred soldiers deployed with him. They didn't know precisely what day he would arrive as—to the surprise of no one—Brahms had neglected to give them a detailed itinerary of his travel plans. Ren did know that he would catch a river boat on the way down, speeding up the journey, so it should be sometime this week. He'd cleared his schedule as much as possible in anticipation, wanting at least one day to catch up with his friend.

After all, there was a lot to catch up on, not all of it pleasant.

The wayward thought tugged his spirits down for a moment. It no longer hurt, what had happened with Deidrick, but it smarted still. Ren had come to the realization some months back that it wasn't the loss of companionship that hurt the most, but the removal of hope. He'd resigned himself for years to being alone in this country, but with Deidrick's approach, a pathway had opened up to him where he'd expected none. The sudden removal of that smarted the most. It ached to go back to that resignation, to let go of the possibility that he might be able to achieve some personal happiness here after all.

Maybe Queen Eloise was right. Maybe he really should go home for a spell and at least try to find someone. If nothing else, he could see his brother and sister-in-law, see his new nephew. He'd gotten word of the birth last month and sent home a few presents and some money to help. Shiirei's economy still recovered from the war; he knew how hard it must be to afford the upkeep of a family right now, and didn't want them to suffer for the lack of money. Takahiro was too proud to ask for help, but he never once tried to return what Ren sent, which told him clearly enough his brother needed the help.

Shaking his head, he pulled himself back into the present. Alright, castle secured. He didn't feel like eating in tonight. The chefs here were amazing, but sometimes he just wanted a different flavor in his mouth. Venturing out of the side door on the east side, he went down the stairs, heading for the main gate. He debated as he went, offering a casual salute to the gate guards as he left the palace compound and hit the main street. What was he in the mood for?

"Ren."

Even if he were deaf, he'd know that voice. With a wide smile on his face, he spun about and found Brahms right behind him. In the near two years since they'd seen each other, the other man hadn't changed an ounce. He looked a little tired, perhaps a little thinner, but still as big and straight faced as always. Well, no, right now he had that lift at the corners of his eyes and mouth, as if he were on the edge of smiling, an expression he wore when he was happy.

"Brahms!" Ren leaped the three steps necessary to close the distance with hand outstretched. "You rascal, when did you get in? I wasn't expecting—whoa. Hugs. Hugs are new."

The arms around his waist tightened enough that it lifted him up onto his toes, Brahms' head buried into the crook of his neck. Never, in all their years together, had Brahms been this physical with him unless one of them was injured. It stunned him for a full second before he relaxed into the embrace. It might be a little strange to hug Brahms like this, but his heart purred at having those strong arms banded around him. Ren hugged him back, burying one hand into Brahms' hair, hearing the words that weren't spoken. "I missed you too. Terribly."

"Too long," Brahms sighed into his neck, the words so low as to be nearly inaudible. "I'm not deploying again without you."

"Why? Was everyone making you talk?" Ren teased him. He had to tease or succumb to his own strong relief of finally having Brahms back. "You poor baby, all those nasty words to confront. Whatever did you do, make Robert talk for you? Wait, you didn't actually do that, did you?"

"He didn't mind."

"For the love of—seriously? You made your batman do all of the talking for you? Tell me the truth, now; when you were a child you were a complete chatterbox, weren't you. And your parents despaired of having any peace and quiet so they started charging you per word, and then you went the opposite direction and became a miser instead. Am I right?"

Brahms didn't laugh aloud, but his shoulders silently shook with it. "No."

"You sure? I find I like the theory; you'll have to tell me the truth, otherwise I'll believe my own story."

Slowly easing Ren back to his feet, Brahms took a half-step back, separating them by four inches, but kept a hand on Ren's arm. "Over dinner, I'll tell you."

"Fish and chips from Yorkshire House, bottle of wine, dinner at my place?" Ren offered.

Brahms nodded, the last bit of tension easing out of his shoulders. "Perfect."

"I thought you might feel a little anti-people at the moment," Ren stated knowingly. Brahms could do everything his job demanded but needed at least a little time to himself each day or risk sanity. After a solid three weeks on the road traveling back home, he had to be thoroughly sick of crowds of any sort. "Alright, come with me, I'll order it and have it delivered."

They didn't talk on the way, as Ren knew when to push and when to leave be. Now, he needed to leave it be and let Brahms take it at his own pace. He enjoyed the silence, companionable as it was, and walked with a spring in his step. As much as he loved this country, and the people in it, it hadn't felt quite right to live here with Brahms away. Perhaps some part of him considered Brahms a necessary component to stay in Aart.

He ordered dinner, and since he was a regular, they promised a quick delivery. Then they returned to the palace and the apartment he had on the first level of the east wing. It wasn't anything fancy, and certainly the kitchen area didn't have space for more than two people, so they settled into chairs near the hearth and enjoyed the fire to chase away the spring chill.

Only then did Ren think to ask the obvious. "Did you already report in to the king and queen? Excellent, so you're free to while away an evening with me. I'm glad you're here, we've been anticipating your arrival the past several days."

"Long trip, but it went smoothly," Brahms told him with a sigh, lifting his feet up to rest on the ottoman.

"I'm glad to hear it. That whole deployment was already a disaster, it wouldn't be fair if the trip down was also rough. How long can you stay? I expect your family is missing you terribly and want you home again."

Brahms gave him an unreadable look, which said something. "I'm not in a hurry."

Not quite sure what that meant, Ren decided to take it at face value for now. Brahms would tell him in his own time. He always did. "You're probably sick of traveling anyway, at the moment. Stay and play with me for a few days. I've been bored without you."

Snorting, Brahms corrected, "Bored without me to tease."

"Well of course, I live to tease you, it's my sole purpose in life. Imagine how devastated I've been for two years without you. I've nearly gone into withdrawals." Ren laughed at the look that earned him and put his hands up in surrender. "Alright, alright, I'll stop. But tell me about Kassmeyer. I trust that when you rebuilt it, you put adequate fortifications in this time?"

"It will hold," Brahms assured him, then added darkly, "It'd better."

"As you refuse to go back up there? I don't blame you, neither of us handle cold weather all that well, and Kassmeyer gets very cold indeed. What did you do in the winters, anyway? Freeze?"

Brahms made a face and gave a sour grunt, fully sprawled into the chair. "Asked Robert to set me on fire once. He wouldn't do it."

Ren could somehow picture this, how his friend would ask his batman with a completely serious face to please set him on fire, and the batman adamantly refusing. He doubled over in laughter. "Did you really? You were that cold? I missed such a priceless moment. Damn, they really should have sent me along with you."

"It would have saved you some heartbreak."

The laughter stilled in his chest as he looked sharply up at Brahms. Anger lurked in those dark blue eyes, banked and smoldering. "You, ah, heard about that already?"

"Nn."

Giving a gusty sigh, Ren looked at the fire crackling in the hearth. He found it a little hard to look at Brahms. The whole fiasco still embarrassed him. "After seven months, I would have thought that story old news. But the rumor's still circulating around, eh? Maybe because that bastard's banishment is over, and he's back in court again. Don't give me that scary face, it hasn't been that bad. I have no feelings for him anymore, just a lingering sense of embarrassment for being caught up with him. Even his ex-fiancée has moved on. She and I still chat with each other if we're at the same social events. I met her new man, Lord Kastner, and he's a much better catch. I actually know him personally, as he's the Minister of Finance. Has six years on her, but he's as solid as the earth itself, and clearly adores her. I don't blame him; she's a good woman. She seems quite pleased with how things turned out."

Brahms watched him quietly. "Do you hate him?"

What an interesting question. "No. No, I find that I don't. I did at first, for hurting me as he did, but then I realized that by hating him, I was still emotionally connected to him. That was unbearable, I hated that. They always say that the opposite of love is hate, but I find that isn't true in my case. I don't hate him. I'm indifferent to him."

The anger and concern in Brahms' face faded, replaced with an intense scrutiny. "You mean that."

"I do." Ren leaned on the arm of the chair and returned the scrutiny. "If I said otherwise, you were going to go right now and gut him, weren't you?"

"Gutting's messy," Brahms denied with an enigmatic twitch of the lips.

"That is not a denial." Ren jabbed a finger in Brahms' direction. "Don't think I don't realize you're still contemplating murder on some level. I know you. You are strictly banned from killing him on my account. There will be no sneak attacks, no assassinations, or anything of that sort. I don't wish for it. Besides, it isn't necessary. Giles was mortally embarrassed by the whole affair, punished by both Queen Eloise and his family, and still hasn't been able to put it past him. I know this because he glares at me whenever I see him, which does put a sparkle in my day, let me tell you. What? I said I was indifferent to him, not that I don't enjoy seeing him reap his just desserts."

Snorting, Brahms finally relaxed. "So, you're over it."

"Completely. But I have learned my lesson from it. No more

trying to seduce straight men, especially not in Aart. It clearly doesn't work."

Alarmed, Brahms shot up straight in his chair, brows beetled together. "Don't say that."

Waving him down, Ren assured him, "It's alright, I'm more or less resigned at this point. Queen Eloise has been making noises for months about sending me to Shiirei for a while to give me the chance to find someone there, although I'm under strict orders to return. She doesn't want me permanently staying over there. I turned her down at first, because no matter what she thinks, I'm not *that* charming, and finding someone in a three-month time span is a near impossible task. But I might take her up on the chance anyway just to see my family. Oh, there's our food."

"No, but—" Brahms cut himself off when Ren got up to answer the door. He held in his protest until Ren had paid the delivery boy a tip and brought the baskets back inside. "Ren. It *is* possible."

Ren gave him a smile, although he felt a little sad at his own denial. "You and Queen Eloise. Such faith. It's alright, I tell you. Now come, let's change to a different topic and eat the food while it's still hot. Did you hear about the trouble we've had with Princess Alexandria?"

"Some," Brahms allowed, and while he looked ready to keep arguing, he let the matter go. Settling at the small table, he helped divide out the food onto the white napkins. His brows lifted, his nostrils flaring as he breathed in deeply. "Missed that smell."

"No one else fries fish as well as they do," Ren agreed wholeheartedly. "I got a lot; dig in. Only some news? What did you hear?"

"That she was attacked on the way in; you had to escort her from my family's fortress. There's been some trouble in the palace since." Brahms broke open one of the fish, adding a squirt of lemon and a dash of salt, looking at Ren from under his eyebrows as his hands moved. "How bad?"

"More annoying than bad, at least so far." Ren mimicked his friend's movements, taking a large bite of the fish with a moan of pleasure. The tenderness of the meat, the hot flavor of the oil, it all lingered pleasantly on his taste buds. "People who have no business in the palace keep getting in, somehow. It's driving me mad. They never do anything, at least not that I can find, but it's the security breach they represent that's giving me migraines. Frei and I started tracking the seals and who's vouching for these people to get them past my guards, but it's been a slow process of information gathering. We've been marking anything strange and questionable, of course, but I hope I can sit down with him soon and comb through it properly, see if we can figure out who's doing this and why."

Brahms paused with a chip halfway to his mouth, a little wrinkle appearing between his brows. "You think they're testing the defenses?"

"Maybe? Frei's opinion on this is they're trying to discredit me." Ren shrugged, as he didn't know, and it could very well be both.

Every line in Brahms went rigid, shoulders and jaw taut. "Are they now."

Ren eyed him with a certain amount of caution. His friend's body language screamed anger right then. Nothing good ever followed when Brahms looked like that. "Don't worry, I'll manage this. It's not like anything serious has happened—"

Someone's fist loudly pounded on the door, and Fillmore's voice came through the wood. "Sir! There's been an attack on the prince!"

8

Ren more or less sprinted for Charles' bedroom, Brahms right at his heels with Fillmore doing his best to keep up. At this time of the evening, most people either lingered at the formal dinner on the main floor or sought their own beds. Ren encountered precious few in the hallways, and no one but guards once he reached the royal family's wing.

Charles' bedroom door stood wide open and Ren immediately went through, assessing the situation with a glance. The huge canopy bed's sheets looked mussed, so Charles must have been in bed when this happened. Nothing else about the room appeared disturbed, the table and chairs near the balcony doors still upright, the fire in the hearth still going strong. Charles himself stood near the foot of the bed, staring at a young woman with irritation, a tic jumping at his temple and a robe hastily belted on. His right hand held a sword he clearly wanted to use, the knuckles white under the force of his grip.

"My Prince," Ren greeted, slowing to a halt in front of him. "Fillmore reported an attack by a girl?"

Pointing to the young woman not three feet away from him, firmly held by Chaz, Charles spluttered, "She just climbed straight into bed with me!"

Ren turned to look at the girl in question, feeling a headache coming on. She was a pretty sort, certainly, with a slightly upturned nose, and tumbling blonde locks over an ample figure her dress did very little to conceal. The nature of the thin and clingy dress silently testified to her profession. Not at all worried about being caught, she gave Ren a sultry wink and smile.

Patience. He couldn't just strangle her because she'd interrupted a long-awaited reunion with Brahms. "And who might you be?"

"Name's Stacey," she introduced herself with a splayed hand to her breast and a coy bat of the eyes. "My, a foreigner. They say the warden of the palace is from a far east country. That you, handsome?"

"That's me," Ren agreed levelly. "I'm Warden Ren. Now, Miss Stacey, I have two questions for you. Who sent you? And how did you get in?"

Lowering her voice, she leaned a little toward him, as if confiding a secret. "I'm here to pleasure the prince. A pre-wedding present, of sorts."

That answered neither of his questions. Ren wondered how much she had been paid to keep her mouth shut. A sizeable sum, certainly, to risk doing something this stupid. "You're not going to answer my questions, are you?"

Dropping the coy act, a hint of shrewdness entered her eyes. "They also say that the warden of the palace has no interest in women."

"That is also true," Ren admitted frankly. "So I'm sorry, I'm sure you're lovely and tempting to the men in this room, but you have too many curves for my taste. Seducing me isn't the right tactic."

With a pout, she shifted, her manner becoming more of a brisk businesswoman. "I don't know who paid me. A thick stack of money was delivered with instructions of what to do and how to get in."

"Instructions alone wouldn't get you past the main gate," Ren denied, advancing on her until they stood toe to toe. "You need a seal, and someone to vouch for you. Whose?"

Looking him dead in the eye, she reached down the front of her dress and pulled a flat wooden seal from between her breasts. Ren took it from her, knowing what it was with a glance. His headache announced its presence. "Thank you, Miss Stacey. I'll need to detain you and question you further, I'm afraid. Have you eaten dinner yet?"

Eyes narrowed in confusion, she gave a tentative shake of the head. "No."

"Chaz," Ren directed his young guardsman, "take her down to the first holding area and feed her dinner, then settle her in for the night. We'll need to investigate this properly, but everyone's gone home to their own beds at this point; it'll have to wait until morning. Tell everyone that I want this woman untouched. *Completely* untouched, do you understand me? If I find out otherwise, heads will roll."

"I'll guard her myself, sir," Chaz swore with a sharp salute. "Come along, you."

Ren didn't watch them go, but turned back to Charles, brandishing the seal as he did. "She had very high credentials. It's a day pass, but a lord or lady would have to sign for this. No wonder she was admitted through."

Charles stared at the seal, jaw dropped. "I know the lords here regularly call for ladies of pleasure, but we've had enough trouble with security the past few months, I would have thought the guards would question her."

"Unfortunately, most of them don't dare, or risk inciting a lord's displeasure," Ren sighed. "I'll investigate this further, but I'm afraid I don't have a good way of putting a stop to this."

"What?" Charles asked in dismay. "Then you mean someone can try sending a girl into my bed again?"

Ren winced. "Well—"

"No." Charles reached out and latched onto Ren's arm with both hands. "Ren. You have to sleep with me from now on."

Brahms choked on his own breath, staring at the prince with eyebrows arched. Ren just looked at Charles, half-resigned. "My Prince."

"I know, I know, you don't want to." Charles gave him a winning smile. "What if I propose, then it'll be alright, right?"

Ren opened his mouth to respond, words cutting short as two arms like bands of steel wrapped around his waist and forcibly moved him outside of the prince's reach. Startled, he tilted his head up, and saw Brahms had his jaw clenched so tightly a vein throbbed.

Glaring at Charles, Brahms growled, "No."

Charles stared at him, nonplussed. "You don't have to be so huffy about it, General. When did you get back into town, anyway?"

"Oh, I see how it is," Alexandria stated as she stormed into the room. Jabbing a finger at Charles, her tone went flat. "So, you propose to share your bed with women *and* men, eh?"

Now more alarmed than he had been upon finding a prostitute in his bed, Charles quickly back peddled. "No, wait, dearest, it was a joke—"

Alexandria wrapped her robe tightly around her chest and flounced back toward the door. Ren felt a little alarmed as well by this, frantically trying to remember if anyone had explained the code to her. Charles didn't use it nearly as often as Roslyn, but he did employ it from time to time. If they had, Alexandria seemed to not have remembered. He opened his mouth, intending to correct the situation, but paused when she gave him a subtle wink in passing. Then he had to bite his tongue to keep from laughing. That minx. Pulling Charles' leg, was she?

Charles frantically chased after her, explaining as he went, and Ren breathed a little sigh of relief. Alexandria no doubt planned to keep Charles with her tonight, which really was the best way to ensure both of them stayed safe. Galvath wouldn't let anything past her door.

Belatedly, Ren realized Brahms still held him in a firm grip. It felt nice, certainly, to be held like this. Ren loved hugs and didn't get enough of them. But it also felt strange, as he didn't normally have this much contact with Brahms, and now marked the second time in three hours Brahms had held him. "Ah, Brahms?"

The arms around his waist eased open, releasing him, and Ren took a step to the side before looking up at his friend. A dark thundercloud still raged over his face, his mouth tight lipped and drawn down at the corners. Ren would have to address that in a moment, before Brahms got the wrong idea. Turning to Fillmore, who patiently stood by at the door, he requested, "Take the seal and track down when it was issued, then write a note to Frei and put it on his desk. I'll follow up with him in the morning."

"Yes, sir." Fitzgerald saluted, took the seal from him, then immediately left at a quick pace.

Standing alone now in the prince's bedroom, Ren could focus on his friend for a minute. "Brahms. It's a joke."

"This joke didn't exist two years ago," Brahms responded, tone a semi-accusation. The downward turn of his mouth became an outright frown. "Charles does this regularly?"

"Roslyn does as well." Ren waited for that to sink in, and it stopped Brahms in his tracks, his frown easing into a more thoughtful expression. "It's something of a game that Roslyn started, but it's come to be a signal of sorts for them. If they're proposing, something has happened to make them highly uncomfortable, and they want me to stay with them."

Brahms studied him for a long moment. "And how often do you get proposed to?"

"A little too often," Ren admitted glumly. "The palace has been strange ever since Charles and Alexandria became engaged. I expect things to settle when they actually get married, we just have to survive it until then. At least, I hope them being married solves the problem."

The general did not look sold on this. Ren wasn't either, truthfully, he just hoped for it.

Shrugging, he set that aside. He needed to focus on the more immediate problem at hand. "Sorry our dinner got interrupted. Go ahead and return to my apartment; feel free to stay the night. I likely will be out the rest of the night until I get to the bottom of this and implement a few security measures to prevent a repeat."

Brahms cocked his head a little, his stance changing to a parade rest that indicated he did not agree with Ren and had his own opinion he would stand firm on. "I'm not going to bed while you stay up."

Protesting, Ren waved both hands in the air. "Wait, wait, you just got home! You're bound to be tired, and truly, I can handle this."

"The two of us can handle this faster," Brahms argued, chin coming up in that mulish way he had. "You can investigate, I'll set up new security."

Sighing, Ren rubbed at his temple. "You're so stubborn. Alright, alright, I know better than to argue when you're like this. Security is ground level at the moment."

"So, fourth point of contact?" Brahms double-checked.

Ren choked, spluttering. Five years in this country, but hearing people innocently use this term still got him every time. They meant it as a fourth level of security, where guards would be posted on the outer wall, at the main doors, at the occupant's room, and a personal bodyguard being designated the 'fourth point of contact.'

In Shiirei, that fourth point meant something very, very different.

Brahms' eyes narrowed slightly. "Are you ever going to explain to me what that means in Shiirei?"

"Someday," Ren promised. Never. He would explain that never. "Let's go. The sooner we get this done, the sooner we can rest."

※

They didn't return to Ren's apartment until well after the witching hour. Ren collapsed in a chair near the hearth, then groaned when he realized it had burned down to embers. He really needed to fall into bed, but he had to prepare a place for Brahms to sleep first.

Striding past the chair, Brahms knelt down and stoked the fire back up, putting more logs on. Then he sat back on his heel, lingering on the hearth's stone for a long moment. "I need to stay."

Ren blinked at him, tired brain struggling to make sense of that cryptic statement. With his back to Ren, the usual visual cues were cut off. "What? Stay? Brahms, you've been away from home for two years. I know for a fact how much your family has missed you; your mother especially is very excited you'll be coming home soon. You can't mean to stay here in the palace—"

Turning, Brahms stayed in his kneeling position, one knee on the floor, a very odd look on his face. Or maybe the flickering light from the fire made it seem so. "You've had nothing but trouble here for months; someone is scheming to reach the royal family, and you want me to leave?"

Ah. Ren could see the simmering anger, now. He had to be careful how he phrased this. "You know that I wouldn't choose anyone else to guard my back. But Brahms, it's been *two years*. If I selfishly keep you here, your mother will personally strangle me."

"Selfish," Brahms repeated, tone pensive. "You think it's selfish."

"What else would you call it?"

"Smart." Brahms hands clenched into fists, head bowing under the pressure, jaw working. "Ren. I can't leave your back unguarded like this. I *can't*."

The one thing that had carried them safely through the war was each other. They knew, without looking, that the other person had their back. Ren had missed that sorely while Brahms was deployed. Most days he felt like a functioning amputee, especially during all of this chaos. He dearly wanted Brahms to stay with him even though he knew it to be a very selfish wish. But now, seeing the emotion over that normally stoic face, he realized how deeply it affected Brahms to be separated. To return and find Ren with trouble on his hands he couldn't readily solve.

His head coming up, Brahms stared him down, words delivered in a bass rumble. "I'm not leaving."

A vice constricting Ren's heart eased and fell away. He collapsed a little more bonelessly in his chair, his tension easing. "I really am a selfish bastard. I don't even want to argue with you. But are you sure? Your parents are not going to be happy about this."

"I'll send them a note," Brahms responded placidly, his previous anger dissipating.

"A note. A note that says more than twenty words?" Ren teased, feeling a little giddy now. Sleep deprivation did that to him. "How about I write the note and you sign it? They'll thank me for it."

Shrugging, Brahms agreed and finally stood. Putting both arms above his head, he stretched hugely, then relaxed again with a content look on his face. "Bed?"

"I'm all for it. Let me pull a pallet out for you—"

Brahms waved this away, already heading for the back bedroom. "We can share."

"We, ah, can?" Ren felt a little off hearing this casual declaration. They'd shared a tent many times in the past, but rarely a bed, and that only under very strange circumstances. In a place with multiple unoccupied bedrooms, including a set of rooms for military staff, there was absolutely no need to share a bed.

Perhaps he thought too deeply about all of this. Brahms just wanted to roll into bed as soon as possible; the man had to be exhausted after the day he'd had. That must be it. Ren stood as well, teasing as he moved, "Well alright, but don't blame me if you wake up with me cuddled on top of you. I'm a cuddler, remember."

Brahms paused in the doorway and turned his head to give Ren a mischievous waggle of the eyebrows. "Promises, promises."

Ren blinked at Brahms' back as he exited out of view. Since when did Brahms do tease-flirting? His libido piped up with several encouragements to follow up on that, but knowing very well Brahms didn't lean in that direction, he shunted all suggestions to the back of his mind. Being more physically demonstrative did not mean Brahms wanted *that* from him.

His libido wailed a protest. Ren ruthlessly shut it up, as he always did when it wanted his friend, and followed Brahms through the door.

Two years had certainly changed things. And yet, in other ways, nothing had changed at all. Brahms was as always steadfast in his support of Ren when Ren needed him most. Truly, his friend couldn't have picked a better time to return home. Happy, he stifled a yawn, fully planning to cuddle-attack Brahms at least once. Just because.

9

Arman had forgotten that when Sho Renjimantoro went to sleep, he did not stay still in slumber. The man didn't snore, but he fidgeted a little, mumbling half-uttered words. It always amused him, watching Ren sleep. Sometimes, he would lean in and ask him questions, as he'd discovered early on that Ren would agree to any question asked. He didn't feel the urge to tease this morning, though, his mood far more tranquil. For a moment, in the dawn light, he lay next to his friend and just watched. In his sleep, Ren lacked the resting face suggesting he plotted minor mischief. His mouth hung a little slack, no trace of tension found anywhere in his body, perfectly at ease with the world.

He envied his friend's rest, as he hadn't been able to sleep well. Partially because he wasn't in the habit of sleeping next to someone else, and partially because too many worries preyed on his mind. Seeing Ren so peacefully asleep made Arman want to poke him. On the other hand, he knew Ren needed his sleep. He really should behave himself.

Ren snorted a little, his eyes fluttering open. On instinct, Arman shut his again immediately, acting as if he were still deeply asleep, curious to what Ren would do.

Of course, it was something mischievous. Ren made good on his plan from last night and rolled on top of Arman, squashing the man with his weight. His victorious chuckle cut off when Arman quickly wrapped two arms around him to hold him in place.

"You're awake," Ren stated suspiciously.

Arman took in a deep breath, eyes still closed, keeping up the charade.

"No, don't try to fool me, you're awake. You don't move at all in your sleep; you don't even fidget. This 'I'm latching onto Ren subconsciously' routine you're pulling will not work. Let go." Ren squirmed, to no avail. Arman had his arms completely pinned and short of kneeing Arman in the groin, Ren wasn't going to win free anytime soon. "You big ape, let me up!"

"Don't wanna," Arman denied, eyes still firmly shut. He quite liked a squirming, wriggling Ren on top of him.

"'Don't wanna'? What, are you twelve?"

"Says the person who cuddle attacked me."

"You were asking to be cuddle attacked. Besides, I warned you last night, didn't I?"

A part of Ren's anatomy nudged hard against Arman's stomach, and he could hear the slight unease in Ren's voice, could feel it in the way Ren tried to carefully lever his groin away. Arman actually liked feeling it, this silent proof Ren found him attractive, and wasn't about to let him up. His gut clenched in reaction, a tingle starting as his own arousal stirred. Perhaps he could start his campaign a little earlier than planned. Acting completely oblivious to Ren's internal struggle, Arman pulled him in more firmly. "Cuddle attack revenge."

Snorting, Ren let his head flop down on Arman's shoulder. "How did you just say that with a straight face?"

"Practice."

"That's some sort of practice, right there." He relaxed into a waiting game.

He no doubt thought Arman would get tired of this much weight pressing against his chest and let Ren go. And perhaps he would, but not anytime soon. Arman pulled him in a little more snugly, situating them more comfortably together, making no move to release him. Ren allowed this, laying his ear against his chest, breath settling into a steady rhythm. Arman had always told Ren things more through actions than words. Would Ren listen and hear loneliness, years of it, and a fierce longing for home?

That's what Arman heard listening to Ren's body language. He really had been missed, hadn't he? Had Ren felt the same way, like an amputee, able to function but with a sympathetic pain of separation?

Ren burrowed in a little more.

Arman went slightly taut, as Ren had never displayed this kind of need for comfort from him before. His embrace tightened just that bit more in response. Licking dry lips, Arman considered his plan, then decided to chuck it. Right now, Ren was vulnerable and open to him. Surely now would be the time to state his intentions. He formed the words in his mind carefully, voice husky from sleep. "Ren. There's something—"

Three loud knocks vibrated Ren's front door. "Warden!"

Groaning, Ren forced himself off, rolling smoothly to the floor. Arman felt like raging. Morning had barely started. Why was there an emergency already? Ren stumbled out of the bedroom and toward the door. Arman could hear him throw it open and growl in a half-teasing, half-resigned tone, "Just tell me the roof isn't on fire."

"And nothing's blown up." Arman knew that voice. Wilkes, wasn't it? "Sir, we just received a report that someone sabotaged Princess Alexandria's horse."

"Is she hurt?"

"Fortunately not, sir. But King Gerhard and Queen Eloise are up in arms about the whole thing. Prince Charles is just swearing. I volunteered to fetch you."

"Smart man," Ren congratulated him. "I'd take the excuse to run for it too. Alright, I'm coming. Where are they?"

"Stables, sir."

The stables were not technically part of Ren's domain. He had little oversight of it aside from general security, but Arman knew right now his monarchs wouldn't look at things that way. Resigning himself to a perfectly terrible morning, Arman took a moment to relax in the bed, as it might be the only time today he'd be off his feet.

He heard Ren promise, "Go back to your post. I'll be there in a minute."

Arman slammed a fist against the mattress, his frustrations boiling over. Ren was dead tired—Arman could hear it in his voice. That usual smooth baritone contained a scratchy catch to it that Ren only got after pushing himself to the edge. What he needed was sleep, a day of rest, not another emergency.

Returning to the bedroom, Ren gave him a half-smile. "Sorry, have to run."

"I'm going with you," Arman informed him, rolling out of the bed and reaching for the clothes he'd hung on the armoire door the night before.

Ren opened his mouth to protest and Arman glared him down. A fleeting expression of relief passed over Ren's face before he turned away. "Alright. I can't say I don't need the help."

When Arman finally got his hands on the people responsible for this nonsense, he was going to bash their skulls together.

When Ren arrived at the stables, dressed but with a little stubble still on his jaw, he found three-fifths of the royal family waiting near one of the tack rooms. Roslyn was missing, likely still in bed at this hour. Brahms stayed right next to him as he crossed the paved stable yard and gave the waiting royals a quick bow. "My Queen, My King, I'd offer you a good morning, but I have a feeling it's a bad one. Where is Princess Alexandria?"

"Changing," Queen Eloise responded, deep lines of anger around her mouth. "She was wet and muddy from what happened."

"What did happen, exactly?" Ren pressed.

Charles came out of the tack room with a dark expression on his face. "It's just her gear, as I feared. To answer you, Ren, we went for a dawn ride to get away from everyone for a little while. We'd reached the shallow creek just past the first marker when Alexandria's horse started skittering sideways and bucking. Fortunately, she was able to dismount without injury, although it meant landing in the creek to accomplish it. We checked and found an itching powder all along the bottom of the saddle blanket."

The stable master, Fredrick, stood nearby, wringing his hands together over a wide stomach, mustache quivering. "Warden, I really don't know how this happened. No one without the proper credentials is allowed near my stables, and certainly not my tack rooms! You know this."

"I do, Master Fredrick," Ren assured him patiently, lifting his hand to stall the man. "I do, calm yourself. This is not the first incident we've had, unfortunately. My Queen, My King, I will bet you anything you care to name that Master Fredrick is proven correct and only people with the right pass came through here. I've locked down security twice already to prevent just this sort of shenanigans."

King Gerhard's expression became pinched and troubled. "I don't think I like what you're insinuating, Ren. Do you mean to tell me that my own people are sneaking these troublemakers in?"

"I know for a fact they are." Huh. That question suggested that their son had not mentioned the night's events. Sidling near Charles, Ren whispered, "You didn't tell them?"

Charles shook his head vehemently, eyes pleading for Ren to do it.

Why did he always get the dirty jobs? Resigned, he faced the royal parents and stated baldly, "Someone sent a prostitute into your son's bed last night."

Queen Eloise went beet red, from either embarrassment or outrage, he couldn't tell. King Gerhard just went grey from anger, his rage boiling below the surface. The king demanded in a harsh, low tone, "They did what?"

"Worse, she had a high security clearance to admit her. I double checked the records and a total of fifteen day passes were issued yesterday to admit people. My King, Frei and I have been tracking the issue of the passes for the past few months, trying to narrow things down. With your permission, I'll sit down with him this morning and see if I can't pinpoint who is behind all of this nonsense."

"I insist you do, my Warden," Queen Eloise declared. "Really, the nerve of them! Trying to break up my son's engagement by putting a whore in his bed. Oh, don't look so shocked, any of you, the ploy is obvious enough. Charles, you did explain matters to Alexandria, I trust, as she went riding with you this morning."

Charles relaxed visibly at his mother's question. "I didn't need to. She also saw through it. I, ah, stayed in her room last night."

And likely her bed. Ren knew they all thought it, but no one chose to say it aloud.

Ren knew what they needed to do. They needed to increase security levels from first point of contact, which was just basic security on the walls, to second point of contact, where each door was locked down and people searched before granted entry. Clearing his throat, he moved the conversation along. "My King, I hate to say this, but I really think we should lock the palace down and declare second point of contact."

"We can't afford to," King Gerhard denied, shoulders slumping for a moment. "There's too much politically going on. We'll just have to tighten security. Ren, I've heard multiple statements from my nobles that reinforce their unease with this marriage alliance."

"That's what lords do, after all," Charles muttered to no one in particular. "Drink, whore, and complain."

His father ignored him, still issuing instructions. "I know you've been investigating, but I think it's time to put your focus on them instead of doubling security every fortnight. Lord Julek, Lady Wioleta, and Lady Karina have all been very vocal in their displeasure, to name a few. I'll put together a list for you. Start there."

"I think it's more than that," Brahms put in, a growl in the words. "I think they're trying to get Ren removed as well."

King Gerhard grimaced and assured him, "I know they are. I am not inclined to place the blame on my warden, however, as he is doing exactly as he should; and I can trust him, at least, to be a neutral party in this hotbed of politics."

Brahms inclined his head, agreeing, his eyes on Ren. "I think your idea of tracking down the passes a good one, but I bet it won't answer everything."

"They'll have mixed legitimate people in with the troublemakers, making it hard to discern who's really at fault," Ren acknowledged. He felt the desperate need for some hot tea right about now. "I know that, why do you think I've been sitting on this for months? The more information I have, the better."

With a wave of the hand, Brahms indicated he hadn't gotten the point. "We need a spy."

Ren cottoned on, instantly knowing who Brahms meant. "Feliks? But you don't like him."

"He flirts with you too much," Brahms grumbled, glancing away. "But he's a good spy."

"I can't refute that, he's an excellent spy." To the confused royals, Ren explained, "Feliks was the spy we used during the war, and I believe he's still on the army payroll. There is nothing this man can't find out. I know you have your own spies in place, My King, but they clearly need a little help, as they haven't been able to get to the bottom of this matter yet."

King Gerhard held up a hand, forestalling him. "You don't need to convince me; I'm perfectly willing to bring another spy on. This Feliks, have him report directly to you. I don't want anyone else in charge of him. General Brahms, thank you for the suggestion. It's a good one. I confess I'm surprised you're still here, however. I would have thought you'd leave for home."

Settling into that stubborn stance of his, Brahms informed the king, "I'm not leaving Ren until things are settled."

"Well, I do admit that relieves me in a way, as I know that Ren has missed you dreadfully." Queen Eloise looked curiously between the two of them, her own thoughts written plain on her face that she wondered over this protective attitude of Brahms'. "And that creature is back in court, as well. I trust you can make sure he won't stab Ren in the back. But isn't your family missing you, General? Surely a short trip to the fortress won't hurt?"

Brahms went even more immovable, like a castle of stone, jaw set in stubborn lines that suggested the world could spin backwards before he'd shift his stance. "I'm not going unless Ren goes with me."

Ren stared at his friend, slightly taken aback by his adamancy. Not in the statement itself, but in the something lurking under the words. Some emotion, or tension, something he rarely heard from Brahms. Unease? No, something deeper. Brahms turned his head and met Ren's gaze square on, and while he might have his face locked down, nothing obscured the emotions in those deep blue eyes. Those eyes spoke of fear, desperation, and rock-hard resolve.

Ren took two steps closer to him, a hand lifting to touch Brahms' arm. He moved without thinking, drawn to him subconsciously, their eyes locked. "You're afraid. Why?"

Reaching up, Brahms covered the hand with one of his own, squeezing the fingers gently. "It's escalating. They're running out of time and getting desperate."

"The engagement party in Scovia," Charles said in realization, running a hand roughshod through his hair and sending curls in every direction. "Damn, I should have realized. Of course, that will be the breaking point. They'll have a much harder time stopping the alliance once we have the marriage agreement signed by both kings. Of course they'll do everything in their power to stop things before then."

Ren didn't think it was just that. True, things were certainly getting worse, the attacks coming closer together, but he didn't think it just this that troubled his friend. Something else was in play here, but Brahms apparently didn't want to speak about it in front of this audience. He'd have to ask again later. "Well, if you're staying, I'm putting you to good use. Track down Feliks for me; let's get him in motion."

Nodding sharply, Brahms gave his hand one more squeeze before turning and heading off at a ground-eating stride. Ren watched him go for a moment, strangely uncertain on how he felt. Normally he knew exactly how to respond to his friend, but Brahms seemed to be redefining how they interacted with each other, and he didn't know how to react in turn. He liked it, certainly, but it made things dangerous. Ren kept an iron lock on his fantasies even on the best of days. This new Brahms held the power to erode the lock completely if Ren wasn't careful.

Queen Eloise frowned after him, a thoughtful finger just below her mouth. "I don't remember our general being that physically demonstrative."

"He wasn't," Ren answered, dragging his eyes away once Brahms vanished from sight through the palace doors. "I'm a bit puzzled by it myself."

"Perhaps it's due to the long separation?" she suggested, although doubt colored her words. "Does he know about the Giles situation? He does? That's it, then. He's trying to offer comfort for a broken heart."

But Brahms knew Ren had recovered, that he no longer had any attachment or feelings for Giles. That couldn't be it. Ren decided not to argue with her about it, as he had other, more pressing matters demanding his attention. "Perhaps so. I take my leave of you for now. Hopefully I'll have better news to report this evening."

Frei proved the saying that old people never slept. Unless Ren visited his office at some godforsaken hour, he could find the head chamberlain there, sitting in his chair with stacks of reports and papers surrounding him. This morning proved no exception, and when Ren slipped through the open door, Frei looked up and reported smoothly, "Princess Alexandria is no worse for wear, except the loss of her riding habit. I understand it took the brunt of the impact with some very spectacular tears."

"I love how I never have to report anything to you, and instead you give me updates," Ren responded, coming about to drop heavily into a chair. "One of these days, I'll surprise you, though. I'm determined."

"You're a hundred years too early to pull it off," Frei retorted, a raspy chuckle in his throat. "Now. How's our favorite general?"

"Strange." Ren took a moment to relax, crossing one leg over another, and desperately wished he'd stopped by the kitchen for more than a roll and a hot cup of tea. Why had he thought that to be a sufficient breakfast? "He's very physically affectionate, which he's never been before, and something is preying at his fears. He says it's this situation I'm in, but...."

"But you think it's something else." Frei tapped at his desk with a fingertip, an idle fidget. "What do you suspect?"

"I haven't the foggiest, which is what puzzles me. Normally, I can at least take a guess, as Brahms keeps no secrets from me. But he's hiding something now, and I never seem to catch him for more than fifteen minutes alone before some disaster strikes, so I can't drag it out of him." Ren brooded at his kneecaps. "He refuses to leave the palace unless I go with him. Is the situation that bad, Frei? Have I become so scatterbrained, leaping from one emergency to the next, that I can't see the picture for what it is?"

Frei shrugged, an eloquent lift of the shoulders. "Perhaps, in part. Or perhaps General Brahms is still on edge after spending two years on the border, and finding us under a constant barrage of attacks has kicked his paranoia up a notch."

Now that seemed entirely feasible. Why hadn't Ren thought of that? He knew what living near enemy territory was like, the way it slithered into a man's subconscious, not allowing him to relax even after he left for a safer area. "Then let's get this solved so we can all relax. You received the message from Master Fredrick about who had access to the tack room over the past two days?"

"I did. Are we certain about that timeline?"

"The itching powder's properties decrease after a certain amount of time spent in the air," Ren explained. "After two days, its effectiveness would have dropped by half. So yes, fairly sure."

"Hmm..." Frei flipped over one stack of papers and reached for another, a thick collection bound by ribbon, almost the size of a novel. "Here are all of the records for the day passes requested in the last month. I suggest we go through and mark any lord who requests a day pass more than three times in a week."

"That seems reasonable; most of the time a lord doesn't need to request day passes at all. Unless he's sneaking in prostitutes."

"Or people of nefarious character," Frei agreed. "Here, I'll take half, you take half. Let's see if we can't put together a list of suspects at the very least."

10

Brahms found them hunched over the table surrounded by multiple stacks of paper roughly four hours later. He entered with a picnic basket in his hand, a very familiar face trailing him. Ren, glad for a break to avoid having a permanent crick in his neck, immediately stood up. "Feliks! I haven't seen you in years, how are you?"

"Sneaky, underhanded, and devilishly charming, as usual," the spy modestly responded, batting his dark brown eyes at Ren like a courtesan would a mark. "Former general, you do look dashing as always."

"And you as humble as usual," Ren responded, laughing. Feliks had devilishly handsome good looks, and knew it—hence his preferred method of getting close to people and charming information out of them. Ren honestly doubted the spy's ability to converse normally with someone; flirtation was so much a part of his speech patterns. "I see Brahms found you quickly enough; good work, my friend. You're here for information?"

Feliks leaned his torso in, coming closer to Ren. "And a kiss?"

Without a flicker of emotion, Brahms slammed a closed fist not too gently on the top of the spy's head.

"Ow!" Darting to the side, Feliks rubbed his abused head and pouted at Brahms.

Pointing a stern finger at Ren, Brahms rumbled, "He's off-limits. Remember?"

"Alright, alright, I won't flirt with him." Grumbling about him having no sense of humor, the spy shifted carefully back to the table. "Chamberlain Frei, you look quite commanding today."

"I look old and tired," Frei corrected with a smile, "but thank you for the compliment; they're rare at my age. How much did General Brahms brief you on?"

"Everything he knew," Feliks responded promptly.

Ren hadn't told him everything, but certainly enough for that to be rather inclusive. "Alright then, let's update you on what we've figured out the past four hours. Both of you, sit."

To no one's surprise, Brahms took the seat next to Ren and glared the spy into sitting on the opposite side of the table. Since Feliks had no compunction about draping himself over Ren's back, he actually felt grateful for his friend's commanding presence. Brahms could keep the spy in check. Ren didn't have quite as much luck in that regard.

Frei cleared his throat and began, "As you no doubt have heard, there has been some discontent since Prince Charles announced his attention to wed Princess Alexandria."

"Some discontent is a very mild way of stating it," Feliks disagreed casually, leaning back in his chair and crossing his feet at the ankle on top of the table. At Frei's glare, he carefully put his legs down again. "There are people ranting about it down at the pubs, and some of the lords are outright screaming their puny throats out, swearing they won't let it happen."

So, Feliks already had his ear to the ground on this, eh? Ren wasn't surprised. "Has anyone said why? The marriage alliance terms are quite favorable to us."

"Oh, they are, taken at face-value." Feliks paused and met Frei's stare with a baffled shrug. "What, you didn't expect people to just accept an alliance without finding an ugly spin to it, did you?"

Frei sighed. "Nonsense, why should they suspect a conspiracy? Go on, Master Spy."

Grinning, Feliks patted him on the back. "There, there. Anyway, it's the underlying message that worries the lords. The Mongs are making lots of unhappy noises about the marriage, threatening to go to war if it goes through. With us on this side of the Z's, and Scovia sharing borders with the Mongs, the lords are afraid we'll be pulled into a war on two fronts."

"And if the Mongs go to war, our northern neighbors will join them?" Ren rubbed at his jaw, thinking the implications through. "True, those two like to ally with each other. I can't imagine the Mongs are recovered enough from the last war to consider another one just yet, though."

"You'd know," Feliks responded, for once not being flirtatious or sarcastic. "Anyway, I also heard rumor that the Mongs seem to think there will be a trade monopoly formed when Scovia and Aart tie the knot. They're really nervous about it."

"There isn't," Frei denied thoughtfully, "but I can see why the idea would unnerve them. Their economy is fragile as it is. So that's the rumors going about the pub houses right now, eh? You mentioned some lords are screaming. Which lords?"

"Haven't gotten any specific names," Feliks admitted sourly. "Can't get anyone to give me one. I'd need money for that and I wasn't willing to spend my own coin to satisfy my curiosity. So, you have a list of names for me to spy on?"

Ren turned over his page, a list of five names neatly written out. "I can't swear it's the head of the household on this, it could be any member of his family. We have our own list and the one that King Gerhard put together of lords who are very vocal about their displeasure. Don't take it as a complete list, these are just the ones we've discovered so far."

Feliks took in the stacks of reports with an understanding 'ah.' "'So far'; got it. Wow, I didn't expect such a lofty list. Lord Julek? Really? Lady Wioleta, Lord Piotr, Lady Karina Cuyler…no, surely not the fair Karina. What did they do to get on the bad-boy list?"

"A whole list of things. They've attempted to disrupt Prince Charles' engagement through nefarious means—"

"Define nefarious," Feliks demanded instantly, eyes bright with anticipation.

"Whores in Charles' bed," Ren clarified.

Feliks let out a whoop, smacking his hand against the table. "Wicked! What else?"

"We're sure one of them has attempted an attack on Alexandria's life several times. On the way here and during a riding accident earlier, as well as some other attempts that never got past her bodyguard. We've had one poisoning attempt as well that didn't make it past our security checks." Ren rubbed at his forehead just thinking about it. "It's a strange mix of very serious attempts at harming her, or semi-serious attempts at just embarrassing one or the other in public."

"More incidents than we care to name," Frei observed darkly. "And it's part and parcel of the security breaches the palace has been experiencing for the past several months. Some of those names, Master Feliks, are likely not linked to the darker attacks we've suffered through. Some of them we suspect of having another motive altogether, one of discrediting Ren and removing him from his position."

Feliks flicked the page up and read it through again. "And what have they done?"

"Let in people on a very frequent basis for some rather flimsy reasons," Frei answered dryly. "And no, young man, I'm not referring to just prostitutes. I mean sending in their valet to check on their suite's decorations. Or sending in a household maid to inquire for the dinner menu. Things of that nature."

"Suspicious." Feliks drew the word out in a hiss of sound, looking positively delighted. "So very suspicious, I love it. I'll work on the list immediately. Ren, can I have money?"

"You can, but there's a specific thing I need you to look for. Some three months ago, an architectural set of blueprints for the palace went missing out of the palace archives. The area has restricted access which makes the situation even more alarming. We've investigated, nigh turned the palace upside down, but we can't find them. I have a suspicion that someone on this list might be in possession of them."

Feliks whistled low. "That sounds problematic. I'm not a builder, tell me what I'm looking for."

"They'll be massive, as long as your torso, with the palace seal as a watermark in the bottom right corner," Frei described, hands coming up to illustrate. "There should be five pages altogether. It's vital we get those back, young man, so do keep a sharp eye out."

With an elaborate bow from his seat, Feliks promised, "I will endeavor to serve, Chamberlain."

"I appreciate it."

Drawing a clean sheet of paper to him, Ren wrote out a note to the accountant and made very sure to sign over the date. He knew Feliks' tricks, such as rubbing out the date and writing a new one in. He also made sure to put a cap on the spy's funds in the note. "There. Take that to Accounting—I'm absolutely sure you know where that is—and try to spend the amount wisely, alright? If you use it all in the next two days, I won't give you anything more."

"So, three days is fine." Feliks beamed at his scowl and popped out of the chair. "Lovely talking to you, as usual, but I have people to flirt with and secrets to steal. See you later, my handsome general."

Brahms turned to call after him, "Only report during daylight hours!"

Ducking back into the doorway, Feliks made a face at him. "You always take all the fun out of things. Fine, fine."

When he disappeared again, Frei arched a brow at Brahms. "I take it that he's tried reporting in the dead of night?"

Grunting sourly, Brahms looked disgusted just at the memory alone. "Only once."

"Brahms broke his nose," Ren reported, laughing, although he tried to subdue it. He, after all this time, found it funny. "I don't think he'd actually dare do it again. Brahms, I am dying of curiosity over here, what is in that basket? It smells wonderful."

Opening the basket, Brahms lifted out several white bowls with lids on them and placed them on the table, neatly avoiding the stacks of paper. "Kitchens reported you hadn't eaten yet."

"Bless you," Ren responded fervently, hastily clearing the rest of the table so that no food could splatter on their hard work. "I'm famished, I just couldn't stop working; I felt we were close to getting an answer. Here, Frei, take a plate."

Frei took the plate, regarding Brahms with a smile that didn't touch the speculative gleam in his eyes. "It's kind of you to think of feeding us, General. In truth, I was about to send a runner for lunch. You've saved us the trouble. You'll eat with us?"

Nodding agreement, Brahms took a plate for himself and filled it with the beef stewed vegetables, mashed potatoes, and thick biscuits. Ren poured him a glass of water from the jug, passing it over, which Brahms took with a slight smile and grunt of thanks.

Ren took the first bite, savoring the thick, creamy sauce and the slight hint of pepper on his tongue. Truly, real food was blissful. He focused only on his plate for a spell, too hungry to think of anything else. Then he noticed the portion on Brahms' plate and frowned. He knew his friend's appetite well, and just those portions would not satisfy him. Reaching for the bowls, he scooped up another spoonful of the beef stewed vegetables. "I know you're worried, but you need to eat."

The corners of Brahms' eyes tilted up in a smile. With a happy sound, he ate a spoonful of his new serving.

Satisfied, Ren went back to eating, and when Brahms offered him another serving, he gestured for another spoonful of everything, which his friend obliged him by doing. Frei seemed to think something of this exchange of food, if his arched eyebrows were anything to go by.

Ren didn't know how to explain this culture quirk to the Aartan. In Shiirei, if you were especially close to someone, like a lover or family, it was a sign of affection to put food on their plate. Brahms had started doing it off and on about three years ago. Ren had always done it, ever since the first night they'd shared a tent.

Deciding he didn't care to go into a culture lesson, he swallowed the last of his lunch and beamed at Brahms. "Thank you, that was delicious. Want to help us wade through the rest of this? Maybe you'll see something we've missed."

"Mmm." The general stood and cleared the table of dishes, putting them all into the basket with Ren's help. Frei called for a runner to return the basket to the kitchen. With all of that taken care of, Brahms returned to his seat and held out a hand, ready for his part.

Relieved to have another mind to bend to the problem, Ren passed half his share of the daily reports to him. With Brahms helping, they now stood a good chance of getting done before midnight.

Assuming their enemies didn't throw another disaster their way today, of course. Ren didn't hold high hopes he'd be able to finish this. His enemies never did things for Ren's convenience.

11

Ren would dearly love to spend all of his time investigating, just so he could put an end to the madness, but couldn't. Hartmann did his best, but they had both a warden and deputy warden for a reason, and eventually Ren had to resume his normal duties. He retreated to his office towards the end of the work day, ploughing through the paperwork that had stacked up while his back was turned, which included an anticipated report from the palace postmaster. Ren picked that one up first.

Postmaster Diede was the crotchety, anal sort of man who kept records of absolutely everything and knew the rules of his job to a fault. Ren had clashed heads with him before, as Diede refused to let any letter or package go to a foreign country without him inspecting it first. The first time Ren had tried to send either letters or packages home, it had devolved into quite the argument, although they'd managed to work around the issue. Most of the time he dreaded dealing with Diede, but this time hopefully he would have good news to share. Breaking open the seal on the report, Ren read it through.

So, nothing had been posted through the palace post office from their suspects, eh? Ren read it through again, his emotions mixed. On the one hand, if they had, Diede would have caught them well before things got to this point. On the other hand, it confirmed what Ren suspected, that the nobles were smart enough to not do all of their shady business here under the king's nose.

He pulled out a blank card and wrote a note of thanks to Diede, then dropped it in the outgoing box for the runners to pick up.

A knock sounded on his door and he looked up, face lighting up in an unconscious smile. "Brahms."

"Have a dinner invitation for you," Brahms informed him, coming in to lean a hip against the corner of Ren's desk. "Konrad, Marcin, and a few of the others want to meet up for drinks. Come with me."

"That sounds perfect," Ren agreed and immediately grabbed another card. "Let me send a quick message to Frei so that he knows where to find me, just in case, and then we can go. Actually, can I invite someone as well?"

Brahms cocked his head in query, a silent 'who' on his face.

"Galvath, Alexandria's bodyguard," Ren explained. "He's become a friend since his arrival. We typically go drinking together."

Shrugging, Brahms allowed that was fine, so they headed up toward the second level. Galvath's room adjoined Alexandria's by design, and Ren nearly knocked on it until he heard his friend's voice coming out of Charles' room. They must be in there. He changed to the last room in the hallway and gave the open door a quick rap with his knuckles. The four occupants looked up from the card game they had splayed out on the round table. Alexandria, Charles, and Roslyn all had cards in their hands and a healthy amount of snacks nearby, the platter half devoured. Galvath stood sentry near the window, a little bored—or he had been until Ren's entrance.

To Alexandria, Ren gave his most charming smile. "I want to steal Galvath."

"Only if you give him back before the morning," she returned readily, folding her hand so that no one could sneak a peek at her cards. "And not completely hungover."

"I can manage the first, but the second is up to him." Ren shrugged, not accepting any blame, future or otherwise.

Alexandria twisted in her chair, studying her bodyguard. Galvath pleaded openly with his eyes. With a sigh, she waved him on, and the big man nearly bounded out the door like a puppy finally let off leash.

As they walked, Ren made the introductions between the two men, because as far as he knew, they'd never been formally introduced. They exchanged hellos, both curious about the other, but asked no further questions. They made it all the way to the end of the hallway before Ren drawled, "Don't you even want to know where we're going?"

"Of course," Galvath responded, tone indicating he didn't really care as long as it got him out of that room.

Snorting, Ren shook his head. "That bored, were you? Well, Brahms has a get together with some of his officer friends, and we're invited along."

"Sounds smashing," Galvath agreed with a winsome smile.

They headed out of the palace in an amiable mood, Brahms walking close enough that their arms brushed several times. Ren decided to put Brahms' close proximity down to his paranoia that they'd be attacked, as Ren refused to view it as any sort of flirtation, and let it ride.

Brahms directed them to a pub three streets down from the palace that Ren knew very well. The officers loved the place as it served excellent ale and good food, and offered semi-private rooms on the second floor for the larger parties. Ren hadn't patronized it the entire time Brahms was away, which was odd, now that he thought on it. Ren had his own friends among the Aartan army, didn't he? Why hadn't he reached out to any of them for a get together in the past two years?

A large hand settled at the small of his back, silently guiding him through the crowded tables, past the long bar at the back of the main taproom, and up the narrow wooden stairs. Ren glanced at Brahms, considering. Still in a very protective mood, then. Right.

Galvath picked up on it as well, catching Ren's eye and mouthing 'what?' but Ren just shrugged, as he really didn't have an explanation for it.

They turned toward the back as they crested the stairs, to what Ren had always thought of as 'their' room, as they inevitably took it when the officers gathered for a night of fun. They only had part of their usual group tonight, it seemed, but Ren didn't find that surprising. Most of the men had likely returned home for a well-earned rest by now. Konrad noticed them first and lifted a hand. "There you are! Glad to see you, Ren. Good job, General."

Ren extended a hand and caught Konrad's in a firm clasp. "It's good to see you, Konrad. I didn't think your wife would let go of you this soon, though."

"She's visiting her parents; I escaped for a night," Konrad confessed with an impish smile.

"Lucky you, then." Turning, Ren leaned over the table to shake hands with Marcin. "How are you doing, Marcin?"

"Relieved to be down here," Marcin responded in his gravelly voice that reminded Ren of landslides. "Two winters up north is enough for any man. Glad to see you, Warden, although I'm sorry to hear you're having such trouble up at the castle."

"We'll sort it out shortly," Ren assured him. He even half-believed his own words. "Egon, you devil, what are you still doing in Castel-de-Haut? I would have thought you home by now."

Egon looked a little mismatched in this atmosphere, the only one in uniform, and one of the few men of a smaller stature than Ren himself. He made up for the lack of brawn by being one of the most intelligent fighters Ren had ever crossed paths with. He grimaced as he responded, "I was all set to go home when my sister sent word to headquarters she was actually here. She's got complications of some sort with her baby, and came here for the doctors to look at her. Now they've put her on strict bedrest until she delivers. I volunteered to stay with her, as no one else in the family can afford to miss work."

"Tough luck," Ren commiserated. "Will she be alright, though?"

"She and the baby both, as long as she doesn't move much in the next month," Egon assured him. "She kicked me out of her room tonight, told me to go have fun."

"Then do that," Ren encouraged him. "And let me know if I can help, maybe send something to pass the time with."

"I will, and trust me, she'll likely need it. My sister is not good at just lying about. But here, sit, we've ordered food and drinks already. Who's your friend?"

"Everyone, this is Galvath," Ren introduced grandly. "He's Princess Alexandria's bodyguard, a good sparring partner, and a drinking buddy. He's here to get drunk, make friends, and relax."

"Galvath, welcome," Egon welcomed him, waving him into the seat next to his own. "You poor sod, do you really spar with Ren on a regular basis?"

Ren missed Galvath's response as he sat at the end of the table, Brahms taking the seat right next to his, leaning back and extending an arm to wrap around the back of the chair. This protective mood of Brahms' would ease once the party got properly started; Ren just had to be patient until it passed.

Food arrived along with the promised golden ale Aart favored, and Ren happily consumed both. Between one thing and another, the only thing he'd eaten today was a hastily scarfed down lunch, and his stomach threatened mutiny if he didn't fill it soon. His friends started telling him stories about how horrible building a fortress was while fighting off ambushes in snowdrifts tall enough to bury a man on a horse, and some of the funnier pranks they'd pulled on each other to ease the monotony of it. Ren nearly snorted ale up his nose a number of times, he laughed so hard. Galvath actually did.

They shifted about, the seating changing as they moved to more easily talk to each other, some of them splintering off into more private conversations. Brahms went to order more ale and Konrad took his vacated seat promptly, planted a forearm on the table and leaned in to confide, "I will never deploy with him again without taking you."

Ren paused with the tankard halfway to his mouth. "Was he that bad?"

"Worse. A wounded bear with a thorn in its side would have been better company. We didn't even dare talk to him the first month. I have literally never seen a human being carry around a dark thundercloud until that point. He eventually settled, stopped being so snappish, but he was very unhappy the entire two years we were up there. And I don't know what happened six months ago, but he heard something from the army courier that set him off again, and it was worse than before. He refused to say a word for two weeks." Konrad shuddered, the gesture only partially exaggerated. "No thank you. I've learned my lesson. If we can't take you, I'm not going. I'll resign my commission first."

Konrad's words floated about in Ren's head, suggesting several things to Ren, but surely that wasn't right. Ren had been lost and dismayed as well, but not to such extremes. He wanted to ask if Konrad perhaps exaggerated a little, as what he described would be more suitable to Brahms missing a lover, not a friend.

A familiar quickness doubled his heartbeat and Ren silently castigated himself for a fool. After five years, surely his heart should understand it couldn't have what it wanted. Brahms was a friend. A dear one—a brother—but still a friend. Ren couldn't have him as anything more. Shaking his head, he firmly forced the hope aside. "Have you ever seen him depressed before, Konrad?"

Head tilting back, the colonel pondered. "I don't think I have, not until this last deployment. Angry, sure, but not depressed. He doesn't do depressed well. Comes off enraged, most of the time. But truly, I don't know what he heard six months ago, but that wasn't depression. I thought he was going to murder someone in cold blood."

Ren grimaced and confessed, "He learned about a certain bad love affair of mine at that point."

"Oh," Konrad drawled in understanding. "Yes, that would do it, alright. I wondered. We heard later about the trouble starting up around the palace, and that got him worried all over again, so we were all very happy to finally get on that boat and go home."

"I don't doubt it." Ren felt a little bad for Brahms' officers. Normally they were a tight knit group, friends as well as subordinates, but they must have hated serving the past two years in that kind of atmosphere.

"Speaking of palace trouble..." Konrad lowered his voice even further, so that he could barely be heard over the ongoing conversation at the other end of the table. "I heard something strange. My cousin's friend is a locksmith, and a good one, and he took on a job that worried him enough he passed word of it to me. He said it was odd enough at the time, but recent events made him question it even more. He had a noble lady come in with a set of six keys to have duplicated. He wouldn't have thought much of it, I don't think, except the keys' fobs had the palace crest on them."

Ren nearly choked on the ale in his mouth and had to pound his chest to clear the airways. "Are you certain?!"

"I spoke to the man myself, and he seemed sincere, not to mention worried. He said he creates duplicate keys all the time, as people inevitably need them, but he's only handled palace keys once before because there's a locksmith in the palace itself that normally handles such matters." Konrad's ginger brows twitched together in a deepening frown. "I didn't like the sound of it. I thought it best to tell you."

Snapping the tankard sharply to the table, Ren caught his hand and urged, "Can you take me to him tonight? I need to speak with him."

"Of course," Konrad assured him with perfect understanding. "He's only one street over, but his shop is likely closed already for the night. I think he lives about the shop, though; we might be able to meet him still."

"Let's try it," Ren insisted, already standing. "If nothing else, I'll know where his shop is and I can try him again in the morning."

Brahms entered at that moment, saw their clasped hands, and went abruptly still. His nostrils flared before he lost all expression, turning so rigid that his tendons popped out. Ren took in that expression and didn't know what to make of it. If he didn't know better he'd say Brahms was...jealous? No, that surely wasn't it. Releasing Konrad, he in turn caught Brahms' arm and whispered quickly, "We might have a lead. Konrad knows something. I'm leaving with him now to follow up on it."

Nodding, Brahms turned and exited, body language stating he'd go with them. Ren couldn't in good conscious just leave so he turned back to the other men and pinned a smile on his face. "Something's come to my attention; I need to go, but let's do this again soon, alright? Galvath, are you fine on your own?"

"Go, go," Galvath encouraged him, the words slightly slurred. "I'm having a marvelous time."

Military men that they were, they understood duty, and made no arguments. With good nights ringing in his ears, Ren hurried down the stairs on Konrad's heels.

The shop really did sit one street over, on the opposite side of the street from the pub, with no light shining through the front picture windows. It was clearly closed for the evening. However, the second story of the building had lights on, indicating someone might be home. Konrad went to the side of the building, down a narrow but clean alley, and up the narrow stairs that led to the top story. He knocked in a triple beat staccato on the white washed door while Ren and Brahms waited on the ground.

A few moments later, a petitely built man with glasses perched on the end of his nose opened it, blinking at his visitor in some confusion which quickly became recognition. "Oh. Colonel Konrad, welcome back. My matter, did you—?"

Konrad pointed to the bottom of the stairs. "I have with me General Brahms and Warden Ren. They are highly interested in hearing your story, sir."

Alarmed, the locksmith stepped out of his doorway to peer down at them. "Dear me, is it really that serious?"

"It might well be," Ren called up to him. "Master, can I hear the story myself?"

"Of course, of course," the man assured them, stepping out and taking the stairs rapidly. "Let's go into the shop, I can show you the molds, as well, that way."

Ren really didn't want to discuss this on an open street, so amiably followed the man through the back door of the shop. It had all the earmarks of a workroom, with multiple tables and benches with half-finished projects strewn about. The room contained a sort of organized chaos, a feeling that the master of the place knew where to find everything, but a visitor would be hopelessly confused. It smelled strongly of metal, fire, and a sort of brine that made Ren's nose twitch.

"This is Master Gibbons," Konrad introduced properly once they had the door shut behind them. "Sir, just tell them what you told me."

Gibbons, even in the single lantern's light, still looked very alarmed to have such prominent men visiting him, but drew in a shaky breath and launched into the tale. "I had a noblewoman visit me some five months ago. She wore a thick veil over her face, and gave me a false name, so I'm not sure to her identity, but she paid in cash up front. I was in desperate need of funds at the time, as the store had experienced an unfortunate fire the month before, and I took the job even though it made me uneasy. She had with her six keys, all bearing the crest of the palace on the fobs, and said she needed duplicates made of each immediately. Two duplicates, to be precise. I told her it would take me five days, which it did, and she collected them promptly on the fifth day. I haven't seen her since."

Ren felt a headache brewing right between his eyes. "That does sound very suspicious. You're absolutely positive it was a noblewoman?"

"Her dress, her speech..." Gibbons elaborated with a helpless splay of the hands. "If she wasn't a noblewoman, she was a very credible actress. The whole business bothered me, of course, so I kept the molds when normally I wouldn't have bothered. Then I heard about some trouble up in the palace, and how it was getting worse up there, and thought maybe it had something to do with the keys. I knew Colonel Konrad was due in, so I thought to wait for him and tell him the story, see what he made of it."

Unease radiated from the man and Ren sought to reassure him, "You were right to be worried and I'm grateful you reported it. You've perhaps solved part of the mystery for me. Can I see the molds?"

"Of course, of course," the man hastily assured him, turning to the far table. From underneath it, he pulled out a wooden crate with white plaster molds stacked inside. He lifted them free and then paused. "You're not going to see detail well in this lighting. I can make a wax mold for you in a few minutes, if you'd like to wait?"

Ren considered that, then requested firmly, "Please do. I'll likely have to take all of this as evidence back with me and the wax versions will be easier to display."

"Just a minute," Gibbons promised and flew into activity.

Leaning into his side, Brahms whispered into his ear, "We wondered how they got in so readily even into restricted areas."

"The keys would explain it," Ren whispered back grimly. "Not difficult to get the keys, either. The maids still have to get in to clean, so they have keys. Find the right maids, buy them out, easy as that. Unfortunately, almost anyone can be bought." Bitterly, he added, "I can keep the palace properly secure if I could just eliminate all the people."

Snorting at this complaint, Brahms pointed out drolly, "They wouldn't need a warden for an empty building."

"True enough." Ren bemoaned that he hadn't finished off that tankard of ale earlier. He felt like he'd be able to take this new revelation better if he were tipsy, at least.

Good to his word, Gibbons presented them with six wax keys made in a slightly grey tint to help bring out the pattern on the fob better. Ren lifted them up, angling them to catch the light, and felt his heart sink. "Well this isn't good. Archives, east side gate, kitchens, west entrance, armory, and stable tack room."

"You can tell just by the shape of the keys?" Konrad demanded, a little incredulous.

Shaking his head, Ren gestured him closer and tilted the fob so he could point out the detail along the edge. "They're all labeled. See the letters there along the bottom?"

Konrad whistled low, eyes in narrow slits as he peered. "I can barely read that. Makes sense they're labeled, though."

"Causes confusion otherwise." Ren's burgeoning headache arrived in full force. "I don't know what disturbs me more—that they have access to the armory or can enter through two of the outside gates."

"Both," Brahms growled, eyes flashing in anger. "Can you change the locks?"

"Yes, but it means tipping our hand, and I have a feeling we shouldn't do that just yet." Rocking back on his heels, Ren tried to think the situation through, anticipating what his enemy would do next. "Master Gibbons, I'd like to preserve you as a witness to all of this. I need you to keep very quiet about everything for the next short while, can you do that?"

Gibbons nodded hastily. "Wouldn't dream of doing otherwise, Warden. If this business gets out too much, it might ruin me."

"It won't come to that," Ren promised him. "If anything, your conscience has possibly saved us. I'll take the molds and wax keys with me tonight; just stay mum about the situation until we call for you."

Leaning in again, Brahms queried softly, "Report to the king tonight or in the morning?"

"King tonight, Frei in the morning," Ren answered quietly. "And pray that at some point, we'll be able to find our beds."

It had to be past midnight by the time Ren stumbled into his apartment. Exhaustion didn't begin to cover it. His very bones protested being upright. King Gerhard had not been pleased with Ren's discovery, although Queen Eloise did most of the shouting for both of them. Ren had to repeat the story three times and display all of the evidence before they ordered it all locked away, in a place they knew the maids didn't have a key to, of course.

Ren paused in the doorway and blearily looked about to find Brahms right behind him. "Are you sleeping here tonight?"

"Yes," Brahms answered simply.

Too tired to care or protest, Ren just waved him to shut the door and headed for his bedroom, stripping off boots and coat as he went, carelessly tossing them aside as he moved. "Pallet?"

"Don't bother," Brahms grunted, also stripping out of his coat and boots. "Bought a massage oil bottle earlier?"

Tired he might be, but Ren knew that if he tried to sleep now, he'd end up with a crick in his neck come morning. The tension had turned his shoulders and neck muscles into a locked iron grid. He'd taught Brahms the fine art of massage during the war, to keep them from both locking up in pain, and he congratulated himself now for the forethought. It was definitely paying off. "Please?"

"Down," Brahms instructed, heading for his bag near the foot of the bed.

Something about him having a bag of his own things here teased at Ren's mind, suggesting that he should question that, but he didn't have the energy for it now. Tomorrow. Assuming he could remember to pursue the matter tomorrow. Shrugging out of his shirt, he flopped face down on the bed.

Then nearly rolled out of it in a blind panic.

"Down," Brahms instructed again, a hand flat between Ren's shoulder blades as he straddled Ren's hips.

"Uhh." Ren felt he should protest this position. Vigorously. He had not taught Brahms to sit on someone while massaging them, he would swear to that in a court of law. The position made him stir a little, anticipating, even as his rational mind knew better.

Warm hands and oil smoothed over his naked skin, sending warm tingles down his spine, and Ren buried his head in a pillow before his expression gave him away. He absolutely couldn't reveal just how much he liked this, it would give Brahms the wrong impression, and— "Owwwww."

"Knew it," Brahms grunted, thumbs finding every knot in Ren's shoulders and pressing rhythmically to release them before sweeping onward, warming and relaxing the muscles. "Could tell from the way you were carrying yourself."

The pain killed whatever ardor Ren felt, which mostly relieved him, and he tilted his head to the side so he could breathe better. "You're not much better."

"Do me next," Brahms requested, then paused and dug his thumb into another knot.

The following few minutes were a strange mix of pleasure and pain until Brahms finally released him and climbed off Ren's hips. He still felt sore but also like he could fully turn his head. Turning it this way and that, Ren gave his friend a tired smile of thanks. "Better. Alright, your turn."

Stripping his shirt over his head, Brahms went face down on the bed, and Ren very pointedly did not straddle his hips but stayed properly to the side. He loosened up that back with a quick chopping motion back and forth, then snagged the bottle of oil from the chest and liberally coated Brahms skin with it. Working with these muscles was always a challenge in strength, as Brahms didn't really have muscles, more like steel ropes masquerading as such. Ren had to put in serious effort to work him loose every time.

This time was worse than any he could recall, likely because it had been two years since Ren had been able to massage him. That and two years of tension gathering up into knots. It took three applications of oil and several sweeps of his forearms, judicious use of his elbows, and more than a few chops to get Brahms to relax. He slowly went boneless in the mattress, breath deepening out.

Then a faint sound, a borderline snore.

"Did you seriously fall asleep on me?" Ren muttered, tilting his torso over to stare at his friend's face. "Yes, you did. I knew you were exhausted."

Shaking his head, he maneuvered the blanket free and draped it over Brahms, then climbed into loose trousers and took his hair down. That relieved some of the pressure in his forehead, and Ren worked his head back and forth on his neck to loosen it a little more. Of course, his headache likely stemmed from sleep deprivation at this point. Climbing in, he settled on his right side, studying the back of that curly dark head with a sad smile. Very quietly he whispered, "This is a dangerous habit you've developed, my friend. I'm growing too accustomed to having you here. I won't be able to sleep by myself soon if you keep sharing my bed like this."

Perhaps Brahms heard him, as he frowned in his sleep.

He'd have to talk to Brahms about this at some point. Not tonight, of course, but at some point. Closing his eyes, Ren let himself relax and enjoy at least one more night of indulging in a fantasy.

12

If left to his own devices, Arman would have avoided the formal dinner that night. His distaste for ceremony and social events bordered on the pathological, and despite his rank and birth he'd never grown truly accustomed to them. It probably had something to do with the incessant chatter about inane topics that drove him mad. Arman would rather stab himself in the eye than talk about the weather.

Ren, however, thrived on conversing with people. He truly enjoyed it, speaking with others, hearing their thoughts, sharing their emotions to events. In this, like so many ways, they were night and day different from each other. Arman loved watching him in moments like these, when Ren blossomed in happiness. It reflected in everything Ren said, everything he did, his expression animated with humor and affection, manner engaging. All lighting suited him, but candlelight turned his skin golden, his waist length hair a lover's fantasy. The memory of last night, with Ren naked from the waist up and under him, rose into his mind's eye. He'd glowed gold dust and raven's wing in that gentle lighting, warm and intoxicatingly close. Each moan and hitch of breath Arman incited with a sweep of his hands quieted the voice that said Ren might reject his touch.

Suspicious, Arman turned his gaze to eye his glass of wine. He was thinking poetically. That might be a good sign he should stop imbibing. Besides, any more of *those* thoughts would show up quite visibly, which he'd rather not reveal at a formal dinner.

Roslyn giggled at something Ren said, drawing her mother's attention, and then Queen Eloise giggled in a very similar way as Ren repeated it. Arman had always harbored the suspicion that it was Ren's conversational skills and charms that landed him the position of castle warden as much as his martial arts prowess. Certainly, of all skills, the castle warden must possess the ability to speak comfortably with every class of people.

Fortunately for all concerned, Arman didn't have to really talk much that evening as he shadowed Ren. No one really expected him to chatter, and he could comfortably let his friend do the talking for both of them. Instead, as Ren spoke, Arman listened.

And he didn't like what he heard.

The u-shaped table housed a full contingent this evening, the wood nearly groaning from the weight of the food it supported. Every candelabrum had been lit, casting the room in bright lights, giving no room for shadows. On the surface, it looked like any other formal dinner with its brightly-dressed attendees—the women all smiles and flirty with their fans, the men discussing serious topics as was their wont. It took at least the first course before Arman realized where the problem stemmed.

People whispered to each other behind hands or fans, their eyes cast toward the head of the table every few minutes before hastily averting their faces, as if afraid to be caught staring. The furtive movements caught Arman's attention and he strained his ears, listening.

"—said that the warden was in the prince's bedchamber late in the night—"

"—Princess Roslyn put forth a petition to the queen to marry Warden Ren, can you imagine—"

"—both siblings are being seduced by him. What are the king and queen thinking leaving such a man here?"

"—perhaps they're right. Someone needs to call for the warden's dismissal—"

That statement won his unwavering regard and he stared at the woman who'd said it for a long moment. A heftily built matron, hair turning slowly to grey, she flinched when she saw his eyes on her and hastily diverted her face, dropping the topic with the woman next to her altogether. He didn't immediately recognize her, but then Arman had never made it a point to learn all of the families. Still, she looked familiar. He'd crossed paths with her at some point.

"What are you staring at so intently?" Ren asked, reaching for his wine.

"Woman on the left, grey dress. Who is she?"

Ren stared at him, eyes shrewd and evaluating. "You're asking me who someone is. Are you running a fever?"

Dammit, why did he have to be so sharp? One of the reasons

why they worked so well together was because of Ren's observational skills, but Arman did curse it at times. Like now. Leaning in closer, he whispered, "I'm hearing snatches. People are saying you've seduced both prince and princess, and that the king should dismiss you."

"Ah, that rumor."

Arman waited for some kind of emotion. Outrage, disbelief, anger, something. All he got was resignation. Staring at Ren incredulously, he demanded, "How long has this been going on?"

"About as long as you've been gone?" Ren offered. He thought about it, lips pursed, then shrugged. "Somewhere around there."

Part of him wanted to wail out a plaintive why, but he didn't need to. Since Ren's appointment, there had always been some discontent among the lords. In part because they had their own candidates they wanted to put in the warden's position. In part because Ren had no political affiliation with any of them, and so couldn't be bought or swayed into overlooking certain indiscretions. In part because of stupid bigotry that dictated a Shiirein man, no matter how qualified, shouldn't hold a highly ranked position in the palace.

The surprise came not from the mutterings of unhappy people, but that it had grown to the point that they would openly discuss it at a formal dinner.

Roslyn, sitting on Ren's left side, leaned forward enough to meet both of their eyes. In a voice pitched to carry, she gave Ren an apologetic smile and said, "Sorry. I'm afraid I made it worse, what with me mock-proposing all of the time."

Making a snap decision, Arman used the opening she gave him. Not missing a beat, Arman put his arm around Ren's shoulders and leaned into him, assuring her, "It's alright, Princess. They'll soon learn I'm not the type to share. That will put the rumors to rest."

He could feel Ren tense under his hand, beyond startled. Before he could give the game away, Arman turned his head against Ren's ear and breathed, "Play along."

Roslyn's head came up, jaw dropped in astonishment. Gesturing to both men, she asked, "Ah...when did this happen?"

Proving he could adapt on the fly, Ren grinned at her and relaxed back into Arman. "The very night he came home, he stayed with me. Things sort of, ah, developed from there."

All true, if misleading. Arman applauded this as Ren was a very terrible liar. Truth would serve them far better. From the corner of his eye, he saw that most of the lords and ladies seated nearby had turned to watch, their attention fixated on the two of them. Arman didn't think of himself much of an actor, but in this, he hardly needed to act. "So, no more proposals from you, Princess. He's mine."

Holding up both hands, she stayed his mock-anger with a giggle. "I'll stop teasing him, promise. Aw, you look so sweet together."

"Naturally we do," Ren responded with confidence.

Even though an act, Arman's heart skipped a beat. He liked hearing those words out of Ren far too much. Reluctantly, he withdrew his arm so that Ren could eat, only to be confronted by a murderous glare from a young lord at the end of the table. He had direct line of sight with him, and judging from the description Frei had supplied Arman with earlier, he knew exactly who it must be. Lifting Ren's free hand, he brought it up to his mouth, acting as if he put a kiss to the knuckles although his lips never made contact. He didn't dare push Ren too far in public—the man's nerve would break at some point.

But the lord in question didn't see it for a false kiss, and his expression darkened to a purple hue of fury. Abruptly, he slammed his wine glass down on the table, threw his chair back in a screech of wood on tile, then stormed out of the room.

Ren, of course, caught all of this and gave him quite the look, somewhat chiding for Arman's childishness, but amused nonetheless.

Shrugging his innocence, he let Ren's hand go. This interaction did not escape the rest of the room, and the whispered conversations changed to remark upon it. Arman listened hard, then grunted in satisfaction. No one could squash a rumor—not anything in the world had the power to do that—but changing the rumor? Easily done.

Hopefully it stayed changed.

Arman knew good and well Ren wouldn't leave the dinner incident alone. As they walked back to Ren's apartment, his friend chortled merrily. "Their faces! Ah, if only I painted, I'd record it for history. You're a superb actor, Brahms; not one of them suspected a thing."

He watched in amusement as Ren nearly skipped along at his side. "You're going to act like we're lovers in public just to see people react."

"And I won't even feel guilty about it." Ren cackled, rubbing his hands together in wicked anticipation. "Especially not after seeing Giles' reaction. Ah, that was sweet revenge. Lady Harriet told me once that there's no better revenge than gaining the arm of a better man in front of an ex-lover. I now understand exactly what she means."

Extending an elbow, Arman offered mock-courteously, "You may flirt with me anytime."

Ren promptly linked arms with him, batting his eyelashes up at him. "Why, sweetums, I thought you'd never say so."

Arman had to bite the inside of his lip to keep from laughing himself, as he couldn't take that face at all seriously. Just who was Ren imitating? He found this playacting dangerous, and the longer they did it, the more he played with fire. While he had stolen moments, initiated flirtations that Ren seemingly responded to, Arman still had found no opening to put his plans into motion and the impatience wore at him. Warmth laced with a touch of arousal lanced through him and he resisted the urge to pull Ren in even closer. Ren seemed in a happy mood now. Maybe he could at least broach the idea tonight? Not here in the hallway, of course, but when they reached Ren's apartment.

"Ah, Warden?" a man called uncertainly behind them.

Dropping Arman's arm, Ren turned immediately. "Fillmore. What is it?"

"Bad news, sir, sorry," the guard apologized, still giving Arman an odd look. "Two of the maids found a mace trap in one of the linen closets."

Ren's demeanor did an abrupt u-turn from flirtatious and silly to deadly serious. "Was it sprung? Is anyone hurt?"

"Thankfully no, on both accounts," Fillmore reported, already turning, ready to lead the way. "We didn't dare touch it, sir."

When Ren looked at him in a silent request for help, Arman instantly nodded. It took two to undo such traps safely, and it went best if those two knew what they were doing. He and Ren had undone many an enemy trap in their time and it would be best if they handled this one.

"Show me," Ren requested of Fillmore.

As he followed, Arman's previous anger during dinner surged anew. Couldn't they let Ren have even a single night of rest? Were they deliberately attacking near the dinner hour to make sure Ren couldn't get a full night's sleep? Or was this trap set far earlier and only now discovered by chance? Either way, this went beyond trying to sabotage Ren's career, as the trap could very well have hurt the staff.

When he finally got his hands on these buffoons, they'd pay dearly. Nothing was worth innocents being hurt.

They left the main halls and went into the staff area, away from the nobility and closer toward the kitchens. Two young girls, neither older than twenty, stood hovering in front of a linen closet. At Ren's approach, they looked a little relieved, one of them calling out to him, "It's this one, Warden. We shut the door again as soon as we saw it."

"Smart thinking," Ren assured them. "Can both of you stand well back?"

Both women immediately backed off and to the side, giving their warden plenty of room to work in, but hovering out of curiosity.

"It'd be best if I had a shield to duck behind while I opened the door," Ren muttered to himself.

Arman tapped him on the shoulder and then hefted the sword hanging on his belt pointedly.

"Oh. Certainly, that will work." Ren bent low, crouching, his hand on the door. "Ready?"

Drawing his sword, he held it in both hands parallel above Ren's head, prepared to block. "Ready."

"Opening now." Ren slowly opened the door, trying not to go too wide for fear of triggering the release. When he had it fully open, and the ball of wooden spikes still hadn't moved from its bed on the sheets, he stared upwards in confusion. "Brahms?"

Since he could see better from his standing position, Arman gave it a careful study, craning his neck about so he could see it from all angles. "Not set."

"So, it's just sitting there?" Ren sighed gustily as he stood. "Damn thing nearly gave me a heart attack. Fillmore, get a report on when someone last opened this closet, I need the time frame for this narrowed down."

"On it, sir."

"And double check all of the other linen closets and chests, I don't want any other nasty surprises."

Fillmore's expression darkened. "I'll do that personally, sir." With a salute, he turned and jogged off.

Standing in-between Arman and the mace trap, Ren carefully

reached up and grasped it by the base of the spikes. Whoever had built it certainly knew the correct method, as it possessed the right number of wooden spikes jutting out from every angle like a ball, with the weight of a stone tied to the center using a judicious amount of rope. Arman had seen many of them during his time with the army. With the right timing, they could injure someone seriously, if not outright kill them.

He heard it before he saw it, the snap of a rope as it released, the movement enough to throw up the top sheet in the back of the closet. "Ren, down!"

Ren dropped immediately, as if his legs had been cut out from underneath him. Arman raised his sword again in a horizontal bar, a hand braced on either end, and caught the mace trap and the other one behind it with the flat of his blade. Muscles bulging and bunching, he strained to keep it from launching outwards, feet sliding a few inches on the carpet.

Rolling to the side, Ren gained his feet and retreated two steps. "I'm free, let go!"

Not able to hold this position indefinitely, Arman saw sense in releasing it, as long as everyone was safely away. He ducked to the side himself, his torso caught by Ren's hands and jerked sharply out of the swing's path. Sometimes he forgot how much strength resided in that wiry frame of Ren's until he started throwing Arman's weight casually about.

The trap had a spring to it, one powerful enough that it threw the mace trap against the far wall, where it impacted the stone and splintered. It hit with the force of a cannon ball and Arman swallowed hard, his mind conjuring terrifying visions of Ren trying to disarm it himself.

The arms around his torso tightened, almost reflexively, as Ren swore aloud. "Damn these bastards to the lowest hell! No matter their issues with me, they could have killed someone."

Arman resisted the urge to grab Ren up and haul him somewhere else, somewhere he'd be safe and people wouldn't conspire against him. A sick feeling churned his gut, thinking of what Ren had faced this entire time. If Ren's reflexes were anything less than stellar, he would have been injured before now.

Dammit, this was *not* how he'd planned for things to go once home. In fact, it was so far from his plans that Arman had to wonder if he'd done something to anger the gods. He should never have introduced Ren to the queen and king five years ago. He should have followed his selfish impulses and made him the castle warden of Brahms Fortress. If he had, none of this would be happening now.

Sounding exhausted right to the bone, Ren let go of him and said quietly, "I'll report this to the king and queen. Get some rest, Brahms."

Arman sent him a glare hot enough to melt steel. Did he really think Arman could cheerfully go to bed and ignore the potential hotbed of problems this trap represented? That he would be able to sleep while Ren ran around the palace looking for other booby traps?

Adequately reading the look on his face, Ren protested, "This isn't your job."

Damn idiot. Grabbing Ren's head with one hand, he drew him up and in, close enough for a kiss. Which is what he would prefer to be doing at the moment, dammit. "Nothing is more important than you."

Ren's expression softened into the sweetest, most affectionate smile, one reminiscent of the smile he'd worn when Arman invited him home, all those years ago. "What did I do to deserve you?"

"Something terrible," Arman said through a dry throat, forcing himself to let go, although he couldn't help but let his fingers linger a little, brushing against Ren's cheek before letting his hand drop.

Laughing softly, Ren agreed dryly, "No doubt. Alright, come with me to report, then let's shake this place down and see what else pops out at us. Miss Gloria, Miss Hania, spread the word amongst the staff that absolutely no one is to open any door without a guardsman present, and do so cautiously, alright?"

"Yes, Warden," both women agreed with a relieved curtsey.

"And let's all hope," Ren added with a grim set to his jaw, "that this was the only one."

❖

King Gerhard and Queen Eloise did not receive the news of the mace trap in their linen closet well. Queen Eloise turned so purple with outrage she looked like a wine bottle ready to blow its cork. King Gerhard just slumped in his chair, cradling his face with both hands.

"Warden," Queen Eloise demanded from her favorite chair in the king's study, "I do not like traps in my palace."

"My Queen, I loathe them," Ren responded in perfect accord

with her.

"I am extremely tired of my family, staff, and guests being in danger," King Gerhard added, lips curling to bare gritted teeth. "Alexandria being in danger is bad enough, but these security breaches have escalated from an annoyance to a serious danger. If not for General Brahms' reflexes, someone might be missing a head right now."

"This is the outside of enough," Queen Eloise declared, face flushing with anger. "Tell me who's doing this."

"I can't give you an exact name," Ren responded with an apologetic splay of hands, "as we're still narrowing down the suspects."

Trying to relieve the burden a little, Arman pried open his mouth and spoke. "I sat with Ren and Chamberlain Frei, Your Majesty and reviewed the daily reports. No one on it had the military expertise to build something like this."

Queen Eloise gave him an odd look for speaking without being prompted, but didn't question it openly. "Who would know how?"

"We have divisions in the army specifically for booby-traps, that are called 'Setting Units.' Creating and setting booby-traps usually fall under their domain more than anyone else's, so it's a semi-technical skill that not everyone in the army would know. That said, the suspects for doing this can't be restricted to just active duty personnel. Anyone retired could also so it," Ren clarified. "That leaves us with a rather large possible list."

"So, we might not be able to find the man that actually set the trap," King Gerhard commented. "That's alarming, Ren. I'd rather not have someone setting random booby-traps in my palace."

"Trust me, My King, it gives me nightmares. I don't want this situation to repeat either. It gets worse, as we know that the armory key was duplicated. The trap could well have been supplied by the palace armory. I've had it under guard ever since I discovered the situation but—" Ren shrugged, not sure what he could say. "They could have removed what they needed and I wouldn't know. Hartmann reports the last inventory was done three months ago. Permission to take a detailed inventory?"

"Granted. But Ren, there's absolutely no way that you can stop it?" Queen Eloise pressed. "Isn't there something you can do?"

"Short of declaring second point of contact? No." Ren shrugged helplessly. "The protocols in place allow people to carry in luggage, crates of supplies and so forth inside without it being thoroughly examined. Anything can be smuggled inside."

The king flexed his hands several times, nostrils flaring as he breathed in deeply. "I can't institute second point of contact right now. But you're allowed to implement a safety check on the larger crates and suitcases for anything dangerous."

A semi-state of second point of contact? Arman thought that smart. Ren apparently shared the opinion as he nodded in open relief. "Yes, My King, I'll do so immediately."

"What of Feliks? You've received no report from him?"

"Not as yet, but I didn't expect one, either. He needs at least a few days to make the rounds and charm people into divulging their secrets. Feliks only reports when he actually has something to report."

It was one of the few reasons why Arman liked the spy. That and he got the job done.

"Our own lords, upsetting the security in the palace just to push their own agendas," Queen Eloise fumed. "And they're going about it so stupidly. They seem to think they can kill two birds with one stone by attacking Alexandria in this way, and discrediting you in the process. Why they think we'll blame you when you're following our commands is beyond my understanding."

Arman didn't think Ren quite saw it that way. If he knew how the lords were sneaking people in, Ren surely felt like he should be able to stop it. But short of locking the palace down completely, there was no sure way of managing it. Thinking hard, he pondered the problem, but he could really only see one way out of this mess. "Your Majesties. I have a thought."

"We dearly need another opinion," King Gerhard encouraged. "What is it, General?"

"Treat this like a military campaign." Looking to Ren, he offered, "Bait and trap?"

Ren's face lit up in a blazing smile, one with a distinctly feral edge to it. "Oh, I like that. My King, he wants you to noise it about that you've grown impatient and are thinking about dismissing me. Give them encouragement to come forward."

"Bait them into coming out into the open, you mean," King Gerhard translated, his expression also becoming rather crafty, like a cat spying a mouse hole, "and then trap them when they've done so. Ren, how much evidence do you have right now?"

"I've reported to you everything we've found. I think we have enough for a conviction for at least some of them. For the rest, all I have is some circumstantial evidence they'll be hard pressed to explain away."

"Call your spy in for an update. If he's found enough to handle the rest, I'll start the rumor tomorrow." King Gerhard sat back in his chair, tired and creased after a long day, but with the composure of a king. "I think it's time we put an end to this."

13

Preparing for the trap would mean another sleepless night, where he might catch four hours and be lucky for even that. Ren worried about Brahms, as his friend's mood became increasingly sour as time went on, and the dark circles under his eyes could make a panda proud. Ren might be the type to function well for long periods of time on little sleep, but Brahms needed a full eight hours, otherwise it got ugly. He really wanted to send Brahms home to the fortress, let him rest. He'd just gotten off a two-year deployment; the man had to be exhausted, but every time Ren tried to bring it up, Brahms snapped at him.

His friend's loyalty and concern touched him, of course. But still, there was no reason for both of them to be driven into the ground by exhaustion. Perhaps he should write Brahms' parents, get them to convince him?

Not the time for such thoughts. Ren propped his shoulder against the back wall of the palace gardens and tried not to yawn. Openly. Where was his illustrious spy, anyway?

A heavy weight draped along his back and a deep voice crooned into his ear, "Ren, my lovely—owww. Owowowowow, my ear, my ear!"

Too tired to even react, Ren just turned and watched Brahms haul their spy away forcefully, his ear higher than the rest of his body. It really did look like Brahms would tear it off at any second. Should he stop him?

Nah. "Feliks, what do you have to report?"

"I'd like to remind you," the spy squealed out, hitting a pitch probably unvisited since puberty, "that ears are very important in my business. Vital, one might say."

Brahms shook him once, then let go. Even in the mellow lighting of the nearby sconce, his expression looked thunderous. He really had no sense of humor when tired.

Apparently, Feliks realized his life had crossed over into 'endangered species' territory and he became very brisk, almost business-like. Or as close as his jovial manner could get. "Of the names you gave me, I can prove that three in question are in up to their pretty little necks. I have a copy of their bank records for the past three months, proving that they've either received or drawn a large amount of money to pay for their shenanigans, and with one of them I have correspondence from a Mong official."

Not sure whether he should ask, but unable to resist, he queried, "And where did you find all of this?"

"People should learn not to lock things in desk drawers," Feliks mourned, shaking his head in disappointment. "It's like painting a sign on it: Important Secrets Kept Here. And they should really, really, stop confiding in their mistresses."

Ren wondered if Feliks had seduced the mistresses in question, but judging from that glint in his eye, the spy likely had. And enjoyed every moment of it. "You have it all on you?"

Taking a wrapped envelope from his jacket, he handed it over solemnly. "Did I do good, Master?"

"You did very well," Ren praised patiently. "And timely, too. We'll be starting a bait and trap campaign of our own soon. Keep your ear to the ground and eyes peeled. You might see a few more come out of the woodwork, or see the others we suspect make some sort of overt move."

"Will do. I—" Feliks gave Brahms a considering look and visibly changed what he meant to say. "—won't ask for a kiss, that's suicidal. I'll let you know if I hear anything else. Night!"

Ren watched the spy slip through the side gate and disappear from sight, then went and locked the door behind him. Pocketing the key ring, he headed for his own apartment, not even intending to look at the information. He did not have the energy or the concentration powers necessary to process any part of it. As he walked, Brahms kept pace with him like a very large shadow.

Something bothered Ren, a sixth sense murmuring that another factor played into Brahms' bad mood, but he couldn't begin to guess what it might be. Brahms wasn't the most demonstrative of people on a normal basis, true, but he also wasn't known for being touchy or irritable. In fact, the man lived on a pretty even keel most of the time. Seeing him so strained and upset hurt Ren's heart. Brahms needed to relax and appreciate being home after a hard deployment, not deal with even more stress piled on top.

It might not be the right time to bring it up again, but Ren didn't think a good opportunity would magically appear anytime soon. He cleared his throat as they hit the main hallway leading up to his apartment. "I know you don't want to hear me say this, but you really should consider going home soon—"

Brahms turned and caught him by both shoulders, dragging him in and up so they stood toe to toe with each other. Eyes burning, he looked moments away from shaking Ren so hard his teeth would rattle.

"No."

"Brahms—"

"No." Hauling him in the rest of the way, Brahms caught him up in a fierce embrace that threatened the integrity of Ren's ribs. His voice broke as he swore against Ren's hair, "I'm never leaving you alone again."

Guilt. *That* was what Ren had missed before. So, it wasn't just stress? That relieved Ren a little, although he still felt responsible for his friend's dark mood. Relaxing into that hard chest, he stood there and just breathed for a moment. "You really think that if you'd been here, you could have prevented all of this madness?"

"I'm not that arrogant."

Snorting in dark humor, Ren translated wryly, "So you think you could have prevented about half of it."

"Mmm."

Half the trouble he had now. Ren admitted that held an enticing appeal. Brahms may or may not be right, and it didn't matter if he was, as there was no point in what-ifs. He wanted to argue, but didn't at the same time. His eyes started to close and he forced them open. Being near Brahms always relaxed him, as absolutely nothing could catch his friend unawares. Part of him just wanted to burrow in and sleep against that broad chest, but that wouldn't be fair of him, would it? Brahms was exhausted too; he couldn't make the man cart him to bed.

With a sigh, he pulled himself free before he really did fall asleep standing up. It wouldn't be the first time. "Alright, I won't suggest it again until this is settled. Fortunately, I think we can at least get the palace security issue dealt with in the next few days. The pump is primed for it, after all. For now, let's go to bed."

"I'm sleeping with you tonight," Brahms announced as they resumed their trek.

Ren cast him an odd look. "Again? You have a perfectly nice apartment of your own, you know. And what does poor Robert think, being abandoned by his master all of the time?"

"Robert understands," Brahms answered cryptically and wouldn't say another word on the subject.

It took three days for the rumors to fully spread. Ren and Frei spent a good deal of time tiding up their reports and making them more logically progressive so that an outside party could follow the thread of evidence. Feliks came in with a few more tidbits, mostly signed witness statements, including one from the prostitute who had invaded Charles' bed. They were able to line up her hiring with the withdrawal of another lord's account and match the handwriting on the note given to her with another sample from the lord in question. It made for a very neat case.

Ren went to Frei's office the morning of the fourth day, the latest present from Feliks in hand, a cup of coffee in the other. Saluting Frei with it as he entered, he asked, "How goes it?"

"I just received a formal petition by fifteen lords to have a hearing with His Majesty today," Frei announced with a smile reminiscent of a gambler with a winning hand. "I'm about to forward the request to him. I think I can fit this in before lunch."

"Knowing King Gerhard's opinion on this, you'll likely be doing it right after breakfast," Ren disagreed, a surge of anticipation racing up his spine. Finally! Finally, those fools had fallen for the trap. "If that's the case, give it to me. I have a little more from Feliks to pass along to our king. And send word to Brahms for me, he's at the general's quarters this morning."

"Of course, of course." Frei promptly handed it over before adding seriously, "Good luck."

"Thank you, my friend, but I highly doubt I'll need it. Not with this much evidence." With a slight bow, he took off at a fast walk, knowing very well where the royal family would be at this time of the day. They always took breakfast in the same garden during good weather, and today certainly qualified. Puffy white clouds dotted a clear blue sky and the weather stayed surprisingly mild for early spring.

He passed staff, servants, guards, lords, ladies, and the odd visiting dignitary as he walked, to whom he offered cordial good mornings. It took bare minutes to reach the right garden, and Chaz let him through with the announcement, "Warden Ren, Your Majesties."

"Ren, this is unexpected," Queen Eloise greeted, dabbing her mouth with a snowy white napkin, lines of concern around her eyes. "Good or bad news?"

"Good. For us, at least." Coming around to stand at King Gerhard's left, he offered the formal request and the spy's packet with a toothy grin. "They've made their move."

King Gerhard's face lit up in a similar smile as he took it, eyes scanning through the request. "Ha! So they have. I see a few unexpected names?"

"I think some of them are capitalizing on this petition, ones that didn't have any involvement in the sabotage attempts," Ren admitted, although the words felt rotten in his mouth. "Giles, for instance."

"People who have a grudge against you," Alexandria stated knowingly. "How many people do you have evidence against?"

"Three I have very firm evidence against. The others I have circumstantial evidence with, and they didn't actually do anything criminal, just stupid. Our suspected eight are all on this list as well as four from your list, but I leave this up to your discretion, My King. I can't legally prove they did anything to deserve punishment."

Queen Eloise leaned sideways to read over her husband's shoulder. "I'm inclined to punish them just for giving us all headaches."

"My dear…" King Gerhard sighed, giving his wife a weary look. Clearly, he'd heard this opinion before.

"I know, I know, but I do feel we should do something to curtail this behavior. A warning is not enough."

"I'll think on it," he promised her. Ren's ears cocked, as the king didn't sound placating, but as if he actually meant it. Oh dear, even their mild-tempered king had lost all patience.

"Perhaps a limitation?" Charles offered thoughtfully, smearing jam over another biscuit. "Ren, as I understand it, there's no limit to how many day passes a lord can request, is that right? I thought so. Well, to those who have acted suspiciously and caused trouble, tell them they can only have, say, ten passes a month for the next year. They'll have to prove their good behavior before they have Our trust again."

Ren's ear caught that royal 'our' and from the look on his parent's faces, so had they. "I personally feel like that's an excellent suggestion, My King."

"I do as well." King Gerhard gave his son a proud smile. "I'll use it. In fact, Charles, Alexandria, I want you to sit in on this hearing. It'll be good practice for both of you, and I feel like it's only right you have some say in this, as it's directly impacted your safety on more than one occasion."

"Thank you, Father, we shall," Charles responded, catching Alexandria's eye and getting a firm nod from her.

The king lay the information next to his plate and informed Ren, "I'll review all of this now. Inform Frei that I will hear them in an hour."

In other words, shortly after breakfast. Ren had been right. "I'll do so, My King."

The Royal Audience Room saw more traffic than the king likely wished for. It might have been intended for something else in the past, but now it functioned as a courtroom. Any crime or grievance that occurred on palace grounds, or that impacted the royal family, went to trial in this room. Because of this, the front of the room had a raised dais with two thrones and four other chairs extending out to either side for the prince, princess, and any other dignitary the royal family recognized as being their equal.

Two tables sat perpendicular to the dais, for the plaintiff and defendant, with two small rows of chairs behind each table for their witnesses to sit. Other than that, it hosted little in the way of furniture, just a few rows of chairs for waiting petitioners, all facing the raised dais. Behind the dais and the red curtain, a door led directly out of the room, offering a discreet entrance and exit should the royal family be inclined to use it. Ren hoped they wouldn't need to use it, but the atmosphere of the room made him distinctly nervous. People looked either smug, vindictive, or angry. Not a good mix of emotions for one small room.

Everyone on their list had shown up, predictably enough, but more than just those fifteen came. He counted heads twice and came up with over thirty people, although with everyone moving around it made it hard for him to be sure of a precise number. Ren recognized palace staff amongst them, maids and servants for the most part. He didn't dare believe that everyone involved with the schemes came today, but hopefully the majority of them did. Ren rather liked the idea of catching the lot of them in one fell swoop.

He caught Brahms' eye, gesturing toward the crowd with a tilt of his head, and Brahms nodded back in grim understanding. He stood on guard near the royal dais, acting like a statue, as if only there to be a token military presence. Galvath stood on the other side, near Alexandria, in an official stance of royal bodyguard. In truth, they'd stationed both men there in case this became ugly. Ren didn't really think the perpetrators would attack the royal family so blatantly, but then, he'd never thought they'd compromise palace security just to further their own goals.

Ren stood behind the defendant's table, double checking he had all of his witnesses and taking stock of the plaintiff's. He knew the players very well by now and could recognize most of them. Most of them leaned in to each other's spaces, engaged in furtive conversations that still carried in this tiled room. They didn't say anything overt, of course, not in front of the king himself, but they certainly sounded peppy. So sure they'd finally get their way?

Fools. They clearly had evidence to present against him, but that street went both ways.

From behind the curtain, the royal family made their entrance, their body posture stiff and chins high. A staff hit the tiles three times in a sharp clack of sound, Frei calling the trial to order. "The petition against Warden Sho Renjimantoro will now commence. Presiding is our good King Gerhard of Aart with our royal mother, Queen Eloise. We are blessed with the attendance of Prince Charles, Princess Roslyn, and Princess Alexandria of Scovia. All rise."

A rustle of cloth as everyone in attendance stood.

"All may be seated. Lord Julek will speak for all of the petitioners."

Julek promptly moved to the accuser's table, although he didn't sit, just stood behind it before bowing to the dais. He had the classic features so popular in Aart—eyes a warm brown, hair sun-kissed and swept off his face in a neat side part—and he wore a doublet so close to black in color that it gave only hints of maroon as he moved, the light catching on individual threads. He looked handsome, in control, and he knew it.

"Your Majesties, Your Highnesses, thank you for hearing us." Julek tried very hard not to sound smug. He failed at it. "As stated on the petition, we wish to request the removal of Warden Ren from his post."

"Yes, so it says," King Gerhard responded, tone so neutral a statue couldn't have said it with such little inflection. "What are your reasons?"

"Why, both Princess Alexandria and Prince Charles have been in danger due to his lax security in the palace! And I understand that a trap of some sort was found in a linen closet this past week. Surely you can see that he isn't up to the job anymore, if he ever was."

Ren dug his fingernails into his palm, clawing for patience. Wait. Wait.

"We are certainly not pleased by the security breaches we've experienced for the past several months," Queen Eloise stated coldly. "And certainly not the attacks to our future daughter-in-law."

"You see? We have other, highly qualified people that surely will do a better job in the position. I have a list of complaints, four in total, to present to you."

King Gerhard looked tired already and the trial had barely started. He waved Julek to continue with a flap of the hand.

Either oblivious to the king's attitude or too certain of himself to care, Julek faced Ren squarely, smirk widening. "I have two witnesses who state that the warden has violated a national law several times by sending both correspondence and letters to a foreign country."

Ren blinked. Of all the things he had expected to come out of Julek's mouth, he least anticipated that one.

Tone saccharine sweet, Julek purred, "Do you deny this, Warden?"

He knew better than to answer that question directly. "I call Postmaster Diede as a material witness."

Julek paused, spine straightening, eyes narrowing in suspicion. "The accused must answer me."

"And I will, with Postmaster Diede present and able to verify my statement," Ren stated firmly.

Queen Eloise snapped her fan quite loudly. "I am absolutely positive that if Ren has done such a thing, it is because he was in contact with his family, Lord Julek. If that is the case, then certainly, we will not hold him to some archaic law. But by all means, let us call and hear Postmaster Diede's testimony regarding this."

He didn't like it, not one bit, but Julek had better sense than to argue with the queen. "While we wait for him to arrive, Your Majesty, may I move on to the second point?"

"Please do," she responded coolly, with the manner of a parent indulging a bad-tempered child.

"I have a witness who can testify that Warden Ren uses a stamp as his legal authorization to sign documentation, and that he mailed such a stamp to Shiirei. This is in violation of our code as it aids and abets forgery."

A murmur ran through the room. Ren went very, very still, the noise in his head zeroing in on a single point. He'd only ever shown four people in Aart that stamp and of those four, only one would be willing to betray him: Deidrick Giles. He hadn't seen the bastard come into the room—he still didn't see him—but he was clearly allied with these people in some way. How else would they know about it, otherwise?

Brahms caught his eye, puzzlement and concern relayed with a downturn of the mouth and a quirk of the eyebrow.

Ren grimaced at him and wished he had time to pull his friend aside and explain all of this without the audience. He felt mortally embarrassed to be caught with his metaphorical pants down. Why had he trusted Deidrick enough to tell him anything, even minor little cultural things like that?

King Gerhard, a little concerned, asked Ren, "Can you explain this?"

"In Shiirei, we do not sign our names, but have a stamp carved with the characters of our name to use," Ren answered, his back brain frantically trying to think of a way around this. "I sent it to my brother almost seven months ago with a letter authorizing him as my legal guardian in Shiirei to deal with some family matters. Such a situation is common in Shiirei and is not illegal by any means."

"So you say," Julek sneered. "But what proof do you have of that? And what proof do you have that someone hasn't used your stamp to authorize matters here in Aart? I have several documents with such a stamp on them, approving requests!"

"Show them," King Gerhard commanded brusquely.

Julek left the table to take a stack of papers from another lord, one Ren recognized. Two accounted for. He returned to the dais and respectfully handed them over.

King Gerhard flipped through them, frowning, then gestured for Ren to come up. "This is your signature in Shiirein?"

He fully expected a poor copy but instead found a crisp, clear stamp in red ink on the bottom of the page. Ren puzzled on that for a moment, as he never signed anything in red ink in Aart, so why would they—oh. Of course. The one letter he'd sent to his brother in front of Giles, he'd stamped it in red ink first. That must be why. "It looks like it, but there are two flaws to this forgery, King Gerhard."

"Forgery!" Julek scoffed. "Are we to take your word on that?"

"You can take mine," Frei announced calmly, also approaching. He took one look at the page in Gerhard's hand and scoffed. "This isn't Ren's. He doesn't use the stamp on palace documentation, and for the exact reason you stated, Lord Julek. The stamp would be too easy to copy and misuse. Ren signs everything and uses the Aartan alphabet to do it in. He also never uses red ink but black."

"How can you prove that?" Julek cross-questioned, still certain they couldn't.

"This document you have in your hands as proof is dated five months ago," Frei observed with an audible eye roll. "If he really did send off his stamp to his brother seven months ago, he couldn't possibly have used it on a palace document two months later. Even the fastest ship would be hard pressed to bring it back to Aart that quickly. Ren, where is your stamp now?"

"Still in Shiirei," Ren answered calmly. "My brother hasn't returned it yet."

Stabbing the paper, Frei enunciated clearly, "Forgery."

How could he possibly prove he didn't have that stamp? Ren thought hard and fast but couldn't think of a way to do it. He'd only mentioned it to Giles in passing, he certainly wasn't in the habit of confiding family problems to anyone on a regular basis. Except for Brahms, of course. His eyes naturally went to his friend as he thought, even though Brahms wouldn't be able to provide any support on this.

To the surprise of everyone in the room, Brahms cleared his throat and addressed everyone on the dais. "Your Majesties, I believe we can pause this question as well until Postmaster Diede comes. He would have a record of when Ren mailed the stamp home, and if it had returned."

Julek rounded on him. "You are not a witness!"

Brahms stared him down, lip drawn up as if he had spied a pustulant maggot. "Lord Julek, do not be obtuse. I might not be standing at the defendant's table, but there is not a man, woman, or child that is in doubt of where my loyalties are."

Before Julek could snarl something else, King Gerhard spoke, voice pointedly raised to override whatever the lord might say. "Lord Julek, General Brahms is here in an official capacity to serve as a witness of the trial. He may, therefore, interject if he feels that key testimonies or evidence should be presented. He also in this case makes a valid point about waiting for Postmaster Diede to arrive."

Grinding his teeth together, Julek barely managed to refrain from snarling at his own monarch. "King Gerhard, do you not think it unwise to appoint this man as a witness? He very clearly stated that he is Warden Ren's ally."

"Lord Julek," Charles stated sarcastically, "General Brahms is not the only staunch ally Ren has in this room. He is, however, the one we trust to keep a rational outlook on the situation as the trial proceeds. Be thankful for it. In his place, I would not be as forbearing."

Having lost steam on two different accounts, Julek cleared his throat and rallied. "Very well, I shall not argue the point."

Frei pointed to the two tables. "Please return to your positions."

Ren and Julek did so, although Julek made a show of obeying. Ren had to wonder where this theatrical manner came from. Did he only know about trials from plays? Ren had been involved in so many at this point that they tended to blur in his memory.

"I have other concerns to bring up to this august body," Julek announced, fingertips splayed and lightly resting on the tabletop, "regarding the matter of Warden Ren's conduct with Prince Charles and Princess Roslyn. We as a body find it unbecoming. He is obviously attempting to seduce them and such an attempt is working, as we have heard both of them propose to him on multiple occasions. I have four witnesses that can attest to this—" Julek turned, gesturing to the maids sitting behind him.

King Gerhard lifted a hand, staying them. "There is no need to call your witnesses. I'm well aware of it."

Spluttering, Julek demanded, "How can Your Majesty allow such behavior?"

"Because we know what it truly means when we hear those words leave our children's mouths," Queen Eloise informed him archly. "Deputy Warden Hartmann, step forward and relay to this—" her eyebrows arched pointedly as she mockingly used Julek's own words "—august body what it means if you hear the words 'marry me' out of Roslyn or Charles."

"It means there is a situation going on that makes them uncomfortable, or could be dangerous, and they require the warden or myself to stay nearby until it is properly resolved," Hartmann responded immediately, standing a little uncomfortably near the witnesses. He eyed them sideways, especially the maids, and the expression on his face promised that they wouldn't like what happened after this.

Roslyn slapped a hand to the wood of the armchair, the sound loud and jarring. "Really, Lord Julek, we've been using that signal for almost two years now. I came up with it myself, and while we might use in a less serious vein at times, it was the perfect way to cue up both Warden Ren and Deputy Warden Hartmann that something was amiss without tipping our hand. Now because of you, I'll have to think of something else to use."

Julek stared at her, aghast. "You proposed to him as a signal?"

"Of course," she responded, exasperated, voice climbing in both range and volume. "Ren is quite frankly unmoved by women. Why by the gods would you accuse him of trying to seduce *me*? Your cause might be aided if you got your facts straight before throwing out such baseless accusations."

"We were not unaware of what the words truly meant," King Gerhard informed him, his aging face settling into lines of cold stone, like an angry gargoyle. "Lord Julek, I find the behavior of my warden to be beyond reproach. My children have not done anything to embarrass me either, for that matter. Kindly drop this matter before We lose Our tempers."

Hearing that royal 'we' quite clearly, Julek paled and immediately ducked into a bow. "A thousand apologies, Your Majesty, of course I did not mean to suggest such. May I move—"

The door to the room opened and a rough, raspy voice called out, "Your Majesties, you summoned me?"

Ren had never been so relieved to see the crotchety old man in his life. The whole room turned to look at Diede who strode in, head held high and a hard look in his eye that Ren recognized well. The postmaster had been in place almost as long as Frei, but he had aged more gracefully and moved with a spry step toward the dais. Every line of his palace uniform lay crisp and neat against his thin body and he stepped directly to Ren's side.

"We have, Postmaster," Queen Eloise greeted with a warm smile. "Thank you for coming so quickly. We have questions regarding post security. Lord Julek accused Warden Ren of sending correspondence and packages to Shiirei. Is this true?"

Diede turned, glaring at Julek as he did so. "Lord Julek, are you accusing me of a dereliction of duty?"

Glaring at him in return, Julek gritted out, "Perish the thought, Postmaster. I accuse Warden Ren of corresponding with a foreign nation."

"*Through* my office," Diede stated, hackles rising. "Which in turn accuses me of a dereliction of duty. I have never been so affronted. Of course I know the law that you're spouting, although it has been since revised, considering it was established well over two hundred years ago. 'Any person living in Aart may not have unsupervised or unauthorized contact with a foreign country unless given permission by the reigning monarch to do so.' That is the law you're referencing, I take it?"

Julek stiffened, nearly vibrating with anger, a ruddy hue splotching his face. "Yes."

"I am aware of it and of course took the necessary precautions. Warden Ren never seals any correspondence or packages until I, personally, have a chance to review them. Only then do I mark it in the ledgers, seal it, and post it." From under his arm, he took a stab bound ledger and handed it to Ren. "I submit this as evidence."

Ren thankfully took it and handed it over to King Gerhard himself, and the royalty on the dais lost no time in flipping it over and scanning the contents.

"They're very detailed," Queen Eloise stated approvingly. "There's no question with these notes what the contents were. Postmaster, you can witness that Ren sent his personal signature stamp to Shiirei as well?"

"I can, Your Majesty. I believe that to have been seven, nearly eight months ago. I can find the entry for you, if you wish?"

"Please do," she requested, handing the ledger back.

Julek bristled like a cat with its tail stepped on. "Do you mean to suggest, Postmaster, that you aided this man in sending a personal stamp to another? Do you not understand that by doing so you are aiding and abetting forgery?"

The postmaster paused in flipping through the pages, fixing a harsh look on Julek. He spoke slowly, patronizingly, as if to a child. "Lord Julek. In order to fulfill my duties in the palace, I must be aware of *all* national laws in order to know what can be safely transmitted to another country. In other words, I have a book of law for every country in the world which I reference with every package. It is not, in fact, illegal for Warden Ren's stamp to be used by another as long as he has given the authority to use it. He has not violated that law nor have I allowed any dishonor to touch my office. *Furthermore—*"

Ren liked the way Diede said that, as he obviously meant 'fuck you.'

"—I can testify and show record that he did indeed send his personal seal to his brother Sho Takahiro precisely seven months and thirteen days ago, and that it has not returned. And yes, Lord Julek, before you can ask, I review all letters and packages coming *from* Shiirei as well before the warden receives them. Here is the entry."

Charles actually left the dais to look over the postmaster's shoulder and read through it quickly. "So it is. Father, I'm quite satisfied."

"So am I," King Gerhard declared.

"Your Majesty," Diede turned to the dais with a slight bow, "does that sufficiently clear up the matter?"

"It does," King Gerhard agreed with a wide smile at that thinning head. "Thank you for your diligence, Postmaster. We are blessed to have you."

Diede sniffed at the praise, glared once more at Julek, and retreated to the defendant witness chairs to take a very pointed seat at the front of the row.

Julek's hands clenched and unclenched at his sides and the faintest sheen of sweat appeared on his forehead. He had obviously expected that accusation to work, that Ren wouldn't be able to refute it, and felt somewhat at a loss now. Clearing his throat, he struggled to pull himself together. "Your Majesty, may I move on to the last point, then?"

"If you must."

Julek glanced back at his cronies, found some moral support there, and straightened his spine once more. "Your Majesty, our final cause for concern, and this takes all of our safety into account, is the protocol of the palace operations itself. When the multiple security breaches occurred, the palace should have immediately been put under second point of contact until the culprit behind such actions was caught. Warden Ren failed to do so."

"We denied him his request to do so," the king answered, eyes snapping with aggravation. The entire room went very still and quiet, the silence rolling over the room like a tidal wave. King Gerhard's voice sounded thunderously loud in comparison. "Do you know why? We didn't imagine you did. We denied it because at first, We didn't want to believe it, that Our own lords would put their petty grievances above the safety of Our family. Above the safety of their future king and queen. And when We realized Warden Ren was completely correct, We wanted to make sure We gathered together *all* of the individuals responsible for this nightmare."

If the silence had been grave before, it was absolute now. Ren bit the inside of his cheek to keep from cackling. The idiots just realized they had walked into a trap of their own making. Some of the lords and ladies fumed, others looked deathly pale. One or two even swayed, as if fighting the urge to faint.

"We gave Warden Ren two months to glean all the possible suspects," Queen Eloise picked up smoothly from where her husband left off. "I'm very proud to say that I believe he's caught most of you in that time. Warden Ren, you have been accused. Please address your accuser."

He bowed to her in turn before facing the gathered lords and few ladies in attendance. "We have evidence to indict Lord Jacobe Kacper, Lady Karina Cuyler, Lord Pieter Mateusz, Lord Ernst Piotr, Lady Melina Natalka, Lord Thomas Julek, Lady Leonie Wioleta, and Lord Jurgen Szymon for deliberately sending non-essential personnel onto the palace grounds. Deputy Warden Hartmann, will you submit the logs in for evidence?"

Hartmann dutifully took the many months of daily logs and showed them to the queen and king. They'd already seen them, of course, but for the trial to be fair Ren had to show them in public as well.

From his position near the dais, Frei bowed to the dais and added,

"Your Majesties, if I may add my testimony? I have also confirmed that the personages called out by the warden are guilty of such offenses and can further testify that all of the reports indicating their crimes came to me first."

Ren silently applauded Frei's testimony, as it neatly cut the protest that Ren could have fabricated the evidence.

King Gerhard skimmed through them and his expression went taut and grim. "So I see. Is that all, Warden?"

"Far from it, My King. I wish to call Master Niles Gibbons as witness."

Gibbons nervously stood, taking the crate of molds and wax keys sitting in the chair next to him, and came to stand next to Ren. He cleared his throat apprehensively before executing an awkward bow. "Your Majesties. I'm Niles Gibbons, a locksmith on Central Square."

"We wish to hear your story, sir," Queen Eloise encouraged him with a smile. "Please, tell us what you know."

The smile reassured Gibbons enough that his spine straightened and he managed a smile back. "Yes, Your Majesty. About five months ago, a noblewoman came into my shop with six keys she wanted duplicated. I thought it strange as she wore a dark veil over her face, and wouldn't give me her name, or even a means to contact her. The keys she wanted duplicated had the palace crest on them—"

Several in the audience gasped, then furtive conversations broke out, only to be quickly hushed when Frei glared at them.

Gibbons gamely continued with nothing more than a glance at the interruption. "—which worried me, but I couldn't imagine that someone who had access to the palace keys would do anything illegal with them. So while it unsettled me, I did as requested and made two sets. The noblewoman picked up the order and I didn't hear another word about it. Still, it seemed so odd, I kept the molds just in case."

"And then?" Ren prompted when the man didn't seem to know what else to say. "You reported it?"

"Well, yes, after about a month I'd heard that the palace was having trouble. Security issues, and such, and I thought, well..." Gibbons trailed off, indicating the bow of key molds helplessly. "What if that noblewoman's intentions weren't so pure? Were the keys I made causing trouble? But I didn't know who to report it to, or if I should, so I waited until a friend came back from deployment and asked his opinion. Colonel Konrad is his name. He told me that it was highly suspicious and that he knew Warden Ren personally and would pass my story along. Warden Ren came to see me about four days later, asked to hear the story, examined the molds, and declared that the keys I made had been used to infiltrate the palace. I promptly turned everything over to him and was sorry I was involved in the whole business."

"Thank you, Master Gibbons." Ren encouraged him to sit again. "My King, the keys in question accessed the palace archives, east side gate, kitchens, west entrance, armory, and stable tack room. I submit the molds for evidence."

"We will receive it," King Gerhard responded formally, mouth in a flat and unhappy line. "Warden Ren, have you found the duplicate keys?"

"We have, My King. My spy found them, I should say. I request the right to keep the identity of my spy anonymous."

"Granted."

Lord Julek let out a sound that would have been at home in a boiling kettle. "Your Majesty, I protest! How do we know that this spy even exists?"

"I've met the man," Frei announced dryly. "In fact, he's General Brahms' spy. Warden Ren borrowed him to investigate. Since he's part of Army Intelligence, we cannot risk unmasking this man. It's a matter of national security."

Queen Eloise inclined her head graciously toward Frei. "Quite so, Chamberlain. Thank you. I too, have met him, Lord Julek. He's quite real. Continue, Warden."

Ren really couldn't help the evil smile as he looked Julek dead in the eye. "The spy discovered key rings that are the exact duplicates of the six palace keys in the homes of Lady Karina and Lord Julek. Just having them is a criminal offense."

Julek staggered back a step, truly sweating now, face going ashen in color.

"Furthermore," really, that was a satisfying word to use, Ren would have to remember it, "the maids responsible for those keys are in your witness area, Lord Julek. One of them gives entrance to the royal archives, and we found a set of palace blueprints in your study with the watermark of the palace crest at the bottom of them. The link between the two is obvious enough, I believe, or should I explain it further?"

They all suspected that the attack on Princess Alexandria during her riding incident was done on Lord Julek's orders but couldn't prove it. The trap found in the linen closet could have been done by either Lady Karina or Lord Julek. They both had the right access to the palace, but Ren still hadn't found their expert, and likely wouldn't. Feliks swore the lady of pleasure sent into Prince Charles' chambers was also ordered by Lord Julek, but all they had was a bank statement in the right amount and a handwriting sample to link him. It was circumstantial evidence at best. Ren chose to leave it be. He had Julek dead to rights on everything else.

Indicating the rather large stack of paper on the table, Ren continued, "We have bank statements, witness statements, even a few letters from a Mong official in your case, Lady Wioleta. As Lord Julek has already explained in great detail, that's a very serious offense. Postmaster Diede, has Lady Wioleta submitted any letters into your office in the past year?"

"None," Diede stated firmly.

Ren nodded, not surprised, then faced Wioleta with a calm expression he did not feel. He leaned onto the table's surface, staring hard at her, and watched her flinch with perverse satisfaction. "In your case, no one with the right authority reviewed your letters for security concerns, as Postmaster Diede is the only one authorized to review foreign correspondence. The contents of the letters indicate your general unhappiness that Princess Alexandria arrived here safely. Would you care to explain that?"

Lady Wioleta looked around wildly for support and found none, even her own compatriots shying physically away from her, afraid her sins might be catching. "I-I-it's a misunderstanding," she babbled out, voice trailing off as she failed to find any reason to explain it all away.

Ren continued calmly. Or at least, he tried to keep calm; the situation made him shiver with anger. "A misunderstanding, is it? Fifteen letters in the course of a half year is a misunderstanding? Love affairs don't produce that much correspondence."

"Misunderstanding or not, We find this highly unforgivable, Lady Wioleta," King Gerhard informed her, a low growl in his voice and a hard look in his eyes. "No one has any reason to contact the Mongs in Aart."

Wioleta sent a desperate, pleading glance to Julek.

Julek stirred, rallying desperately, aware that if he didn't speak now he wouldn't get another chance. "How can you possibly know what is or is not within Lady Wioleta's study? Or my study for that matter?" Julek thundered back at him. "This spy of Warden Ren's—he could have planted them!"

"Because our royal spy went with him and entered your study to retrieve them," Charles informed him flatly. "They moved as a unit to serve as witnesses to each other. Oh yes, Lord Julek, we have suspected you for some time. All of you, in fact."

Julek staggered where he stood, his expression so deathly pale and grey that a corpse looked healthy in comparison.

"This whole affair angers Us," King Gerhard growled at them, making everyone flinch. "Whatever your opinions or concerns about the royal engagement or my warden, you do *not* push your agenda by threatening the security of this palace or the ones who live in it. You've threatened the life of my future daughter-in-law on more than one occasion, embarrassed the Heir Apparent, and opened the palace to the possibility of enemy attack. It that were not bad enough, you've nearly hurt Our staff on several occasions, innocents who have nothing to do with your power plays. This angers Us considerably. Be thankful We are not going to move on circumstantial evidence, because We are highly inclined to punish everyone in this room."

Ren really had to swallow the urge to beam at his king. It wouldn't be at all appropriate, even if it did bring joy to his heart to see his enemies get their just comeuppance.

"Lord Julek," King Gerhard continued, anger blazing across his face at near cataclysmic levels. "You are hereby stripped of your rank, and your cousin will be appointed in your stead. You are not allowed to have any use of the family's estate, funds, or any of their means. You are banished from Aart, and will be executed immediately if you step foot in this country again."

Julek swayed and fell into his seat, staring at the floor, expression ashen.

"Lady Wioleta, you are stripped of your rank and will be imprisoned for the rest of your natural days. We will not harbor someone who engages with Our enemy or plans to harm one of the royal family."

Wioleta let out a wail of protest, collapsing into the arms of the man next to her, who did his best to hold up her not-inconsiderable girth. Ren couldn't see through the rows of people clearly, but he assumed it to be her husband. Likely ex-husband, soon, as Ren rather doubted the man would wish to remain married to a criminal.

"Lady Karina, you shall also be stripped of land, title, and wealth, and exiled from Aart. We cannot prove what you did with those keys, but We don't need to, as having them is a serious infraction of the law. If you return to Our country, you will also be put to death on sight." King Gerhard ignored it when Karina fell out of her chair in a dead faint and addressed the rest of the audience. "For the other lords and ladies who deliberately sent non-essential people into Our palace, your freedom to come and go is hereby restricted for the next year. You and anyone of your household are only allowed admittance to the palace five times a month, and you will be under tight guard the entirety of your stay. You must prove yourselves again to Us, regain Our trust, before We will allow you entrance to Zonhoven Palace." The king rose to his feet, casting the entire room a look of utter disgust. "As for the rest of you, I would put considerable distance between yourselves and this body. Your association with them troubles Us and We can promise you will be under surveillance for some time to come because of it. This hearing is dismissed."

Frei clacked the staff against the tiles, signaling for them to rise. "All rise!"

In a somewhat dramatic sweep, the royal family left the dais and exited out the back. Ren dearly wished to follow, but he had to make sure that this lot properly went to holding cells or were escorted off palace grounds before they did something even more foolish.

Brahms came to him, a rare smile on his face. "It's finally over."

"Almost," Ren agreed with an answering grin. "Help me sort this lot out, would you? If you could take Julek, Karina, and Wioleta to the palace holding cells, I can get Hartmann to help me usher the rest of them off palace grounds."

A wicked gleam in his eye, Brahms promised, "I'll handle them."

As Brahms walked toward the three, Ren belatedly called to him, "Don't use excessive force if they resist!"

Brahms turned, casting a glance back over his shoulder that looked full of mischief, and then carried on his task without another word. Ren had this feeling the man would define the term 'excessive force' very loosely. He thought about following Brahms, ensuring his good behavior, then shrugged it off. After all the grief those three had caused, he wouldn't feel bad about any bruises they collected along the way to their cells.

Turning, he regarded his two key witnesses. "Gentlemen, you did an amazingly good turn for me today. Thank you."

Gibbons gave him a bashful duck of the head. "I'm very grateful you didn't throw any accusations at my head, Warden. What I did was foolish; you would have been well within your rights."

Shaking his head, Ren denied, "I couldn't possibly reward your honesty that way. Besides, you gave me the key evidence I needed to put those three away, no pun intended. I've no desire to reward you with jail time. You have my heartfelt thanks."

Gibbons shook hands with him firmly and then walked away with a spring in his step that wasn't there before. He felt like a lighter man with all of it out in the open, and Ren was glad for his sake.

With a sniff, Postmaster Diede stated tartly, "I'll accept no thanks from you. Those fools thought to use my work against you. Calling me as a witness was my due and nothing more."

Diede had a crusty personality most people couldn't abide, but in this moment Ren could almost kiss him for it. "I wouldn't dream of it, Postmaster. But may I say how glad I am that you perform so excellently in your position?"

Mellowing a smidge, Diede allowed, "Any other warden would protest me pawing through their personal correspondence. I can at least respect a man that puts security above his own feelings. Don't read so much into it, young man."

Ren watched him leave with a bemused smile. Had Diede just given him an extremely backward compliment? Shaking the thought off, he put himself into motion, helping Hartmann gather everyone in the room, and herding them like disobedient sheep off palace grounds. He received several lethal glares from them, but some stayed in such shock that they couldn't even manage to look up from their shoes.

Ren called on a complement of guards to escort people out, riding herd on all of them until the last was settled. Only then did he return to Frei's office and report, "That's all of them settled. Thank you, my friend, you were quick on your feet today."

"I wanted to make sure they didn't drag things out in a meaningless muddle," Frei responded easily. Archly, he added, "It was reported to me that Lord Julek somehow acquired a broken nose on the way to the holding cells."

He kept his face bland with effort. "Really? How did that happen?"

"Your general lost his temper, I expect," Frei responded with a snort. "I'm amazed he held it in as long as he did, all things considered. That business with the seal, do I need to worry about that?"

Ren shook his head grimly. "I'll take care of it. I know who was behind it."

After a moment of studying him, Frei dipped his head, agreeing and letting the matter go. "I wish we knew who was behind all of it. The issue with the mace in the linen closet is still unanswered, as is the poisoning attempt on Princess Alexandria. We're still not sure who attacked her on the way in, as well."

"I feel like we only caught half of the players today, and not even the important ones," Ren admitted morosely. "It'll come back to bite us later if we don't figure it out soon. You know it will."

"I do, but we've exhausted our clues at the moment. It's a waiting game now to see what our spies can turn up." Frei looked older beyond his years, like an ancient gnome. With a visible shake, he changed topics. "King Gerhard has issued orders regarding you. I contacted your deputy and Hartmann said he would cover for you the rest of the day. You are under royal command to take the next three days off and rest."

Ren sent a silent prayer to the heavens on the royal family's behalf. "Bless them for it. I'll take it. If something does happen, though, I'll likely be with Brahms out in town getting thoroughly drunk."

Chuckling, Frei waved him on. "After the past seven months, I think you deserve it."

Feeling lighter than he had in some time, he left the room and nearly ran straight into Brahms. Unable to keep the smile from his face, he said, "That went better than I hoped."

"I'm in favor of getting drunk," Brahms responded, half of the worry lines from his face fading, leaving him more relaxed than he'd been in weeks. "They're all out, then?"

"I escorted them myself." Ren suspected he would have to deal with Giles sooner or later, but he didn't feel like pursuing it right now. He had a rare holiday given to him, after all; he could enjoy it first, and slowly prove Giles's culpability later. Clapping a hand on Brahms' shoulder, he invited, "Let's go out for lunch, get drunk, and be totally irresponsible for the rest of the day."

"You really can?" Brahms asked in surprise.

"Frei informs me I have the day off. Hartmann's covering for me." Too impatient to stand there, he caught Brahms arm, tugging him back around. "Let's go, let's go. We can finally spend a little time with each other without interruptions threatening."

"Mmn," Brahms agreed, content, and readily followed.

14

Day drinking had always agreed with Ren, likely because he rarely got to do it, so sitting in a private room at one of his favorite upscale restaurants with an open bottle of superb wine put him in a very good mood. The addition of Brahms as company bumped it up to an excellent mood, and he couldn't suppress a silly smile as he poured a glass for both of them.

Brahms sipped and sighed like a man who tasted nirvana. "Perfect."

"I do love this vintage," Ren agreed, sipping at his own glass. He especially liked drinking it here, with no prying eyes or ears, and a door firmly shielding them from the outside world. Granted, the door had no lock to it, and anyone could enter, but he liked the illusion. Brahms always chose this place for that very reason—Ren knew he did—but he sometimes indulged his fantasies a little by pretending it was a date. The mellow lighting from the wall sconces, the lute music floating down the hall, and the atmosphere of the restaurant lent itself to romantic flights of fancy.

Today especially he had to keep those wild thoughts firmly in check as he knew alcohol loosened his tongue in unfortunate ways. Better not to let his mind even consider such a thing, much less daydream about it. He'd done very well the past five years at being strictly Brahms' friend and he saw no reason to spoil their relationship now.

Toying with the glass, Brahms inquired dryly, "Alright, when did the royal siblings start proposing?"

"I think it was literally the week you left," Ren answered slowly, casting his mind back in an effort to recall. "I was in a perfectly foul mood that week. I didn't know what to do with myself when off-duty, as we'd always spent such time together, and I might have been moping. And drunk."

"How drunk?" Brahms asked knowingly, mouth quirked in amusement.

"Smashed," Ren admitted ruefully, the memory almost making him chuckle now. "Charles brought out some vintage wine from the cellars that we probably shouldn't have opened for anything short of a royal wedding, and we poured Roslyn a half-cup she had no business drinking, and we sat there and drank ourselves stupid. I honestly only remember bits and pieces of that night. It started out with us both bemoaning our favorite people were too far away from us—Charles was seriously crushing on Princess Alexandria at the time—and ended up with us crying on each other's shoulders."

"You've always been an emotional drunk," Brahms allowed, eyes squinting in open amusement.

Ren loved it when his friend reached this stage, when he felt comfortable and relaxed enough to express everything he felt candidly. The man had a strange sense of shyness, as if displaying emotion embarrassed him on some level, and Ren always felt privileged to see Brahms at his most emotive.

"Anyway, Roslyn declared that there was no need to be sad, as she would marry me. Then Charles protested, said I couldn't possibly be interested in marrying a woman, that it was better he marry me. And of course it dissolved into a sibling fight from there. I think I avowed at some point I'd marry both of them. Or at least, they claim I agreed to marry both of them. I really don't remember that part."

"So they've been proposing to you ever since?" Brahms responded a little doubtfully.

"It started out as a running joke, and then it took an interesting turn about six months later," Ren explained, relaxing fully back into his chair. "Some visiting dignitaries' son took a liking to Roslyn and kept following her around. Even I found him obnoxious. Roslyn was ready to kill him. She started using me as a shield to avoid him, which worked for a short time, then he found a way to catch her when she wasn't near me. Had to teach her self-defense because of that brat."

A frown tugged at Brahms' mouth. "Queen Eloise allowed this?"

"I'm not sure how fully aware she was of the situation," Ren allowed slowly. "And truly, the boy wasn't doing anything, just making a pest of himself. Roslyn complained about him, but I don't think anyone really took her seriously at first except me, because he was on his best behavior in front of the parents. I saw his true nature, as did Roslyn, but no one else did. Not at first. I taught her self-defense as he frankly worried me. That, and Roslyn needed to let out some steam before her temper exploded. Training seemed the safest outlet for it."

"And then?" Brahms prompted, tone suggesting he knew very well the story didn't end there.

"And then we were at a formal function, and he started pressing her to dance with him. Roslyn refused, quite politely given the circumstances, and said she would dance with me. He didn't like it, demanded she dance with him instead, and insulted me in the process. Well, you can imagine how well she took that."

Brahms snorted as he lifted the glass for another drink. "That is to say, not at all."

"She informed him flatly, at the top of her lungs, that she wanted to marry me and no one else. It caught King Gerhard's and Queen Eloise's attention, of course, but the boy's back was to them. He didn't realize half of the room was paying attention to them now. When I heard my name, I had a feeling what would happen, but I was halfway across the room and couldn't get there quickly enough. The boy finally lost his temper and shouted back at her that she couldn't marry some common foreigner—"

The look on Brahms' face suggested he didn't believe at all that was what the boy had said.

"Well, alright, he might have thrown in a few more insults, but I forget all he said," Ren admitted lightly, as none of it troubled him. "It enraged Roslyn, though. She punched him right in the gut, doubling him over. I don't think anyone expected her to be so physical with the attack, much less her ardent suitor, who lay on the ground trying to get his breath back. Roslyn marched straight to me, latched onto my arm, and announced that if he came near her again she'd put a boot up his fucking arse. Her exact words, mind you."

Brahms nearly choked on his wine as laughter shook his frame. "Sorry I missed it."

"I was too, believe me. Anyway, that's when the whole proposal thing became semi-serious. If either of them is proposing to me, I take it as a sign of trouble more than affection. Although, fortunately, it doesn't happen often. If it did, I think the royal parents would be asking me some very uncomfortable questions."

Lifting the bottle, Brahms topped off his glass. "Startled me when I heard Charles do it. I thought you'd seduced another Aartan."

Shaking his head, Ren denied, "I haven't even seduced one, thank you very much. And I regret the one that seduced me sorely. I've given up on straight men anyway. I don't need to repeat that particular experience to learn my lesson."

A strange look flitted over Brahms' face, there and gone again before Ren could decipher it properly. "You succeeded with more than one."

"Oh sure, if you believe the rumors, I seduced you too," Ren drawled, almost instantly regretting the words. It depressed him utterly, as they both knew it to be untrue. He downed half of his glass in one pull then belatedly realized that getting drunk right now might not be the best idea. Better slow down after this cup.

"Maybe you have," Brahms suggested, an enigmatic smile toying at the corners of his mouth.

Ren just looked at him over the rim of his glass, blatantly disbelieving the gall of the man. "You are mean to tease me. Why are we friends, again?"

Usually Brahms would shrug this off and crack a joke, but not this time. His smile didn't falter, just deepened, his eyes remaining on Ren's. "Am I teasing?"

"You know damn well you are," Ren accused, stabbing a finger at him. He'd unfortunately chosen his left hand to do it with, which held his wine glass, so the wine sloshed a little. Mourning the loss, he carefully emptied the cup before putting it safely aside. "I've been naked or near naked in front of you multiple times. If you had even the slightest inkling of an interest, you would have jumped me before now."

"If I had tried that, you would have retaliated. I'd have woken up in a corner somewhere with a ringing head."

No, he wouldn't have. Ren would have been delighted, in fact, and promptly dragged him into the nearest bed. Well, alright, maybe not. He'd have been too worried about what it would do to their relationship to engage in casual sex.

Unless, of course, Brahms had approached him seriously....

Ren cut off that traitorous thought right there before it could tumble out of his mouth. "Moot point, we both know you're teasing. And the joke isn't funny, thank you very much. Ah, damn, I'm drunk enough that Queen Eloise's offer actually sounds tempting."

Confused, Brahms cocked his head.

"You know, her offer to send me to Shiirei to find a lover," Ren clarified impatiently.

Brahms jerked upright in alarm. "You wouldn't actually try it."

"Please, we both know that's impossible to pull off. But I can go back, see family, and hire a male courtesan for a month of diabolical pleasure." It would be an empty, hollow relationship but at least he could let off some sexual steam. "Do you think if I stayed drunk the entire voyage there, that it would still seem like a good idea by the time I arrive?"

The open expressiveness vanished abruptly from Brahms' face and his hand tightened on the glass to the point of threatening its integrity. "No."

Ren frowned at him, not understanding his friend's abruptly dark mood. "Why not? It won't hurt anyone."

"It will hurt you," Brahms responded tightly. "And me. No. You're not going."

That almost sounded like a confession—no. No, that was the wine talking. Ren mentally pulled himself back from that dangerous edge before he could fall into hope. Again. No, Brahms didn't mean it that way. He likely meant that after two years of separation, having Ren gone for four months would be painful, and he didn't want to experience that again. "Relax, I'm joking."

"You're not," Brahms denied softly, worried now instead of angry. "Ren. Loneliness is eating at you."

Too true. Ren pushed himself unsteadily to his feet. "I'm fine. I'm just an emotional drunk, that's all. I best stop here. Let's go back, alright? No, wait, I'm craving fish and chips. Let's get an early dinner and finish the bottle later."

Brahms didn't let it rest there. He came around the table and pulled Ren to him in a firm, comforting embrace. Ren wrapped both arms around his waist, letting his eyes fall shut for a moment, indulging in the hug.

Against his temple, Brahms said softly, "You're not alone. I'll never leave you alone again."

Tears pricked at the back of Ren's eyes and for a moment, he let himself lean into those arms. But only for a moment, because it was too tempting to try and make this into something more. He pulled free before he could do or say something they'd both regret, pinning a smile on his face. "From the day we met, you never have. Now come on, something hot and greasy is calling to me, and I need a walk in fresh air to clear my head."

Brahms looked as if he wanted to say something, but Ren had a feeling Brahms would say something his heart couldn't accept right now. He stepped quickly through the door, into the outside air and breathed deep, shoving off the somber mood like an unwanted cloak, deliberately putting them on a different topic. He had an entire evening to properly enjoy and he refused to ruin it with drunken doldrums.

15

Arman had hit his limit.

He knew this because none of his plans implemented the tactic of lying naked in bed with Ren. In fact, he couldn't even decide what letter plan he implemented now. G? M? Did it even matter? He'd tried multiple times to talk to Ren, to properly propose, and they'd all utterly failed. It was so rare that Ren didn't hear him. Arman knew their situation could be blamed for it—if Ren weren't overworked and exhausted, he'd pick up on the cues that Arman had something important to say. Even in a war zone, Arman had never failed to gain Ren's attention, which said something about the fiasco in the palace right now.

It admittedly caused Arman to flounder, unsure of how to garner Ren's full attention. Words had utterly failed to work. Blasted things rarely did their job in Arman's case anyway. So he fell back to the tactic he knew would snag his friend's undivided attention.

Action.

After Ren passed out, partially from the wine, mostly from exhaustion, Arman carefully undressed him down to his smallclothes and slid him into bed. Ren barely did more than grumble about cold sheets before snuggling in. Arman stripped down to pants as well and slipped in behind him, pulling the covers up over them both as he moved. He slung an arm around Ren's waist, searching for his hand and finding it, lacing their fingers together to lay against Ren's stomach. He slid one leg between Ren's, ankles twining together and pressed his chest up against Ren's back. He nearly groaned aloud at the feel of Ren firmly cuddled into him.

Shit. This might have been a bad idea. Arman didn't know if he could control himself. Two years of repressed emotion surged through him, all headed to his cock, which was all too eager to make Ren's acquaintance. Arman nearly pulled back and came up with another plan, but found he couldn't force himself out of the bed. He'd wanted to be like this with Ren for far too long, cuddled together in an intimate embrace.

Swearing to himself, he stayed, his hand carefully not moving any lower. He told himself severely that he wouldn't seduce Ren until the man had at least a full night's sleep. A sleep-deprived Ren was not the most reasonable of creatures, and Arman stood a far better chance of actually getting his proposal out if Ren finally got some rest.

He nearly settled in completely until his nose brushed up against Ren's ponytail. Oh, right. Ren hated sleeping with his hair still up. Arman undid the tie, tossing it onto the chest, then combed through the loose hair with gentle fingertips. It felt like silk against his hands, cool and free. He played with it, letting it slip in and out of his fingers, indulging in a fantasy he'd often harbored while deployed up north. Ren seemed to enjoy the sensation, as he smiled and nearly purred in his sleep. A small smile played around Arman's mouth at Ren's reaction. His Ren really was a tactile creature.

Would he be able to do this again when Ren awoke?

The question scared him. Arman didn't know the answer. He prayed for it, but would Ren be able to see him as a husband? Five years ago, Arman knew his friend had liked him, wanted to be lovers, but Ren had never pressed. Never even suggested. Teased, joked, mock-flirted, yes. But never seriously. Arman had felt flattered Ren thought him handsome, returned the loyalty and friendship, and assumed the crush would fade with time.

He'd been an utter fool.

Arman remembered a time when he could look at Ren and see a friend, but that was such a distant memory he could barely recall it. Now his heart always beat a little harder when he stood next to Ren. His pulse raced for a moment, hands ached to touch, and he wished for nothing more than Ren's undivided attention. How could he not have seen it, the potential for everything they could be? Now Arman faced the loss of something offered, something he'd failed to take, and he didn't know if his heart could withstand the dearth if Ren didn't accept him.

If he could do something to go back five years, see Ren the way he saw him now, Arman would pay the price in a heartbeat. Five years later might be five years too late, especially after Ren's recent heartbreak. Ren seemed to have given up on any possibility of gaining a partner, which terrified Arman.

Snuggling into Ren's back, Arman dropped a kiss against his bare shoulder and whispered against his skin, "I love you. You have to hear me, Ren. Right now, I don't know how to reach you."

Ren settled into his embrace fully with a satisfied sigh. Taking hope in that reaction, Arman let his eyes close and tried to sleep as well.

Sleep came in fits and snatches, but sometime in the wee hours of the morning he must have fully dropped off. Ren stirred against him, tensing, which woke him abruptly. He waited with bated breath for Ren's reaction.

"Brahms?" Ren called softly, sounding uncertain and on edge.

Not changing his position, Arman responded in an equally soft tone, "Yes."

"Why are we spooning and in bed with each other?" His hand flexed uneasily in Arman's grip, trying to loosen. Arman reluctantly let go, his hand instantly cold from the loss.

How best to answer that question? "I need your attention."

"And being cuddled together was the best way to get it?" Ren responded doubtfully. He tried to move, shift so he could see Arman.

Arman didn't know how to face him just yet, so he put his hand back on Ren's stomach, pinning him in place. "I've been trying to talk to you for days. We're always interrupted. I need to prove something to you, too."

"Brahms." Ren let out a patient sigh, the sound a little pained. As it should be, considering the man likely had a hangover. "You know what, when I'm half-naked and in bed with you, I'm calling you Arman. Arman, dearest friend, I have a hangover. Please let me up."

"Not yet." He had ten seconds before Ren's impatience with the situation made him throw Arman's ass out of bed. He debated what actions, what words, would get through to Ren with best effect in a lightning quick analysis. "Ren. I promise to explain, just stay like this for a few more minutes."

Grumbling, Ren subsided, although he stayed taut in Arman's arms. "Alright, I'm listening. What?"

No, he didn't fully have Ren's attention. Ren leaned ever so subtly away from him, shifting his legs away and toward the edge of the bed. His friend was looking for a way to escape. Frustrated,

Arman decided he'd have to do this out of order. Working the signet ring off his pinky, he snagged Ren's left hand and slipped it onto his ring finger. It fit near perfectly, to Arman's relief.

Ren froze, staring at it. "Arman. What the hell?"

Ha, finally. Now Ren was truly listening. "I want to marry you."

With an abrupt flip, Ren twisted so he could look at Arman, his dark eyes searching Arman's face. Arman met his gaze levelly, not trying to hide anything, letting all the love and affection he felt for this amazing man show.

For a moment, a split second, Ren looked incredibly happy. Then his eyes shuttered, closing off that emotion. "Why? This makes no sense; why are you proposing?"

Shit. He really didn't want to fall back to words, useless things that they were, but he might not have a choice. "Because I love you."

That did not have the effect he anticipated. Ren's expression grew affectionate but exasperated in equal measure. "Arman Brahms, I know you love me. That is not what I asked. You didn't come up with this idea because you think I need a lover, did you?"

Arman couldn't help but flinch slightly. He'd initially thought of this plan precisely because of that. Hell, the man knew him too well.

Ren sighed and looked away, levering up to an elbow. "Arman, I swear, you—"

Desperate, Arman snatched him back down, drawing Ren so he lay smack against him. "Dammit, Sho Renjimantoro, would you listen to me?"

Startled, Ren's attention snapped up to him, surprised to hear his full name out of Arman's mouth. It had been years since he'd used it. Ren lay on top of him, flushed and trying to keep their groins away from each other. Arman shifted and yanked until he had Ren pressed fully against him. Ren's breath caught in his throat as he felt Arman's hardness against him, almond shaped eyes flaring wide as they caught Arman's.

Framing his face with both hands, Arman leaned in a little, their noses almost brushing. "Listen to me," he pleaded, not sure what else to do, what else to say. This whole thing had gone so poorly, not at all as expected, Arman feared he'd lose any hope of it working. "I want you. Not as a brother, not as a friend. A lover. A partner. I'm *in* love with you."

Ren stared at him, searching for what felt like eons, barely breathing. "Holy shit, you're serious. When did all of this change? Why?"

Those questions, at least, he knew how to answer. "Two years ago, right before I deployed, I decided to propose. You're right. I initially decided to propose because you don't handle it well, being alone. I thought I could be what you needed, a lover as well as a friend. I was a fool. I didn't realize…" Arman found it incredibly hard to continue, the words rasping out of his throat. "I didn't realize until I heard about your affair with that bastard. I wanted—want—to kill him for touching you. Imagining any man's hands on you other than mine—I hate it. I realized in that moment, if I'd just said something, if I'd *asked*, you'd be in my arms. My lover. I want that. More than I want air, I want that."

Arman heard Ren's breath hitch and stutter. In a barely discernable whisper, Ren said, "You seriously—"

"I do." Arman stayed still and silent, not knowing what else to say. If all of this didn't get his sincerity across to Ren, nothing would.

A shudder ran through Ren's frame, emotions warring over his face. "You've never been attracted to men before. You've joked about it, I've teased you about it, this is well established, dammit. And now you're saying that you've suddenly decided you like men after all?"

"No," Arman answered honestly. "Just you."

Ren abruptly rolled for the other side of the bed. Arman caught him around the waist, hauling him back, which took serious effort. Ren fought hard to get away.

"I want out of bed for the rest of this conversation," Ren snarled at him, trying to break his grip. "Let go. Let go, dammit."

"Not until you tell me you hear me."

Swearing furiously in his mother tongue, Ren abruptly changed directions, pushing with both palms against Arman's chest, hard enough he actually shifted six inches on the bed, putting him dangerously close to the edge. Ren was panting, face flushed, anxious for reasons Arman didn't understand. "You really think you want me. Alright, prove it."

Ren likely expected this to make him pause, as Arman had never been with a man before, but in truth he'd had to stop himself ever since he'd come home from reaching out to Ren, from seducing him. Arman didn't even hesitate and flipped them both, Ren's back hitting the sheets with a slight bounce, a happy smile on his face.

That expression shocked Ren to stillness, as very little in the world could get Arman to smile. Arman couldn't help it. He had two years of repressed emotions bursting free, and he didn't need to keep any guard up with Ren. He'd half-hoped that he could do something more romantic with their first kiss than prove a point, but Ren was nothing if not stubborn, so Arman really should have expected these events.

Arman cupped the sides of Ren's face to tilt it back, fingers tangled in Ren's glorious fall of hair, and leaned in for a kiss. Using judicious amounts of tongue and teeth, he poured six months of lust and passion into every nip, every swipe, every crush of lips. Messy and aggressive, Ren gave as good as he got.

Arman's lips tingled with the force of their kisses, the rasp of stubble against his skin strange at first, but a welcome sensation. Ren tasted like morning breath and leftover hints of ale, of *want* and *please* and *finally*. Arman pulled back to see Ren's pupils blown, face flushed, hair a tangled halo across the pillows. Joy filled him to bursting, and Arman nearly trembled with the overwhelming force of it, so unbelievably happy to have this man finally in his arms.

He dove back in for another kiss, a benediction and plea, the feeling of *right* and *home* and *mine* spiraling through his thoughts to dispel all reasoning and restraint. Their tongues tangled and retreated, played and explored. A moan escaped when Ren sucked hard on Arman's tongue, teeth scraping lightly, so of course Ren did it again.

Arman broke away to trail his lips down the side of Ren's neck, questing. When Ren whimpered in a sharp breath, one hand clutching the hair along Arman's nape, the other gripping his upper back, Arman sucked heat into the spot until the noises flowed from Ren's throat.

Ren's hands yanked on Arman's hair to pull him up, and his hips rose to meet Arman's. Arman echoed Ren's groan, and he settled his weight more firmly onto Ren, while he went with the implied request to kiss Ren again. He willed himself to slow down, to show that this was more than just lust, but an all-encompassing need. That he wanted more than just to maul Ren, but to savor and appreciate him.

But Ren had other ideas.

He raced his hands over Arman, tracing muscles and curves. He palmed Arman's ass, soothed and swept along his ribs. He wrapped a leg tight around Arman's waist and undulated his hips up to align them properly. Fire, hot and bright, flashed through Arman's veins, the catch and slide of their cocks undiminished through the fabric of his pants.

Pants. Pants definitely had to go. Arman struggled to remove his without breaking the kiss, kicking back the blankets to the end of the bed to give him room to work with. He got his pants off before his hands found Ren's waistband and worked the buttons free.

Ren tore his mouth away, breath harsh as he panted for air. "Arman, we should—"

"Later." Arman growled against Ren's neck before he nipped him none too gently. Hell no, he finally had this man naked and under him. With a yank, he got the pants down over Ren's hips, not caring when they carelessly hit the floor.

Not deterred, Ren tried again. "I know I said to make love to me, but you've never been with a man, right? I don't know what you'll be comfortable with—"

"Yes."

"No, no, no, yes is not an answer. I have not asked a question that 'yes' works with, just—" His words choked off when Arman wrapped a tight hand around Ren's cock and gave it a tug. Arman might not know much about making love to another man, but he felt perfectly confident in two skills: kissing and handjobs. Admittedly, having someone else's cock in his hand took some adjusting, and he had to lever his body a little to the side to give himself the right leverage. But he knew he'd hit the right angle and pressure when Ren rocked into it instinctively. "Yeeeeeees."

Arman chuckled, the sound rich and throaty. "See?"

"That's not cheating fair," Ren gasped, trying very hard to hold onto indignation, reason, something, and then groaning and giving over to Arman's demands without another protest.

For a while, Arman just focused on making his lover feel good. He'd heard things over the years, of course; being friends with Ren made that kind of talk inevitable. Some of what he'd heard sounded absurd, some of it painful, and some had to be wishful thinking. He felt hesitant to put into practice anything he'd heard. That wasn't the point of this, anyway; Ren knew him to be inexperienced. Right now, the goal was to brand into Ren's skin that Arman wanted him.

So he paid attention to the clues Ren's body gave him: breathy moans spilled from his throat and eyes scrunched tight when he twisted his grip. Ren's spine arched when he pumped tight and fast.

Fingers scrabbled in the sheets and precome dribbled when Arman rubbed circles of varying pressure under the crown.

But of course Ren couldn't just lie still and enjoy it. He wasn't that kind of man, to only take. Ren twisted a little, putting his mouth near Arman's nipple and giving it his undivided attention for a moment. Arman's eyes fell to half-mast as the pleasure zinged through him, tugging at his groin in a way that surprised him. Damn. He'd known women enjoyed such attentions, but he'd never suspected men would as well. Arman could see Ren cataloging each hiss and hum from him with lust-darkened eyes, reading him the way he'd always done.

Breath catching, mind hazing over the more Ren played, Arman desperately wanted to connect them a little more properly. Arman hadn't the necessary things to do anything serious, if rumors and drunken talk were to be believed, and it probably wasn't a good idea to try full lovemaking on the first go around anyway. But if touch without pants had felt so good, he wondered....

"Oh gods," Ren rasped out and banded an arm around Arman's waist as Arman shifted to bring their cocks together. "Yes, like that, Arman."

Arman's elbows briefly buckled, his forehead coming to rest against Ren's and they both panted there for a moment, breaths intertwining until the overwhelming rush of pleasure abated enough to move again.

Ren grabbed Arman by the ass, instigating little rocking motions, and Arman caught on quickly, wrapping a hand tightly around both of their lengths. Ren's hips snapped forward, catching the head of Arman's cock. The heat and friction dragged out a noise Arman hadn't known he could make, and he chased the feeling with hips and hand, using the precome that leaked from them both to ease the way.

In counterpoint to the fireworks lighting up his blood, he lowered his mouth an inch to gently kiss Ren, lingering, savoring. He tried to show Ren without question the way he felt, kissing him the way a man did to someone he cherished and desired above all else. He poured everything he was, every drop of love he felt into the kiss, and prayed Ren had received the message. He pulled back with a pant of air and gazed into the eyes of his beloved.

Ren's expression reflected unbridled love and delight.

Arman's breath caught in his throat, and all motion stopped. He'd only seen that expression once before, years ago, when Ren agreed to come home with Arman. It was the same joy, the same delight, as if Arman had just granted something Ren dearly wished for.

Arman felt his own smile spread across his face, joy and relief shining through. "Ren," he whispered against kiss-swollen lips, and Ren shuddered in response.

"Arman, please," Ren whimpered, bucking his cock through Arman's lax grip. Arman quickly tightened his hand, and their thrusts became that much harder, that much faster. Ren kept both hands firmly on Arman's buttocks to drive them both. With emotions running high on both sides, they didn't last much longer. Ren's spine bowed, muscles trembling, words tumbling out incoherently as he spilled across Arman's fist. One more gliding stroke sent white heat shooting up Arman's spine, clouding his vision, and he fell over the edge.

They lay tangled together, chests heaving, neither moving.

Vaguely worried about his weight on the slimmer man, Arman asked into the pillow where his head had landed, "Can you breathe?"

Ren stroked his back with an idle palm. "That's my line. Can you breathe?"

"Mmm."

"That's fine, then."

Aftershocks of pleasure thrummed pleasantly through his body and he let himself drift for a moment. Perhaps he should say something at this juncture, but Arman had learned that when Ren was presented with something shocking, he needed to mull it over. If he was content to let Arman use him as a pillow while he mulled, he wouldn't protest.

As his body calmed, his mind returned to the discussion that had led to all of this, and Ren's protest. Surely, Ren now had no doubt in his mind that they would be perfectly compatible as lovers, especially after he had a chance to show Arman the ropes. The question he faced now was: did that mean marriage was automatically the right answer? Arman knew his friend's history well enough to know that Ren had honestly never thought about marriage in a serious vein before. He'd never had a relationship last long enough to get to that point. Hell, Shiirei didn't even allow same-sex marriages.

For years, Arman's parents had tried to introduce him to suitable young women. He'd never been moved by any of them. Not that he found men particularly alluring, either, truth tell. He'd wondered from time to time if there was something wrong with him, something that prevented him from finding a person he wanted to spend his life with.

His deep connection to Ren offset the question, as surely he wouldn't feel so strongly about the man if he were incapable of attachment.

Eventually, another thought had formed. Even if there was no desire there, Arman fully hoped to live alongside Ren for the rest of their lives. From what he understood, through observation and advice he'd heard from other married couples, the optimum marriage was built on friendship. 'Marry your best friend' or so the adage went.

Ren certainly fit that bill, and he didn't doubt that they'd live together quite companionably. They'd already tested that in a war zone by sharing the same tent for a straight year. He knew it hurt Ren to be celibate and live without any possibility of finding someone in Aart, so wouldn't it suit both of them to be married? It all seemed rather obvious after a while.

After he realized his feelings were not at all platonic, the plan he'd hatched gained a new dimension to it. Arman now had no doubts that this was the right person to marry.

But did Ren see it all the same way?

The laxness of post-coital bliss faded, and Ren's frame under his slowly went taut. At first, he thought he had lain there too long, and cut off his lover's air supply, but his breathing didn't really change. Worried, he murmured, "You're tensing."

Ren forced his body to relax again. "Sorry. You've just given me a lot to think about, and I suddenly don't know how to answer you. You just proved that we have excellent chemistry in bed—which surprises me, I don't know why, it just does—and I already know that we get along well even at the lowest points in life, so I think I can marry you without wanting to kill you within a month. Or a year. And certainly, I love you, you're one of the dearest people in the world to me, but I'm not at all convinced this is the right path to take. Part of me thinks that this is a wonderful opportunity to have a life partner who cares about me. Another part feels like it's a leap of faith, and I'm torn on which to go with. Sorry, that's likely not the response you wanted."

Arman's heart gave a hard lurch in his chest. As he feared, Ren's analytical brain was taking over, and in exactly the sort of way Arman didn't want it to. He lifted himself up to see Ren's expression.

With some trepidation, Ren looked back up at him, clearly regretting his words. He'd always just babbled with Arman, saying whatever crossed his mind, but he seemed to feel this was a terrible time to follow that habit. No doubt he didn't want to hurt his friend, especially after Arman had gone to such lengths to get the sincerity of this (admittedly strange, not at all normal) proposal across.

Arman didn't go far, just up onto his elbows, transferring half of the weight off Ren and allowing him to breathe a little easier. How to convince him? How did he begin to take everything he'd felt, everything he dreamed and planned and hoped for the past two years, and somehow cram it into completely inadequate words? How did he convince his friend that he really was the love of his life, and that this wasn't strictly for Ren's benefit, but for his own as well? He stared down at Ren with an unfathomable expression for a long moment before it cracked, showing nothing but desperation underneath. "Renjimantoro."

Ren jolted at hearing his full name. Arman only used it when the situation was truly serious.

"Renjimantoro," Arman repeated, pleaded. "Please."

Ren's eyes went wide, breath stuttering as if even breathing was beyond him in that moment. "Please is not cheating fair."

That expression gave Arman hope and he ducked in to kiss Ren, gently, the same way their last kiss had been. "I love you. Please."

Ren closed his eyes, shuttering his expression from Arman for a moment. Arman didn't try to press him, just stayed still and waited. He could only push Ren so far. At some point he had to retreat enough for Ren to come to his own terms on this. When Ren opened his eyes again, they held a look of determination, accentuated by a tender smile. "Five words. You've overturned all of my objections, doubts, and fears in just five words. Alright, Arman. I'll marry you."

Delight exploded once more, feeling like an adrenaline surge, and Arman ducked in to kiss him passionately. Ren returned the kiss with just as much ardor. Arman really wanted to stay in bed, but he found himself too impatient to get the rest of his plans finalized. In a blink, Arman was gone, up and off the bed, ducking into the small toilet area in the next room. He returned with a wet cloth, which he used to quickly clean up with, then tossed it to Ren.

Confused by this, Ren used it, slowly wiping all away all traces of their love-making earlier.

Without pause, Arman turned for the foot of the bed, reaching for his clothes. When he realized Ren hadn't immediately followed him, he turned, his legs barely in his trousers, gesturing impatiently. "Let's go."

"Wait, you mean now?" Ren asked incredulously. "You want us to go get married right now?"

Arman gave him his patented 'yes of course now, don't be obtuse' look.

Scrubbing at his face with both hands, Ren pulled himself up into a sitting position. "Arman, listen to me. People do not propose and get married in the same day, alright? They propose, and then they tell the family, and discuss dates, and buy fancy clothes, and why are you pouting at me? Seriously, you're pouting at me, you look like you're five. Stop that, it's unbecoming of a general."

"You said you would," Arman mumbled, pout deepening.

"And I'm not reneging, I'm just saying that shouldn't we tell people first? Plan a ceremony? Alright, alright, stop pouting, come here, I can see that you have your heart set on doing this today." Rising from the bed, Ren took him into his arms, holding him around the waist. Several emotions darted over Ren's face, ranging from concern to shrewdness, as if he knew very well Arman had some sort of master plan and he mentally schemed on how to get the general to admit to it. "Look, I'm protesting only because I'm worried. Your mother especially has been looking forward to you getting married, and I know her, she'll want to throw a grand party to celebrate it. I do not want my future mother-in-law mad at me from day one, alright?"

Despite the fact that Arman stood a half-head taller, he still somehow managed to do that expression his sister-in-law Richelle had taught him, and looked up through his lashes, looking pitiful and earnest all at once. Ren swallowed visibly, protest dying in his throat. Wow, that had worked better than he expected. He'd have to remember this one.

Ren shook a finger at him, commanding, "Stop that. With the eyes, stop that right now, you're killing me. I'm not the one being unreasonable here, it's you, and…oh for the love of all that is holy. Dammit, fine, we'll get married today, but only on one condition."

Arman immediately perked up, hopeful and expectant.

"When your mother does find out about this, you will own up to the fact that this was completely your idea, and when she starts throwing out plans for a grand party, you won't argue with her." Ren pointed a stern finger at him. "You let her do what she wants. Deal?"

"Deal," Arman agreed promptly, feeling like happiness poured out of skin. He couldn't believe he'd gotten Ren to agree like this.

Had his earlier suspicions been correct? They must have been.

"Fine. I want to wash up, then we'll go. Wait, can we even get married today? I'm not clear on the procedures, but isn't there paperwork and a request for a license that you have to do first?"

"Already did it," Arman informed him smugly.

Ren rolled his eyes and muttered, "Of course you have."

16

Arman took him by the hand and left the main palace, heading directly toward the adjacent army headquarters, ignoring all of the strange looks they garnered on the way. Due to the wine and the whole situation, it was now mid-morning, so they saw a number of people as they traversed the hallways. Ren greeted them as they passed, acting as if nothing were wrong, even though his heart thumped so hard it threatened to leave his chest altogether.

He'd said yes in the heat of the moment and with Arman's pressure, but now, outside of that room, he had to wonder all over again: Was this right? Was he insane to agree to this? Just because they were friends, and had good chemistry in bed, didn't mean they'd automatically have a successful marriage. Part of Ren feared going ahead with this, as it had the potential to blow up painfully in their faces. Arman didn't even have a good understanding of what it would mean for them both, to have a man as a partner.

And yet…oh gods, and yet the possibility of having Arman was far too enticing. Ren had harbored secret fantasies over the years of being with Arman, but never like this, never with them officially bound together by laws and oaths. He'd never even considered the possibility. It spoke deeply to Ren's psyche, tantalizingly, offering him exactly what he never imagined he could have. Ren wanted it so badly he nearly shook under the force of the desire. It scared him all over again, because this had to be a dream. A cruel dream, showing him what he wanted, if only he had the courage to accept it.

Only Arman's grip on him kept Ren sane and grounded. The hand in his held him firmly, not allowing any possibility of escape. The ring on Ren's finger pressed against his skin, a tactile reminder. Arman said he'd had it made two years ago. It shouldn't surprise him that Arman would make preparations that far back. He was always one to be prepared when he decided to go through with something. But still, the idea that he had worn that ring on his pinky for two years, just waiting for the time he could put it on Ren, tugged sharply on Ren's heartstrings, and Ren held on to that. Maybe this was new and sudden to him, but not to Arman; if the man had spent two years planning this, then he certainly had considered what he was getting into.

They went straight through the side entrance and up into the general's quarters. Robert had laundry out on the main table he was folding when they came in. He took in the sight of their clasped hands and obvious relief flashed across his face.

Arman only paused long enough to give Ren a quick look, to make sure he hadn't changed his mind and would bolt, then turned to Robert. "The paperwork."

"Of course, sir."

With that order issued, Arman ducked into the next room, presumably to change out of yesterday's clothes.

Even the general's quarters only consisted of four rooms, so there wasn't much space for a confidential conversation, but Ren lowered his tone and tried for it anyway. Following Robert to the desk in the corner, he hissed, "Robert. Did you know about this?"

"I did, sir," Robert admitted with a weather eye on the bedroom door. "I helped him prepare the necessary paperwork. Did he tell you he's been planning this for two years?"

"Yes, he did."

"I was quite astonished at first," Robert admitted to him, retrieving a thick envelope that looked as if it had been shipped out to sea and back. "I didn't understand what motivated him, as to my eyes you two have never been anything more than close friends. And then I realized he was worried about you. He could tell that the lack of, ah, intimate partnership bothered you. I think he was afraid it would wear you down eventually and force you to return to your home country."

"So he decided to marry me, and give me what I needed in order to stay." It was so Arman.

"Yes, sir, that's my take on it. Of course, I didn't suspect anything more than that and was quite worried about his decision, as I didn't think you'd take it well once you figured out his motivations. Not until six months ago, at least. One of the couriers who came in shared some gossip with me, as is their wont, and one of the things he mentioned was your interaction with young Lord Giles. The general was furious hearing it. He barely spoke for two weeks."

"And at that point you realized he actually was in love with me."

Robert's faintly worried frown cleared. "You understand that too?"

"It took me a minute," Ren admitted ruefully. "But for all that he doesn't like to talk, he certainly knows how to use words to devastating effect. Robert, I have to ask, who else knows about this?"

"I don't think anyone else does, sir. Or at least, the general hasn't confided in anyone else on the matter." Robert handed him the envelope as he spoke, still with a weather eye on that door. His master changed quickly; they didn't have much time until he reappeared. "In regards to his family, I don't believe they know his intentions. I certainly didn't dare speak of it."

In case things went horribly wrong? Ren clapped him on the shoulder. "I appreciate that, Robert, thank you. Now, what all is in the envelope?"

"A marriage license, partially filled out. It just needs the priest's name, signature, and date. There's a copy of your citizenship certification and his. I put in the license fee too. You should be able to just hand it to the priest; he has everything he needs to file a notice." Dropping his voice even further, Robert took out a second packet, smaller and in the form of a jeweler's pouch. "Sir, just in case, I did prepare a wedding ring for him as well."

Taking the pouch, he shook the ring out into his hand and let out a low whistle. Robert had somehow managed to find Ren's family crest, the stylized four-petaled cherry blossom surrounded by two thin rings. He hadn't spared any expense, either, as the ring was solid gold and obviously fitted to Arman's finger. "I owe you, Robert."

"Think of it as my wedding present to you," Robert requested, relieved that his gesture of good will had been taken so well. "I'm honestly delighted the general's plans turned out as he had hoped. I didn't want to consider what would happen to both of you otherwise."

"Besides, with me at his side, you'll have a live-in translator when he gets especially cryptic?" Ren stated wryly.

Robert chuckled. "And that, sir. Your ring, does it fit? We had to take an educated guess at the size."

"Fits well," Ren assured him.

"Good," Arman declared, striding back into the room. He was not in uniform, but dressed in the white shirt, black pants, and black fitted coat that he favored. "Robert, come as a witness."

"I'd be pleased to, sir," Robert assured him, brightening at the invitation. "When is the ceremony?"

Eyes on Arman, Ren answered, "Right now."

Robert blinked at him, then at his master. "Now?"

"Trust me, I argued with him about it, but he won. We'll get married now, file it, then let his mother do a celebration later." If his mother approved enough to offer them that. Ren wasn't at all sure she would. Arman's family liked him, thought well of him, but there was a difference between being welcomed as a friend and being welcomed as a son-in-law.

Perhaps Arman saw the flash of uncertainty on his face. Arman strode to him, captured the back of his head with a cupped palm and placed a gentle kiss on his forehead. "It'll be fine."

Blowing out a breath, Ren argued, "How do you know? Arman, you haven't said a word to your family about any of this, so how do you know they'll blithely accept that their son chose a man as his partner?"

"My mother said she didn't care who, as long as I got married," Arman said seriously.

"And you're taking her at her word?" Ren didn't buy that, but he knew very well Arman would use her words to justify the matter. Not that he wanted conflict, he just didn't know how to anticipate how people would react. Same-sex relationships didn't even exist in this culture, so it could well be that even Arman's family wouldn't know how to react at first.

Studying his face, Arman's eyes narrowed an nth degree. "You promised."

"I did, and I will, I'm just a little worried. You can't blame me for being worried; you're pushing this ahead so quickly." He pocketed the ring carefully. Then he looked up into a pair of blue eyes he knew so very well and saw the worry in them—worry that Ren might try to wriggle out of this somehow. Whatever fears or concerns Ren might entertain, the one thing he knew for certain was that Arman wouldn't change his stance. The man could teach rocks how to be stubborn once he set his mind to something. He leaned up a bit to give Arman a quick kiss, reassuring him.

Perhaps reassuring them both. "I have no idea why it's so important to you that we get married today, but I can see that it is, and

I won't argue. Let's go."

Arman gave him that small smile, the one that lit his whole face. Ren heard Robert's breath catch, seeing it, and knew it was the first time the batman had ever seen his master with that expression. Ren had seen it now three times in the space of a morning and it made his heart skip a beat each time.

Wasting no more time, Arman led them out of the building, and then to the one next door. Ren should have expected that they would go to the army chaplain. Why not? He was conveniently placed and wouldn't dare disobey or argue with a superior officer.

And Ren expected arguments.

Bertwin, who still wore his chaplain robe, stood at the altar and rifled through a large book in front of him. At their entrance, he looked up, tipping back the cap on his head before it could slide out of place. "Ah, General, Ren, it's unexpected to see you here. What can I do for you?"

"Bertwin," Ren greeted, clasping his hand briefly in a handshake before letting go. It was strange to see him in that billowy blue robe instead of shirt and worn-in trousers. "As to that, we'd like to get married."

Bertwin's jaw dropped slightly, brows furrowing into confusion. "I'm sorry, I might not…that is, I don't think I understand. You and…?"

"Me," Arman informed him, not entirely patient with the question.

Bertwin had seen combat on two different continents, served as chaplain for nearly twenty years, and had heard any number of outrageous things from people in that time. Ren had been drinking buddies with him for about three years now, confided in the disaster of his love affair with Giles, and he knew that he'd completely shocked the man.

"He's not pulling your leg, it's not a prank, and I was just as surprised as you are when he proposed," Ren assured the man.

Bertwin stared at Ren in open astonishment. "He proposed?"

"Just as surprised, trust me," Ren repeated, starting to see the humor in all of this. "I did not see this coming. But we are absolutely sure about it and have all the paperwork prepared. Will you do the honors?"

It took a minute, then Bertwin nodded to them firmly. "I wouldn't miss the opportunity for the world. Alright, let me see your paperwork.

Do you both have rings?"

"We do." Although for the ceremony to go right, Ren would have to take his temporarily off. He handed over the paperwork first, then passed the ring over.

Arman studied him with some perplexity. "You have a ring for me?"

"You can thank your excellent batman who planned ahead," Ren informed him. "He had a ring made for you that has my family crest on it."

That pleased Arman immensely and he turned to tell Robert over his shoulder, "You need a raise."

Robert chuckled. "I won't argue, sir."

Bertwin quickly flipped through the paperwork, teeth worrying at his bottom lip as he did so. "Everything is in order. General Brahms, forgive the question, but I do need to make sure. By any chance, did you look up the regulations for weddings and ascertain if this is legal?"

"I did. The regulation reads 'two consenting adults of legal age' and is not gender specific."

Were they going off the theory that as long as it wasn't specifically prohibited, it must be legal? Although Ren felt impressed Arman had thought to look up the regulations for it, as he certainly wouldn't have.

Relieved, Bertwin nodded. "Then I have no objection. Gentlemen, you have your rings in hand? Good. Witness, state your full name and occupation, please."

"Colbert Robert, batman to General Arman Brahms."

"Thank you." Bertwin fell into a more formal cadence. "Batman Robert, witness this ceremony so that no man may deny it afterwards. Arman Brahms, do you take this wo—erhm, excuse me, man, to be your lawfully wedded husband, to have and hold until death do you part?"

Arman forgave the chaplain the slip of the tongue and answered solemnly, "I do."

"Sho Renjimantoro, do you take this man to be your lawfully wedded husband, to have and hold until death do you part?"

It was happening. It was really happening. Only in his deepest fantasies had he ever imagined having a life partner, and never once did he really think he'd get any sort of wedding ceremony. Maybe a commitment ceremony, but never more than that. Now here he stood, in a proper church, with a chaplain reciting the vows. He looked up at the man about to be his husband and Arman stared back at him. Incandescent joy shone in those deep blue eyes, the force of it nearly robbing Ren of breath. Ren hoped he reflected the same joy back. He felt a little dazed, perhaps overwhelmed by the magnitude of the choice he was making, as he answered, "I do."

"Please exchange the rings."

His hands shook a little, just a fine tremor, as he carefully slid the ring onto Arman's left ring finger. Arman's stayed rock steady as he returned the ring to its proper place on Ren's finger.

"Let no man deny the promises that have been exchanged here, nor try to rip asunder what has been blessed. May harmony, peace, and abiding joy stay with you as you live your lives together. I now pronounce you husband and…" Bertwin paused, not quite sure how to end the formal phrasing. "…husband."

Bailing the poor man out, as he really was adjusting the vows on the fly, Ren asked teasingly, "Do I still get to kiss him even though there's no bride?"

Laughing, Bertwin gestured for him to go ahead. "I insist."

Cupping Ren's face with both hands, Arman leaned in the few inches necessary and kissed him slowly, caressingly, with the same banked passion that Ren had tasted that morning. He had to remind himself, firmly, that he was in a church with witnesses and he couldn't just push the man down and have his wicked way with him.

Lifting free, Arman beamed at him for a moment, shocking them all into silence, before getting his expression back under control and addressing Bertwin with something like his normal tone. "Thank you, Chaplain."

Bertwin might have questioned it before, but not after seeing the love radiating from that smile. Something of a fine mist hovered in his eyes as he answered, "It has been my honor, truly. Not to mention I'm very glad for the bragging rights, as this is definitely a story to be shared. Please come sign the certificates, so that we each have a copy, and then I'll handle the rest."

Ren obligingly put pen to paper, then paused. He'd been in this country for so long that he automatically used their alphabet to write his signature with. And certainly, that was still his legal name, but somehow putting down that signature sat ill with him. If there was ever a time when he needed to be completely honest in signing his name to something, this was surely it. Decisively, he wrote his name out in his own language, which certainly looked a little odd compared to the rest of the words on the license, but he felt better for it.

Everything signed, the fee delivered, they thanked Bertwin again before leaving as unobtrusively as they'd come. Robert cleared his throat and addressed them. "Gentlemen, congratulations. I'm sure you have many things you want to do today, so I only ask one question before taking my leave. Who's moving where?"

That was an excellent question. Ren didn't have the foggiest. Looking at his newly minted husband, he said uncertainly, "I don't think I can leave my apartment in the castle. People have to be able to find me in case of an emergency."

"I don't want to stay out here anyway," Arman assured him. "Robert, move everything to his apartment."

"Understood, sir."

Ren added, "Try to take your time. Tomorrow's soon enough."

The batman knew very well what he hinted at and assured him, "I couldn't possibly move everything over before late tomorrow morning."

He knew he liked this man for a reason. "You are a saint, Robert, and we don't deserve you. See you tomorrow."

Robert winked at him before sauntering off back toward headquarters.

Arman looked at him hopefully. "Back to bed?"

"I demand food first," Ren informed him, tracing a line along the top of Arman's waistline, dipping a finger underneath the waistband just to tease the man a little. "And we need to pick up a few essentials from a pharmacist, and then, my husband, I have absolutely no objection to spending the rest of the day with you."

Those blue eyes went stormy and dark. "If you don't remove your hand, you're not going to make it to either of those places."

He was serious, too. A thrill raced up Ren's spine at the predatory look in Arman's eyes. It took willpower to remind himself that they really did need lubrication of some kind or risk injury. Retrieving his hand, he calmed his breathing, wrangling his libido back under control. "As much as I love the idea, are you sure that you don't want to notify your family first?"

Shaking his head, Arman took his hand, lacing their fingers together. "Today, all I want is you."

Squeezing back, he lifted up to kiss him gently. "Well," he said, voice husky, "I can't argue with that."

17

Arman let him do exactly the two stops he requested and no more. Ren made sure to eat well, as apparently he would need the strength soon. This side to Arman wasn't one he knew, and it surprised him but only in the best of ways. Was this how Arman reacted to a lover? A spouse?

He had to admit, he rather liked it.

Once they returned to Ren's apartment, he put the bag of goodies on the bedside chest and turned, feeling a little awkward about inviting his husband back to bed. They'd gone from friends to lovers so quickly his head still spun a little. He turned to ask, something at any rate, only to be silenced before he could get a word out by a very demanding kiss. An arm came around his waist and drew him in to a tight embrace while another reached up to play with the long tail of his hair.

"Bed, now," Arman whispered against his mouth.

"No problem," Ren assured him fervently. He paused only long enough to toe off his boots before hopping onto the mattress and scooting over to the middle. Considering how they were this morning, he wanted plenty of room on both sides. Nothing killed the mood faster than accidentally dumping your partner on the floor.

Arman followed suit, toeing off boots before he knelt and crawled over to him, lying down at Ren's side. They repositioned for another kiss, tongues darting out to tangle with each other. Unlike the hurry of this morning, Arman took his time now, savoring every breath, kissing him with a slow, patient greed. Ren moved to straddle his waist, enjoying the attention immensely, threading his hands through that thick hair.

In slow movements, they unbuttoned each other's shirts, pushing them off, heedlessly tossing them onto the floor. Skin on skin felt even better. Ren always wondered what it was about skin contact that intensified love-making so much for him. He never quite could decide on an answer.

Part of Ren still hesitated in reaching for Arman. His friend (gah, husband now!) had been completely and unquestionably straight for thirty years, after all. No one could flip their sexuality overnight, even if he was completely in love with Ren. Being intimate with a man had to be strange for him on some level and Ren didn't want to just assume he was fine and push things in a bad direction. He didn't try to put his hands under Arman's waistband at first, just let fingertips find and trace the cock underneath.

He got no more than two strokes in before Arman reached for his trouser buttons, efficiently undoing them and pushing the waistband down. So, still not shy at all about being naked and in bed with him. Ren was relieved. This morning had been a heady concoction of repressed desires and emotional highs, which could push anyone into sex. He was glad to see that this, at least, didn't change even with their minds being in a calmer headspace.

It took some maneuvering, flipping, and such to get pants off. One leg caught on Arman's ankle, drawing a dark look from the man, and Ren had to rescue it before it was just torn off. That look amused him vastly and he bit back a chuckle.

Arman drew him back down, cradling him a little between spread thighs, and resumed kissing him senseless. Ren's heartbeat kicked up a notch, skin heating as passion built. It was hard to catch his breath, hard to really focus, but he wanted to make this good for Arman. He disengaged to reach for the goody-bag, fumbling to pull the glass jar out. His stretch had put his right nipple in proximity to his husband's mouth and Arman took full advantage. Breath wheezing, Ren finally grazed the glass with his fingertips and latched onto it. He sat upright and promptly uncorked it, dipping fingers into the oil. Rising to his knees, he spread his legs wider, reaching around with one hand to start preparing himself. A slight hiss escaped as he slid a digit in at the awkward angle.

Arman propped himself on his elbows in confusion. "What are you doing?"

As Ren had already explained the mechanics of this process on the way to and from the pharmacist's, he was confused by the confusion. "Preparing myself?"

"I've never done this before. It's better that I be bottom first."

Ren stopped, lowering to his heels, and really looked at Arman. Nothing about Arman's expression indicated he was trying to be accommodating, or doing this for Ren's benefit. He merely stated his opinion about the best course of action. It slowly dawned on Ren that for the first time in, well, ever, he was in bed with a man who had absolutely no prejudices about the roles in bed.

Tensing, Arman's expression closed off a little. "You don't want to."

"That is not it at all," Ren assured him hastily, running a soothing hand down Arman's thigh. "It's, ah…damn. How to explain this. I just realized that you have no ingrained perceptions where top and bottom is concerned. It has mentally thrown me."

"Perceptions?" Arman repeated blankly.

Ren realized he really had better explain this. Not that it would matter much between the two of them, but they did sometimes travel outside of this country, and Arman needed to be prepared. "In most of the world, the man who takes the top position is considered to be the dominant one. A man who takes bottom is submissive to him. It's normally understood that a man who prefers the bottom position is by nature weaker."

Arman gave him an odd look. "That makes no sense."

"I absolutely agree, it never has to me either, but you see why I'm a little thrown? Because normally, I wouldn't be having this argument at all with a man if I offered to bottom. And really, truly, I don't mind. I'm an equal opportunist, I like it either way."

Confusion cleared, Arman nodded understanding. Ren did not expect for Arman to lie back and spread his legs wide open. Not that he didn't find the view enticing—Ren damn near swallowed his tongue—but, but, "Are you absolutely sure this is a good idea? Granted, it would be a hands-on lesson if I did you first, I can't argue that, but the first time is a little rough. It isn't painful, but it isn't painless, if you get my meaning. Takes a while for a body to get used to it. I've done it before—" Ren stumbled to a halt when he realized it had been nearly a decade since he'd had anal sex. Hell, had it really been that long? He'd basically be like a virgin down there, then.

Arman got that obstinate set to his jaw, lips tightening.

"I just hit your stubborn switch, didn't I," Ren groaned. "Why are you so stubborn when I don't need you to be? Alright, alright, we'll try this your way. But you listen to me, this is not a competition, and if it hurts, *say something*."

"Mm."

Still feeling like this was not the best decision, he placed the oil on the bed and gamely bent to it anyway. With hands and tongue, he began a program of distraction. He lay a kiss on Arman's inner thigh, gave it a nip, and nuzzled his way up to where thigh met groin. He spent a couple of breaths there tracing patterns with his tongue and used his hands to stroke up and down Arman's thighs, feather light. Arman panted and tried to shift Ren's attentions further over. With a smirk, Ren let him, and drew the head of that lovely cock into his mouth. He kept the pressure light—just little flicks of the tongue, little hints of suction. He used one hand to fondle Arman's balls and let the other drift down and behind to stroke his perineum and hole. Arman tensed for a moment, but Ren kept the pressure light, merely rubbing light circles over it. As Arman relaxed again, he began to add hints of pressure, gently pressing the tip in, retreating, pressing.

"Ren," Arman rumbled, "stop teasing."

"But teasing you is so much fun, husband," Ren said with a smirk and put more oil on his fingers. He sucked Arman back into his mouth with force this time and he slipped his finger in up to the first knuckle. Arman gasped and let out a groan that shuddered through his whole body. The sheets under them abruptly went taut as Arman clenched both hands into them. Ren let his finger rest there a moment, letting Arman get used to the feeling. Meanwhile, he used the flat of his tongue to work the long vein from the base of Arman's cock to the tip.

After a moment, Arman nodded, and Ren pressed the rest of his finger in. When he met no resistance, he started thrusting it in and out until everything relaxed, and then he slowly worked a second finger in.

"Feel okay?" he asked.

Arman was quiet a moment before saying, "A little weird. Not bad," he assured when Ren immediately stopped moving, "just weird pressure. Keep going."

Ren eyed him, but took Arman at his word and started searching for the one thing he knew that would change that feeling. Finding it, he crooked his fingers and Arman's hips shot off the bed, a garbled shout falling from his lips. And because Ren loved to play, immediately tapped the spot again, just to hear the noises that spilled out of his lover's throat.

Eyes wide, Arman stared at Ren incredulously.

"And now you know why I like to bottom," Ren informed him smugly. "Want me to hit it again?"

Arman nodded frantically, so Ren set about playing, changing up rhythm and force to keep Arman on edge. Maybe Arman had saved up all the held back vocals for his lover, maybe that was it. He certainly didn't hold back now, and every moan and gasp and whimper lit Ren's desire that much more. He felt his own cock twitch in response.

Gods, he loved Arman.

Using those sounds as a guide, he nibbled here, licked there, swirled his tongue just below the crown, played with the slit, and did his utmost to distract as he scissored his fingers and worked a third in.

Hissing, Arman flinched a little.

Ren stopped immediately. "Did that hurt?"

"Burns a little," Arman admitted, chest heaving for breath. "Don't stop."

Stretching meant some discomfort. He could deal with a low-grade burn. It was actual pain Ren wanted to avoid causing. With a watchful eye on Arman, Ren worked both channel and cock for some time. His husband definitely had girth, but Ren wasn't small either. Arman's back arched at a particularly wide stretch, breath keening in the back of his throat. Ren paused again, studying every nuance of his expression. Discomfort, but no pain that he could see. "Still alright?"

"In me. Now," Arman begged in a voice that sounded like gravel.

Had Ren really pushed him to the breaking point? He'd been trying not to. Well, sort of trying not to. The sounds were to blame. He hadn't been able to resist pushing all of Arman's sensitive buttons repeatedly. "Alright. Up. Roll over, that's it, up on your hands and knees."

Arman came up, legs shaking a little, then he went abruptly still. "No."

Withdrawing both hands, Ren waited, heart beating an unsteady tattoo. So he'd finally hit Arman's limit. "Alright. We don't have to."

"I don't like this position." Arman sat back on his heels, reaching for Ren's hand. "Choose one where I can see your face."

Oh. That was the objection. Granted, Ren didn't prefer mounting from behind either, but it was easier on the one bottoming in some ways. Thinking quickly, he offered, "I can lie on my back? You can straddle me and come down that way. Take your time doing it, you have full control in that position."

"Mm," Arman agreed, satisfied.

Ren scooted around, putting two pillows behind him to support his back, then waited with his feet braced for Arman to straddle him. He did so with his usual lack of modesty, not seeming to realize just how much this full-frontal view turned Ren on.

Of course, his cock advertised the fact by twitching, and Arman paused, looking at it, before a feline grin spread over his face. "You like this position."

"I have my sexy husband on full display, of course I like this position," Ren drawled. "I'm not quite hard enough to give you a good ride, though, you might want to—ngghhhh. Yes, that. Your hands are wicked, I love them, where did you learn to do that?"

"Very boring summer when I was fifteen," Arman answered dryly.

"Are you seriously telling me that you spent an entire summer learning the best techniques of—ngghh. No, seriously, stop, you're not going to have anything to mount if you keep doing that."

What sounded suspiciously like a chuckle drifted from Arman's mouth but he did withdraw his hand, keeping only one in place to help guide Ren inside. Ren paused him only long enough to slather a good amount of oil on himself before gesturing the other man to proceed. He wiped his hand on the sheets, then placed both hands on Arman's hips, mostly as a safety measure because he just knew that Arman was going to try and take him all in one go.

Arman started to sink down, and sure enough, Ren had to guide him.

"Slowly. Slowly. Damn, you feel good. I always forget how good this feels. Are you alright? No pain?"

Arman's eyes fell to a half-mast as the head of Ren's cock breached him, mouth open and panting. His thighs trembled with the strain of staying there. "It's a little odd; no pain."

"Good, no pain is good," Ren managed. "Ready to continue?"

Arman slowly lowered himself with exquisite control until he settled firmly into the cradle of Ren's thighs. They both took a moment to breathe, exhales shuddering out in near tandem. Ren fought tooth and nail not to thrust into tight heat. He flexed his fingers into firm skin, curled his toes into the sheets.

Arman's interest in the proceedings hadn't flagged, which was a good sign. "Alright, ready to move?"

Arman answered by slowly rising up and then going back down again. He repeated the motion with a grunt, chin falling to his chest. Ren let him do so, catching a rhythm, hands firmly on his hips the entire time. When he felt like Arman had settled into it, only then did he angle his hips, searching once again for the spot inside that would rock his husband's world. And he knew exactly when he hit it, as Arman's spine arched back, a fine shiver racing over his skin. His groan vibrated throughout his body into Ren's cock, and Ren couldn't help the buck of his own hips and the moan that slipped out.

Arman braced himself against Ren's chest and lifted up and down again, faster this time, searching for the right angle himself.

It might have started out awkward, but it was getting fun now. Unable to keep a grin off his face, Ren obligingly shifted his legs, gaining the leverage he needed, then angled to strike that spot repeatedly. Bitten off cries, groans, gasps, and incoherent words spilled out of Arman's mouth. Their pace increased again, sweat beading on their skin, both of them breathing hard. The bed squeaked a little with each hard thrust, a counterpoint rhythm to their own.

Ren's eyes roved over Arman's face, capturing every detail of this moment for future recall. Initial awkwardness or not, this first time was more than he ever dreamed it could be. Love slid through him, vibrant and warm, when Arman's gaze locked with his and gave him a smile.

He reached for Arman and stroked him, timing it with their thrusts. Snapping his hips down, once, twice, Arman seized tight, shuddering and spilling out over Ren's belly. The moan Arman released swiftly became Ren's favorite noise to date. Ren stroked Arman through it, enjoying the man's expression of pure bliss. Then he grabbed his hips again and rocked into him, demanding, chasing his own release. Arman grunted with each thrust, rebalancing himself with his hands on Ren's chest, watching avidly.

Pleasure burst through his system as he came, fireworks of light dancing behind closed eyes, and he let himself go completely. For a moment, he focused on getting his breath back, and only then did he open his eyes again.

Arman still sat straddled over him, even though they were no longer joined, an expression of perfect contentment radiating from him.

Grinning, Ren levered himself up to steal a kiss. "I don't need to ask if you liked it. It's written all over your face. But did you like it well enough to do it again?"

"Any time," Arman stated firmly, "and no, I'm not hurting."

"Just a little sore and aching, right?" Ren stated knowingly. "Don't try to say otherwise, I know better. Here, come down, cuddle with me until we get our breath back."

Arman promptly did just that, snuggling into his side, pillowing his head on Ren's shoulder.

And this was another reason why Ren felt very glad that Arman didn't have any of those silly prejudices ingrained in him. Ren loved to cuddle but most men found that too 'feminine' and avoided it. After the sex was over, they'd get up and leave. Being able to keep Arman close without bargaining for it, that was a blessing.

"Teach me how to do that next."

Turning his head a little, hair shifting on the pillow, he craned his neck so he could see Arman's expression. "Do which?"

"Take you in my mouth," Arman answered, tongue flicking out to lick his lips.

Ren's flaccid cock twitched in anticipation. Oh hell, they were going to thoroughly wear each other out, weren't they?

Morning came, as it always did, and found Ren face down in the bed, sprawled under the covers. Arman had gotten up at some point, and Ren's body felt a weird mixture of pleasantly sore and absolutely exhausted. He had never, not even as a teenager, had that much sex in a twenty-four-hour period. In fact, he was vaguely impressed he'd been able to get it up that many times. Granted, he'd been somewhat deprived for the past five years—Bastard Idiot excluded—but still.

Arman came over to drape himself on Ren's back, kissing the side of his neck. "You need to get up. Robert's coming soon."

"Get me a pain powder from the chest," Ren pleaded.

Alarmed, his husband demanded, "Did I hurt you last night?"

"No, I'm hungover."

Silence, as Arman paused and tried to make sense of that. "We didn't have any wine last night."

"Sex, man, I'm hungover from too much sex. You were insatiable last night. Which, now that I think about it, is extremely odd in a way. For thirty years you're straight, then you decide to marry me, and now you're suddenly gung-ho on having sex with a man. Does that not strike you as odd?"

"No," Arman denied dryly. "I had to restrain my desires for six months with no outlet."

"Oh. Didn't think of that. Granted, that would make anyone horny." Ren made an effort to turn over, mostly because his stomach growled at him petulantly. "Help me get up. I have no energy. My only hope is that breakfast will restore me."

Arman did not give him a hand like he expected, but maneuvered his arms under Ren's shoulders and knees and actually lifted him with a grunt of effort.

"Whoa!" Ren flailed a little before latching onto a rock-hard set of shoulders. "I didn't say do a bridal lift! I'm not a bride."

Pausing, still with Ren cradled against his chest, Arman stared off into space with a slight furrow between his brows.

Knowing well what he was thinking, Ren drawled, "You're now wondering if that makes you the bride, aren't you?"

"Mm."

"Well, that depends, are you willing to wear the dress at the ceremony?" Ren bit his lip in an effort to keep his face straight and not give the game away.

Arman gave him an appalled look. Then his eyes narrowed suspiciously. "You're laughing."

"I am not. See? Not laughing." Ren was totally laughing on an internal level.

With the speed of a cobra, Arman darted in to play-bite at his nose, making Ren laugh outright. "Can't fool me."

"Never can," Ren agreed, still chuckling. "Alright, let me down. Is there any water left in the washbasin or did you use it all?"

"Still half left."

Blessing him for small favors, Ren went into the toilet area and closed the door, as he needed five minutes of privacy just then. This being married thing was nice, no question about it, but it didn't mean he'd grown used to it overnight. Some parts of it still felt a little awkward. Or rather, he'd expected awkward morning-after syndrome and wasn't getting it, which conversely made him feel awkward. Ren had to wonder, was it because of their experience in living with each other? They basically had no secrets at this point, and were in a very committed relationship. So, naturally, there was no unease the next morning? That might be it. If that's all it was, Ren would count his blessings and take it.

As he washed, he spotted several marks on his skin, and was that…? Yes, it was. That was a hickey. Now when did that get there? At least it was in a spot that could be hidden by clothes. If Roslyn saw it, she would surely ask inappropriate questions, and he really didn't want to go there with her. Her parents would kill him if he taught her anything else. Wrapping a towel around his waist, he stepped back out, passing a comb through his hair as he moved. He'd need to wash his hair soon, but it would have to wait; he didn't have the patience for that now.

He came out to find Arman had stripped the bed already and laid new sheets on it. Military habits were indeed wonderful that way. Going to the armoire in the corner, he drew out a clean set of clothes and dressed right there, not bothered that Arman got a free show. Even before their marriage, they'd seen all there was to see anyway. In the army, there was no such thing as modesty.

Picking up the comb again, he moved to the washstand mirror and combed his hair up and into his habitual high ponytail. Satisfied the tie would hold, he stepped back out, searching for his boots. He'd kicked them off near the end of the bed somewhere. Ren refused to walk around his apartment in just stockinged feet. Despite the rug on the floor, the stone floors underneath were freezing.

A knock sounded on the door and they both called, "Enter!"

He couldn't see it, of course—a wall and door blocked his view of the main room—but he could hear Robert come in and greet his master. Finally finding his shoes, he slipped them on and stamped them once to settle his feet firmly inside before joining the other two in the main room. "Good morning, Robert."

"Good morning, sir." Robert greeted him with the most pleased smile he'd ever seen from the man. "I took the liberty of asking for another armoire to be moved in here, and they're arranging for one to be brought out of storage. For now, the general's chests are being ported over."

Really, what would they do without Robert? "Thank you, that's splendid. Does anyone know about the marriage yet?"

"I've given no reason for the move, sir," Robert answered carefully, glancing between them. "I thought it was your news to share and not mine. Chaplain Bertwin and I did have dinner together, as he was avidly curious how this happened and I saw no problem sharing the story with him."

"He's a confidant of mine and a friend, that's fine," Ren assured him. "Alright, good. I didn't want our monarchs to find out about this through the rumor mill. But this is the castle, after all, people thrive on rumors here more than food. It would be better if we moved quickly. Arman?"

Arman shrugged his agreement, not looking at all concerned. "Now?"

"Might as well," Ren agreed. He personally didn't know how this news would be taken. That they would be happy for him, he had no doubt, but this marriage threw into question his own position here as warden. Brahms Fortress was a good two days' trip outside of the capital city. As the eldest son, and the one with formal military training, Arman was set to inherit it. If he followed Arman home, it wouldn't be possible for him to do his job here. It was a sticky problem he had no immediate solution for.

Shaking his head, he tried not to borrow trouble ahead of time. "I think I know where the queen will be, at least. She normally takes her morning tea in the West Morning Room at this time. Let's try there first."

18

Queen Eloise was indeed in the West Morning Room, along with Princesses Alexandria and Roslyn. The three made a pretty picture around the white wrought iron table, the sun streaming in through the floor to ceiling windows, the air rich and fragrant with the scents of food and flowers. It looked like a fairy tale painting. Ada opened the door and announced them with a smile. "General Brahms and Warden Ren, Your Majesty."

"Ah, good, two of my favorite people," Queen Eloise greeted warmly. "Come, sit. Have you eaten breakfast? No? Then Ada, please serve them both. I didn't expect to see either of you this morning. Is something the matter?"

After all that they'd been through for the past several months, he understood why she asked the question. "No, My Queen, rather we came to tell you good news."

"Oh? I'm always open to good news. What is it?" She smiled at him, expression open and curious.

Ren felt his nerves sing with tension. This was far more nerve-wracking than he'd anticipated, which said something, as he didn't imagine it would be easy. In many ways, this was his adoptive family in Aart, closer to him than his own biological family in Shiirei. He knew exactly what reaction his news would receive in his native country but in Aart? He couldn't begin to guess. He didn't believe they'd outright reject him, but could they accept it?

Perhaps Arman sensed his attack of nerves, as his husband pulled a chair out for him and settled beside him, then tangled their fingers together under the table. Ren shot him a look and found Arman completely at ease. Well, no, he looked very determined, actually, but not on guard. Ren held onto that, gripped those warm fingers firmly, and decided he better ease Queen Eloise into it, especially since she had just taken a sip of her tea. "Arman surprised me yesterday. He proposed."

Queen Eloise froze, the tea still in her mouth, which made her look rather like a chipmunk with nuts in its cheeks. Unfortunately, Roslyn didn't have the same control and choked on the scone she'd just taken a bite of. Even Galvath, standing guard in the corner, choked on his own breath.

Ren shot him a quick glance before he leaned over, helpfully smacking Roslyn in the middle of the back. "I know, I know, I didn't expect it either. Breathe, Princess."

Finally swallowing, Queen Eloise pressed a hand to her chest and looked between the two of them as if doubting her ears. "The two of you are terrible pranksters when you're together, so you do understand if I can't take you seriously right now?"

Considering some of the stunts he'd pulled with Arman in the past five years, he rather deserved that.

Growling in aggravation, Arman caught him by the back of the neck and leaned in, mouth taking his in what was so very obviously not a first kiss. Ren responded, enjoying the kiss, but hyper-aware that they'd stunned the room silent in the process. When Arman withdrew, he glared at them all, as if upset they hadn't automatically believed Ren.

"I think he's serious," Alexandria breathed, eyes darting between the two men. "Oh. Oh, my. How did this happen?"

"Wait, General Brahms actually proposed?" Roslyn demanded in growing excitement. "I would have thought it the other way around!"

Queen Eloise popped up from the table and rushed around it to throw her arms around Ren's shoulders and squeeze him to death. Swaying back and forth in excitement, she exclaimed, "I'm so happy for you, Ren! But you can't just announce something like that when we're all not here. Ada, go fetch my husband and son. I don't care what they're doing. They need to hear the story."

Happy his news was being taken so well, Ren put up with being squashed against an ample chest. Breathing wasn't important; it was fine.

Retreating a half-step back, she released him just enough for him to breathe. "General Brahms, I've never seen you look so content. I'm happy for you as well, although confused on how this came about. After five years, I'd quite given up any hope that you might fall for our Ren."

Brow quirked a little at that 'our,' Arman corrected, "I wanted to propose two years ago."

"Oh. Ohhh," Queen Eloise said in realization. "Hence why you were so upset when I wouldn't let him go with you. I'm so sorry, if I had only known—no, wait. *You* should have explained yourself better. Let this be a lesson to you, General: use your words."

Ren couldn't help himself and laughed out loud. Truly, his husband had really stabbed himself in the foot in this regard. Arman poked him in the side in reprimand for laughing, which of course made Ren laugh even harder.

"You have to admit, she's got you there," Ren told him, then dodged when Arman tried to poke him again.

"Boys, boys, not at the table," Queen Eloise reproved. "Oh good, Gerhard, Charles, you came quickly. We have such excellent news!"

"I should hope so," King Gerhard responded, a little exasperated. "I was about to head into a meeting."

"An accounting meeting," Charles elaborated with a wink to his mother. "So, thank you for your excellent timing. What's the news?"

"Ren and General Brahms are engaged," the queen announced, as happy and satisfied as if she had arranged the match herself.

Well, no, that wasn't quite right. Ren frowned a little, realizing that he probably should explain that better.

"Really?" Charles responded, giving Ren no opening to speak. "That is amazing. Ren, what made you propose?"

"No, no," his sister corrected gleefully. "General Brahms proposed."

King and prince looked at Arman incredulously. In unison, they spluttered, "You did?"

Put upon, Arman looked to Ren for support, expression a little disgruntled.

"Of course it's surprising; you're not known for liking men," Ren responded to him in a low tone. "And most of the castle had you pegged for a man sliding into confirmed bachelorhood. Why do you think your mother was so anxious to get you married off soon?"

Expression clearing, Arman conceded this with a provisional nod and one shoulder shrug.

"Ah," Charles intoned with sudden realization. "But when you're married, doesn't that mean Ren will have to be released as warden?"

Queen Eloise abruptly looked horrified, as did Roslyn, and they stared at Ren in growing consternation. Rubbing the back of his neck, Ren responded helplessly, "Brahms Fortress is a two-day journey from here. I think it's a little too far to commute in. And, ah, actually—"

"No," Roslyn stated flatly. "No, absolutely not. Papa, stop him. We can't lose Ren; the castle will fall down if he leaves."

"Really, daughter, that's an exaggeration," King Gerhard replied, although he clearly didn't like the idea either.

"It's not much of one," Queen Eloise stated in growing agitation. She almost glared at Arman. "While I'm happy for Ren's sake, I'm mad at you. You may not have my warden, General."

Arman cocked a challenging eyebrow at her, then lifted his left hand in the air along with Ren's, showing them all the wedding bands on both their fingers.

"As to that," Ren stated with a sigh, as he just knew this would start a whopper of an argument, "We're already married."

That set the royal family off at once, talking over each other loudly. Only Princess Alexandria refrained, seeming quite surprised at this turn of events, but entertained by it as well. After their first night of drinking, Ren had gotten to be rather good friends with her, so he mouthed hopefully, "Help?"

Grinning, she shook her head no and sat back, for all the world enjoying the show.

Some friend she was. Writing off all help from that quarter, Ren turned to Galvath, only to find him grinning without the slightest intention of interrupting such excellent entertainment. Ren had perfectly terrible friends. Resigned, he stood and lifted both hands, trying to calm them down. "Quiet, quiet, I can't even understand all of you. Yes, we're really married; Chaplain Bertwin did the honors yesterday morning. Yes, we still plan to have a full ceremony later. We moved that quickly at Arman's insistence, which I now understand." Turning to his husband, Ren asked tartly, "You knew very well you'd get this response, didn't you? And you didn't want any arguments on whether you could marry me or not, so you removed that from the equation."

Smugly, Arman told Queen Eloise, "My Ren."

Queen Eloise spluttered indignantly, quite ready to pick up the nearest heavy object and chuck it at her favorite general's head. Well, previously favorite. Ren had the notion she would cheerfully demote him right now.

Hoping to find some chink in the armor, Queen Eloise demanded, "But he only just proposed. Surely you didn't already consummate the marriage?"

"Consummated," Arman confirmed, lips curling in a very feline manner.

"Very, very consummated," Ren affirmed, trying to keep his face straight. "Sorry, My Queen."

Roslyn leaned in and whispered, "Good?"

"Roslyn!" both of her parents chastised, scandalized.

Subtly, Ren gave her a wink and thumbs up, which made her grin like a demented elf. Galvath choked on a laugh, poorly disguising it as a cough instead. Ren had the notion he'd be invited out for a drink at the soonest possible opportunity, and grilled.

Feeling like someone needed to head this off before it became an outright argument that ended with beheadings—Queen Eloise had those assassin eyes again that normally preceded lines like 'off with his head'—Ren cleared his throat. "My Queen, My King, please calm yourselves. We have no way of knowing if I'll be able to live in Brahms Fortress at this point in time. We have not had the opportunity to inform Arman's family about this. We don't know how they're going to take the news."

Immediately switching to his defense, Queen Eloise demanded, "Surely you don't think they'll disown him? Or reject you as their son-in-law?"

"I'm a man," he reminded her patiently. "They have high hopes on him marrying, yes, but also producing more children to join the rest of their grandchildren. They likely won't know what to make of him marrying me instead."

Queen Eloise got a stubborn set to her jaw. "They had better accept you. I won't take it well otherwise."

"My Queen," Ren groaned, not sure whether to hug her for that statement or be worried about his immediate future. "You can't force people to love you."

Charles cleared his throat and rescued the conversation before it spiraled into threats. "I think what he was trying to get at, Mother, was that they might end up here by default depending on how the Brahms family takes this. Even if his fears aren't proven true, I don't think we need to immediately find a new warden. General, correct me if I'm wrong, but I believe your father to still be in good health?"

"He is," Arman confirmed with a nod. "Knees are troubling him some, but he's well other than that."

"I would imagine he could manage the defenses of Brahms Fortress for some years to come," Charles added pointedly for his mother's benefit. "Say, perhaps even another twenty years? Excellent. You see, Mother? Ren can still serve here for at least another two decades before we'll have to find a replacement."

"Certainly, we will be glad to keep him longer," King Gerhard stated, also eyeing his wife cautiously, as one would a snake poised to strike. "Eloise, dearest, I know you're upset at the possibility of losing Ren, but you've also been worried about him for years. He's found happiness with a man that we can all trust. Isn't that wonderful news?"

Deflating, Queen Eloise admitted, "Yes, of course it is. I just... oh, bother. General Brahms, I wish to strongly impress on you that I want Ren to stay as warden for as long as possible."

"Easily done," Arman assured her, mellowing now that he was getting his way.

"The last time I saw him, Lord Brahms swore up and down he'd never retire," Ren added in, hoping to bank her ire even further. "He said we'd have to put him in a grave first. So I think I can remain here for some time, My Queen."

"Good. But General, what is your take on this? Do you think your family will object to your marriage?"

Proving he'd already thought about this, Arman instantly shook his head. "He's already a son to them."

"So you think they'll be accepting of this. I believe you to be right." With a knowing look at Ren, she offered, "Perhaps it is your experience in your home country that inclines you to believe that you won't be accepted here?"

Ren really wished he could refute that, but she might very well be right. "I hope it is only that, at least."

"I trust that it is until proven otherwise. I will consider the matter settled for the moment, then." Queen Eloise relaxed her shoulders, tension easing out of her, and stared at Arman for a long moment before admitting, "I am glad. Truly. I would not have parted with him for anyone else. You, at least, I can trust to cherish him properly."

"Yes, Your Majesty," Arman agreed simply. "After all, I loved him first."

"That you did. And brought him home with you, and then shared him with us, and I'm grateful for that. Grateful enough that I won't murder you for taking him away again, tempting though that is." Queen Eloise didn't entirely sound as if she jested.

Alexandria finally proved to be a friend and diverted the topic. "General, Ren, you say that you haven't notified your family yet? Do you have any plans for how you wish to publicly announce your marriage, or when you'll hold a more proper ceremony?"

"None," Ren admitted. "Part of our deal was that he would give his mother full reign in that department. If she doesn't wish to, then we'll think about it."

"If she doesn't wish to," Queen Eloise informed them tartly, "then I will."

"Of course we will." King Gerhard seemed relieved the worst was apparently over. "But I think we should give Ren at least some time to go and visit his new family, don't you, dearest? Will two weeks be enough time, Ren?"

"I would imagine so, My King," Ren agreed equably, trying not to show how nervous that idea made him.

"Then two weeks it shall be. I'll let you arrange your substitute with Frei. In the meantime…" the king came around and offered a hand, which Ren took in a strong grip. "My heartfelt congratulations. To you as well, General. I never would have expected it, but am both relieved and delighted that you chose each other. Many blessings upon you both."

Touched at this free acceptance, Ren beamed back at him. "Thank you."

19

Of course, after that, the whole palace seemed to know that he was married, and to whom. Ren couldn't go five steps without someone congratulating him. Some were confused, others curious, and a few downright lewd in their speculative questions. Ren patiently responded to the first, answered the second, and gave ridiculous replies to the third.

Not his fault they really believed you could only have sex while bent over and touching your toes.

Alright, perhaps a smidge his fault.

He'd feel bad about it at some point. After he stopped snickering.

Still, all of these claps on the backs and hugs and congratulations warmed his heart considerably. How differently Aart looked at this versus the rest of the world. Here, they looked at a man newly married, and felt happiness that he'd found someone to spend his life with, and nothing more. It perversely saddened him. Couldn't everyone else see it the same way?

Shaking off the thought, he focused on organizing things so he could leave. He'd spent the last week organizing his affairs here so he could take his vacation and go to Brahms Fortress. Ren dearly wished he could just pack a bag and go, but unfortunately, he had too much paperwork to do, and loose ends to tie up before he could manage it. If he hustled, he felt reasonably sure he could handle the bulk of the work in about two days, and then hand the follow-up to Hartmann.

Although, he still had to deal with Deidrick Giles, too. Which would involve telling Arman about how his seal came up during the trial, which he really, really didn't want to delve into. But he couldn't put it off much longer, either. Dammit.

"Ren."

Turning in his chair, he spied his deputy warden and waved him in. "Speak of the devil. I was just thinking about you."

"Why are you in your office at seven in the evening?" Hartmann asked him with considerable asperity.

Pushing away from his desk—carefully, as the stacks of paperwork threatened an avalanche—he turned to regard the man face on and sniped back, "Because if I leave you with all of this work to do, you won't get home until midnight for the rest of the week, and your wife will murder me."

"And if you don't go home at a reasonable time to *your* husband, what do you think he's going to do to me?" Hartmann retorted, crossing his arms over his chest and giving Ren a hard glare. "And for the record, I'm more scared of your husband than my wife."

"Why, because he's armed?" Ren personally wouldn't put it past Heidi to chase Hartmann around with a butcher knife. She had that kind of temper.

"No, because he has a whole army at his beck and call."

Snorting, Ren agreed, "You make an excellent point there. Don't worry, I know how to distract him."

Giving him a look of abject pity, Hartmann shook his head. "You haven't been married long, so let me give you some advice. Not all problems can be solved by sex."

"Hartmann," Ren responded patiently, "I wasn't referring to just sex. Remember, I've known this man almost six years. Even when we were just friends I could still distract him."

An odd look crossed over Hartmann's face, as if he didn't quite believe this statement. "You really weren't lovers at all during that time?"

Having run into this question more than once, Ren had already grown heartily tired of answering it. He dredged up patience from somewhere. "We really weren't. He surprised me as much as anyone with the proposal. In fact, we'd never even kissed each other until the morning he proposed."

"Huh. We all could have sworn…" Hartmann trailed off thoughtfully. "But now that I think of it, it makes sense. You'd never have gotten involved with Giles if you and General Brahms were intimate."

"Thank you for realizing that. Most of the palace hasn't. Now, why are you here this late, anyway?"

"Ran an errand for Heidi, and remembered halfway home that

she had a question for you," Hartmann admitted. "She wants to know what to get you two for a wedding present."

Ren didn't even have to think about that one, not from Heidi. "Can she make us a large quilt like the one you have on your bed?"

"You really want that?" Hartmann asked in surprise. "Granted, it's very comfortable, but you've got the finest seamstresses in the palace at your disposal."

"That quilt is beautiful and your wife's skills are on par with theirs," Ren assured him. "And you can tell her I said so. One just like it, please, but maybe with a bit more blue?"

"She'd be delighted," Hartmann assured him. "She's always looking for a project. She won't be able to get it to you anytime soon, though. A quilt that large takes her about four months to make."

Ren shrugged this concern off. "We'll have a formal wedding ceremony in several months; she can always give it to us then."

"So, you are going to properly celebrate? Good, that was her other question. Alright, I'll pass the request along." Shaking a stern finger at him, Hartmann ordered. "I realize that we have a lot to do to prepare for Prince Charles and Princess Alexandria returning to Scovia, but stop for the night. Go home before your husband comes looking for you. Trust me, it's not pretty when they lose patience and come after you themselves."

"I will, I will," Ren flapped a hand, waving him off. "Go home. No wait, did you get that formal request for help off to Bhodhsa?"

"Well, I delivered it to Postmaster Diede, but I don't think he sent it out yet. Why?"

"I had a thought." More than one, in fact. Ren knew that the Scovians wanted to do their own version of a formal engagement party for the two upcoming royals, and that Alexandria had her own loose ends to tie off at home before she could formally marry Charles and move to Aart. But having the two of them travel back to Scovia before they knew who was after her gave Ren grey hairs. If they absolutely had to travel a month from now, he either wanted full cooperation from the country they were traveling through, or the culprits from the first attempt caught. Preferably both. "As it happens, I'm very well acquainted with one of their generals. I'd like to drop a hint that we'd prefer to work with him when forming up a guard for the trip through Bhodhsa."

Hartman blinked in mild surprise. "I didn't know you had friends in Bhodhsa. And their general, really? When did you meet, during the war?"

"Precisely. I made friends with a lot of people during the war. In-between fighting people, all you had to do was long marches and camp chores, so it left a lot of time on a man's hands. We ended up talking to each other by default, and made fast friends in the process. I'm not just saying I want O'Broín here because he's a friend of mine, though. He's got a good head on his shoulders, knows the lay of the land, and I trust him to protect people properly. If I have a choice on who to protect Prince Charles and Princess Alexandria's backs, I want O'Broín."

"Did you say all of that to Charles?" Hartmann inquired.

"Just now thought of it," Ren admitted, feeling somewhat sheepish. He really should have considered it before, when Alexandria informed him of her decision to go home for five months, but he hadn't. Too many details cluttering up his brain space, clearly, as he really should have. "I'll pass it along to everyone in the morning, I just thought it might be best if the request went through right the first time instead of an amended letter chasing after it."

"Well, we can send a runner to Diede, asking him to hold the letter for now. I'll do it, but only if you leave that chair right now."

"I just have to sort the last of this correspondence, and then I'll be caught up with today." Ren waved the last letter in illustration, picking up the letter opener and slotting it under the flap.

Hartmann planted his shoulders against the doorframe. "I don't believe you. I'm supervising until you actually leave."

"Such a cynical, mistrustful man you are," Ren mourned, ripping up the last inch of the envelope and setting the opener aside. As he pulled the folded sheet out, a fine powder escaped at the same time. Opening the page, he stared at the blank sheet, perplexed. "How odd, there's nothing—"

The powder touched his fingers and he paused, staring at it hard. The fine grains with a yellow tint to them sparkled dully against his skin. He hadn't seen it in years, hadn't thought about it in nearly as long, but Ren recognized it readily. "Damn it all to fucking hell!"

Hartmann jerked away from the door jamb, coming to him. "What?"

"STOP," Ren barked, halting his friend in his tracks. "I've just been poisoned."

Hartmann stared at him in alarm, eyes wide as he stared at the letter still in Ren's hands. "Are you certain?"

"I wish I wasn't. No, it might be good I recognize this. Hartmann, send for the palace doctor immediately, tell him that I need belladonna, and I need it now. Also, spread the word that any letter with no sender's address on it is to be immediately set aside and not opened."

Nodding shortly, Hartmann sprinted out of Ren's office, his footsteps echoing through the hallway, overlaying his calls for help.

Ren carefully put the letter on a side table, on top of a clean cloth he kept there. He wanted to preserve the evidence but also give them a safe way of carrying it. He didn't have much time, perhaps an hour before he started to feel the effects. Dammit, it just figured. He finally realized his fantasy of marrying a good man and he'd end up dead a week later.

Although if he knew his husband, Arman would raise him from the dead just to kill him all over again for falling into such a trap.

With the letter set aside, he went to the other corner and divested the vase of its flowers, using the water inside to rinse his hands. It did not do a thorough job, but hopefully took the worst off. Ren was at least confident he wouldn't spread the poison about if someone carelessly touched him. Still, he'd feel better once he thoroughly scrubbed his skin with a brush and some strong soap.

Worried about his ring, as his fingers already seemed to be swelling a little, he slipped it off and put it into a secure pocket. He didn't want to be forced to cut it off later.

Fucking hell, who had poisoned him? Ren had been lulled into a false sense of security as they had supposedly caught the troublemakers, and there hadn't been any incidents the whole week. They'd obviously failed to catch everyone. Or had they? With a letter, this could be a very long ranged attack.

Worry resonated in his chest like a living heartbeat. Would the physician have enough belladonna on hand to treat him? They wouldn't have a lot of time to send someone out into the city, and this late at night, most of the pharmacists would be closed. Treated quickly, this shouldn't be fatal, but time was not on Ren's side.

Three sets of footsteps returned—Hartmann, Chaz, and a young man Ren recognized as the palace physician's assistant. Hartmann's face was flushed from all of the exercise, expression grim. "Ren, you're not the only one poisoned. Princess Alexandria's been hit as well."

Arman knew fear intimately well. He'd faced it on battlefields most of his adult life, he'd faced it as a child whenever the Zaytsevians attacked his home, and again recently on a personal level, afraid Ren wouldn't accept him. But all of that seemed to pale to the fear coursing through him now, as he took the stairs up to the second level of the palace at breakneck speed. The fear tore at his heart, strained his nerves, and threatened to send him to his knees altogether. It ate at every thought so that he couldn't think of anything but getting to Ren.

He burst into Princess Alexandria's room just ahead of the runner who'd been sent to fetch him. The princess lay on her bed with the physician's assistant hovering over her, washing her hands for some reason. Ren sat at the foot of the bed, a basin in front of him, his hands damp and a yellow tint to his skin. The physician hovered near him, taking quick notes on a piece of paper. The rest of the royal family gathered near them both, keeping clear to not impede the frantically working men.

He went straight for Ren, barely stopping himself from crushing the man to his chest.

Ren cut himself off as he spied Arman and issued a warning of, "Wait, don't touch my hands. I haven't been completely cleaned of the poison yet."

Heeding the warning, Arman sank to his knee and reached for Ren's face instead. He didn't like the way sweat rolled from Ren's temples and down his front, soaking his shirt, or the labored way Ren's breathing rattled in his chest, or the hunched way he sat, as if sitting straight proved too much effort. Pinning the physician with a glare, he growled, "You'll save them."

"I can," the physician assured him strongly. "Fortunately for us all, Warden Ren recognizes what this is and knows how to counteract it. Warden, after I strain the leaves, then what?"

"Soak it in alcohol for ten minutes, then set it in a hot pan of water. We need to breathe in the fumes for fifteen minutes. We might have to repeat that process up to three times. It's a matter of timing, after that. You have to keep us breathing. This poison directly interferes with the lungs. If you can get at least the first dose of the antidote into our lungs fast enough, you'll win half the battle."

With a nod, the man wasted no more time discussing the situation, but immediately stood and ran from the room. Arman assumed he would head for the tools he needed to follow Ren's instructions and paid him no more attention. The poison affected breathing? Was that why Ren's breath came out in those harsh, wet-sounding pants?

Bending, Ren went for the basin at his feet and picked up the brush and bar of soap near it, scrubbing at his skin carefully. "Sorry, Arman. I was a bit careless."

Terror still shook him hard enough Arman didn't quite trust himself to speak. His voice wavered as he asked, "What happened?"

Hearing that, Ren paused and looked up at him, regret in his eyes. "Someone sent a letter to both me and the princess. Inside was a powdered poison that came into contact with my skin as soon as I drew the blank letter out."

"How dangerous is it?"

"Normally it isn't, not really. My people use a variant of this, a milder form to deal with insects. It's only dangerous if you're in contact with it for long periods of time, or you carelessly breathe it in. We were all taught how to safeguard against it in the army—just in case—as we're always tramping through fields during the war." Ren stopped scrubbing for a moment, a green cast to his face. "Damn, I forgot about the nausea. Princess Alexandria, if you feel like throwing up, do. It's one of the side effects."

"Now you warn me," Alexandria groaned from the bed.

Sensing his husband's need, Arman quickly fetched an empty bowl from a nearby table and brought it over. Ren promptly made use of it, although he didn't throw up much, having not had a meal in several hours. Grimacing, he wiped his face. "Thanks. Gods above, I'm going to murder the bastard who did this with my bare hands."

"You'll have to beat me to it," Charles promised darkly from his position near Alexandria.

Coming closer to the bed, King Gerhard inquired, "Ren, what other side effects are there?"

"Lung paralysis, sweating, cramping, loss of strength in the muscles, twitching, diarrhea," Ren rattled off promptly, giving the occupants on the bed a sympathetic smile. "All the fun things."

"It amazes me you can joke in a time like this," Queen Eloise fumed, pacing back and forth in short strides, her expression drawn and pinched.

Arman could have told her that Ren had a terrible habit of cracking bad jokes under tense circumstances. He'd always been torn between laughing and hitting the man for it. Right now, gratefulness won out, because if Ren could joke, he knew how to handle the situation. When Ren went quiet and still, that's when they were really in trouble. "You'll live."

Giving him a soft smile, Ren assured him, "We'll both live and we won't have any major side effects from this. The one upside to it is if we survive the night, it won't damage us the rest of our lives. We're fortunate that the physician keeps a good quantity of belladonna on hand."

"I'm confused on that point," Charles admitted, shifting up enough to see Ren more comfortably, although he maintained his grip on Alexandria. "I thought belladonna a poison?"

"In large quantities, or in a concentrated form, it certainly is. But most medicines are poisons if used in the wrong way," the physician's assistant answered absently. "Princess, I believe your hands are safe now. Warden, how are you?"

"I think I'm safe as well. I've been over them five times."

"That should do it," the assistant agreed, pushing scraggly blond hair out of his eyes. "General, if you'll take your, ah, husband and sit him over there on the couch? Support him against your own body, it will help when the weakness hits. He needs to stay semi-upright to help with the breathing."

Glad for something to do, Arman immediately lifted Ren to his feet, supporting him as they shuffled the short distance over to the couch. He sat first, pulling Ren down with him, and his husband settled against his chest with a grateful sigh. Ren felt entirely too hot and damp to his liking. He'd seen Ren injured before, of course, but that didn't mean he'd become accustomed to it. If anything, this time was worse compared to previous times.

Roslyn came over with a damp towel in hand, leaning in to lightly clean the sweat from Ren's face, her bottom lip caught between her teeth.

"This changes matters," King Gerhard said to the room at large. "We thought we'd caught whoever was behind the attacks, but clearly we missed at least one."

"They were too clever to appear openly," Queen Eloise commented, her eyes spitting fire. "And it was shrewd of them to send this attack from afar. But it also gives us something to trace them with, I think. General, is your spy still available?"

"He is, Your Majesty," Arman answered tightly. "I'll set him on this immediately."

"I think we need to do more than that," King Gerhard disagreed, his eyes staring blankly at the far wall, a hand scratching idly at his chin. "Ren, as of right now, you're off-duty for the next month. Don't look at me like that, Roslyn, I have to. He's now a victim. Legally speaking, he can't investigate his own attack."

"Oh," the princess acquiesced in a small voice.

"Besides, I think he's due some recovery time and he certainly is due the two weeks I promised him," Gerhard tacked on, more for his daughter's benefit than anyone else's, as they understood what he meant by the order. "A month will hopefully be sufficient to catch who did this. I hate that it's come to this, but I think we need to finally put the palace grounds under second point of contact and thoroughly investigate. I want this person rooted out of my country."

"It will be hard for just Hartmann to manage," Ren objected.

King Gerhard gave him a reassuring nod. "I realize that. Is there someone who you can recommend to aid Deputy Warden Hartmann in this task?"

"Colonel Konrad," Arman answered immediately, not even needing to think.

Ren nodded against his chest. "I second that, My King. Konrad is infinitely trustworthy and knows how to get the job done. I can hand your safety off to him without a single qualm."

"Then General, I request and require that you give Colonel Konrad orders to support Deputy Warden Hartmann as he investigates, and aid us in Our time of need."

"Send a message now," Ren murmured. "It's alright, I'll be fine for a few minutes."

Arman knew that. Forcing himself to let go of Ren, that was the problem. Every time he let Ren out of his sight, something increasingly terrible happened, and the fear now lived in him that the next event would make him a widower. He pushed the fear aside as unreasonable, as this room had all of the protection that could be offered, with multiple guards and bodyguards in every corner and at every entrance. Galvath especially looked ready to commit murder at the slightest provocation. With a nod, Arman placed a quick kiss against the top of that silky dark hair, then pulled himself free long enough to borrow pen and paper from Alexandria's writing desk and scribble out a note. Roslyn leaned in to support Ren when he moved, and he cast her a grateful look, which she returned with a determined, if worried, nod.

Not feeling up to writing a full letter explaining, he only stated that Konrad was to come at once to the palace and wrote in a pass at the bottom of the letter instructing a guard to escort him directly to Alexandria's room. Then he took it to Ren for his signature, as only the warden could authorize such a pass.

Ren took it, eyes skimming over the words, then sighed in resignation. "Husband, do we need to revisit Rule One? When giving orders, said orders must be more than a location."

Why was he being so nitpicky on the details now, of all times? "We'll brief him when he gets here."

With a long-suffering look at him, Ren added in a few more lines of his own, then deigned to sign the bottom of the page. "Fillmore! Come take this, deliver it, and escort Colonel Konrad to us as quickly as possible."

"Yes, sir," Fillmore assured him, taking the folded page and immediately rushing out the door.

Not knowing what else to do, Arman slipped back into position behind Ren. He frowned when, this time, Ren entrusted more of his weight. No, more like, he didn't have the strength to sit up on his own without straining. Where was that damned physician?

They waited in a tense silence for several minutes before footsteps and sloshing noises heralded the return of the physician and two more assistants. They had steaming kettles, large brass tubs, and towels in their hands. The physician went directly to Ren, prying open the lid of the glass jar and displaying the contents, which looked like shredded leaves floating in pure alcohol. "What do you think?"

"Perfect," Ren assured him, breathing now very strained. "It's the right color. Strain out the alcohol and tip only the leaves into the water."

Roslyn left the couch so that they had room to maneuver. Low stools were brought into position and Alexandria moved to a chair so she could sit. Then the two victims leaned over the bowls with towels draped over their heads, encouraging the steam directly at their faces. Arman held Ren steady through this process, ready to crawl out of his own skin. He knew Ren was comfortable with basic medicinal practice; he'd seen him use it in the field. But this wasn't just trusting Ren's knowledge. It was seeing the person he loved most suffering, and Arman had no defense against that.

The only thing that helped him from losing his mind entirely was the way Ren's breathing went from strained to a deeper, easier rhythm. He didn't sound normal, not yet, but he no longer sounded like a leaking blacksmith's bellows either. The antidote was taking effect.

"Time," the physician announced, pulling the towel off Alexandria's head. "How are you both feeling? You sound better; not as labored as before."

Ren sat back, the top of his head now completely damp and sweaty, trusting his full weight to Arman. "I do feel better, but I think another dose wouldn't hurt."

"I still feel very nauseous and weak," Alexandria admitted.

"Once more, then," the physician agreed, coming around to check Ren's eyes with a practiced air. "But let's give you a minute to cool. N-o sense getting overheated and dizzy with it. I'll have more hot water brought up from the kitchens."

As the physician moved off again, Ren tilted his face so he could whisper against Arman's jaw, "I won't leave you just yet."

"You'd better not leave me at all," Arman responded, voice hoarse from shoving the words through a constricted throat.

Smiling, Ren pressed a kiss against his chin. "Not until we're old and grey, I promise."

20

Arman did not sleep at all that night.

He couldn't. The physician offered up one of his assistants to stay and watch Ren, and they kept the man nearby, but Arman spent the entire night propped up against the headboard, watching his husband's chest. Up, down, breath in, breath out. It unnerved him, how close Ren had come to being unable to do such a basic bodily function.

For a moment, after getting the message that Ren had been poisoned, Arman had faced the possibility of the love of his life dying. Nothing but the abyss had stared back at him. He never ever wanted to be that close to madness ever again.

Charles had given them his bedroom so the physician could stay on hand for both patients. The prince refused to move from his fiancée's side anyway. From Arman's position on the bed, he could see the mantel clock ticking away the time. With each passing hour, Ren's breathing became steadier, easier, no longer a labored effort. By the time dawn flirted on the horizon, his skin no longer contained an unhealthy cast, and he'd ceased sweating.

The physician's assistant—Arman never had gotten the man's name—trundled over to the bed in a tired manner, checking Ren's temperature and listening to his breathing, then gave Arman a satisfied nod. "He's fine, General," he whispered. "He's past the crucial stage and well into recovery now. I dare say he'll be up and running about as normal within three days."

Arman's eyes closed in relief. "Thank you."

"Rest," the assistant suggested gently. "You need it now more than him. Your husband is fine."

Nodding, Arman waited for the man to leave and only then maneuvered around until he lay flat against the bed. Then he thought better of it, reaching up to tie a lock of Ren's hair around his wrist so the man couldn't quietly sneak out of bed without alerting him. Satisfied, he snuggled up against Ren's back and immediately fell asleep.

What felt like seconds later, a pained yelp woke him, and he jerked upright, disoriented and unfocused. "Wha'?"

"Arman," Ren scolded, tugging at his wrist. "Why did you tie my hair to you? It's a poor time for a prank."

"Never a poor time for pranks," Arman argued without thinking about it. Then he blinked his eyes into focus, gathering his scattered wits through what felt like a fog of fleece. "And I did that to keep you from sneaking out of bed."

Ren paused in untying his hair, giving him a look that balanced between being tender and exasperated. "You're tired, you need more rest. You probably didn't sleep until well after midnight, when I passed through the crucial stage. It's barely eight now. Go back to sleep."

"The hell I will." Arman glared right back at him. He'd slept, what, four hours? Sufficient to be going on with. He reached over to throw back the covers.

Ren slapped a hand down, keeping him under the blanket. "Arman. You're barely able to focus your eyes. You've been in crisis mode ever since you came home, scarcely getting enough sleep, and then last night drained whatever energy reserves you had left. Sleep. I promise I'm not going far."

"No," Arman argued stubbornly.

"Arman—"

"No."

"Will you be reasonable?"

"No."

"You are seriously violating Rule Four right now. You're not allowed to argue with just one word."

Arman eyed the crossed arms over Ren's chest, the stubborn lift of his chin, the way his eyes narrowed to mere slits, and re-evaluated pissing off his husband at this juncture. Even though he really wanted to maintain the 'no', as Ren had never figured out how to effectively argue against that. "Every time I turn my back, someone attacks you. I can't risk it."

Ren opened his mouth on a protest, thought about it, then subsided with a year's worth of sighs. "It certainly feels that way. Alright, I understand your worry. All I was going to do was check in with Hartmann and Frei, perhaps catch Konrad up to speed."

"Done and done," Arman assured him. "All three came in last night after you fell asleep and we conferred with each other. They'll come here if they have questions."

"So, they're already working the case?" Ren's irritation eased at this reassurance. "Alright. There's not much I can do to help them, unfortunately. King Gerhard is right, I can't be involved or it will jeopardize the evidence, and I truly don't want to do that."

Relieved he saw reason, Arman grunted agreement.

Getting that shrewd look in his eye, Ren offered, "How about this? I'll take a long soak in the tub, get detoxed, and wash all of this sweat off of me. I'll sit down after that and write a full report of everything I remember for them to use as evidence. While I'm doing that, you keep sleeping. I promise not to eat anything, open any letters, or let anyone in the room while you're asleep. Deal?"

That sounded better than Arman could hope. Ren could be ridiculously stubborn when he set his mind to something. It took him a moment to realize that Ren was actively trying to compromise with him to keep them from arguing. As much as he wanted to be up while Ren was up, he also recognized he was not functioning at his best. A few more hours of sleep would do them both good. "Alright."

"Good. Then lay back down, darling, and sleep."

Arman had his head on the pillow before the obvious hit. Catching Ren's arm, he drew him back. "Wait. Darling?"

Uncertain, Ren responded cautiously, "No good?"

"I like it," Arman whispered. It was the first time Ren had addressed him with an endearment.

A small smile on his face, Ren leaned in to press a kiss to Arman's forehead. "Then I'll call you that way. Sleep."

Content for the first time in what felt like years, Arman let his eyes close.

◆

When Arman woke up the second time, he found Ren had been good to his word. No visitors, no food, just a handwritten report and a clean Ren. They ordered food—which was rigorously tested for poison even before it reached their plates—and ate a quiet lunch. Arman needed quiet. He needed the space to just be with his husband without a threat breathing down their necks. Arman might have lived twenty-five years without Ren, but he no longer remembered how he'd done that. He had no desire to relearn the skill.

Ren, of course, needed to turn in his report and check in with his two deputy wardens before they could follow orders and prepare to leave for Brahms Fortress. Arman didn't mind a quick stop in at the office on their way back.

Reaching the office, he found Hartmann in his chair with Konrad hovering nearby, both of them staring at the same piece of paper.

Stopping in the doorway, Ren called out, "Knock, knock."

Head coming up sharply, Konrad turned to greet him with a relieved smile. "Of course you're already on your feet."

"Of course, I'm invincible, you know that," Ren riposted neatly. He held out a hand to the man, clasping forearms strongly. Konrad's tight grip looked borderline painful. Arman knew Konrad must have been worried, as the concern was still clear to see.

"It's good you two came when you did," Konrad informed them, steering Ren to a chair and practically forcing him into it. "I have a bone to pick with you both. Did you really get married without even a word to us?"

Without compunction, Ren pointed to Arman, who perched on the side of his chair. "His fault."

Arman gave him an exasperated look which Ren returned, wrinkling his nose in a childish gesture. Ren had warned him the morning he proposed he wouldn't shoulder any of the blame for the fallout. He obviously meant it. With a brief eyeroll, Arman admitted, "It was mine. There was a reason for it."

"We'll celebrate it properly in a few months," Ren tacked on with a smile for his friend. "Don't worry, you can celebrate with us then."

"I'd better," Konrad warned them, softening a little. "Still, glad to see the two of you together officially. We'd just about given up all hope of it happening."

Arman had doubted it himself, more than once. It pleased him that no one questioned their marriage. Mostly because statements like that put a smile on Ren's face every time.

"Konrad, thanks for coming. Truly. I can't think of someone I'd rather have here."

"I'm very glad you did call me," the colonel responded darkly, "as I want first crack at this. We've gathered up all the evidence;

we're going over it now. Hartmann was thankfully able to give me an eyewitness account."

"And I wrote a formal statement." Ren handed it over, torn about doing so. He'd made it clear earlier to Arman that part of him still really wanted to pursue the matter himself. Still, he understood the reasons why he couldn't, and Konrad wouldn't rest until he either got to the bottom of the matter or had no avenues left to pursue.

"Thank you, that will help." Konrad perused it, reading through quickly.

Biting his lip, Ren shot Arman a look that he unfortunately knew well. That half-wince of anticipation; the way his hand latched onto his hair, gripping it strongly; implied Ren worried about a future reaction of Arman's. It spoke of trepidation. Arman dreaded that particular expression, as it never prefaced anything good. He couldn't imagine what Ren would hesitate to say in front of him. Arman stroked the back of Ren's head and down before resting on his shoulder. "What, love?"

Ren leaned into the touch for a moment, gathering in a breath. His jaw firmed into a determined line that Arman could read blindfolded. Whatever this was, Ren hated it but would force himself to face it anyway. "I might have an idea of who was behind the poisoning. Even if it isn't him, there's something I need you to investigate. I started the investigation myself, trying to find solid evidence, but since I'm leaving, you'll have to pick it up and continue."

"Alright...?" Konrad drew out, encouraging him.

"You heard that one of the issues brought up in the trial was my signature stamp?" Ren didn't really wait for a response, although Konrad nodded, confirming this. "There's only a few people who even know what that is, much less have seen it and know where I keep it. Out of those people, only one would ever wish to betray me."

"Giles," Konrad and Hartmann realized in unison, Hartmann resigned, Konrad angry.

Arman went very, very still. He realized immediately why Ren hadn't wanted to say this in front of him. Ren might regret the whole affair but he'd largely put it behind him as well. However, he knew that Arman hated any mention of it, that it hurt him on some level. For his sake, he wouldn't breathe a word or reference that time unless it was strictly necessary.

Like now.

"He saw me use it once. Right as I was posting it to my brother, actually. He asked what I was doing, and I...told him."

It didn't take much in the way of imagination. Arman could see how it had likely played out. Of course Ren hadn't thought anything of it. Why should he? He was just writing his brother, sending along his stamp. It wasn't anything earth-shattering.

"And no one else knows about it?" Konrad double checked, voice very carefully neutral.

Shaking his head, Ren kept his gaze locked on Konrad. "Arman, Frei, and you are the only other ones who've even seen it. Well, and Postmaster Diede, of course. I know it wasn't any of you."

Dead silence fell, stretching out, eerily similar to a sepulcher. Arman felt like killing something, so the mood was accurate. Hartmann took one look at his face and moved two careful steps backward, out of range. Konrad, made of sterner material, grimaced but held firm. Ren tilted his head slightly toward Arman with a tight expression on his face, not needing to look to see how Arman took this news.

Hartmann, proving to be a man of unquestionable courage, cleared his throat and spoke first. "It might be hard to prove the link, as it will likely fall to his word against yours, but we'll investigate it. If nothing else, it tells us that he still carries a hard grudge against you and is willing to work with your enemies. He might prove to be a weak link into the group, which we need at the moment."

Ren nodded. "Thank you, my friend. That's all the dark secrets I have to share with you today. Hand me that stack of paperwork on the side; only I can handle it."

"How about I send it to you tomorrow?" Hartmann offered. "I don't think you should be working today."

Ren couldn't exactly debate that, as he'd already promised several people that he wouldn't. "Alright. I'll make sure it's all sorted before I leave. Hartmann, my office is yours."

"I'll try not to destroy it," Hartmann joked, his tone strained. "I'll keep you updated on our progress."

"Thanks."

It felt rather like Ren had lit a cannonball and handed it to him. Arman wanted to drop it, but didn't dare. He had to handle it properly or it would blow up in both of their faces. Ren left the office with Arman hot on his heels but neither man spoke until they'd gained Ren's—their—apartment. Only then, with the door behind them, in a quiet space with no audience, did Ren face Arman squarely.

Arman stared back at him, jaw clenched, a tic spasming near his eye. "You didn't tell me this on purpose."

"I was…." His eyes skittered off to the side, as if he suddenly found himself incapable of looking Arman in the face.

Shit. He never wanted Ren to react like that around him. Arman took in a deep breath, regaining his temper. Anger and harsh words would do nothing good right now, and he loathed fight with Ren. About anything, much less this.

"Ren." Arman's hands shaped Ren's face, bringing his chin back up, his anger calming but not dissipating. "Look at me, love."

With some difficulty, Ren managed. "I'm sorry. I know I should have told you. I just—"

"That whole affair hurt you, I know it did."

"And embarrassed me," Ren agreed, tired and strained. "But it's no excuse. I still should have said something to you."

"I understand why you didn't. I'm not very forgiving where Giles is concerned."

Ren lifted a shoulder in a brief shrug, agreeing, but his expression said he didn't fully concur. "It's more that whenever he's brought up, it hurts you. And every time I see that flash of anger and hurt on your face, I feel like I've betrayed you somehow, and it's *that* I can't stomach."

Dammit. He really had to control his reactions better. Or make peace with it somehow. Arman absolutely did not want to run Ren through a grinder repeatedly over one mistake, nor did he want Ren to develop the habit of keeping things from him. They'd managed a perfectly healthy and accepting relationship before getting married. He refused to have his jealousy mess that up now. "It's not you I'm mad at."

"It's Giles, I know," Ren agreed, nodding, still not looking directly at Arman.

"Mostly myself," Arman sighed. "My regret of not saying something two years ago runs very deep." Arman dropped a kiss on the top of his head, arms snug around Ren's shoulders. "This is as much my fault as yours, Ren."

Shaking his head, Ren leaned into the embrace, sighing as if Arman had lifted some heavy burden off his heart. "I vote we stack all of the blame on Giles, where it belongs. I don't think either of us deserves to be punished for that idiot's poor life decisions."

"Motion carried," he agreed, relieved. He'd avoided that exploding bomb after all. Thank all the gods Ren knew how to talk problems through with him.

Seizing the sides of his face with both hands, Ren looked squarely up at him, dark eyes fierce with emotion. "He has no part of my heart."

"I know," Arman soothed, voice low and caressing. "Shh, love, I know."

Ren folded himself into Arman's arms and held him tightly. Against his shirt, Ren whispered, "If I had known you were coming home to me like this, I would never have let him touch me."

"I know that too." Which was the other reason why Arman kept kicking himself. He could have had Ren for *years,* and avoided this whole fiasco if he'd just realized what was in front of him. But he needed to let it go, let all of it go, or risk hurting Ren again. Of the two of them, Ren had dealt with the lion's share of the pain. Arman shouldn't be adding to it. He deliberately relaxed his shoulders, pressing a kiss against that silky hair as he whispered, "No matter what happens, remember to tell me."

Ren nodded. "Promise."

"Good. Come lay down."

They might have barely been up three hours, but in truth, Ren still looked like something half-dead the cat had dragged in. Arman had rarely seen him so drained of energy, and having this semi-argument had done nothing to help Ren's recovery. The offer wasn't just for Ren's sake, as Arman needed an excuse to cuddle. Perhaps Ren sensed this, as he didn't protest. They stripped off jackets and boots, slipping under the top quilt to curl into each other.

As he lay snuggled against Ren's back, Arman fervently wished that every memory of Deidrick Giles would go straight to the ninth circle of hell. If he never had to deal with the man again, it would be too soon.

Hartmann lost no time in settling second point of contact over the palace. He and Konrad were on a warpath, questioning everything that happened, looking for any clue. Ren and Arman investigated everything in their own apartment with white gloves, but found nothing suspicious. Whoever attacked hadn't thought to try their apartment in the palace, at least.

Relieved to have a safe space still, Ren brought some of his paperwork from his office and tried again to tie up those loose ends so that Hartmann wouldn't have to deal with it. Arman wouldn't hear of them leaving for another two days, giving him time to get his usual health back. Hopefully, it would be enough time to finish the work off.

While he did that, Robert and Arman packed for their month-long jaunt. Ren wanted to pick up a few things for his new mother-in-law, as he knew that she liked certain creams and perfumes from Castel-de-Haut. He hadn't the time to get anything for her on his last visit, due to its emergency nature, but he could now. Ren felt well enough that he almost went directly out into the city to shop, then realized that he should probably get something for Anthony too, but what?

And Arman hadn't been home in over two years. Surely he'd want to buy presents for his parents as well.

No, he'd better meet up with his husband first, then go shopping.

Exiting the small study room, he found Robert in the process of unpacking the trunk, clothes in stacks all over the carpeted floor. The batman looked up at his entrance and greeted, "You're already finished, sir?"

"Ha! I wish. It'll take another day at least before that happens. I'm a little confused, aren't you supposed to be packing? Not unpacking."

"There's an odor coming from the bottom of the trunk," Robert explained, glaring at the beat-up black trunk in question. "I am trying to determine from where."

"Ah. I'll leave you to investigate, then. Where's Arman?"

"In the bedroom, sir."

With a wave of thanks, Ren stepped through to the other room. Robert had been very busy, as not only did another wardrobe reside next to his, but another shaving stand, and proper nightstands on either side of the bed. Ren had been using his chest to serve as one for so long, seeing it switched still surprised him. "Arman?"

Arman came out of the bathing room in nothing but pants and boots, his hair, neck, and part of his face damp. His hair had also noticeably gotten a cut, the loose curls now tamed back to a wave on top and a close cut along the sides. Ren let out a whistle. "Looking sharp, husband."

With a completely straight face, Arman stepped out of the

doorway and did a slow spin, like a model showing off.

Chuckling, Ren reached up to touch the shorter length, enjoying the bristly feel of it against his fingers. "I like it. You didn't like the scruffy look? Whyever not? It made you fluffy, like a cute little puppy. Why are you glaring at me; I'm complimenting you!"

Of course, Arman didn't believe that blatant lie. He moved in and stole Ren's mouth in a firm kiss before backing off with a smirk. "I like this new way of shutting you up."

"Me too," Ren agreed, licking his lips. "I'll have to give more smart-ass comments."

Rolling his eyes, Arman went back to rinsing the soap out of his hair. Ren almost hesitated, then realized he was being absurd and followed him in to the tiled room. "So, Robert gave you a haircut? That's a great idea, I think I'll ask him to do the same."

Arman froze and gave him a frown that bordered on a glare. Firmly, he shook his head.

"My hair is literally down to my hips," Ren pointed out, finding this protest absurd. "Any longer, I'll be sitting on it all the time. I've let it go too long; I need to lose a few inches."

Arman's frown deepened to a scowl.

"Seriously? Since when did you have a hair fetish?" Ren had not expected an argument about this, of all things.

Dropping the towel, Arman stepped away from the sink, then all the way in, caging Ren against the wall, their bodies pressed firmly together. It was the first time since his poisoning that Arman had initiated anything. Ren's heartbeat spiked, body tingling in anticipation as he really, really liked this position. Faces aligned to an almost-kiss, Arman whispered against his mouth, "Since I had that hair over me caressingly."

Ren shivered, as he knew the exact time Arman referred to, specifically the other night when he'd been deep inside the other man and enjoying every minute of it. He almost responded to the memory alone. Then, of course, Arman decided not to leave it at that and gave a subtle roll of his hips, teasing Ren's mouth with a kiss that promised everything.

It took a long minute for him to get his breath back, then of course he realized Arman's game plan. "You bastard. Did you deliberately give me a boner so I would be too embarrassed to go out there and ask Robert for a haircut?"

"Worked," Arman responded smugly.

Ren hit him for that, which did not have the desired effect, as Arman just dodged, chuckling. "Why did I marry you, again?"

Arman shrugged his ignorance, eyes sparkling, and returned to his hair.

He might have thought he'd won, but Ren was not a former general for nothing. Coming up from behind, he slid his hands slowly around Arman's waist, plastering himself against the man's back. Arman tensed, sensing Ren was up to something. Tilting a little on tip toe, Ren reached up and nibbled on Arman's ear, tasting soap ever so faintly but mostly him. As he did so, he slid his hand down to lightly dance his fingers between Arman's legs. In a throaty purr, he whispered, "How about you give me three inches? Just three inches, so I can actually sit without jerking my head back. I promise you won't miss it."

"Just three?" Arman asked suspiciously. He responded to Ren's touch, helpless not to do so, but that didn't mean he would fall for things so quickly.

"Promise." Ren slid his hands under the waistband, hunting for treasure. "Just three."

Grunting, Arman relaxed into Ren's embrace, enjoying the grip. "And you claim I don't play fair."

"Now who do you think I learned it from?"

※

Poor Robert probably knew what they'd gotten up to while he was hunting in a trunk for terrible smells. Judging from that indulgent smile, Ren had not been as successful in staying quiet as he thought he'd been. Oops. Right now, they were in the honeymoon stage, which inclined forgiveness, but that wouldn't hold out forever.

For the first time, Ren realized he really did have to get a bigger apartment. Or another suite of rooms for Robert. Something. Maybe he could maneuver to get one as a wedding present?

Deciding he would play dumb, Ren pinned a bright smile on his face and asked, "Robert, would you cut my hair too? Just three inches shorter, please."

Walking past, Arman amended, "Make that two."

Ren aimed a kick at his backside, making Arman laugh. "You

agreed! Three."

Nodding confirmation, Arman said, "Yes, two."

"You are a scullion," Ren accused, shaking a finger at him. "A false, disloyal man, who has all of the shame of a hump-backed alley cat. Three."

"Two."

"Three, you cream-faced toad."

"Two."

Ren threw up his hands and decided to ignore him. "Three inches, please, Robert. And afterward, I'll step out into the city and buy a few presents. I was going to ask my husband to go with me, but he's currently being a rat fink, so I suppose I'll go alone."

"Presents?" Arman queried, his teasing fading into a tone of confusion. "For whom?"

"Your mother and father, of course. Maybe a little something for your brothers as well; they're both expecting children soon."

Arman's eyes narrowed and he came to stand next to Ren, close but not quite touching. He studied Ren closely, in that penetrating way he had that made Ren feel as if he could see right through to the back of Ren's skull. "You don't need to buy anything."

Realizing Arman might have caught on to him, Ren tossed this aside, evading him. "Nonsense, I always pick up a few things for Mother. And it's only fair I do that for the rest of the family from time to time. I like them too; she's just easier to buy for, as I know what she wants."

This easy litany didn't fool Arman in the slightest, and he turned to Robert and gestured him toward the door.

Picking up the hint, the batman lifted a load of clothes, and brightly said, "I'll just be at the laundry. I'll cut your hair on my return, sir."

Dammit. Of course he couldn't fool Arman, why had he even tried? Ren couldn't bring himself to look at him, just stared at the glowing embers in the fireplace, hands crossed defensively over his chest.

"Ren." Arman cradled his head with both hands, gently bringing his head up. "Talk to me."

"That's rich," Ren snorted, still not able to meet his eyes. "For once, it's you asking me to talk instead of the other way around."

"Renjimantoro."

"Ouch, full name, huh." Ren blew out a breath and still couldn't meet Arman's eyes, instead staring at the far wall. In a small voice, he confessed, "I might be a little nervous."

"You're scared," Arman corrected, baffled. "I've never seen you scared before."

"Everything else I've ever faced, I knew how to face it." Ren felt like he really needed alcohol to take the sting out of this conversation. Where was an open bottle of rice wine when he needed one? "But this…Arman, I don't know how to face this. I know these people. I love them dearly. If they reject me—us—it'll hurt, and I don't know if my heart can take it."

"They won't."

Losing his temper, Ren's eyes finally snapped up to his. "You're so sure? I'm not. My parents didn't speak to me for two years when I told them I liked men. My mother cried, my father blamed himself. I left the house and joined the army just to get away from it all. This from the people that raised me. I know your parents think of me like a son, but it's so, so easy for people to turn their backs on each other. I'm afraid for me, but I'm mostly afraid for you because I don't want that to happen to you. I don't want you to lose them because of me."

"Shh." Arman dropped his hands to wrap him up in a tight hug. "Remember, they've already accepted you as you are. I don't think this will be any different."

Ren clutched him, burying his face into Arman's shoulder, choking back the urge to burrow in and never come out again. Arman was so sure that they wouldn't face any heartbreak, and he prayed it would play out that way. They'd already been so readily accepted here, that it gave him hope, but he couldn't silence the fears. Those fears lived in the back of his mind every moment, eroding his faith, wearing him steadily down.

Placing a kiss on the top of his head, Arman whispered against his hair, "You're worried about your brother too."

Sighing, Ren admitted against his shirt in a muffled voice, "It's illegal for men to get married in Shiirei. He accepts me, but I think our marriage will confound him."

"I think he'll be glad his younger brother is happy."

Since Arman had actually met his brother and knew him, Ren took some heart in these words. "You really think so?"

"He asked me to take care of you, last time I saw him."

"Wait, what?" Ren demanded sharply, pulling away enough that he could see Arman's face. "What were his exact words?"

Arman had to think for a moment to recall, "I leave Renjimantoro in your care."

"Holy hell," Ren breathed, stunned. "That's the traditional thing you say to someone who's engaged. Are you telling me that he knew, even then, that we'd…."

When he trailed off, Arman grinned at him. "See? Nothing to worry about."

"Holy hell," he repeated, his mind not producing any other words than that. "No, wait, that means he thought we were together back then. He thinks we've been together for *five years*."

Arman canted his head to the side, expression asking, 'what's your point?'

"Don't be obtuse, don't you see? He thinks that I literally eloped with you five years ago! That I followed you to this country because we were lovers."

"Ah." Arman thought about that for another moment. "That's good."

"That's good," Ren repeated in despair. "That's good, he says. I need to sit down. I can't believe that my brother seriously gave you permission to take me away to a different country. Worse, he thinks that I didn't have the guts to confess to him that we were lovers, but he still gave you permission anyway. I can't figure out if he's a complete idiot, or if he just loves me that much."

"Second option," Arman counseled, amused at his shock. "Takahiro's not an idiot."

"Not by any stretch of the imagination." Ren had to agree with him there. Out of the two of them, Takahiro was the brain of the family. Ren definitely weighed in on the 'brawn' side of the equation. He collapsed into a chair with a whoosh of displaced air. "Oh hell. Part of me is super happy about this; it means he really accepts you as my lover, but that also means I'm going to have to straighten him out on the whole thing. And he's finally going to ask the question that he should have asked five years ago: why by the gods would you follow a friend into a totally different country and not stay with your family?"

"You had a crush on me," Arman stated factually.

"How do you know that? I never said anything and I wasn't obvious."

Arman cocked an eyebrow an nth degree and just looked at him.

"Shut it, I was not! I played it off; people just thought we were really close, and I flirted just to tease you. Don't give me that smug look, you so did not know that I crushed on you back then."

His husband had the gall to reach over and pat the top of his head like a puppy looking for a treat.

"You did know," Ren groaned, defeated. "How did you know?"

Settling at his feet, Arman propped his folded arms on top of Ren's knees, looking up at him comfortably. "You kept feeding me."

"Ah?" Ren frowned, trying to remember from five years ago.

"You still feed me," Arman revised, eyes warm and affectionate. "Remember, how you explained the importance of food in your culture?"

Slowly, the memory came back to him. Right, Arman had seen a man taking bits of meat and vegetables from his own plate and putting them into the bowl of the woman sitting with him. He'd asked if that was something serious, as the woman kept blushing every time he did it. Ren had explained that feeding people in that way was a silent way of showing your love for the other person. He'd explained a lot of his culture to Arman in those early days and had paid little attention to his own words.

And then he'd developed a teensy crush for his friend, even though he'd known it wouldn't go anywhere, and couldn't resist showing him in some way that he cared for him. He'd developed the habit of putting choice pieces of meat or things he knew Arman liked into his bowl whenever they ate with each other. Realizing his mistake, Ren covered his eyes with one hand. "I did do that, didn't I? All the time."

"That's how I knew," Arman stated, reaching up to tug his hand down. "Don't be embarrassed."

"I am totally embarrassed. You realize that I didn't follow you here with any expectations, right? I didn't think for a minute we'd be lovers back then. I was honestly trying to be a good friend to you, and nothing more."

Arman kept his hand, twining their fingers together a little, not allowing him to duck away. "I know."

Despite how things turned out, Ren still wanted to go find a hole somewhere and bury his head in it. Then a thought struck, and he rolled it around in his mouth for a moment, testing the words, before releasing them. "I've still fed you off and on for the past five years. Did that habit give you hope I'd accept a proposal from you?"

"Yes."

Ren looked at his husband with new eyes. So, he'd assumed, all this time, that Ren liked him? That certainly put a different spin on things. "If you knew, then why….No, let me rephrase. You decided to marry me for my sake at first. But if you thought that I liked you, why would you believe that I would leave Aart?"

Glancing away, Arman took a moment to formulate his answer. "It's very hard to have feelings for someone when they aren't returned."

His eyes closed in understanding. "Oh dear. Arman, my darling husband, the act of feeding someone else does not always mean *romantic* love, you know."

Arman froze, eyes widening slowly. "…what?"

"I did have a crush on you at first," Ren clarified slowly, not sure how much he should say, as Arman now looked a little horrified. "But I had to let it go. You're right, one-sided loves hurt. I had to come to terms with the fact that we'd be friends, nothing more. But I do love you, so of course I kept up the habit of feeding you."

For the longest time, Arman sat there, turning all of it over and over in his head. In a voice so quiet that it almost couldn't be heard, he whispered, "That's why you didn't immediately agree."

"I didn't immediately agree to marry you because I thought you were proposing for all of the wrong reasons. I was half-right, mind you. And I can see from the look on your face that you're now doubting whether I wanted to marry you at all. Stop that right this instant. If I didn't want to marry you, I would have tossed your naked ass out of my bed, and this ring wouldn't be on my finger."

The rising tension in Arman eased although he still looked a little troubled.

And now he'd planted doubts in his husband's mind. Terrific. Ren resisted the urge to go to the nice stone wall and bang his head against it repeatedly. Growling a curse, he brought Arman's head up with a hand under his chin. "Arman Brahms, look at me. Am I the sort of man that accepts someone into his bed just because he's lonely?"

Arman's expression cleared slowly. "Never."

"So you do know me. Good. Do you believe that I would rather lose all of my limbs rather than hurt you?"

"Of course." As an afterthought, Arman requested, "But please don't."

"Like my limbs attached, eh? So do I. Do you understand what

I'm saying? I hesitated in answering you because I was very afraid that by saying yes, I might hurt you. Because I needed to make sure you were asking for the right reasons. That I was agreeing for the right reasons. You have a terrible habit of sacrificing yourself for others, I couldn't let this be one of those times."

Arman's hand lifted to trace the side of Ren's jaw with gentle fingers, eyes searching his. "If given other choices, you'd still choose me?"

"A hundred times over," Ren said firmly, meaning every word.

The last of the shadows faded from Arman's eyes, and he leaned up for a soft kiss. Ever so relieved, Ren kissed him back and swore to himself that he'd do a better job assuring Arman that he was very happy to be married to him. He shouldn't be able to shake his husband's faith in their marriage like this so easily. Although it was probably just as well they'd had this conversation, all things considered.

Ren couldn't take this distance between them, even if it was nothing more than a few inches. He slid down into Arman's lap, straddling him, hiding his face in the crook of Arman's neck. For an indeterminable amount of time, Ren held Arman close, letting them just be for a while. In all of the hustle and bustle since the wedding, they hadn't been given enough time to find their balance with each other. Knowing each other as friends and knowing each other as spouses were two very different things.

"When it's all settled, let's visit Takahiro," Arman offered quietly against Ren's hair.

Smiling, Ren dropped a kiss against Arman's neck, tightening his arms around him. "I'd like that very much. I still can't believe he thought we eloped five years ago. What kind of piss poor brother does he take me for, anyway? If we were lovers back then, I would have told him!"

"Isn't it better he assumed it?" Arman rumbled in amusement, his normal good humor restored. "That assumption led my heart to you."

Ren opened his mouth, only to slowly close it again. It was rather hard to argue with that.

21

They set out early in morning, both of them riding, with Robert in a cart with their luggage. In no hurry, they didn't travel to Brahms Fortress at the same breakneck speed Charles had demanded in the last trip. Which was just as well, as Ren still tired easily. He didn't suffer from any shortness of breath, fortunately, but there were times when he had to stop and just breathe, as his body felt taxed. Ren could not wait until he'd fully recovered, as just riding shouldn't be this tiring.

It took a full two days for them to make the trip, and they chose to push a little on the last leg so they didn't arrive after sunset. It shaved an hour off, leaving them plenty of light to see by as they thundered across the bridge.

Even at a distance, the guards on top of the walls recognized Arman, and the horns blared out a welcome. He waved back, the three of them pausing long enough for the gate to rise before they entered.

People poured out from every conceivable door, shouting out welcomes. Arman greeted them with handshakes and a few hugs, radiating contentment in being home after two years. Ren stayed mounted a little while longer, taking advantage of the higher vantage point to watch. His husband never complained about being homesick, but he obviously had been, as he looked lighter in this moment than he'd ever been.

"Master Ren!" Sam greeted, taking hold of the reins near the bit. "I'll take him. Welcome back, sir."

"Thank you, Sam." Ren threw a leg off and slid down, glad to be out of the saddle. He really didn't ride enough in his job as warden to keep in practice for it. Trips like this always left him a mite sore. "Give me the saddlebags, though, I have presents in those."

"For the mistress? Oh, she'll be glad for that, sir. She's been threatening to go off into town by herself, she's so low on her creams," Sam confided easily.

"I had a feeling that might be the case."

"ARMAN!" Eida called out, rushing out of the main door with arms outstretched.

Turning, her son handily caught her, picking her up and giving a quick twirl, setting his mother to laughing. "You should have sent word; I don't even have your favorite foods prepared! What took you so long?" she demanded of him.

Shrugging, Arman set her down and answered in his usual fashion, "Things happened. Came as fast as I could. Father."

Anthony hip-checked his wife a little, forcing her to give way, which she rewarded with a slap against his back. Ignoring that, he caught his son up in a fierce hug for a long moment. "Missed you, son."

"Missed all of you," Arman responded softly. Drawing back, he caught his mother's hand, looking at both of them seriously. "I have something important to tell you."

So, he'd decided to do this right off the bat? Ren's nerves thanked him. He didn't know if he could manage to eat right now with the butterflies careening around in his stomach. "Why don't you three catch up? I'll take a walk in the garden, stretch my legs out a little."

Arman frowned at him, head canted in question. Ren gestured for him to go on, feeling that it would be better if Arman told his parents in private.

A little baffled, but amiable, Eida led them inside. "Let's sit in the Morning Room, then. It's nice and warm. Bertie! Prepare Arman's favorite cherry pie, would you?"

"Of course, mistress."

Presents needed to wait, apparently. Ren handed them off to the staff to carry up to his room, then made his way to the garden. With the three of them in the Morning Room, he actually could stay nearby without being intrusive.

The garden didn't have much size to it, especially compared to the ones in the Zonhoven Palace. Still, it had a square footpath to follow, which he did. Eida favored more medicinal type plants than anything purely decorative, but still, she'd laid it out in a way that looked attractive. He tried to appreciate the beauty of it, only to fail miserably. Ren could only think of one other time he'd been this terrified—nearly two decades ago, when he'd confessed to his parents women held no appeal to him. The parallel was understandable, as Anthony and Eida had become his foster parents here. He'd lived at Brahms Fortress for nearly two months before being introduced to the royal family. They'd been amazing to him ever since his arrival in this country and the idea of losing that relationship…the fear brought bile up to his throat. He lifted his hands, found them to be shaking, and tried to still them by clenching them into fists. When that didn't work, he pressed them against his thighs. Deities, but his first battle hadn't been as nerve-wracking as this. His eyes kept drifting back to the Morning Room. Windows basically formed the outer wall of it, giving him a clear view inside, and voices sometimes could be heard. Just tone, however; the glass muted the words to an indistinguishable jumble.

He didn't need the words. Body language said a great deal. Arman sat on one chair, his parents in two others facing him. He said something, and his mother reared back in shock, his father going unnaturally still. Then both parents asked multiple questions, leaning toward him, hands gesturing wildly, but whatever Arman responded with didn't appease them.

Agitated, Eida left her chair in a flurry of skirts, heading for the door leading into the garden.

Oh gods. This didn't look good. Ren turned toward the door, bracing himself.

"Ren," Eida stepped out into the garden, frustration drawing her features into a pinched expression. "Come in this instant. Arman is being more difficult than usual."

The ball of nerves lodged in his throat developed spikes. Ren prayed for patience, for courage, as he desperately needed both as he followed her in. A part of him—a large part—felt like he was on a torture rack made of his own fears and nerves. He'd deliberately told Arman to speak with his parents alone because he didn't know how to face them and tell them all of this. He'd already confessed something similar once before in his life, and it had been an unmitigated disaster, with their relationship never being the same afterwards. He had no faith he'd do a better job of it now, because all he had was the truth, and he didn't know if that would be enough.

If the truth could ever be enough.

Entering, he saw Anthony had risen to stand next to the hearth, frowning at his eldest.

Arman stood as he came in, gesturing him in closer, which Ren appreciated because he couldn't fathom relaxing enough to sit down right now. Leaning into his side, Ren demanded in a low tone, "Let me guess. You said something along the lines of, 'I decided to marry Ren, we already have a marriage license, but he said you can do a ceremony if you want to.'"

Arman nodded agreement, head canting a little to the side as if to ask, 'what more did I possibly need to say?'

"Of course that's all you said," Ren groaned, head dropping forward. "Why, why did I think it was a good idea to let you talk to your parents alone?"

"That is an excellent question," Eida said tartly, reclaiming her chair in front of them. Worry gathered around her eyes, and her mouth stayed in a flat line, unhappy. "You should know better, Ren. Now, what is this about you two being married?"

Those expressions, they said without words that Eida and Anthony weren't happy at this news. Despair careened through him, as Ren couldn't see any light at the end of this particular tunnel. Still, he tried to hold onto some hope that once he explained, they'd be able to at least accept it.

Ren settled into an automatic parade rest, then mentally cursed himself for it. Not the impression he wanted to give, but he couldn't seem to draw himself out of it, either. Arman slid an arm around his waist, offering him support, which should have relaxed Ren but instead made him more tense. His eyes flitted to Anthony's face, then Eida, taking in their reactions. They both looked startled, as well they should; he and Arman had never been physically demonstrative with each other before their marriage. This, more than anything, would tell them a great deal about how much had changed.

Against his temple, Arman murmured in Shiirein, "Relax, beloved. You're so tense you're about to bite your own tongue."

In the same language, Ren gritted out, "This is one of those times I really wish you would talk for yourself." Although he liked hearing 'beloved' from Arman, he'd never been on the receiving end of that endearment before. It almost thawed his nerves enough he could mentally climb off that torture table.

Not relinquishing his hold on him, Arman faced his parents and requested, "We'll explain, just stop frowning. You're scaring him badly."

Eida shared a shocked glance with Anthony before focusing on Ren again. "We're scaring you?"

"Mother," Arman chided in exasperation. "Consider Shiirei's culture. What Ren's told you about his parents' reaction to his liking men. You think this feels different to him?"

Realization dawned, and Eida's mouth formed a perfect 'o' of understanding. Then she moved, coming directly for him. Ren's instincts suggested fight or flight, choose either, but *go,* and it took considerable control on Ren's part to not put up a defense or run for it when she closed in. He didn't think she'd hit him, but—

Eida put both arms around his waist and hugged him tightly to her. Ren froze, not at all sure how to respond to this. She wasn't angry—thank all the gods—but hugging?

"Ren," she chided him gently against his chest. "Whatever the reason for this, I won't be angry, and we certainly won't reject the two of you. Anthony, come here. Hug him too. He's literally shaking."

Was he really? Damn, he was. Ren would take going to war over standing here right now, he was that terrified, and wasn't that a mixed-up state of affairs? To rather face armed men out for his head than his own family. He tried to get words out, but his throat constricted to the point he was fighting for air, much less coherency.

A pair of strong arms closed around his side, and he knew them, even though he'd never felt them before like this. Anthony had obeyed and hugged both Ren and his wife strongly, his body brandishing heat like a roaring fire. "Ren," he said against the top of Ren's head, "breathe. Before you pass out, breathe."

Parental love. Ren had had it once, then lost it. But now, between the two of them, he felt it again. Despite knowing what he was, what he'd done, he had it again. His fears ground to a halt, confused, then retreated as budding hope took over. He blew out an explosive breath and drew another in, his lungs expanding under the force of it. Over Eida's head, he met Arman's eyes and found his husband smiling back at him, the expression soft and full of encouragement. Arman hadn't moved from his side during all of this, and Ren felt fiercely glad for that support, because even though he now understood Anthony and Eida weren't angry, he still found their lack of reaction to this strange. Well, no, not lack of reaction. They clearly were confused and waiting on an explanation before deciding how to react.

Stepping back, Eida looked up into his face, studying him. "Good, you have a little color back in you."

Anthony shifted away as well, expression regretful. "Ren, I'm sorry that I didn't think about this from your perspective. Considering Shiirei's culture, of course you'd be unnerved telling us you're married to our son. I just need to understand; I'm not condemning you. Why are you two married?"

Right, that was a good question. Ren logically understood that, because Anthony and Eida had only ever known them to be friends; brothers-in-arms. They'd not think of them in a romantic sense at all.

Arman finally decided to actually talk and answered the question. "It's for love, of course."

His parents' confusion ramped up another level or ten. Anthony gestured them into chairs. "I think you'd better sit—Ren definitely needs to sit—and then we'll start at the beginning."

Ren dared to really believe, for the first time, that this conversation wouldn't turn out badly for him. For either of them. The patience, the unwavering affection from both parents, shored up his hope in that regard. He took a seat on the couch, Arman settling in close enough their hips pressed together. Ren took his hand, as he needed that extra support, and Arman gave it with another small smile of encouragement. Lifting his head, he faced them squarely, drawing on whatever courage he could scrape up. With an internal prayer, he started talking.

"From the beginning, then. Apparently, Arman decided two years ago that he should marry me. He had the hair-brained idea that if I didn't find a partner soon, I'd give up living in Aart and leave. So he planned it all out without telling anyone but Robert and bided his time. Then, almost seven months ago he learned about my disastrous affair with Deidrick Giles—"

"Bastard," Arman corrected, hand clenching in a brief show of anger.

Inclining his head, Ren accepted the insult as due. "—and realized that there was nothing platonic about his feelings for me. That he had, in fact, convinced himself to marry me for all the wrong reasons and none of them were how he truly felt. After he returned, he proposed."

Both parents looked at their son incredulously. Granted, they had every right to feel that way, but Ren didn't know which part astonished them most. That Arman had fallen in love with another man, or that he'd decided to marry Ren just to keep his friend from leaving. Not that Ren had ever really considered leaving, but that was beside the point at the moment.

"You?" his mother demanded, beyond shocked. "You actually proposed? See, you can talk when you want to!"

Oh. That was the point she was stuck on. "Well, when I say proposed, I mean he put his signet ring on my finger."

Anthony gave an aborted laugh. "Now that's more believable. For a moment, I wanted to ask how drunk he was."

Eida pinched the bridge of her nose and took in a deep breath before releasing it again. "Of course he did. Ren, I'm quite amazed you know all of this. How did you drag it out of him?"

"Drag?" Arman objected, a twinkle in his eye.

Ren ignored him. "A lot of wrestling, threats, and stubbornness. So, usual tactics." Except not really. Naked skin and sex had gone into it, too. Ren decided he would never, ever, tell them that. Some things parents didn't need to know.

"Took some fast talking to get it through I was sincere," Arman tacked on, his smile rueful. "But I eventually did."

Ren, remembering that early morning scene, smiled back at him. "When he finally convinced me that he was sincere, that he really wished to be lovers as well as friends, I couldn't refuse him. I didn't want to refuse him."

His mouth stumbled, as Ren didn't know what else to say at that point. When Arman stated earlier that they'd married for love, his parents no doubt thought it was for a friendship sort of love, not *romantic*. No one in this room had ever suspected Arman would want Ren in that way, least of all Ren himself, so he couldn't blame their surprise. But the suspense of their reaction damn near killed him. Would they be able to wrap their heads around this? Would they be able to accept Ren as a son-in-law fully?

Eida reached over to take both of his hands. "My dear, I think you are very worried about what we think, is that right? I admit I'm very confused, as I never once suspected this might happen, and I'll need a little time to adjust to the idea. But in some ways, it doesn't change anything. You were already a son to us. Now we can legally call you our own, that's all."

The relief nearly bowled him over. That spiked ball in his throat disappeared in a rush and he sagged for a moment, unable to believe his good fortune. He'd married the heir of a fortress, in a land he barely had claim to, and yet he'd been readily accepted by his new parents. Had he been dropped into some sort of fairytale? Had he died of poisoning after all, and this was this afterlife? It was so blissful, he couldn't believe it, but he had no intention of pinching himself and testing it for a dream. Ren would cheerfully sleep away an eternity if this was his reward.

Ren couldn't contain his joy, and swiftly left his chair and joined her, hugging her tightly. She readily hugged him back, hands around his waist. "You have no idea how happy that makes me."

"I admit I'm confused as well," Anthony admitted frankly, ruffing the back of his head. "I'll definitely need to sleep on it. I'm mostly mad at my son for not talking to us about any of this before forging ahead."

Arman did not quail when both of his parents glared at him, just shrugged. "I couldn't put it into a letter. I didn't have the words to explain."

Glare growing harder, Eida demanded, "What is so difficult about writing 'I realized I'm in love with my best friend. I'm going to propose the minute I'm home. Please give me your blessing?' Even for you, that's doable, it's only twenty words or so!"

"Twenty-two," Arman corrected her promptly.

Still holding tightly to Ren, Eida complained to her husband, "I should have drowned him at birth. I'd have fewer grey hairs right now if I had."

"I'm just as glad you didn't; where would we be now without Ren?" Anthony responded with a quick smile to his new son-in-law. "Whatever we might think of their marriage, Ren has done us all good service. We'd be in trouble if he hadn't come into our lives."

"That's true enough." A thought hit, and Eida brightened perceptibly. "Maybe this is the gods' way of an apology. They gave me a son that won't talk to me, then a son-in-law who will make up for it."

Arman found this very amusing, as he shook silently with laughter.

"Don't laugh, it's not funny, I did teach you how to speak," his mother scolded, wagging a finger at him. "And I'm very, very upset that you didn't wait so that we could be there for your wedding. Why didn't you?"

"Couldn't," Arman responded frankly. "Queen wouldn't have given me permission."

Brows drawing in, Eida turned to Ren, her worry mounting. "Why not? Was she against this?"

"Not for the reasons you're likely thinking," Ren assured her. Look at that expression. Eida was like a lioness, determining if she had to go in defense of one of her own or not. It made him ridiculously happy to see it, to be included as one of hers to protect. "On a personal level, the whole royal family is perfectly delighted. But on a professional one, they realized that our marriage meant I would move to Brahms at some point, and that was the sticking point. Queen Eloise was especially wroth about it, as she's loath to lose me as her warden."

"Don't blame her," Anthony acknowledged. "Their previous warden did the job alright, but it took two deputies and an assistant to help him. You're doing the work of three people and managing better than he did besides. You did tell our monarchs that I don't need you to move here anytime soon? I think I can manage another fifteen years before Arman needs to return home."

"That was our guess, and yes, we did tell them that. It soothed her ire considerably. She's still a little miffed, but her reaction made me realize why Arman was so insistent to marry first, then inform people. He wasn't willing to take chances."

"Easier to get forgiveness than permission?" Anthony gave a rueful nod of acknowledgment. "In our case as well, I suppose. You were that dead set on having him, then?"

Arman's eyes went to Ren, softening perceptibly. "I love him. I couldn't take any chances."

His mother put a hand to her heart, touched beyond words at this declaration. Rising, she went to hug her oldest, all previous frustration forgotten. "I never thought I'd see the day with you happily married. Alright, I'll forgive you, but only if I can throw you a proper wedding with a reception afterwards."

"He will let you do anything you want in that regard," Ren guaranteed. Mentally, he jumped up and down, and did a few flips. This conversation had gone far, far better than he'd feared it would. In fact, he now felt almost silly for fearing their reactions at all. Well, not silly, but as if he had done them a disservice by doubting them. "That was our deal. We could register the marriage immediately, but he can't argue with you on the ceremony."

"Excellent!" Eida beamed at him, then her look went shrewd. "You know, Anthony, it occurs to me that Arman might have done us a wonderful favor by marrying Ren."

"In that when our son is being difficult, we can at least depend on our son-in-law?" Anthony finished his wife's thought dryly. "I admit that thought just occurred to me as well."

Ren thought about that for a moment before offering, "Happy to help?"

Picking up her son's hand, Eida asked, "Where's your signet ring?"

Arman inclined his head toward Ren. "Used it to make his wedding ring."

"Oh." Eida's hand found her heart again. "Oh, that's so romantic. I didn't know you could be romantic."

"You have no idea," Ren assured her. "He's taken me by surprise more than once."

Eida's relief was so strong as to be almost palpable. It seemed she harbored a few doubts on whether her eldest could actually be a good husband to Ren or not. Ren decided not to comment, as time would prove it out. "Is that right?"

Anthony glanced between both men before clearing his throat, drawing their attention to him. "I think it's time to call your brothers, Arman, and share this news with the rest of the family. Eida, how about we plan for a family dinner tomorrow?"

"I think that's a splendid idea, my dear. We'll tell them only that Arman has some very happy news. I don't want to spoil the surprise." Beaming, she popped out of the chair and scurried toward the door. "I'll write up the notes to send now. After that, we really must sit down and discuss dates. We need to start planning for a wedding ceremony, and a reception, oh and we mustn't forget the honeymoon—" Her voice gradually faded as she headed down the hall and out of earshot.

Shaking his head, Anthony stared in the general direction his wife had disappeared to. "We're in for it now. Arman, are you really going to let her do whatever she wants?"

"Worth it," Arman assured him with a slight shrug.

His father gave him an odd look, and for good reason—Arman loathed pomp and ceremony of all types and had to be dragged physically to such functions. For him to not try and duck out this, even if it was his own wedding, was very telling. "Well, I'm going to go impress on her that she has a budget before she gets something ridiculous stuck in her head."

After his father left the room, Arman shifted over to sit next to Ren, pulling him into his lap. Ren felt a little strange perched on the other's knee, but didn't fight it, trying to relax into it instead. With a hand, Arman cradled his head, giving him that soft, barely perceptible smile that melted Ren's heart like butter in the sun. "See?"

"See, there was nothing to worry about after all?" Ren finished the question. "Husband mine, you have no idea how precious your parents' blanket acceptance of this is."

Arman's dark brows twitched together in a brief frown. "Your brother will accept it."

"Likely, yes, but I have extended family, remember."

"And they won't?"

"I don't know," Ren sighed. Giving in, he curled himself up even further, letting Arman support his weight and worries. Just for a minute. He needed that minute after surviving the past half hour. "I really hope so, but I don't know."

Of course, dinner conversation that night mostly revolved around Eida's plans for their wedding. Arman ate and didn't interrupt her, Ren pitched in an agreement or denial in the right spots, and Anthony only stepped in when his wife got a little too carried away, reminding her of the budget.

His father still didn't seem completely comfortable with them, as if he struggled to accept them as a couple. He never said anything to Ren, but the way Anthony watched them with that slightly perplexed look spoke volumes. Arman hoped that given time, he'd adjust to it. For now, he could only be relieved that both parents were willing to accept it.

Ren gave out presents, exchanged hugs good night, then gratefully escaped to Arman's room. Well, their room now. Arman sensed his new husband needed space and quiet after this very stressful day to let his emotions unwind. He didn't even try to stop him and lingered at the dining room table to give Ren a little time to himself. Anthony went up as well, also likely needing a bit of privacy and silence to adjust to today's revelations.

Of course, his mother capitalized on the opportunity this afforded and stayed seated, turning in her chair to face him. "This really wasn't just for Ren's sake?"

Taking her hand, he tried to put the many emotions that tugged and tangled and demanded things of his heart into words that she could understand. Then he realized those words were completely inadequate and frowned. Why was talking so difficult?

"Arman," his mother scolded. "I know it's difficult, but at least try. This sudden decision worries me."

He couldn't think of better words to use, and by default, fell back on the ones he'd first thought of. "It's for us both."

"Why?" she prompted patiently.

"Ren has a great capacity to love. He needs it. He wasn't fine, being alone in Aart."

"Yes, I know." She squeezed his hand lightly, her smile sad. "He always put on a good face, but I could tell that it ate at him. I'm sure you saw it better than we did, as he keeps no secrets from you. That's why you decided to be what he needed, to marry him."

It wasn't a question but he answered it with a nod.

"I understand very well what made you move for Ren's sake," Eida leaned in a little, expression overly patient. "But this marriage wasn't for just his sake. Why yours?"

Again, the words felt very inadequate. How could they begin to describe all of the joy, pain, worry, desire, trust, and need he felt when he looked at the amazing man who'd exchanged vows with him? "I love him."

"Darling son, you have always loved him. That's obvious to a blind man. But you never felt any desire to marry him until these past few years—"

Shaking his head, he tried again, frustrated by this inability to fully express to her what he wished. And people wondered why he didn't like to talk. It was because he never felt like words were properly up to the task. "No, Mother. Not as a brother or a friend. I desire him beyond that. I love him."

Eida stopped mid-sentence, eyes a little wide as she took his meaning. "You're in love with him. That's what you're saying. Heavens, Arman, when did that happen?"

"Don't know," he admitted, bemused by that himself. He'd

thought a lot about that, wondering just when his platonic affection for his best friend had slid into this desire to be everything to him. He couldn't begin to pinpoint a specific event or time. It was an academic question, anyway; it didn't change how he felt now. "I realized it about seven months ago, everything I really felt. But I feel like I loved him before, I just didn't recognize it for what it was."

Eida's face turned slightly so that she stared blankly at the far wall. "Ren's explanation earlier to us made sense, but I thought he'd perhaps made some assumptions. All of this is so very unlike you. I've tried offering you various matches for the past ten years, and not once would you even try to engage with them. You wouldn't even tell me what was wrong with them, why you didn't like them."

Wasn't that perfectly obvious? "They weren't Ren."

"So it isn't that you aren't attracted to women," his mother asked delicately.

Ah. So that was her real question. His mother never could approach a topic directly. "I'm not interested in men, either."

"Just Ren." Her expression turned bemused. "I won't lie; I'm very confused by this, but I'm not unhappy about it. Ren brings out the best in you. Always has. If you feel that being married to him is essential to your happiness, I won't argue. I do have a few concerns, however."

Arman waved her on, already anticipating some of the issues she'd bring up.

"Do you plan to have any children of your own? Through a surrogate mother, perhaps?"

Shaking his head firmly, Arman answered, "Not a surrogate. Perhaps adoption, but I haven't spoken to Ren about this."

"Ah. Well, it's true that with your brothers having children, we won't be short on heirs for the fortress. I'm not worried about that aspect of it, but I didn't want to see you both deprived of the chance to be parents. Ask Ren about it, won't you?"

"I will." Once things had settled down, at least. Arman felt the timing for that conversation would be better off in the future.

"My only other question for now, as everything else we have time to settle, is who is taking on who's name?"

Arman stared at her perfectly blankly for at least three full seconds before the question made sense. Then he swore softly. In the course of getting everything settled, and safeguarding Ren at Zonhoven Palace, that little detail had escaped him completely.

"I don't know who would be considered the, well, 'bride' in this situation." Eida frowned, her fingers flexing in his. "I don't think that's the proper term, either, as you're both clearly men. What would happen in Shiirei?"

This, at least, he knew how to answer. "Names don't change in Shiirei after marriage."

"Really? How odd. Is that a purely western custom? I see. Then will Ren keep his family name?"

Arman shrugged his ignorance. He'd have to ask and be careful of how he asked, as he didn't want to press Ren into anything.

"Well, discuss it and give me an answer, I need to know how to do the wedding invitations and such." With a pat on his hand, she rose to her feet, him immediately following her. "I'll let you go to bed; you're tired, I can tell. I'll see you in the morning. And assure Ren that we truly are happy he's part of the family, just a bit befuddled how it came about."

"I will," he promised, pressing a kiss to her cheek in goodnight before climbing up the stairs to his childhood room. Arman's childhood still remained in traces, such as the wooden horse on the shelf, the wooden practice sword leaning in the corner, and a child's drawing framed above the mantel. The furniture had changed when he hit his late teens, the massive bed suiting someone of his stature. It now would comfortably accommodate both him and his husband.

Arman entered, stifling a yawn behind his hand, then paused just inside the doorway. "You're already in bed?"

"Tired," Ren yawned. He lay on his side, blankets pulled up to his chest, a night shirt on. "I'm not used to riding like that anymore. Your mother stopped you on the way up again?"

Deciding he didn't need a rehash of the entire conversation, Arman shortened it to the necessary bit. "She wanted to know if you'd take on our name."

Ren blinked. Then swore. "I didn't even think of that. Right, in this culture, a wife takes on the husband's name. Did you explain that we don't do that in Shiirei?"

"I did." Arman shrugged, indicating she hadn't exactly approved of the answer. "Told her it was up to you."

"Thanks for that," Ren responded sarcastically. "Now she's going to ask me in the morning and I don't have an answer for her."

Arman moved to the washstand, already stripping off his shirt. "I can take on yours."

"Don't you dare. Your father will murder me in my own bed." Ren sat up a little, propping himself up against the headboard, shoving a pillow behind him to make the position more comfortable. "Is it really that important that we share the same surname?"

"Not exactly. People will just expect it." Pouring water into the basin, he soaped up a washcloth and did a quick cleanup. Arman didn't sound worried, just curious. "I think it's more complicated for you than me."

"You have me there," Ren sighed, his gaze drifting to the fire in the hearth. Arman didn't try to face him, as sometimes it was easier to talk about things like this without forcing Ren to make eye contact. "The Sho family hasn't always been very accepting of me. My brother aside, most of them wouldn't even own up to being my relation until I made the rank of colonel. Then, because I had brought some prestige to the family name, they'd tolerate me. I don't have any strong attachment to the family, but at the same time, I'm not sure if that's a good reason for me to change my name."

Part of Arman had always wanted to meet Ren's family. Just so he could strangle the lot of them. Ren seemed to take the attitude more or less in stride, as if it was only to be expected, but Arman didn't see it that way. Sensing Ren didn't need his anger just then, he shoved it down, keeping his back turned to the bed to hide his expression. Shucking the rest of his clothes, Arman reached for a pair of loose pants and put those on. "Then don't."

"It really doesn't bother you either way?" Ren waited for him to join him on the bed. Arman drew back the covers but didn't climb in all the way, instead sitting with one leg folded up under the other. "I'd completely forgotten about it, honestly. So much has gone on recently that it slipped my mind. I'm not even sure how it would sound together. Ren Brahms…"

Arman's felt his cheeks heat, breath catch a little in his throat. The sound of his name from those lips made his heart skip a beat. He hadn't realized until Ren said it how much he wanted it, for Ren to be a Brahms in name.

"You like it. You like the sound of your name attached to mine."

Clearing his throat, Arman looked away. Damn, and he'd just promised himself not ten minutes ago he wouldn't force his opinion on Ren. "It's your choice."

"Oh, no you don't, do not even try to evade me." Ren leaned in, contorting in an effort to see Arman's face. "I want to hear it. You like it, don't you?"

Sighing gustily, Arman ran a hand through his hair, carding his fingers through it so that it stood up on end. "Ren. I have pushed you on every other point. I won't do it on this."

Ren scooted in so that they sat with thighs pressing. "Are you possibly feeling guilty that you coerced me into marrying you so quickly?"

Arman still refused to look at him, eyes trained on a dark corner, his mouth tightening ever so slightly. Guilty? Yes. Well, no. He didn't regret marrying Ren, not for a moment, but he wasn't blind. He realized that doing it now made Ren's already-hectic life even more complicated. Why hadn't he given them both time? Why had he assumed that just because they'd shared a tent for a year, and had been friends for five after that, that transitioning into married life would be a snap?

"A little, huh. For the record, I don't regret it."

Head snapping around, Arman protested, "You were nervous the whole time."

"Still am, a little," Ren admitted frankly. Then he paused, jaw working, searching for words. "My entire life, I never really expected to get married. It was like a fairy tale to me, a fantasy. I didn't plan for it, didn't even really wish for it, because I never thought it would happen. The best I ever hoped for was a lover that I might care for. And then you burst onto the scene, a partner that I already knew and trusted, offering me that fantasy. I wanted it so badly my heart trembled with it, but I was equally terrified I'd wake up from the dream. That it wasn't real."

Arman's heart shivered. He'd given Ren a fantasy? So, it wasn't that he had pushed Ren too hard, too fast, that made him nervous? Reaching up, he cradled Ren's head in his hand, thumb lightly stroking against his cheekbone in a gentle caress. "Even now?"

"I'm still half-convinced it's a fantasy," Ren whispered. "It's all too good to be true."

Drawing him in further, Arman put a kiss against his forehead, then hovered there with his lips barely grazing skin. "I really should have taken you with me two years ago. I regret that now."

"You think it would have been easier to convince me two years ago?"

"Yes," Arman answered promptly, voice hardening. "Before *he* hurt you. Your heart closed up after what he did."

Ren's hands smoothed up his chest, leaning into the embrace. "You might be right. If anything, it's probably just as well that you fell for me. I wouldn't have been able to trust a proposal from anyone else as being sincere."

"Are you still sure I can't kill him?"

"Certain. And don't suggest that to our queen, either, she's still upset enough to hire an assassin." Tilting his head up, he met Arman's mouth in a slow kiss, more for reassurance than passion. Of course, the plan backfired a little and when they parted, Ren's breath came a little fast. Arman felt his own pulse quickening. His husband was entirely too sexy for comfort. Against his mouth, Ren whispered, "Don't feel apologetic to me. You've given me everything I've ever wanted. In fact, I feel bad, I haven't really given you anything."

"You said 'yes,'" Arman denied immediately. "'Yes' was all I wanted."

"Nope, that argument doesn't fly," Ren denied cheerfully. "I think I should do at least one thing for you. It's decided, I'll be a Brahms."

Growling, Arman gave him a frustrated glare. That was not the point of this conversation, the point was for Ren to think about it.

"You said it was my choice," Ren reminded him with a wicked grin. "I can choose to do things that please you, you know. It's my prerogative as a husband."

Snorting, Arman rolled his eyes before turning serious once more. "You won't regret it?"

"Regret being part of a family that adores me? What's there to regret?"

22

Ren took a turn around the top of the battlements, a cup of hot tea in his hands to help ward off the morning chill. It was definitely getting warmer as the season changed into summer, but the mornings still had a distinct nip in the breeze. He stopped, facing northward, into Zaytsevian territory. In two decades or less, this would be his battlefield, his and Arman's. It would be their duty to protect the northeastern border of Aart. As many times as he'd been here, he'd never once suspected that would ever be the case. It alarmed him, in a way, this sudden responsibility, but at the same time it relieved him. Ren dearly loved having a place that he firmly belonged to.

"Morning, my favorite son-in-law," Anthony greeted jovially.

Snorting, Ren turned to watch his approach. Anthony was dressed for the day in dark pants and an olive-green jacket, his own cup of tea in his hand, bright-eyed and bushy-tailed. "Father, I'm your only son-in-law."

"You're still my favorite." Eyes crinkled up in laughter, he stopped to stare in the same direction Ren had just been facing. "Surveying all your worldly wealth?"

"It's actually a very strange thought," Ren admitted frankly, placing his forearms against the stone. The cold, hard edge bit a little through his sleeves. "I don't think it sank in properly until just now. I was so wrapped up in Arman and all of the palace intrigue, I didn't properly consider it. But standing here, looking at the mountains and the pass, I realize this really will be my life in twenty or so years. This will be home."

"It is home," Anthony corrected him gently. "You're just deployed elsewhere for now, that's all."

Those softly uttered words hit straight in the heart. Ren blinked back sudden tears. He didn't dare face Anthony until he had his emotions back under control. Voice husky, he admitted, "I was terrified coming out here. I didn't know what you and Mother would think of the marriage. I'd hoped you'd accept it. I was very afraid you wouldn't."

Anthony put an arm around his shoulders and hugged him briefly. "Honestly, I'm still adjusting to the idea. But I'm relieved, Ren. So relieved. He's clearly ecstatic being married to you. Arman's a difficult to man to love in some ways, but he's always been open with you. More open than he is with us. He adored you from the start; we could all see it. I don't think he would have accepted any man as your lover; he was too protective of you to handle that situation well."

A thought that Ren had never entertained. Tilting his head, he regarded Anthony curiously. "Really?"

"Lance and I talked about it once," Anthony recalled with a half-smile. "We gave it low odds of you finding someone so amazing that even Arman would accept him. Which made us worry for your sake, of course. You already had the odds stacked against you in this country. I wasn't sure if you'd ever gain someone for yourself. I didn't quite have this solution, mind you."

Recognizing the teasing for what it was, Ren grinned at him. "Neither did I."

"So, for my son, and for you, I'm quite happy how this worked out. Professionally speaking, I'm ecstatic. Two generals to guard the place even after I'm gone is more than I could have hoped for." Anthony gave a general wave with his mug to indicate the land around them. "I feel better leaving it in your hands."

He really had been accepted. The realization left Ren reeling. Strange, how he'd had to travel to a completely different country in order to find his proper home. "Thank you. That means the world to me."

"If dealing with palace politics becomes too much for you, come home sooner," Anthony urged him, concern creating a furrow between his brows and drawing at the corners of his mouth. "I don't want you in danger again like you've been these past few months. You understand me, son?"

The casual endearment made Ren ridiculously happy. "Yes, Father."

"Good." Relaxing a little, Anthony took a healthy swallow from his mug and then made a face. "Damn thing always goes cold before

I can drink it."

Ren had no doubt his own tea was in the same shape, considering the cold air. He didn't even try to verify it. "Let's go back in, get a refill."

"Not a bad thought." As they walked along the top battlement, heading for the stairs, Anthony inquired, "I heard about the trial, but did you ever figure out who all was responsible for what?"

"Unfortunately not," Ren denied in renewed aggravation. "Some of it was pure guesswork. And there are a few mysteries still lingering. We don't know, for example, just who planted the mace trap in the linen closet."

Alarmed, Anthony stopped on the top stair. "The what, now?"

"Ah." Ren belatedly realized he might not have given a full account of everything yesterday. "I didn't tell you about that? Someone planted a mace ball in the linen closet on the main floor. It was set to spring as soon as someone tried to remove it. If not for Arman, I might be missing a head about now."

"Damn." Anthony slammed the side of his fist against the nearest stone, expression dark with anger. "And you have no idea who?"

"I really, really wish I did. I half-hoped that they'd gotten the supplies to make it from the palace armory, as that would have at least narrowed down our list of suspects, but no such luck " Ren continued down the stairs, his stomach grumbling for breakfast.

"Someone snuck in the supplies and an expert and no one noticed?" Anthony queried doubtfully, following him. "I know your guards better than that, Ren."

"Believe me, we're all as baffled. We were extra paranoid by that point. I can't imagine any soldier or veteran just waltzing in with all of the supplies necessary. Only the highest ranking officials weren't being thoroughly inspected by that point."

"So that narrows the field some." Anthony paused on the mid-landing, eyes narrowed thoughtfully.

Ren knew that look and paused as well. "What?"

"It occurs to me..." trailing off, Anthony thought some more before asking, "Didn't you say that Lady Karina was one of the idiots with keys?"

"Yes, why?" Ren responded, fully alert, eyes trained on Anthony's face.

"Lady Karina's grandfather and I served together, back in the day.

General Eanraig Cuyler. As a young buck, that's what he did. Traps."

The information swirled in Ren's mind, tantalizing with possible answers. "You think he still has the skills?"

Anthony batted the question aside as not even worth considering. "They trained those men to be able to make a trap of anything in pitch darkness. Even thirty years later, muscle memory alone would carry him through."

"Father, can you write this all out?" Ren requested urgently. "Everything you know about him and his expertise, and anyone else that you know is related to the group we incarcerated that might have the necessary experience. Konrad and Hartmann are shooting blind right now."

"I'd be happy to, son. Mace balls in linen closets," Anthony growled, his feet in motion once more. "Putting my boys in danger. I'll have the man's head on a pike if he really did that."

It was nice to have a father angry on his behalf. It had been so long, over a decade, since his own father cared enough to respond so, that Ren had forgotten what it felt like. He smiled all the way back to the main level, listening to Anthony growl out curses. Even if this information proved to be misleading, and Cuyler wasn't guilty, Ren found he didn't really care.

The other sons and their families arrived mid-afternoon, a crying toddler in tow, all of them wearing smiles to see Arman. Ren hung back as they exchanged hugs, the lot talking over each other the way they normally did. Perhaps Arman's silence came from never being able to get a word in edgewise while growing up? Certainly his brothers could talk enough for five people.

Eida skillfully managed them, herding everyone into the dining hall. Someone had opened the windows to let in warmth and air, so it felt quite pleasant inside, and the smells coming from the dishes in the center of the table made Ren's mouth water. His nervousness in telling the rest of the family hadn't faded, but it had abated due to Anthony's and Eida's acceptance. He actually felt like he could eat.

The siblings all sat in their usual places: Lance near his father's left hand with his wife Richelle and their son Miles, then the youngest son Marshall with his very pregnant wife Willa. Ren barely knew

Willa, having only seen her on her wedding day, but he knew both parents adored her. She certainly greeted everyone with a wide smile, transforming her somewhat stark features into a pleasant beauty. Arman and Ren settled on the right side, with Eida near the head of the table.

Standing, Eida cleared her throat. "Before we start eating, Arman has an announcement."

They justifiably looked at their older brother in astonishment, as Arman rarely announced anything. Ren half-expected Arman's response to this, so he didn't feel at all surprised when his husband promptly turned expectantly to him.

Ren stared him down, expression saying, 'No part of our wedding vows included me talking for you the rest of our lives.'

Arman quirked a brow back. 'Remember the last time you made me talk?'

Damn. Alright, Ren better handle this. "Mother, I think I better do it, to avoid a repetition of last time."

Grimacing, she waved him on. "Yes, let's please avoid that."

And the nervousness was back. Ren cleared his throat and pinned a winsome smile to his face. "Your brother proposed to me two weeks ago. We're married."

Dead silence.

Lance, an uncanny younger version of Arman, kept trying to talk but no sound emerged. Richelle looked just as stunned, her dark golden eyes bouncing between the two of them as if she couldn't quite decide who to demand answers from. Marshall sat back with a huff, fair brows straight into his hairline, with Willa tugging at his sleeve and whispering quick questions.

"I know, I know, we're all surprised," Eida responded, as if her children's silence could be interpreted into actual words. "They told us yesterday and I still can't quite wrap my head around it."

"Wait," Lance threw up a hand, his expression gradually clearing. "They're not pranking us? They're actually married?"

Arman lifted his left hand to display the wedding ring he wore.

Swearing softly, Lance planted both hands on the table and leaned over the surface. "That's Ren's family crest, isn't it. Holy he—" catching his mother's expression, he swallowed the rest of the oath. "Ah. Ahem. I don't know whether to congratulate you or ask a million questions first."

"Congratulations," Willa offered, her smile a little tentative. "I'm not quite sure I understand how this happened, though."

"None of you are as surprised as I am, trust me," Ren assured the table at large. "He planned this out without telling anyone, and then sprung it on me."

"Sprung it successfully, if you're wearing his ring," Lance observed, watching them thoughtfully. "Arman, correct me if I'm wrong, but I have the feeling you decided to do this before your deployment."

Arman raised his glass and silently toasted his brother for a well-educated guess.

"Ha, thought so." Lance toasted him back.

"Wait," Anthony lifted a hand, stalling any other questions, glancing between his two sons. "Lance, how did you know?"

"My big brother asked me an interesting question right before he left, whether the law in Aart was worded so that it would prohibit Ren from marrying. I thought he was asking on Ren's behalf. I actually expected an announcement of some sort from Ren that he'd found a partner. When that didn't happen, I assumed things fell through and didn't think anything more of it. But it makes more sense now. I take it that you had no trouble marrying, then?"

"None," Ren confirmed.

"So how long have you liked men?" Marshall blurted out. "Do you think it was because you lived in Shiirei for a year during the war?"

Without looking, Richelle reached out and smacked him in the back of the head.

"Ow!" Rubbing his abused skull, Marshall pouted at his sister-in-law. "You're always hitting me."

"You're always asking stupid questions," Richelle retorted impatiently. "Sit down. I doubt your brother has developed a sudden liking for men. I think this has more to do with Ren. The question you should be asking is, is this a real marriage? I have trouble seeing the two of you as anything more than brothers. I know that you're close, but envisioning you as spouses is giving me trouble."

Ren had to allow that was fair. He'd never thought to be anything else to Arman the past five years, and Richelle had not known him during his crush-on-Arman stage. "I'm not sure how to help you on that."

"Kiss each other," she requested, a mischievous glint in her eyes.

Willa clapped her hands enthusiastically. "Yes, please."

Marshall turned an odd look on his wife. "You want to see my brothers kissing? Because I have to tell you, Ren is as much a brother as Arman."

"I want to see two handsome men kissing," she corrected him absently, her eyes ardently on the other side of the table. "I think it will be alluring."

This sort of thing was attractive to females? Really? Ren turned to Arman, intending to ask what he wanted to do, only to jump a little when his husband caught his chin and leaned in for a very not-chaste kiss. Tongue definitely got involved. Withdrawing a bit, Ren murmured, "If you turn me on right now, you will not like the consequences later."

"Promises, promises," Arman whispered back, voice shaking with silent laughter. Releasing his chin, Arman sat back in his chair, giving his sisters-in-law a silent query with an arched eyebrow.

Willa fanned herself with a hand, a blush high on her cheeks. Richelle had a hand over her mouth, amused and perhaps a little relieved. "Thank you, Arman. I can very clearly see it now."

Satisfied, Arman gave her a nod. "Any other questions?"

"Who took on the role of the bride?" Marshall asked seriously, only to flinch when Richelle hit him again. "Will you stop?!"

"You ask one more stupid question, I will throw you out the window," Richelle threatened. "Willa will help me."

"I probably will," Willa agreed cheerfully. "Truly, though, why did you get married without us in attendance? I'm a little hurt."

"Ah, that," Eida fortunately stepped in to explain. "Arman was worried he wouldn't be able to get permission from Queen Eloise and King Gerhard. They adore Ren so, they wouldn't want to lose him as Castle Warden."

"And if he married Arman, he would eventually end up here," Lance finished in understanding. "Did it work? They approved the marriage?"

"After much grumbling, yes," Ren answered, bemused. No one had objected yet, or even looked upset. They only tried to understand the situation. How differently they reacted compared to his own family. "I think it helped that we promised I'd stay in position at least another fifteen years."

"That would do it." Lance sat forward in his chair a little more, head canted as he studied Ren. "You look...surprised. Are we not reacting as you expected? Did you think we would deny the two of you?"

Ren wished he could say otherwise, but couldn't, and stumbled. His courage had been bolstered by Eida and Anthony's acceptance, certainly. He didn't feel the same terror that the rest of Arman's family wouldn't be able to accept them. But the fear always lurked near the surface, suggesting that not everyone could be that amiable, that all it took was one bad apple to ruin the whole cart. To have that fear proved groundless, well, he considered it a miracle. But he couldn't pretend it had never been there.

"Oh, Ren." Richelle left her chair and quickly came around the table, throwing her arms around him so she could draw him in to her for a semi-awkward hug, with him still in the chair. "You poor dear, of course; I forget sometimes that you lived in a country where this wouldn't have been accepted. You must have been worried sick coming out here to tell us."

Ren hugged her back and breathed her in, feeling his eyes burn a little. He and Richelle had always gotten along, and the way she reached for him now so automatically to give comfort meant the world to him.

"Is that right?" Willa asked someone at the table. "Would he really have had trouble in his home country?"

"I don't think it would have even been allowed," Lance answered. "Arman was worried about it, which tells me that he knew Shiirei wouldn't have permitted such a union. Am I right, brother? I thought so. Praise the gods you brought him home with you, then. At least here in Aart you won't have such a problem."

They accepted it. They accepted him. Ren didn't know whether to laugh or cry. He felt like he might do either at any moment, maybe even both, and wouldn't that be a strange sight. Richelle's hand came up and stroked his head, as if comforting a child. "It's alright, Ren. I admit you surprised us. We never thought Arman wanted you in that way. We never thought you would love our brother in that way, either. But you've always been ours, ever since the day Arman brought you here."

"Stop, stop," Ren requested, drawing back. "You're going to make me cry if you keep going."

"And what's wrong with that?" she sassed back, a gentle smile on her face. "You're with family, crying's allowed."

"Sorry, Richelle, but if he cries now he'll forever lose his manly points," Marshall disagreed. "You're only allowed to cry under certain conditions, like if you lose a limb."

Shaking a finger at him, Richelle warned, "I will throw you out of the window, don't think I won't."

"And I will help," Willa promised her husband darkly. With him cowed, she turned back to the men. "I know you were married, but are we going to celebrate it at all?"

"I'm planning a proper ceremony and reception," Eida announced happily. "They've given me free reign. I want to do it three months from now; that should be enough time to send out the announcements and make preparations. Girls, I would dearly love your help."

"Of course, Mother," both women assured her in near stereo.

Before he forgot or lost his nerve, Ren cleared his throat. "Mother, you asked Arman last night about our surnames. I'll take the Brahms name, if that's alright."

That set off a whole new round of questions, most of them overlapping each other, and Ren didn't even try to decipher anything. Anthony finally got them to stop by knocking his knuckles against the wooden table in a loud double-tap. "Stop, I can't hear him. Ren, you'd take our name?"

"In Shiirei, even after marriage, no one's name changes," Ren explained, trying to get the butterflies in his stomach to stop duking it out. He never would be able to eat at this rate. "So I hadn't thought of it until Mother asked. But in all truth, the Sho family has never quite known what to do with me. I think I'd prefer to carry the name of the family that can accept me unconditionally. Besides—" he looked at Arman, a soft, helpless smile curving his mouth upwards "—I can tell he wants it badly, even though he won't ask me for it."

"Father," Richelle informed Anthony firmly, "if you don't say yes, I will disown you."

"Daughter," Anthony retorted primly, "I wouldn't dream of saying no. There will be no disowning in my house. Ren, I insist you take our name. In fact, I will write a letter tonight to send to your family declaring that we've taken you."

"A declaration of war?" Marshall asked in growing excitement. "I like it; can I sign it too?"

Ren didn't know what to make of this odd enthusiasm of Marshall's. He seemed perfectly accepting, if still struggling to understand. "I don't think a declaration is necessary? Besides, the only address I know for certain is my brother's, and he's the only one who won't argue."

Eida put her hand over her heart, relieved. "So you do have one member of your family that will be happy for you? I'm very glad to hear that. Now, are there any more questions or concerns? No? Then let's eat."

As the large white platters made their way around the table, Arman's hand stole into Ren's for a moment, squeezing gently. He leaned in to whisper, "See? It's fine."

Miracle of miracles, it apparently was. Ren looked around the table, taking them all in, and indeed they seemed perfectly alright with this turn of events. His sisters-in-law (ye gods he had two new sisters now) actually looked pleased. Baffled, touched, he asked his husband in a hushed voice, "Are you sure I'm not dreaming?"

Arman darted in for a sweet kiss. "Sometimes, fantasies are real, my love."

"I can pinch you if that will help," Marshall offered. "Ow! Wife, don't abuse me too."

"If you interrupt them one more time, our first child will be our last," Willa threatened. "Excuse him, Ren, Arman, he doesn't have a romantic bone in his body. Clearly the eldest brother inherited the lion's share of that talent."

"Ooh, speaking of, how did Arman propose? I want the story," Richelle requested, an expectant expression on her face.

Ren instantly flushed.

Lance chuckled, the sound rich and warm. "I take it from your expression that he did not do a traditional proposal. Why am I not surprised. Arman, truly, what did you do?"

"I just slid my ring on his finger," Arman denied innocently.

Ren glared at him. He was not, absolutely not, going to answer this question.

"No, truly, what did you do?" Richelle demanded, her grin going wicked. "I didn't think anything could embarrass Ren."

"He might have been hung over, naked, and in bed with me at the time," Arman admitted without batting an eye.

With an indignant screech, Eida smacked Arman's shoulder in

a loud slap. "No wonder he wouldn't tell me! Arman, for shame, I raised you to be a proper gentleman!"

"It worked," Arman defended himself mildly, rubbing at his abused shoulder.

Outraged, Eida looked past him, eyes demanding a rebuttal from Ren.

Wincing, Ren admitted, "It was more like half-naked…" That hadn't made it any better, apparently, as her glare intensified. "Sorry, Mother. I might not have believed him otherwise."

"So Arman did know what he was doing," Lance concluded, voice choked with laughter. "Ah, that's priceless. That's a story for the family legends, right there."

Throwing her hands up in the air, Eida gave up and went back to filling her plate.

Clearing his throat, Anthony struggled to yank a smile off his face before his wife could reprimand him for it. He, at least, found it amusing. "Arman, is it your intention to live with Ren? I thought so. Are you being reassigned duty in Castel-de-Haut, then?"

As they spoke of future plans and such, Ren's eyes moved around the table once more. How had he acquired such luck, to have a family like this? How had he earned it? He dearly wished to know, as he desperately wanted to keep them. Or was this just a blessing, a balance of karma, to make up for his own family?

Looking at his husband, who practically glowed with happiness, the flash of insecurity faded into a content hum. He'd been so worried, coming here, but all of those fears proved groundless. Whether it be luck, or karma, or just a blessing from the gods, he'd somehow acquired a home worth keeping.

❂

Arman settled near the family room's hearth after dinner ended. Most of the family followed in with him, although Richelle and Willa caught Ren and dragged him to the far corner, already discussing wedding plans. Arman appreciated that both of his sisters-in-law knew better than to ask him anything about it. His mother should have known as well, but she kept dragging him in, asking for his opinion. He had to wonder, how many pointless conversations would it take before she gave up?

With a soft huff, Lance settled into the armchair next to his, a cup of steaming tea in his hand. "Well, Arman, you've managed to thoroughly shock the whole family."

Shrugging, he gave a grunt, as he didn't really care about that. Although their reactions had been amusing.

Leaning in, Lance confided, "Mother now wonders if your interests lie more toward men, and that's why you never went along with any of her matchmaking attempts."

Rolling his eyes, Arman informed him, "That's not it."

"I didn't think so. If it was just that, you would have figured it out while in Shiirei six years ago and moved on Ren much sooner. But still, she wonders." Lance took a sip from his cup, eyes on the flickering fire in front of them. "I'm sure you'll get a thousand and one questions about it, so I won't ask, as it seems obvious enough to me. I did hear something disturbing, though. Was Ren really poisoned?"

Just the reminder of that sent a wave of fury through him and his fists clenched in his lap so hard his knuckles shone white. "Yes."

"What happened? I thought him well-loved in his position, not the sort of target for that kind of thing."

He didn't really want to dwell on it, but Arman had learned as a child to tell Lance as much as possible. His brother had connections he didn't, and his analytical mind often caught things that Arman missed. As succinctly as he knew how, he laid out the events, ending with, "Konrad is investigating it now."

"Good man to do the job," Lance agreed, expression troubled. "Praise the gods Ren knows something of poisons and medicines. I don't want to think of what might have happened otherwise. Was he sent out here to recuperate?"

"In part. In part to keep him out of the investigation."

"It won't do to have the victim investigating the crime," Lance agreed and gave his new brother-in-law's back a fond smile. "Not that you could have kept him out of things if he'd stayed in the palace. Your Ren is not the patient sort."

'His Ren,' was it? Arman had to admit he liked the sound of that. "He can be."

"With other people, yes, but not with this sort of thing." Lance paused, drinking and thinking, as was his way. Arman sensed something else bothered Lance and waited him out patiently. Finally, Lance admitted, "There is one matter about him marrying you that does trouble me. Ren's mentioned his desire to go home and see his brother more than once. If he goes, I assume you'll go with him?"

"Barring duty preventing me," Arman agreed, knowing well what Lance was driving at. "You worry his family won't accept me."

"They won't even properly accept Ren, which confounds me, truly. He's a former general, renowned for both his valor and intelligence, and now a very highly beloved warden in an ally country. I thought Shiirein culture put enough esteem in such matters to overlook Ren's nature, but even then, they barely tolerate him. I'm afraid they won't at all accept you."

Arman gave him a bemused smile. "I don't care about them. I would go to support Ren."

"Who, as we both agreed, has a short temper about such matters. Do you really think that he'll watch his family snub you and take that well?"

Ah. Damn, Lance had a good point there. Arman frowned into the fire and reconsidered his decision to go with Ren. But the idea of sending him to Shiirei alone, where very few would move to protect or help him, sent chills down his spine. "I'll keep him from murdering any of them."

"That's probably the best you can do," Lance sighed. "It broke my heart, earlier, how uncertain he was with us. I've never seen him like that before, not even the first day you brought him home with you. Although Richelle seems to have pulled him out of that."

Turning in his chair, Arman watched his husband interact with his sisters-in-law and mother-in-law. Ren said something that had all three women laughing, a wicked grin on his face. Truly, he looked far more comfortable now, acting as if he were home, which in a sense, he was. The four of them made a pretty picture and Arman watched for a moment, enjoying the scene, before returning to his conversation with his brother.

Lance had a smile on his face, his expression borderline smug. Arman cocked his head a little, questioning, and Lance explained, "It's nice to see you in love. I'm not sure if you realize how obvious it is, your feelings for Ren, but we can all see it when you look at him."

"I don't try to be unreadable on purpose," Arman protested mildly.

"Lies," his brother snorted, not believing that for a moment. "Bald-faced lies."

"What lies are we talking about?" Marshall inquired, coming to join them, sitting in the last remaining chair near the hearth.

"Arman claims he isn't unreadable on purpose," Lance drawled.

"Lies," Marshall denied instantly, shaking a finger at him. "You are impossible to read. It's always amazed me how Ren manages it so well. I grew up with you and I have no idea half the time what you're thinking."

"Wait until your life depends on it," Ren advised dryly, coming up to lean against Arman's shoulder, perching on the arm of the chair. "It's amazing what you can learn to do with the right motivation. My darling, I have a question for you. Blue or white?"

Arman didn't see how that question applied to anything he'd been discussing, and had to assume this was a wedding question of some sort. "Yes."

"Yes does not work, remember Rule Five. You can't give me a blanket 'yes' to any question. Now, blue or white?"

Lance chuckled behind the rim of his cup. "Ren, does he really just say 'yes' to you like that often? So often you had to create a rule for it?"

"You would not believe," Ren groused, although a gleam of laughter in his dark eyes suggested he didn't actually find this irritating. Poking Arman in the shoulder, he prompted, "Blue or white?"

Arman decided to go in favor of Ren's favorite color. "Blue."

"You deliberately chose that because you know it's my favorite color," Ren accused him.

Using Ren's words from last night, Arman responded innocently, "I can do things that I know will please you. It's my prerogative as a husband."

"You rat fink." Catching his head in the crook of his elbow, Ren ran a rough hand over his head, making Arman squirm in protest. "You do not use my words against me. You know what, that's a new rule. Rule Nineteen."

"There are nineteen rules?" Marshall demanded incredulously. "You're pulling my leg."

"Really nineteen," Ren confirmed. "Although it's three, five and sixteen he tends to violate the most these days. Now, husband mine, answer me honestly. Blue or white?"

"Black," Arman answered instead, partially just to get another rise out of his husband.

"You are being deliberately difficult. We can't use black for a wedding." Ren let him out of the hold, idly putting his wayward curls back in place with a light brush of the fingertips. Arman liked the attention. Usually, Ren didn't touch his head like this, but it felt quite nice. "You really don't like white? I wouldn't have thought you'd mind it much, as you often wear white shirts."

Arman shrugged, as he usually wore white shirts because they went with his uniform, so he had an abundance of those.

"Alright, blue it is, then." Dropping a kiss on his forehead, Ren hopped off the arm of the chair and went back to the planning session in the corner.

It made him ridiculously happy that Ren would be so casually affectionate in front of the rest of the family. He owed Richelle—he owed everyone—for so thoroughly putting Ren's fears to rest.

With a weather eye on his wife, Marshall leaned in and whispered, "I have to ask, I'm too curious. Is making love to a man enjoyable?"

Arman let his smirk speak volumes.

"Really?" Marshall leaned in a little further. "Give me details. You didn't find it strange?"

"I can hear you, Marshall Brahms," his wife called from the corner with a frosty look in her blue eyes.

"Damn," Marshall swore, sitting back. "She has bat ears, I swear it."

"I can still hear you!"

Defeated, Marshall slumped further into his chair, refusing to look at anyone.

Arman's shoulders shook with silent laughter. He did love Willa.

23

Anthony was far too delighted to have Ren. Ren knew this because nearly every day, his new father-in-law ran him through all of the drills, defenses, and so forth of the fortress, insisting that Ren needed to start learning how to run the place. No matter that it would be another fifteen years or so until he actually took over. No matter that Arman already knew all of this and could do it in his sleep. Ren finally saw the excuse for what it was—a chance to properly bond—and didn't argue. Besides, he enjoyed it too, having a father again.

Of course, Eida stole him away often for wedding plans, which included getting his measurements for wedding clothes. She seemed equally delighted to have another son, especially one that understood a woman liked having her creams, and knew where to buy them. Ren hadn't had such a close relationship even with his own mother, so this startled him at times, but he loved every minute of it.

They got regular updates from Hartmann, usually every four or five days. Most of them stated they'd been pressuring Giles, and the young lord had cracked under the pressure, and perhaps revealed more than he ever intended. Still no solid proof about the stamp, however. Four weeks into their stay, they got the last letter from Hartmann stating they knew who the poisoner was, and it was safe to return. Ren and Arman departed for the castle the next day.

As much as he enjoyed being at Brahms Fortress, it had been emotionally stressful in some ways. Ren enjoyed the time spent with family but he felt like he was slacking, too, and part of him itched to get back to work.

When Zonhoven Palace came into sight, a smile unwittingly came over his face. It made such a pretty picture sitting on top of the hill, the white of the stone shining in the sun. Truly, his second home had all of the beauty and majesty of some fairy tale painting. Had the long-ago architect who had designed this place meant for the green hills around the castle to be such a picturesque backdrop, or had that just been a slice of good fortune?

They came up the steep incline at a leisurely pace, not pushing the horses, and Ren saluted the guards standing to either side of the arched gateway. "Wilhms, Patrick, I'm back!"

Both men waved back, lighting up in smiles. "Welcome back!" Patrick called, leaving his post a little to meet Ren part of the way, then turning to walk with him. "Warden, did you have a good trip?"

"I did, thank you. All's been quiet here?"

"Fortunately, sir. Deputy Hartmann threatened us with death and mayhem if we slacked any. Said you had enough on your plate to worry about, and he wouldn't allow any disasters while you were gone. Colonel Konrad's run a tight ship, too. He's ferreted out a few troublemakers." Patrick rubbed at his red beard and offered, "You might want to check with him, though, sir. General O' Broín arrived yesterday to discuss what happened to Princess Alexandria. I think he really wants to speak with you."

"I'll do so, thank you." With a final salute, they passed through the gates completely and into the main stable yard. As typical for this time of day, people passed in and out, some people returning from a jaunt into the city, others heading into it for some quick shopping before dinner. Ren dismounted from his horse with a sigh of relief, and passed along the reins to the palace stable hands with a word of thanks.

Robert signaled he had the bags and to go ahead. Ren and Arman headed for the main doors that led into the palace proper. Let's see, at this time of the day, it might be easier to go and see Frei instead of Hartmann. Hartmann would likely be on his last rounds before getting off shift; he might just catch the man in Frei's office if he timed it right.

"Ren! Arman!"

Ren stopped with his foot on the bottom step leading into the palace, turning to see Roslyn approaching from the west wing at a very un-princess-like jog, her skirts in both hands to make it easier to run. She looked ready to go out, her usual silk replaced with a more practical linen, if still in blue. She'd pass out of the blue phase eventually. Moving to meet her, he stepped out of the main traffic and stopped in one of the rosebud alcoves the head gardener loved to create all around the footpaths. "Roslyn, I'm home."

"Welcome home. You're in one piece so it must have gone well."

"It did, fortunately."

"Good. Lend me some money; I'm broke and I want to go into town."

Several different parts of that request didn't make any sense. Bemused, Ren asked, "Don't you have an allowance? And why are you asking money from me?"

"Mama and Papa have started charging me for every curse word that I use," Roslyn explained, extremely put out. Crossing her arms over her chest, she muttered, "Which is ridiculous; I'm old enough to swear if I want to."

Deciding to leave that part alone, Ren asked incredulously, "You mean to tell me that you've literally spent your entire allowance this month on swearing?"

"It's that damn bastard's fault," she informed him crossly, eyes snapping with fire. "He was going around saying awful things about you and Arman. I couldn't stand it. I tore him a new one, right there in the hallway. He didn't like that, not at all, and tried to argue with me."

Ren rubbed at his forehead. "I'm just as glad I missed it. How loud were you?"

"Loud," she announced proudly. "The whole palace now knows he's a complete ass."

He didn't know whether to hug her or shake her. "Roslyn, you're surely not coming to me because you expect me to compensate you for that?"

"No, no, it's because you're my husband," she assured him with a brilliant smile.

Arman, not fazed by this, lifted Ren's left hand to wave the signet ring in the air and gave her a pointed look.

"It's fine, you're my husband too," Roslyn assured him with a pat on his forearm. "We can have a threesome."

Arman choked and turned an accusatory look on Ren.

"Why are you looking at me like that? Not everything she learns is from me!" Ren protested.

Roslyn sidled up next to him, lifting a hand to her mouth and whispering behind it, "Actually, you taught me that one."

He had?! Ducking closer to her, he whispered back, "When? I don't remember this."

"You remember that night after we got word Arman was going to have to stay up there until the fortress was built? When you got so drunk?"

Oh. Right. That night. Straightening, Ren cleared his throat before muttering to his husband, "In my defense, I was so drunk that night that I don't actually remember most of the conversation."

Arman just stared at him, resigned, although he looked a little amused by this. Fortunately.

Rocking back and forth on her toes, Roslyn assured him cheerfully, "I do!"

"That's the problem," Ren informed her darkly. "Are you ever going to tell me what all I told you that night?"

Roslyn pretended to think about this for a moment, a finger pressed to her lips. "Mmm, that depends."

Accepting the inevitable, he pulled his wallet out and started forking over money. "You are a terrible, terrible person and I have no idea why I love you so much. Alright, spill. What else did I teach you that night, aside from swearing and threesomes?"

"You told me about your first lover," Roslyn rattled things off while counting them out on her fingers, "threesomes, how to properly swear without repeating yourself, how to seduce a man properly, and how to tie a man to a bed."

Arman choked, smacking a palm against his chest, struggling either to breathe or laugh, maybe both.

Contemplative, Ren realized that it could be worse. He hadn't actually taught her the really, really inappropriate things; thank all the gods for small favors. "Is that why I woke up tied to the bed?"

"Well, I had to practice on someone, and you said it was safer to do it on you," Roslyn explained. She looked entirely too smug about all of this, like a cat that had gotten into the cream long before anyone came along to stop her. "Don't worry, Mama only knows about the swearing."

"Please keep it that way?" he pleaded with her. "Otherwise your parents really are going to kill me."

Arman gave him a Look. "Husband, you are banned from getting drunk again."

Considering that the first time he'd gotten sloshed in this country, he'd corrupted a teenage princess, and the second time he'd wound up half-naked and in bed with his best friend, Ren really couldn't find a leg to stand on. He winced. "Probably a good idea. Alright, Roslyn, I suggest learning how to insult someone without swearing, unless you want to be broke every month."

"I was doing really well until I overhead the bastard," Roslyn mourned. "I hadn't said a single cuss word for three days."

"What am I going to do with you?" Ren asked rhetorically.

"Spoil me," she responded promptly, lifting up on her tiptoes to give them both a kiss on the cheek. "Thanks, husbands! See you later! Oh, and welcome home!"

Watching her run off, heading toward her maid who waited by the gate, Ren re-examined being adopted by Roslynn. Was being adopted by a princess like being adopted by a cat? Was he past the point of no return?

Chaz came out of the palace, saluting as he came. "General, Warden, welcome home. Was it a good trip?"

"An excellent one, thank you, Chaz. How are things here?"

"Running like clockwork," Chaz assured him. "General O' Broín arrived yesterday, and wanted to speak with you once you got in. I believe he's with Prince Charles and King Gerhard at the moment in a conference, though."

"Then I'll try and speak with him later. Do you know what it's about?"

"I believe he's here to discuss the attack on Princess Alexandria, sir."

That would make sense. Anthony had requested him specifically, but they hadn't been sure the request would be granted. Good thing it had. O' Broín wouldn't rest until this problem was solved, and they needed that kind of dogged persistence. "Is Hartmann still on duty?"

"He is, sir. He and Colonel Konrad said they'd stay through the end of the day, and for you to rest."

Bless those two. Ren owed them dinner, at the very least. "I'll check in with Chamberlain Frei. If anyone's looking for me, I'll either be there or at my apartment."

"Yes, sir. Good to have you back, sir." With a salute, Chaz went back to his patrol.

Ren turned to Arman. "I shouldn't be with Chamberlain Frei for more than an hour. I know you're hungry, though, you can eat without me."

Shaking his head, Arman responded with a gentle half-smile.

"I'll wait. I'll follow up with Konrad."

"Alright, see you at home." He closed in long enough to give his husband a chaste kiss before turning and heading inside. Of course, he got wolf-whistles from anyone who saw, but those he ignored. He didn't mean to give anyone a show; he just liked kissing Arman. The man was extremely kissable—not his fault he couldn't resist.

He said hellos as he went through the main hallways, assuring anyone who asked that his vacation had gone very well, that he was feeling fine, relieved he could answer honestly. Ren had almost gained Frei's office when he heard his name hailed from behind.

"Sho."

Turning, he found General Argyle O' Broín coming up the hallway, the man's long legs eating up the ground effortlessly. In the five years since they'd served on the same warfront, the man hadn't changed much, his skin perhaps a touch paler these days. Black hair in a wavy cut down to his collar, cheekbones sharp enough to slice bread with, and a strong figure that would belong to any heroic figure in a child's fairytale, he still made an imposing figure. Unlike those days, however, he wore no armor now, just a simply-cut dark navy coat, and pants tucked into high black boots.

Having very fond memories of the man, Ren felt happy to see him, if a little worried. O' Broín's people did not readily accept men of his orientation, and surely he'd heard about Ren's marriage by now. He read no condemnation on that face, however, no unease, so Ren hoped for the best and stretched out a hand. "O' Broín. I can't tell you how happy I am to see you here."

"Happy to see you—angry for the reason," O' Broín responded in that voice that made Ren think of deep, mountainous caverns. He grasped Ren's hand firmly, then clapped him on the shoulder for good measure. "Heard about all that poisoning nonsense. I was delayed coming in because of it. We wanted to give Princess Alexandria time to recuperate, as traveling back to Scovia's likely to be a hard trip."

"I hear you on that one," Ren agreed. He wasn't surprised that Alexandria's return home was delayed because of the poisoning incident. He just thanked the gods his request for O'Broín had gone through.

"I heard of your marriage, Sho. My heartfelt congratulations to you both."

The clutch around his heart eased and Ren couldn't help the silly smile that took over his face. "Thank you. I was a little worried how you'd take the news."

O' Broín snorted, tossing this worry away with a shake of the head. "I admit, first time I heard about you, I couldn't wrap my head around it. My country has a lot of things to say about men with your orientation, none of it kind. But I served with you, remember? Hell, you saved my life at least once, twice if we're being picky."

"Let's be picky," Ren agreed mock-seriously.

"And there's no way I could believe any of that hogwash after knowing you," O' Broín finished, shaking his head in amusement. "After that, I took things as I saw them, and got a good friend out of it. Just as well I did. Brahms didn't respond well to anyone who even looked at you wrong."

Remembering all of those fights Brahms used to get involved in, Ren couldn't shrug this off. "Eh, true."

"I am upset with the two of you, however," O' Broín informed him, stabbing a finger towards his chest. "Not only did you cost me a hundred crowns, but I don't get invited to the wedding?"

Ren's jaw dropped. "Don't tell me you bet on us!"

"Sho, don't be an idiot. The whole army had a bet riding on the two of you. Whoever could prove that you two were actually lovers would inherit quite the pot, let me tell you. I think the winner was Adams, actually; he got a copy of the ship's register that showed you going home with Brahms after the war. We took that as proof enough at the time."

Not knowing whether to laugh or groan, Ren denied, "We weren't lovers then, though."

"As I now understand," O' Broín agreed amiably. "Princess Roslyn very eagerly told me the story. Well, the safe version of the story. I'm inclined to think there's another version that is not suitable for the genteel sensibilities, shall we say. Aha, I thought so. I'm half-tempted to look Adams up and demand the pot back, but I'm fairly sure he's spent it all by now."

"After five years?" Ren responded, the humor of the situation kicking in. "I would think so. Well, how about you join us for dinner tonight and I'll buy you a round to make up for it?"

"I think I should be buying *you* a round," O' Broín corrected. "To congratulate you both."

"I never turn down free drinks," Ren glanced behind him, toward the open office door, "but I have to check in first. Can we catch up later, say an hour and a half from now at the main gate?"

"Certainly. We'll discuss business tomorrow," O'Broín promised. "At the main gate, then."

"The main gate," Ren agreed. With a wave, he went into Frei's office, happy that he could catch up with an old friend after this. Although, truly, had the whole army known what he and Arman hadn't? Had they felt the two of them to be so inevitable that they'd actually bet on it?

"Ah, Ren," Frei greeted warmly, pushing a little away from his desk, relaxing back into his chair. "Welcome back."

Focusing on the here and now, Ren shoved his speculations aside and took his usual chair next to Frei. "Thank you. Konrad's been sending me updates, and I've been assured twice that nothing serious happened while I was gone, but did anything happen while I was gone?"

"Nothing serious," Frei answered in a rusty chuckle. "No more kitchen fires, magpies stealing signet rings, or anything of that ilk either. A bunch of wagging tongues spreading nonsense, of course, but that's usual in court."

"I would think the whole country suffering from an illness if they stopped gossiping," Ren agreed easily. "And? When I last heard, they'd narrowed the list of suspects on who poisoned us."

"They have indeed, and I think they know who did it. The letter from Anthony Brahms shed some very interesting light on the mace trap as well, which Colonel Konrad eagerly looked into. But I'll let them report the matter. I understand it should be sometime tomorrow, as they've baited their suspect into acting again."

Ren dearly wanted to ask questions but knew that even if he did, Frei wouldn't be able to answer them. For all their sakes, Ren had to stay out of this one. "Is that why the palace is no longer under second point of contact?"

"That's why. That and to give the culprits plenty of rope to hang themselves with. I trust that everything went well at Brahms Fortress, as you came in smiling."

"Very well," Ren assured him, feeling warm just from the memory of it. "I think they were all surprised, but my new mother-in-law is of the opinion that the heavens decided to give her a son that liked to talk to make up for the one who doesn't."

Frei barked out a laugh. "I can see her saying that very thing. Good, I'm glad that my concerns are laid to rest."

"Not as much as I am. Anything change while I was out?"

"Just your room assignment," Frei informed him, gesturing toward the large blueprints of the palace pinned to the wall behind his head. "Queen Eloise informed me that it was inconceivable that a married man, her warden, be confined to a single apartment within the palace. We've moved you to the central building, second floor."

Only one room on that level hadn't already been claimed. Ren blurted out incredulously, "The Stag Room? That's meant for visiting dignitaries!"

Frei shrugged, as if he had nothing to do with this, but the laugh lines around his eyes deepened, giving the game away. "We don't have many apartments that have enough room for a married couple and their batman. The few that I do are in the uppermost levels of the palace and in an auxiliary wing, which is too far out of the way. You need to be in a place where we can readily reach you."

True, Ren had no argument for that. Still, he felt a little floored that he'd been given such an exquisite set of rooms. "I'll have to thank the queen, and you, Frei, for this. Truly, it's more than I expected."

Leaning toward him, Frei confided, "I think this was her way of apologizing for separating the two of you, and perhaps a bit of a wedding present mixed in."

"That does sound like her, alright. Am I already moved in?"

"We didn't dare, not until you got back, but the rooms are aired out and ready for you. Take your time, there's no rush."

"Thank you, Frei. Truly. I'm—" Ren had to pause, emotion clogging his throat for a moment. "I'm overwhelmed by how readily everyone's accepted us."

"I know this wouldn't have happened in Shiirei, so it might be overwhelming for you, even strange." Frei grasped his hand and squeezed it gently. "But you're in Aart, my dear friend, and we take care of our own here. Now, you look over those rooms and tell me what you might need in the way of furniture. We took our best guess, but there might be something you'd like to change. We want you to be comfortable there, so tell us if that's not the case, alright?"

"I will," Ren promised and meant it. "Anything else?"

Hesitating, Frei carefully phrased the words before speaking them. "Konrad and Hartmann have everything well in hand, I think, but do watch your back. The young Lord Giles is proving to be more foolish than wise, and is stirring up trouble against you. Most of them are dismissing him as a lover scorned, and for good reason, but he's gaining some traction with a few of the lords. We haven't been able to truly prove he was part of that group from before; it's still your word against his."

Ren wasn't blind to the political influence he wielded as the warden here. He knew everyone's comings and goings, had authority to detain people as necessary, and could use his direct line to the royal family as he pleased. Many people coveted the position, and would dearly love to put one of their sons in his place. "I understand."

"I thought you would. For now, it's not serious, and I'll alert you if it does become a true issue. I think you've earned the right to take a few days and settle into your new apartment."

Trusting his judgment in this, Ren agreed, "I'll let you watch the situation, then. If either Konrad or Hartmann needs me, tell them I'm available. For now, I'm off to dinner in town with my husband and our old friend. Send word if you need me."

Frei shooed him on, only to call him back as he reached the door. "Ren? You won't leave us for Brahms Fortress?"

Turning back, Ren assured him with a smile. "Not yet, Frei. Not for years yet, don't you worry."

24

Arman sat back in his chair, his arm around the back of his husband's, a tankard in his hand, and a content feeling in his chest. Sitting here with O' Broín was like old times when they were still in Shiirei—although fortunately without an enemy army pounding at their doors. The pub had a nice, mellow air to it, conversations flowing around them like a swirl of music. A sole musician played a well-known love song in one of the corners, its melody adding a counterpoint. Ren was far more relaxed than Arman had ever seen him. He was vain enough to think he might have had something to do with that.

They chatted the first hour, just catching up with each other's lives since they'd last had the chance five years ago. Arman let the two do most of the talking, content to sit and listen.

Of course, O' Broín couldn't let that be, and aimed a pointed look at him. "I see some things never change. Still having Sho do all your talking for you?"

"He's Brahms now," Arman retorted pleasantly, inwardly grinning.

"I'm not calling you both Brahms, that will get confusing," O' Broín riposted cheekily. "And before you ask, I'm not using your first name, either."

Ren chuckled, eyes crinkling in amusement. "That's because you can't pronounce it."

"Damn right I can't," O' Broín declared proudly. "What kind of mouthful is that, anyway? Most of the Shiireins I know, their names are short, not multisyllables."

Shrugging, Ren confided, "I'm not sure how true this is, but my brother is seven years older than I, and he claims my parents fought for months on what to name me. My father wanted to name me after his father, my mother after her father, you get the drift. They finally took both names and crammed them together. Renji and Mantoro. Renjimantoro. Let me tell you, it makes even less sense in my native tongue."

Arman, reminded, snorted a laugh into his ale.

"What?" O' Broín demanded, interest perking. "What does it mean? I know each of those blocky characters of yours means multiple things."

"Right, it has two different readings," Ren explained with a slightly hangdog expression. "My parents really weren't thinking when they used the characters for my name. So, altogether it means: reams of paper from the melting man."

O' Broín stared at him incredulously for a second before busting out laughing. "That's terrible!"

"I know," Ren mourned. "Why do you think I go by Ren most of the time? At least that can be read multiple ways. Multiple, nice ways."

"Makes me wish I'd learned the language properly instead of the phrases to get by with. I'd have gotten a good laugh much sooner." Shaking his head, O' Broín sipped at his ale. "Although I feel like I should learn the language now for a different reason. Odds are we'll be back in Shiirei fighting again soon enough,"

Arman didn't like the sound of this and straightened. "Why?"

"It's not looking good," O' Broín stated with a shrug that was meant to look casual but came off worried. "Haven't you seen any movement?"

"No," Arman denied, still not sure what his friend drove at. "After the war, the Z's blamed their king for the failure to win and had him executed."

"They've been a bunch of headless chickens running around ever since," Ren filled in. "Past two years especially they've been so scattered, they haven't even given Brahms Fortress a good test of the defenses. They've got, what, fourteen different candidates for king right now, according to Father?"

"That's what Lance reported to him," Arman confirmed. "They're not unified enough to march on anyone. But what are you seeing, O' Broín?"

"Not from the Z's, but the Mongs," O' Broín admitted darkly. "They're making…unhappy sounds, to put it mildly. They've been trying to send ambassadors, emissaries, the works to the other countries demanding war reparations. Which is rich, coming from them. Everyone's turned them down flat, and they're not happy about it. The tone coming from them now is threatening, like it was six years ago."

Ren went very still at those words, his eyes searching out Arman's, worry reflecting in them. Arman shared that worry, but not just in the way Ren felt it. "How sure of this are you?"

Shaking his head, O' Broín confessed, "It's more a gut feeling than anything concrete. I see the potential for another war but it's nothing firm enough that we could put a staying hand to it. Still, if I had to put all my money on the culprit for our recent troubles? It would be the Mongs. They're the only ones upset enough to act out like this."

"You're likely right, but if there is another war…" Ren trailed off unhappily.

"Shiirei will be in trouble." Arman felt like those words qualified for the understatement of the century. It would be so much worse than that. They didn't have the resources, manpower, or leadership necessary to fight another war right now. They wouldn't for another decade at least.

"Of course, if Shiirei's invaded again, we'll go to its aid," O' Broín assured Ren, manner suggesting he wasn't just trying to cheer him up, but it was simple truth. "My king's been very firm on that, as I'm sure King Gerhard is. If this happens, do you think Shiirei will recall you?"

"Recall me?" Ren repeated in flat amazement. "O' Broín, I'm not in the army anymore."

O' Broín faltered, looking between them askance. "Oh. I thought you were…well, in reserve. Wait, they really discharged you?"

"They discharged everyone but essential personnel to maintain border security," Ren answered, rubbing a tired hand against his forehead. "Since I've left, three other generals have retired, which leaves only one general still in command over there."

"Wait, *one*?" O' Broín demanded incredulously, ale sloshing over his hand as he jerked forward. "I grant you, Shiirei's not as big as some of the other countries, but it needs more than one general! Holy hell, if the Mongs invade, it'll be a complete disaster. Shiirei really released all of their officers? What the hell were they thinking?"

"That they couldn't pay all of their officers," Ren responded wearily. "Look, I didn't say it was a good decision, but it was the only one they could make, financially. They couldn't even release us with full pay. We all got half-pay and were frankly grateful for even that."

"Shit," O' Broín breathed, the full impact of it all hitting him, his eyes going wide in a rapidly paling face. "Fucking shit, Sho, that's not good. You're the only general I could work with. And now you're telling me that not only can you not go back to your former position, but all of the officers we developed a rapport with are gone too?"

Arman saw the problem intimately well. He'd experienced a great deal of grief while in Shiirei, even after meeting Ren. And the only reason he'd managed to get anything done during the war was because Ren fully cooperated with him. "Something needs to change. If what you're seeing with the Mongs is true, then Shiirei needs to be properly prepared or it will fall."

O' Broín ran a tired hand over his face. "Damn. This is worse than I anticipated, and I wasn't imagining anything pretty. I really hope I'm reading the situation wrong, that they're planning more of a land attack than going to sea again. Most of our reports indicate they're pressing Scovia the most."

"Makes sense, they share a border with it," Arman allowed, although that didn't entirely sit well with him. The Mongs had never tried to attack Scovia before, always taking to the sea first and pestering people along the coast, as it was easier to do hit and run tactics that way. The Mongs rarely went into a full out war unless a very rich prize drew them in. Like Shiirei's spice trade. He felt like he stared at a puzzle but was missing the necessary pieces to see the full picture.

"O' Broín," Ren stated slowly, "I want to talk to you more about what we can do to prepare Shiirei's defenses. I don't want the country caught with its pants down like last time. Before you leave with Alexandria, let's properly sit down and come up with some ideas. I can pitch it to King Gerhard, you pitch it to your king, and maybe we can get somewhere with it."

Arman nodded approval. His Ren's strength was people. Ren could get mountains to move through his connections with people. Arman had no doubt that with Ren's mind turned to this problem, a solution would present itself.

"Of course," O' Broín assured him readily, already proving Arman's point. "Shit, man, but you have no idea how much this scares me. I do *not* want to have to return to Shiirei; that was bloody difficult enough the first time. We'll discuss it properly, come up with some ideas, and you can bet I'll pitch it to my king the minute I'm back home. Let's thwart the Mongs properly this time, yeah?"

"You're the best, O' Broín," Ren responded with a wide smile and toasted the man.

Arman clinked his tankard with the others' and let the topic change to something lighter. There would be time enough for duties. Tonight, he wanted to focus on his friend.

"The problem is," O' Broín stated in open aggravation, "we don't know who attacked the princess. It could be any number of political parties unhappy with this alliance, or the Mongs, or the Z's. They were very careful to leave no trace of themselves behind, and even the princess's people aren't sure. I don't think that we can blithely assume anything."

Ren stared hard at the map on the table, unable to disagree with his friend. Ren, Arman, O' Broín, Prince Charles, Princess Alexandria, Galvath, and Stas Preben, Captain of Alexandria's guard, had gathered this morning for a very amiable breakfast in the Queen's Morning Room. But the dishes were cleared off the table now, a map taking their place, and the topic shifted to business. Looking up at the opposite side of the table, Ren asked, "Captain Preben, not even their fighting styles looked familiar?"

"They very carefully didn't attack us with swords, but with arrows and caltrops," Preben replied, his beak-like nose wrinkling in distaste. "Which sounds less than formidable, but with the caltrops surrounding us on all sides, we found evading the archers difficult."

"I've used just such a tactic before to devastating effect," Ren assured him. "Trust me, I know how deadly it can be. So, they thought to disguise even their fighting style. Interesting."

"Says their fighting style is a dead giveaway," Arman observed thoughtfully.

Preben inclined his head in agreement. "I'd come to that same conclusion. Unfortunately, the bastards—excuse my language, Your Highness—were thorough in their deception."

"I've called them worse, Preben," Alexandria assured him darkly.

"Don't limit your language on my account. Alright, if we can't make any determinations on who attacked me, then what can we do? It will be difficult to guard against an unknown enemy."

"Yes and no," O' Broín replied, turning in his seat to face the head of the table and address her more directly. "Certainly, we can't develop any tactics to confront a specific enemy, but some defenses are universal. I think with the right precautions, we can still get you safely home."

"Such as only releasing our itinerary for departure the night before," Galvath offered to her. "That will give the enemy very little time to move against us. It puts the odds in our favor of slipping past them."

"That and taking some educated guesses on where along our route they could effectively ambush us," Ren added, thinking hard. Although releasing her itinerary last minute would hopefully prevent any other poisoning attempts as well. "If we plan this right, we can have certain people in place at each point, ready to give us aid if we need it."

Arman nodded along with this. "Trap within a trap."

"Precisely," O' Broín agreed. "Your Highness, my king was very upset about you being attacked on our soil. I am authorized to pull whatever resources I deem necessary to safeguard your return. Sho and I talked about this briefly last night, and I think with enough support on hand, we can travel quick and light, perhaps outrun them before they can attack."

"A heavy guard certainly didn't deter them," Alexandria responded thoughtfully, staring at the men surrounding her. "I like the idea of traveling swiftly, but I would assume you would send only the very strongest fighters with us, if we choose this plan."

"To offset the disadvantages, yes, we'd have to," Ren agreed promptly. "But we'll get to that part later. Can we take this as agreement to travel under light guard?"

Alexandria shared a speaking glance with Charles, who responded, "You may. Are we taking the same route back?"

Preben shook his head firmly. "I advise against that."

"Perhaps only in the beginning," Ren counseled. "We know for a fact that it will be safe to go up and through Brahms Fortress, as my father-in-law will not tolerate anything untoward on his section of the roads. I suggest going north and up, toward the main highway, staying at Brahms Fortress for a night, then continuing east along Trader's Route until you get to the Bhodhsa turn-off."

"You came this direction on the way up. If we repeat your steps only to a certain point, and then take you further south again, to the Fifth Highway, then it puts you more squarely in Bhodhsa's territory. From there, I can arrange more protection for the rest of the trip."

In an aside, Ren asked O' Broín quietly, "I've always wondered, why is it called the Fifth Highway?"

"Because the first king who ordered it built was a skin-flint when it came to money and he didn't build it right," O' Broín whispered back, leaning slightly toward Ren in his chair. "It had to be added onto four more times to get it the right size and length to be useable."

"Ah. That would explain it."

Charles stood from his chair to come around and stand in between Ren and Arman, leaning on the table and tracing the map route with his finger. "We avoid the same area she was attacked in last time if we do that, true, but are you convinced this road is any safer?"

"Marginally safer," O' Broín responded carefully. "There are more potential places for ambushes, but those areas all have either garrisoned troops or lord's manors nearby, with one exception. I can arrange for aid to be on standby on this road without much hassle. If you retrace the route Princess Alexandria took on the way in, however—"

"There's not much help to be had up there," Alexandria acknowledged with a troubled frown. "We found that out the hard way. Lord Brahms was our nearest safe haven. Charles, I like the option they're presenting. I trust General O' Broín's judgment in this."

"I do admit it seems the best option," Charles admitted slowly. "General O' Broín, how long will it take for you to set this up?"

"A week?" O' Broín offered. "A week at most, I would say. I can borrow some of your pigeons, send messages out, and have it organized rather quickly. Word spread very quickly about Princess Alexandria's trip here, and my people are not pleased about it; they consider it a slap in the face, so they'll be more than ready to help."

Bhodhsa took their border's security very, very seriously. It was part of the reason why Ren had suggested O' Broín come up. He knew the man would be motivated to make sure an attack didn't happen again. Ren dearly wished they didn't have to take Charles with them on this trip, as in a security sense, guarding two royals provided quite the headache. Unfortunately, the prince was due to not only have another engagement ceremony in Scovia before the end of the month, but to tour the country with Alexandria and be formally introduced to the people. He'd be there for several months. They had to take him now.

The doors to the Morning Room opened and King Gerhard and Queen Eloise swept through. Everyone immediately stood and gave them a bow in greeting.

"Good morning, everyone. I have an announcement to make."

Sensing he had something vital to say, they all stood to hear the news.

"We've caught the poisoner," King Gerhard announced gravely. "Colonel Konrad and Deputy Warden Hartmann presented the evidence against her last night, and today we caught her red-handed in the act of trying to poison the food going to this very table. Alexandria, I am sorry to inform you it was your maid, Ula."

Alexandria let out a gasp, then slammed her fist against the table, making everything on it jump. "That bitch!" Belatedly realizing her manners, she muttered, "Excuse me, Your Majesties."

"I said the exact same thing," Queen Eloise assured her darkly. "The gall of the woman!"

"Have you interrogated her?" Ren pressed, relieved the culprit had been caught, but more interested in her employer.

King Gerhard shook his head grimly. "Sadly, she had poison ready to take should she be caught. She was dead within minutes. We're all very aggrieved by this, as we'd hoped to know our enemy."

Dammit, of course they sent someone like that in. Ren hated when people felt their lives were so disposable. "Princess Alexandria, how well do you know this woman?"

"Not that well," she admitted, still looking irate enough to revive the dead woman to murder her all over again. "She was one of the staff members made available to me. I changed up most of my immediate staff and guards, trying to throw off any enemy and keep them from bribing or threatening their way into my party. The attempt obviously failed."

"Not for lack of trying," Preben stated tiredly. "My apologies, Your Highness, nothing in her background suggested anything untoward."

"Nothing ever does," O' Broín muttered. "I'm sorry for the loss,

Your Majesty."

"Not as much as we are. I'm afraid that the matter of the mace trap in the linen closet will take more time, but Lord Brahms gave us some good information. We'll get to the bottom of the matter." With a shake of the head, King Gerhard moved past the subject. "I see that we've started planning already." The king stopped at the head of the table, near Alexandria's shoulder, and peered toward the map. "What have we decided, if anything?"

"A route, My King." Ren popped up to trace the path they'd take, explaining as he went and concluding, "General O' Broín assures us he can arrange support in the tricky areas along the road, so we're all in favor of a light guard, to help speed the journey along."

"And hopefully outrun our enemies?" Queen Eloise queried thoughtfully. She brought her fan out to play as she took Charles' vacated seat, idly cooling her face. "I am not displeased with the idea."

Addressing O' Broín, King Gerhard carefully stated, "No offense to you or your men, General O' Broín, but I'd feel better having some of my own accompany Alexandria and Charles back to Scovia."

"Of course," O' Broín assured him in that deep, bass rumble. "For that matter, Your Majesty, I didn't bring enough men with me to adequately protect them. I assumed you would include your own guard."

King Gerhard looked a little relieved to have missed stepping on anyone's toes. "Excellent, well, in that case, I think I'll send—"

In the same breath, Charles and Alexandria interrupted: "I want Brahms." "I want Ren." Then they blinked and looked at each other, a little bemused.

Heaving a gusty sigh, the king reminded them both, "They only just returned home, I can't send Ren back out again. Charles, I certainly don't mind if General Brahms accompanies you, however. I think that's a reasonable request."

"You're going to send a newly married man out without his husband? A man that we all know to be one of our strongest fighters?" Queen Eloise objected, snapping her fan shut, a glare building as she stared at her husband. "This, after we separated them for two years? For shame."

"Dearest—" King Gerhard started, already weary with the argument. The poor king hated nothing more than arguing.

"Father, I can't have Ren?" Alexandria asked plaintively, a pout forming. "Are you sure?"

He looked to his future daughter-in-law who openly pouted, to Brahms who secretly pouted (and doing a poor job of hiding it), to his wife who both pouted and glared. Throwing his hands up in the air, he informed the room at large, "I don't care. Do whatever you want, I don't care. It's not worth the argument."

"Ren and Brahms, then." Charles beamed at them. "Sorry, I know you only got back; do you mind another trip?"

Sparing a look at his husband, Ren double checked with him and got a slight dip of the chin in agreement. "That's perfectly fine, My Prince, Princess. I'd rather go with you than you suffer ill on your journey home."

"It'll be more fun with you two along anyway," Alexandria informed them, beaming. Her expression turned a little sly and she added, "Perhaps on that long journey, I can finally get one of you to confess the story of how General Brahms proposed."

Ren shot his husband a look that promised death if he uttered a peep. Arman looked back steadily, a smirk playing around the corners of his mouth.

"It especially makes me curious when you two react that way," Alexandria added, waggling her eyebrows. "It makes me think something naughty went on."

Why, why couldn't have Arman proposed normally? Ren still believed that it took Arman's maneuvering to get him to believe the proposal was sincere, so he didn't regret it. But if Arman had at least tried a normal method first, he would've had a good story to use when people asked the question.

Queen Eloise moved them along with a pleased expression, her fan coming back into play. "Very well, I'm glad that's settled. General, I leave the guard up to you. Ren, I believe Frei and Hartmann managed everything in your absence, but do make sure that everything is handled before you leave. I'll request Colonel Konrad to stay on a little longer and help cover the work until you return. And everyone, I want it understood that we absolutely will not tell anyone about the date of departure until the night before. I want to keep this secret for as long as possible. Is that clear? Good. Now, Alexandria, when do you need to leave?"

"General O' Broín believes he can set this up within a week," Alexandria responded, worrying at her bottom lip with pearly white teeth. "I think nine days from now. I don't want people needlessly waiting on me. And I need to get home; there are certain duties waiting on us."

"Nine days, then," King Gerhard agreed. "Are there any objections to this? No? Excellent. Charles, go through all of the anticipated problems for the journey, and then submit a detailed report to me later. Because we are going through General O' Broín's homeland, I appoint him as the lead on this trip. General, I would take it as a kindness if you escort my people back after Charles and Alexandria have safely arrived in Scovia."

"I wouldn't dream of doing otherwise, Your Majesty," O' Broín assured him.

King Gerhard relaxed a little, clearly happy that he had such competent people working a problem that worried him. "I'll send a letter to King Brayan later to thank him for your services. Ren, do try to return within a month's time. Roslyn is simply impossible while you're gone."

Ren gave him a bow. "I will try, My King."

"Good. Gentleman, daughter, I'll leave you to it." Offering a hand to his wife, the monarchs swept out of the room again.

Resuming their seats, everyone bent toward the map once more. Ren pulled a pen toward him, asking O' Broín as he did so, "Alright, so you'll arrange backup. I must ask, how do you plan to signal for help if we need it? We won't have time to rush off a message."

"Unless you plan to have them wait right on the road itself?" Preben queried.

Shaking his head, O' Broín explained, "We'll use a signal flare. Of course, we'll maintain a fourth point of contact with Princess Alexandria."

Ren tried to not react and failed, his cheeks heating a little.

Giving him an odd look, O' Broín repeated, "A fourth point of contact. You know, a bodyguard."

"I'm aware." Ren wasn't about to explain that he knew what the man meant. It was the *other* meaning he'd first thought of, and the idea of a seven-way orgy had briefly flashed through his head.

"Ren," Charles drawled, a mischievous smile drawing up the corners of his mouth, "I take it that in Shiirei, that means something completely different?"

"Yes, it does." Ren made his tone brisk, no-nonsense, discouraging further question. Ren had already corrupted one princess, he refused to drag Alexandria in as well.

Alexandria caught on and she rolled her eyes. "You're not going to explain as long as I'm in the room, are you? Ren, I am well aware what sex is, you know."

"This would require me explaining gay sex, and I absolutely refuse," he responded sweetly. Clapping his hands together, he forcefully went back to the original topic. "Now, moving on—O' Broín, you know this road better than any of us, where are the best places to set up an ambush?"

Later that night, Ren lay face down on their new bed, naked from the waist up, and receiving a perfectly lovely massage. They were still not fully moved into the new apartment yet, but most of their clothes and personal effects had made it up, so they chose to stay the night up here. Robert, especially, appreciated having a private space away from the two of them.

The new bed was nice. Ren quite liked it, as it had more width than his old one. Not that they were using that extra space at the moment. Arman straddled his thighs, hands oiled up, moving in sure strokes as he worked the knots out. Ren more or less melted into a puddle with every pass. "I love your hands."

Arman chuckled lowly. "I see that."

"No, seriously, I love your hands. Half of the reason I married you was for your hands. I'm so glad I taught you how to do thisssss…. owww. Ow, that's a knot, right there."

Pressing against it with his thumb, Arman slowly pulled one way, then another, working it loose and ignoring his husband's squirms of discomfort.

"I'd forgotten how stressful it is to plan troop movements," Ren sighed as the knot released and Arman moved on. "O' Broín knows what he's doing, as does Preben, which makes it easier. I think we have a good chance of making it to Scovia without any trouble, don't you?"

"Mmh."

"That was not a sound of agreement. You don't think we'll make it?"

"I think we'll be attacked," Arman sighed. "We'll probably make it."

"You've got that gut feeling too, eh? And here I thought it was little ole paranoid me. True, if they tried to attack Alexandria once and failed, they'll not likely give up just like that. And having Charles along will be too tempting of a target for them to pass up."

"Exactly."

"Evil men are so unimaginative and persistent," Ren grumbled against the sheets. "I especially hate them for being persistent. Don't they understand we have better things to do with our time? And why are you taking off my pants?"

"They need taking off," Arman answered innocently.

Slitting open an eye, Ren tilted is head so he could look at his husband. "Are you thinking what I hope you're thinking?"

"Probably."

"Oh good." Ren wiggled and helped as best he could for the pants to go away without doing something energetic, like sitting up. Then he flopped back down, smiling as one of those lovely fingers entered him to start stretching him out. "Ahhh. Mmmm. You could have done this last night, you know."

"You were drunk last night," Arman disagreed.

Granted, he'd been a little tipsy. O' Broín had instigated a drinking contest and Ren had never been able to decline those. Especially not when O' Broín had pulled out a bottle of fine Bhodhsa liquor. Ren licked his lips in memory of the rich taste of the alcohol. "I regret nothing, it was delicious. But for future reference, I'm perfectly fine with drunken sex."

A second finger pressed in, scissoring, only pausing for Arman to use a little more oil before resuming. Ren's channel heated up pleasantly and he shifted so he could push back on those fingers, his cock thickening in response to the stimuli.

Because of his preoccupation with Arman's fingers, it took a second to register that he hadn't gotten an agreement from his husband. Tilting his head again, he studied that beloved face and realized Arman looked a little disturbed. "You don't like the idea?"

Arman shook his head and explained, "Feels like I'm taking advantage of you."

"You really, really aren't. Even if I'm drunk, if I ask for sex, trust me, I'm—ahhhh," Ren's vision went white for a second as Arman's fingers found the right spot and hit it without mercy. Shaking a little, he gasped, "I'll argue this later. In me, now."

Being a disobedient husband, Arman did not follow orders, instead only inserting another finger. Ren thoroughly liked that finger, he had nothing against it, but that was not what he wanted in him just then. Growling, he tried urging Arman once more. "Not with a finger. You. In. Me."

Arman's eyes twinkled and he didn't make a single move to obey Ren's demands.

"Tormenting me, eh? You think this is funny? I'll pay you back for this later, Brahms, see if I don't. You'll wake up tied to the bed one morning with me doing perfectly evil things to you—"

Removing his fingers, Arman draped himself over Ren's back to whisper right against his ear, "Sounds like incentive, not punishment."

Arman had figured out Ren's weakness was his ears several weeks ago and seemed to enjoy pushing that button. Ren wished he didn't react to it so strongly, but something about his husband's husky whispers made every nerve he had tingle. "Arman, so help me—"

Something blunt and hard pressed against his entrance, teasing without entering. Arman chuckled against his ear, hands gliding up and down Ren's sides. "So impatient."

Maybe he thought he could just rest there and drive Ren crazy, but even on his stomach like this, Ren still had his knees semi-underneath him, which gave him leverage. He quickly reached underneath himself to steady Arman's cock and then pushed back, taking Arman in with one hard stroke. This time his husband was the one unable to formulate words, just groan. Ren had to pause for a moment, as that burned a little more than he expected. Perhaps he hadn't been quite as ready as he thought. The sensation passed, leaving him full and stretched. A shiver of anticipation raced up and down his spine.

Arman didn't really like this position, so Ren felt no surprise when he levered them both up so that he straddled Arman's thighs instead, both of them kneeling. It sent Arman even deeper into Ren and a moan caught in his throat. This always felt so amazing. Ren reached up, catching Arman's head with both of his hands, the only thing he could comfortably reach. His fingers played with the short hair on that taut neck.

"Good?" Arman checked, breath coming out in short pants.

"Yes, so good, move, please," Ren moaned, lifting himself up before dropping back down again. Arman's hands came to his waist, pulling him up, then drawing him back down, setting a rhythm they both wanted. Sliding up was a release, coming down was fulfillment, and Ren could never decide which he liked better. A selfish part of him wanted both at once, which always drove them faster, harder.

The bed squeaked in counterpoint to their movements, like a maidenly aunt scolding them. Ren made a mental note to replace the bed after all, then went right back to the bliss of having a thoroughly enjoyable romp with his husband. He could feel the pleasure building, the desire for release screaming through his body, but he didn't want to give in just yet. Arman always came last, which smarted a little at Ren's pride. Today, he wouldn't give in until Arman lost all control and—

Arman shifted a hand over to his cock, stroking it rapidly, and Ren's control shattered. Crying out, his back arched, internal walls clenching around Arman, sending the other man over the edge. Shaking under the force of it, he didn't even try to move, just knelt there with his head resting on Arman's shoulder. Arman put both arms around his waist, letting his forehead rest on Ren's shoulder, their chests heaving as they caught their breath.

"Darling."

"Mmm."

"In case you were wondering, *this* is a fourth point of contact in Shiirei."

For a moment, he didn't connect it to their meeting earlier, then Arman laughed outright against Ren's skin.

25

Ren really, truly did not have time to attend a formal dinner that night, not since they planned to leave in just over a week to take Alexandria home. He had a great deal to prepare to make that happen. But Roslyn insisted, saying since she wouldn't see them for a month, and the least they could do was have dinner with her. So, there he sat at the head table in-between his husband and a princess. Roslyn smiled at everything, in high spirits, and cuddled her head against Ren's chest whenever her parents had their heads turned.

At least he didn't need to worry about finding dinner. The kitchen staff had outdone themselves tonight. Ren paid more attention to everything that came onto his plate than the various lords and ladies sitting about the table. He found the crowded room to be a bit too noisy for comfort, and he couldn't really relax and enjoy the meal properly. Sometimes the U-shaped table had more empty chairs than occupied, but not tonight. Tonight the room hosted at full capacity, the air thick with smoky candlelight, rich aromas, and chatter.

"Ren."

Turning to Arman, he didn't try to speak with his mouth full, just hummed questioningly.

"Giles is glaring at you. End, right side, blue jacket."

It took considerable effort on his part to ignore that glare, lethal even from this distance. The scales for homicidal rage tilted in his favor, not Giles', and being forced to ignore it grated on his nerves.

"That," Roslyn informed Arman acidly, "is typical of Giles. He does it at every formal dinner."

The hand around Arman's fork clenched, going white-knuckled under the force of his grip, threatening the integrity of its shape altogether. Ren quickly slid an arm around his waist, discreetly holding him back, and whispered into his ear, "I do not want blood in my food."

"I can break his neck," Arman rumbled back. "Bloodless that way."

Roslyn grinned like a hungry shark at Giles. "I approve, my husband. Go forth."

"I do not approve," Ren growled at them both, exasperated. "Eat your dinner."

Arman's scrutiny made it feel like he could see right through to the back of Ren's skull. "Wifey approved."

"Do not call her wifey; if the queen hears you she'll strangle us both, and I don't care what Roslyn thinks. I do not want you in jail for murder." Ren hardened his tone, staring Arman down. "Ignore him and eat."

Arman's lips pursed, not backing down, just thinking. "The queen will pardon me."

"She absolutely will," Roslyn promised him hopefully. "Oh, oh, he's moving. He's coming this way."

Arman's chair scraped back, giving him room to stand. Ren looked at the situation and just knew what would happen next. It was almost inevitable that the young fool couldn't leave well enough alone. Just how lonely had he been to get involved with an idiot like this?

As inescapable as this confrontation promised to be, Ren didn't like the timing of it. Politically speaking, having a physical fight right here at a formal dinner would not do him any favors. Even if he did want to bash Giles' nose into the back of his skull. Ren glanced to the main dais, but the queen and king had moved off at some point, likely making the rounds and chatting with people. Alright, so Queen Eloise wouldn't be nearby to egg this on; at least he had that going for him.

Ren really felt torn about this whole situation. As much as he agreed that Giles deserved another punch in the mouth, he'd already been punished publicly once already. Ren didn't see how adding more fuel to the fire would help anyone. And he could tell from the slightly unsteady gait, Giles had imbibed a bit too much at dinner. Drunken fools never made good decisions.

Someone, likely a friend, hastily got out of his seat and scurried after Giles. Catching his arm, he said something urgently in a low tone, but Giles threw the restraining hand off, heading for him anyway.

Making a snap decision, Ren signaled both Chaz and Wilkes

away from the doors, pointing to Giles. They nodded back and moved as a unit, catching Giles by the arms before he could make it another few steps and hauling him directly out of the room. Ren left his chair and followed after, thankful that whatever happened now, at least it wouldn't be a public display.

Old hands at handling drunk and foolish lords, the guards hauled Giles directly into one of the empty antechambers nearby, reserved for this purpose. Ren ducked in after them, not surprised when Arman arrived at his heels, but very surprised to find Frei already seated inside. The chamberlain sat at the only table in the room, dinner spread out in front of him, and he daintily wiped his mouth with a napkin as they burst inside. "Ah, so he did decide on a foolish course. Wilkes, Chaz, thank you for Lord Giles's abrupt removal. Did he make a scene?"

"Warden Ren requested we remove him before he had a chance, sir," Wilkes reportedly in a perfectly neutral tone. Really, it was a thing of beauty, it was so bland.

Ren hastily closed the door before coming around to stand near Frei.

Giles glared up at the guard, still a little unsteady on his feet. "So I can't even call this cocksucker out?"

"One more disgraceful word from you, my lord," Frei warned, expression darkening like an encroaching storm, "and you'll find yourself in very uncomfortable accommodations. Queen Eloise has made her stance on this clear. Whatever your personal feelings, you are not allowed to attack her warden, especially not in public."

Giles craned his head around to give Ren a rich leer, which didn't match the disgust in his eyes. "I see you're using your body to your advantage, as usual. How many times did you have to fuck *him* before he agreed to mar—"

Arman moved so quickly even Ren barely tracked his speed. Giles' head snapped back, blood spurting from his nose, and he would have fallen straight to the carpet if not for the hold the two guards still had on him. Grabbing him by the front of his collar, Arman hauled him back up and breathed, "The man you are so casually insulting in front of me is not only my husband, but the most beloved warden Aart has ever had. He was lead general in Shiirei, and one of the main reasons why Aart's economy didn't collapse due to the Mong's invasion of his homeland. Without him, *my lord*, you wouldn't be living the life of luxury you have now. I can imagine how much it hurt to lose him, as he is a very attentive and affectionate lover, but you lost him through your own stupidity. You have no one else to blame."

Giles glared back at him, but the glare trembled, lacking force, and he looked a little pale underneath the drunken flush in his cheeks. Arman looked angry enough to dismember him, and even through the alcoholic haze, Giles apparently realized that no one in this room would stop him from doing so. In fact, they'd all perfectly be willing to hide the body.

"You're already implicated in falsifying evidence," Frei added sharply.

Giles tried for a growl, but the way his eyes widened gave his fear away. "Like you can prove anything—"

"We know you did," Frei cut through cleanly, voice modulated once more, "but by all means, give me another charge that I can lay at your door. Unless, of course, you want to use this opportunity to confess and lower your sentence?"

Giles' mouth curled up in a sneer. "You're fishing, Chamberlain."

So he knew that. Ren didn't know who had coached Giles, but they'd done a thorough job at it. Aside from being generally obnoxious, he seemed to have a plan he'd stuck to, as he certainly refused to say anything enlightening.

The door opened and Roslyn stepped through, whispering loudly, "Is he dead yet? Oh damn, he isn't. What's the holdup?"

Ren rolled his eyes to the heavens and wondered: why did he have to be the responsible one in this situation? "Wilkes, Chaz, before someone really is murdered in this room, kindly take Giles to the drunk tank and leave him there for the night."

Spluttering, Giles snapped his head around and screeched, "You wouldn't dare—"

"You either go to the drunk tank, or you lose a limb tonight," Ren informed him flatly. "Your choice."

"I've done *nothing* to deserve—" Giles protested hotly, voice rising in volume.

Frei slapped a hand against the table, the sound like a percussive drum. "Lord Giles, Queen Eloise commanded you to show due respect to her warden and to never, ever, make a public spectacle of yourself again. You deliberately have violated that command twice. If not for Warden Ren's quick actions, you would have done it *at a formal dinner*."

Giles apparently had forgotten all of that while wallowing in the bottom of his cups. He paled at the reminder.

"He is being extremely lenient with you by only incarcerating you for the night, and I suggest you take him up on the offer, as his husband looks perfectly willing to tear your mouth off altogether," Frei informed him tartly. "I must say, in his shoes, I might not have hesitated to do so. Now, will you go without a fight, or do I have to finally use that secret passage to smuggle your corpse into the river tonight?"

Giles had no means for defense and no allies. His head dropped and he croaked to the floor, "I'll go."

"Excellent. Wilkes, Chaz, if you will." Frei watched them retreat, Giles stumbling a little over his own feet, then rubbed at his forehead after they were gone. "Young fool. Thank you, Ren, for acting as you did. I know it couldn't have been easy."

"Part of me really wants to whittle him down to size," Ren admitted, "but it won't improve the situation. And I still hope we can use his connection to catch the rest of his nefarious group. Thank you, Frei, for setting up this safeguard."

"I, too, am trying to diffuse the situation before it grows out of hand," Frei responded wearily. "Although Giles seems determined to spoil our efforts. Enough about that. Return to your dinner."

"Wait," Roslyn blurted, eyes shining with excitement. "Is there really a secret passage that leads down to the river?"

Catching both of her shoulders, Ren frog-marched her toward the door. "Forget about it, Roslyn."

"That's not a denial," the princess pointed out hopefully, willing to be led. "There is? There really is? Why don't you ever tell me these things? Where is it?"

With a straight face, Arman informed her, "I'm afraid that's classified."

"I'm a princess of Aart, I can be told classified information!" she retorted. "Tell me, hubby, pleeeeease?"

"Classified," Arman maintained blandly.

"Awww."

Ren left for Scovia in seven days and had far too much on his plate. He felt like one of those street performers, the ones that could juggle multiple balls—only instead of balls, people kept throwing in random things like pigeons and daggers. A palace runner—a new one; Ren barely recognized the face and couldn't for the life of him remember the name—came running his direction at near breakneck speed. The child looked barely old enough to even gain a runner's position in the palace, but he skidded to a halt, and drew himself into an admirably straight posture of attention in front of Ren, like a seasoned veteran. "Warden. A Lady Harriet Kastner is in Chamberlain Frei's office. It's urgent she see you."

Harriet Kastner? It took a second for it to click, as Ren wasn't used to thinking of her with her married name. Harriet Eberhardt, Deidrick's once fiancée. He hadn't seen her at court in at least two months, but Harriet was a friend now, and if she called for him then she certainly needed him. "Thank you."

Ren took off running at a quick clip, not fast enough to wind himself, as he'd need the ability to talk once he arrived. He took a more creative route than pure hallways, traveling through two open windows, along a roofline, across a garden, then up again before gaining the glass doors leading into Frei's office. Frei didn't look at all surprised at Ren's unusual entrance, although Harriet started visibly. "I have been summoned, I believe?"

Gesturing him all the way in, Frei responded, "You have, and you arrived quickly, which is good. I sent out three runners to search for you. Ren, we finally have something to pin that lout with."

That sounded entirely promising, and Ren knew exactly who Frei meant. Giles. First, however, he greeted his friend properly. "Harriet. You look so much more radiant than when I saw you last."

She rose from her chair, extending both hands to him, her face lit up in a smile that truly added beauty twice over again. She no longer wore her curly brunette hair up in a severe bun at the top of her head, but let it fall half-loose in a waterfall cascade of curls around her shoulders, framing her heart-shaped face in a truly flattering way. She seemed far more vibrant now than he'd ever seen her. "If I look that way, it's because I *am* that way, and I largely have you to thank for it. But shame on you for not telling me about General Brahms; I had to hear it through rumor."

"A lot happened," he sighed. "Most of it not pleasant, as you know. Although I'm happy to report that you're right, being married to a good man is incredibly lovely."

"Isn't it?" she agreed in perfect understanding. "Don't you feel like you're on the verge of smiling all day?"

"That's precisely it." Ren couldn't have phrased it better himself. "But what's brought you to me? That louse Giles hasn't tried to start trouble with you, has he?"

"No, he's basically ignored me ever since we formally parted ways," she assured him darkly. "I'm here because I can finally return the favor."

Ren didn't follow this at all. She tugged at one of his hands, leading him to the table, and he went with her, not fighting it. A leather satchel lay on the table, and from it, she drew out a rectangular piece of wood roughly two inches long. Flipping it to display the end, she asked, "Look familiar?"

That was his signature stamp. Ren's mouth dropped open, and he spluttered, trying to form words and failing utterly. No, wait, it wasn't his. Takahiro still had his, but this looked eerily similar. "Where the hell did this come from?"

"This," she responded triumphantly, "is the mockup. The trial version before the finalized product. And I found it in the hands of a young woodcarver living on Deidrick Giles' country estate."

Floored, he stared at her incredulously. "Harriet. Please start at the beginning."

"Gladly." She beamed, entirely too smug about the whole matter. Taking a chair, she waited until he fumbled into one, then launched confidently into her story. "My family and the Gileses aren't really on good terms after everything that happened, but we still see each other socially; it's difficult not to. Roughly two weeks ago, I heard Deidrick bitterly complain that Colonel Konrad and Deputy Warden Hartmann were constantly badgering him about a signature stamp that belonged to you. I caught only bits and pieces of it, but it was enough for me to get the gist. I tracked down Colonel Konrad for the full story, and he explained what had happened during the trial. I think he hoped I'd know something about it, but unfortunately, I didn't. Not then.

"But it occurred to me, in order for them to forge your signature stamp on all of those documents, didn't that mean they'd have to have a stamp made? And the only one who could describe it accurately would be Deidrick. It took me some time to track the right person down—I started with the family's engraver, silly me—but finally I remembered Hans. He's not really an expert in such matters, but his father is a carpenter at the estate, and Hans is very clever with things of this ilk. I went to him, and he admitted he'd done something along those lines, and he had the first mockup still. This," she pulled out a page from the satchel and handed it over, "is his written testimony of what he was asked to do and by whom. I had it witnessed by two other people; I hope that was enough?"

Ren took the page from her hands, angling it so that both he and Frei could read it at the same time, and skimmed it quickly. It was barely more than three paragraphs, but a lovely three paragraphs. "Harriet, if we both weren't married, I'd kiss you."

She giggled, smugly pleased with herself. "Will that do the trick, then?"

Belying his own words, he reached over and planted a kiss on her cheek, making her blush. "It will do more than that, my dear friend. You've just given us the only evidence we can use to pin this on Giles, something I'd nearly given up on."

Harriet blinked at him, astounded. "No! Have I really? I thought you had other evidence on him."

"Just suspicions, but nothing we could solidly prove," Frei corrected. "Ren, give me that, and the stamp. I'll send it directly to Hartmann for safe keeping. You can't handle it any more directly than this, not when you're implicated."

Ren gladly did so, but nearly vibrated under the force of his relief and vindicated pleasure. Finally, *finally*, he could prove Giles' participation in this whole affair.

A touch uncertainly, Harriet added, "I told Hans that he wasn't going to be in trouble for any of this."

"He won't be," Frei assured her. "He had no idea what it was for, after all. He was just a dupe in this particular crime. We might call upon him for formal testimony, but nothing more than that. Lady Harriet, please tell me anyone else who knows what you've been up to."

"Only my husband," she assured him. "I kept this very close to the chest. I wasn't sure who it would be wise to confide in."

Praise this woman's common sense and intelligence. Ren nearly kissed her again. "Please keep it that way. I'll report this to our monarchs immediately and I'm sure they'll move without delay. Harriet, truly, we could not have done this without you."

"I'd have had a perfectly miserable life without *you*, and your help," she responded sincerely. "I feel that all I've done is even the scales. But Ren, before you rush out the door, promise me that you and your husband will be over for dinner soon?"

A slow grin took over his face. "I promise you we will."

With the new evidence, King Gerhard and Queen Eloise lost no time in acting upon it. They immediately called for Giles to come and present himself to the Royal Audience Room. This trial was open to the public as usual, but in truth very few actually attended, perhaps a little over a dozen altogether. It was mid-afternoon; most were out on their own pursuits with few in the palace to hear the announcement of the trial. Ren preferred it that way. The last thing he wanted was to give the rumor mill more to work with.

Ren sat at the plaintiff's table, this time with Arman standing beside him and Harriet as his witness. They hadn't deemed Hans necessary for this, not with his written testimony and Harriet present for any questions.

Deidrick and his father stood at the defense's table, and this time neither Giles looked cocky. In fact, Deidrick's clothes stuck to him under his black jacket, a nervous sweat pouring off him. Being summoned here stated louder than words that Ren finally had the evidence to pin him to the wall.

The entire royal family once again entered from behind the dais, and they kept a neutral expression on, but Roslyn's mask kept slipping as she gave Giles shark-like smiles of pure menace. It rather destroyed the effort everyone else made. Giles stared at her in growing horror, whatever color he had in his face draining so he looked like a three-day-old corpse.

Frei clacked his staff against the tile floors to call the room to order. "The petition against Lord Deidrick Giles will now commence. Presiding is our good King Gerhard of Aart with our royal mother, Queen Eloise. We are blessed with the attendance of Prince Charles, Princess Roslyn, and Princess Alexandria of Scovia. All rise."

A rustle of cloth as everyone in attendance stood.

"All may be seated. Warden Ren will speak of his allegations."

Ren promptly moved to the defense's table. He'd already

rehearsed what he needed to say. "My King, My Queen, thank you for hearing me. Some months ago I was in trial here, and during the proceedings of that trial I was accused of aiding and abetting forgery through the use of a signature stamp. While I was proved innocent in that allegation, the question of how I was accused has remained, as very few people have seen that stamp or knew of its existence. There was also the question of how several documents, allegedly stamped with my signature, came to the trial as my stamp was sent to Shiirei months before the trial started. I now have the evidence to prove that it was Deidrick Giles behind all of these actions."

Linus Giles slammed a hand against the table. "King Gerhard, I demand to know what evidence Warden Ren can possibly use against my son in this case."

He cast a quick, covert glance at Harriet, not wanting to put her on the spot unduly. She gave him a firm nod in return. Well alright then. Proud of her, he addressed the dais once more. "I call for my witness Lady Harriet Kastner."

Harriet came promptly to stand at his side, the wooden stamp and letter in her hands. She gave a deep curtsey to the dais. "Your Majesties, thank you for hearing me. Approximately two weeks ago, I learned by chance that Lord Deidrick Giles was suspected of having manipulated the evidence in a trial against Warden Ren Brahms. I knew nothing about the matter at the time, but knew that if Warden Ren suspected him, that he had grounds for those suspicions. I approached Colonel Konrad, who I knew to be investigating the matter, to get the facts straight. Only then did I know where to look for the evidence. I approached three different people on the Giles' estates that had the skills to duplicate such a signature stamp before I found the right person. The letter I have here is his witness statement, and the stamp in my hands is the mock-up version. May I present both to you?"

"Please do," Queen Eloise invited, extending both hands.

Harriet promptly went up and handed them over before curtseying again and retreating to the accuser's table. Of course, the royals had already seen all of this before, but they read it through again, handled the stamp, and agreed that it firmly evidenced Giles' complicity.

As this played out, Ren studied Giles from the corner of his eye. He looked ready to faint, as well he should be. Imbecile. If he'd only treated Harriet with decency, if he'd not thought to pursue his smarted pride by antagonizing Ren, he wouldn't have landed himself in trial today. But it was too late. His wounded pride came with a very high price. This didn't bother Ren overly much and his mouth curled into a smile, as smug as the cat who'd finally gotten into the cream.

"This is very firm evidence," King Gerhard finally declared, handing it down to Frei. "I am satisfied to its veracity. Thank you, Lady Harriet."

Taking the dismissal, she returned to the witness chairs.

Queen Eloise turned to Giles with those assassin eyes of hers, and truly, it was a miracle the man didn't just keel over on the spot. "This single action of yours has many legal violations, Lord Deidrick. Because you forged Our warden's signature stamp, you've committed forgery and fraud, tampered with evidence in a royal trial, bore false witness in a royal trial, and participated in a conspiracy to commit treason."

His father immediately leapt to his defense. "Your Majesty, surely that last is too much. My son never intended to commit treason against this nation!"

"Your son willingly allied himself with several lords and ladies that did, in fact, commit treason," Queen Eloise corrected with all of the warmth of an iceberg. "He did so in this very room. There is no other way for me to interpret that, Lord Giles."

Giles stared back at her, aghast, then turned a look on his son that was one part horrified, one part enraged. Deidrick refused to look up from the table, staring at it as if it held all of life's mysteries.

"In light of these offenses," King Gerhard picked up smoothly, "we cannot allow Deidrick Giles to remain free in this country. He has proven where his allegiance truly lies. He is hereby stripped of his rank and sentenced to prison for thirty years."

Linus let out a wail, quickly stifled behind his hand. Deidrick didn't even flinch, as if he could no longer comprehend his own native tongue.

King Gerhard lifted a hand and added, "We will alter our sentence only on one condition. If Deidrick Giles will inform us of every person that was involved with the original trial against Warden Ren, as well as the attacks the palace has suffered over this past year, then we will alter our sentence accordingly. He will not be allowed to regain his rank and title, but his sentenced years in prison will be adjusted."

"He will do so, Your Majesty," Linus swore, kicking his son's ankle. "Immediately. Deidrick, say something!"

Slowly, Deidrick lifted his head, staring at Ren as if he'd never seen him before. Ren turned, settling into a parade rest, returning the stare evenly. He felt no sympathy for this young fool, but there was a part of him that remembered that initial approach, that first kiss, and the innocence behind it. How quickly the whole thing had soured, curdling in his stomach. If Ren possessed the ability to go back in time, he might very well choose that moment, and save them all the pain that came from it.

Swallowing, Deidrick tried three times before he could manage to get his voice to cooperate. "I never should have touched you."

"No," Ren agreed, voice equally quiet. "You shouldn't have. Tell us, Giles. Who else was involved?"

"Most of them you know. I never knew them all, either." He faltered, stared again at the table. "They'll kill me when they find out. I can't talk."

And that was the last that Deidrick Giles said to anyone.

26

In the pre-dawn hours, everyone assembled in the main courtyard of the palace, ready for departure. Even though O' Broín had been appointed as leader, Ren couldn't help but take a headcount. Princess Alexandria, Prince Charles, Arman of course, Robert, O' Broín, Preben, Galvath, and two of O' Broín's captains, Caedmon and Devaughn. Most of Princess Alexandria's initial escort had been injured and were sent home via boat months ago. Eight soldiers—well, nine in a pinch—as Charles could certainly hold his own. For that matter, Princess Alexandria had a rather good arm for the bow, so perhaps Ren should think of them all as fighters.

Queen Eloise and King Gerhard hugged people goodbye with promises to see them soon. O' Broín didn't let them linger, loading everyone up onto horseback, Robert taking charge of the single cart laden with luggage and supplies. The wagon had a strong team of four Clydesdales, so Ren had perfect faith that if they needed to run, the wagon would be able to keep up.

They left through the main gate with no fanfare, as planned. With the early hour, most of them still felt a little sleepy, and the quick trot they moved at discouraged conversation. The sun steadily rose on their right as they moved through familiar countryside, leaving Castle-de-Haut behind them. Ren relaxed into the saddle as they moved, enjoying the sunshine and the rolling fields bracketing each side of the road. They weren't in dangerous territory yet, so for now, he could enjoy the scenery without looking for trouble behind every bush.

In truth, he was glad to be out of the palace for a month. Maybe it would calm down while they were gone. The trial for Deidrick Giles hadn't been well attended, but rumors about it spread quickly afterwards. Ren had been nearly ambushed by people wanting the details. Giles went straight to prison, still adamantly not talking, although Ren hoped that would change after he'd been in his cold cell for a while. Then again, maybe not. Giles seemed convinced that he'd be killed the moment he named any names. Just who had that whelp climbed into bed with?

He shook the thought off, as he'd done nothing but ruminate on it for days now, and there was no answer. The air outside of the palace was crisp and clear. Ren determined to enjoy it before the summer heat settled in.

Once far enough out, O' Broín slowed them to a quick walk, not wanting to tire the horses out so early in the journey. Alexandria urged her horse up so that she rode alongside Ren and directly behind O' Broín. Her mare tried to sidle up to Ren's stallion, the roan flirting outrageously.

"Stop it," Alexandria ordered the horse crossly. "You are the most shameless flirt. I don't know why I put up with you. Quit, or so help me, I'll make sure you don't come near another stallion for a year. That's better."

Ren found this exchange amusing, especially since she delivered it in such a way that inclined Ren to think she'd repeated this very speech more than once. "Having a little trouble, My Princess?"

Huffing a stray strand of hair out of her eyes, Alexandria told him, "She's hopeless, she really is, but she has the smoothest gait of any horse I've ever ridden, which is why I put up with her on long trips. Anyway, I wanted to ask, how do you and General O' Broín know each other? You're obviously close friends."

"Yes, we served on the same battlefront during the war," Ren answered easily. "Not the entire time, mind you, but for…how long was it, O' Broín? Nine months? Ten months?"

Twisting in his saddle, O' Broín responded, "Depends on when you're counting from. From that very first meeting, nearly ten months. Although I don't think that really counts, in a way. I didn't think of you as a general at first."

Remembering how they met, Ren laughed, slapping a hand against his thigh. "I can see why!"

A slow smile spread over Alexandria's face. "Charles, have you heard how these two met?"

"I haven't, actually," Charles answered from behind them, urging his own horse in closer to hear better.

"All travels go by faster when people share a good tale," Galvath intoned. "Ren, do us the honors by starting us off on a good note."

"I'd be pleased to," Ren replied, casting back and trying to figure out just where to start. "About a month after Bhodhsa's forces landed, we were scrambling to get the right troops deployed into the right areas. My Emperor called for an emergency meeting near the north shore, asking that every general from each country meet so we could determine who needed to go where. Arman at that point had already been with me about three months, as Aart, as you know, sent troops first. We got word and headed out, only to double back, as the roads were covered in so many traps as to be nigh impossible to pass. Our position was very bad at the time. So we chose to go by boat instead, as a river wound most of the way there, and then we'd hop out of it and walk the rest of the distance. It would make us late for the meeting, but Arman and I didn't see any other way of managing to get there."

"Not that it helped," Arman pointed out sourly. He rode next to Charles, acting for all the world as if he hadn't been paying attention, but he clearly was.

Ren had to groan, the memory of it still a bit painful. "Ye gods, I almost wish now we'd taken the road after all. Arman, two of our officers, and I were halfway there when the Mongs started firing from the trees. I'd packed a bow just in case, but I was the only one, so I had them row hard while I tried to pick off the snipers. But of course, we were all dodging, and in the process of trying to get clear, we lost one of the oars. Then, to add to our bad luck, we hit some rapids, and lost the other oar altogether."

Charles started laughing. "You didn't!"

"I find it very unfair that oars will outpace a boat on a river," Ren noted to the group in general, ignoring the chuckles this earned him. "So there we are, no oars, stuck in the middle of the river, already late for our very important meeting," Ren warmed up to the tale, as he still found it funny, "and Arman looks at me like, well, what do you want to do about this? I asked everyone in the boat, and it turned out I was the only one who knew how to swim—don't worry, I drown-proofed them all later—which left it up to me to fix matters. So I started stripping."

Alexandria's eyes flew wide, hand coming up to cover her mouth. "You didn't!"

"Sure, I wasn't about to get sopping wet. I had a meeting to attend after all. So I stripped down to skivvies, hopped into the water, then latched onto the back and started kicking. The men in the boat paddled along as best they could with their hands, which helped a little. It was slow, but we made headway, and I managed to get us out of the middle of the river and to shore. I figured we could at least get out and take the road the rest of the way in. What I didn't take into account were the rocks along the shore. Very sharp, very pointy rocks. They nearly cut my feet to ribbons. Arman had to come rescue me."

"Which was when I arrived on scene." O' Broín took up the story in a reminiscent tone. "I chose to take the road in, was also running late, and saw this group of allied soldiers climbing out of a boat on the shore. All except one, who strode back into the water and lifted a practically naked Shiirein out in a bridal carry. I'd heard the stories, of course, of some of the allied soldiers taking advantage of their location and hiring some, ah—"

"Rent boys is the term you're looking for," Ren supplied helpfully.

O' Broín glared at him, for some reason. "Paid companions of the male variety, shall we say. Naked as he was, with that long hair he favors, Sho looked the part."

"I was not naked," Ren protested, pretending indignation. "I had underwear on."

"White underwear, yes, that clearly kept your modesty intact," O' Broín drawled with a pointed look at him. "I'll have you know half of my men were discussing the pros and cons to male companionship on the way back to our camp that night thanks to you. Anyway, Brahms put his own jacket around Sho as soon as they got on land and refused to budge until the man was dressed and dry again. In fact, he helped him dry off, like an attentive lover. Then I got a good look at the insignia on Sho's jacket and realized *this* was the Shiirein general I was to work with for the next part of the campaign and about swallowed my tongue."

"As first impressions went, it was something of a disaster," Ren acknowledged cheerfully. "I had to beat half of his staff in a competitive sparring match before they'd take me seriously."

"It took me the longest time to forget that first impression." O' Broín shook his head, laughing at himself. "It didn't help that these two acted like lovers half the time. They could finish each other's thoughts, they were so close. Anyway, Princess Alexandria, that's how we first met."

"That is certainly not the answer I expected," Alexandria responded, blue eyes sparkling with laughter. "Heavens. Then, General Brahms, am I to understand that you and Ren were interested in each other even then?"

"Not then," Arman denied seriously. "We were brothers then."

"Ren had a crush on him, though," O' Broín added factually.

Groaning, Ren slumped in the saddle. "How does everyone *know* that!"

"You were obvious," O' Broín informed him, voice rich with laughter.

"Very obvious," Arman agreed.

Twisting in the saddle, Ren shook a finger at him, ignoring everyone else's amusement. "You, husband, are supposed to be on my side."

Arman pointed a finger at himself, blue eyes wide with feigned innocence.

"Yes, you, don't give me that innocent, injured look. I know that look all too well, you can't fool me. Why do I put up with you?"

With a sultry wink at him, Arman purred, "Yes, I wonder."

Giggling, Alexandria lifted a hand to her mouth and stage-whispered, "General Brahms, maybe you'll tell me now how you proposed?"

"Wow," Ren stated loudly, putting his heels to his stallion's flanks. "I'm just going to scout ahead. All of you keep chatting."

He resolutely ignored any and all laughter from behind him.

They continued the journey without any trouble through Brahms' lands, staying the night and thoroughly enjoying the hospitality afforded at the fortress. Ren had to promise they would visit again on the way back before Eida would let them go. Early the next morning, they continued on toward the east, taking the Trader's Route briefly before leaving it for the Fifth Highway. The first three days passed with no issues, but then, they didn't expect any trouble here.

The problems would start now.

Most of Bhodhsa stayed incredibly flat, at least in this northwestern section. The southern area of the country was made of rolling hills, steep mountains, and rocky outcroppings covered in short grass. But not here. Lakes, rivers, and the occasional copse of trees broke up the landscape, but for the most part the view remained unimpeded for miles at a time. Ren liked the Fifth Highway for that reason—it made ambushes nearly impossible for most of the trip. Only a few places intersected with steep mountains or small forests, and those would be their troublesome spots.

In the flat areas, he remained alert, but didn't try to question everything his eyes saw. It would be impossible to hide anything larger than a fly in this landscape, after all. Still, they chose not to take unnecessary chances, and timed it so they always stayed in a city at night. In the highlands of Bhodhsa, a campfire could be seen for miles in every direction, which would give away their position like a beacon on a hill. In the dead of night, anything could sneak up on them unawares, and no one wanted to risk it. If they felt they couldn't reach the next town by nightfall, they'd stop early instead. It added time to their journey, but no one felt it unnecessarily lengthened the trip.

Three days into Bhodhsa, they stopped at a fair-sized town with a decent inn and an enormous taproom, which adequately showed where most of the inn's earnings lay. It had a cozy atmosphere with low beamed ceilings, dark wood floors, and two separate stone hearths on either side of the room. At this time of the night, most of the working class lingered over a pint, talking to each other in casual tones. Ren remained at the table after dinner with Galvath, most of the party already retiring upstairs to bed. He didn't quite feel like bed himself, not yet, not after five days of doing nothing more than riding, eating, or sleeping. Seeing it was just the two of them, Ren offered, "It's a shame we can't afford to get drunk, otherwise I'd offer you a drink."

"How about a half pint?" Galvath replied, at ease in his chair near the fireplace. Despite being summer, the tap room had a distinct chill to it in the evenings, and all the patrons chose to sit as close to the fire as possible. "I have a high tolerance. That much won't affect me."

"Fair enough. Master! Two half pints, if you please."

The master served it up and passed it down the length of the bar. Galvath stood up and stretched out a hand to catch the handles before passing Ren his and resuming his seat. Ren took a sip and hummed his appreciation. "There's just something about the way they brew alcohol up here. It's tart but pleasant, like a hard apple cider."

"I know it," Galvath agreed, sipping on his own tankard, making it last. "I tried asking for the secret, only to be glared at, so I don't recommend it."

"I wouldn't dream of it," Ren assured him. "Princess Alexandria is faring better on this trip than I expected. She's used to riding, I take it?"

"Travels all over Scovia on her father's behalf," Galvath confirmed. "With his illness confining him to a chair, she's become his legs, although I expect her brother will take up the duty in her stead after she moves to Aart. I think she's actually glad for the excuse to be on horseback instead of in a carriage this time."

"I can see why." Ren had only one experience of being in a carriage for an extended period of time, and he swore he'd never do it again unless the weather was perfectly foul. Even a well-sprung carriage could find every rut and bump in the road and jostle its occupants fiercely.

Leaning in a little closer, Galvath lowered his tone to a more confidential level. "To be honest, Ren, it's you I'm more worried about."

"Me?" Ren objected, pointing to his own nose. "Whatever for?"

"Not the physical part of it," Galvath explained seriously, putting his tankard aside for a moment. "But I know that Bhodhsa and Scovia won't look kindly on you and General Brahms."

"Ah, that." Ren felt touched at his friend's concern but assured him, "It's alright. Well, I'm alright, I'm used to it. If you're going to worry about anyone, worry about Arman. He's not used to it. I mean, he's used to coming to my defense in such cases, but it's never been aimed at him before, and that's a different kettle of fish altogether. I'm not quite sure how he's going to react to it all."

Galvath's brows drew together in a concerned frown. "But how do you think he'll react?"

"With his fists," Ren replied dryly, lifting his tankard to his mouth. "My husband is a man of action, not words."

Looking a little perturbed by this, Galvath protested, "But he can't punch everyone."

"Try explaining that to him, not me." Ren took a sip and realized that Galvath's concerns hadn't abated at all. "My friend, not everyone is stupid enough to insult a man of rank to his face. Our positions offer us some protection, and we use that protection to our advantage, as we don't want a fight with every bigoted idiot in the world. Arman won't go looking for a fight, and neither will I. All I'm saying is, if that fight is brought to us, then we won't shirk from it."

"But you are worried about him," Galvath protested quietly.

"I don't want him hurt." Ren sighed, putting the tankard back down. "I hesitated when he proposed to me, you know. Part of the reason was my worry over him, how his life would change because of me. In that regard, I still don't know if I made the right decision, as certainly he was safer before we married."

Galvath shook his head firmly. "He's happier with you, though. Everyone who knows him says so."

"Which is why I can't regret it. And truly, Galvath, is love not the one thing worth fighting for?"

"I think so. In a perfect world, it wouldn't be necessary, though." Galvath stared glumly into his ale for a long moment. "You know that if something happens, I have your back, right?"

Ren clinked his tankard up against Galvath's, a wide smile on his face. "Of that, I have no doubt."

A pair of hands he knew well landed on his shoulders, and he looked up to find Arman staring down at him. "Hello, handsome. Looking for me?"

"Mmm," Arman grunted in confirmation. "Bed."

"I can't tell," Ren observed to Galvath, pretending confusion, "if that was a command or an invitation."

Arman quirked a brow at him, hands not moving.

"Oh, both?" Ren replied, perking up. "I can work with both."

Galvath snorted into his drink, entertained by the exchange. "Good night, Ren, Brahms."

"Good night," Ren returned. He thought briefly of draining the rest of his tankard, then thought better of it, as he was already feeling a little too fatigued and more alcohol would not help that state. "I'm right behind you, darling husband."

Satisfied, Arman let go and wound his way around the various tables, heading for the stairs. They had the first room at the top of the stairs, at Arman's insistence, as that way he had complete control of who went through the hallway. Since only their party took up this part of the inn, the innkeeper hadn't fought him on that point. Ren felt glad for it, as he, too, felt a little more secure with Arman keeping watch. In the right conditions, Arman could sleep like the dead, but in these situations he could rest as light as a feather, coming awake at the slightest hint of danger. It had saved their lives more than once during the war.

They had a nice room, and Ren took advantage of it, washing off the worst of the travel dust and dressing in light breeches and a billowy shirt to sleep in. By either luck or design, they had a room with a large single bed, and although it dominated the area and left them with very little room to maneuver, Ren was grateful for it. He hadn't been able to sleep next to Arman for five days now and that had quickly worn rather thin.

With a bounce, he hopped onto the bed, then wiggled under the covers. The slightly warm covers. So Arman had climbed in only to get out again to fetch Ren? The thought made him smile.

Arman rolled in behind him, snuggling in at Ren's back with an arm around his waist. Only then did he fully relax with a content sigh.

"You now find it completely impossible to sleep alone, don't you?" he asked his husband knowingly.

"Bed was cold," Arman grumbled against the back of his head.

His chest shook with a silent laugh. "Why are you so adorable?"

Arman went very still. "Excuse me? I am a scary general."

"Adorable," Ren maintained, then yelped when two hands found his tickle spots. Squirming, he tried to roll off of the mattress, but since it had too much bounce to it, he couldn't gain any traction. "Stop, stop, I give!"

Still grumbling about being a fierce general, and generals not being 'adorable' or any of that nonsense, Arman stopped tickling and hauled him back into position like a disobedient pillow. Ren went willingly, snuggling in, but his mind refused to turn off. He lay staring at the polished wood walls, mentally going over their route and all of the contingencies they had planned. Would it be enough?

"Ren. Sleep."

Ren ignored the command and asked, "Are you worried about tomorrow? We'll hit the dangerous area when we cross through Windsong Mountains Pass."

"A little worried," Arman admitted. "We passed through the first dangerous spot without trouble, but…"

"But tomorrow we hit three in a row," Ren completed glumly. "I am not looking forward to tomorrow."

Windsong Pass stretched out along the one mountain range in the center of the continent, starting out as an easy incline that abruptly went steep toward the peak. They reached it mid-morning, giving them plenty of light to travel by, but Ren couldn't help but worry they wouldn't be able to get through the pass and down again before the light failed them. O' Broín was reasonably sure they'd make it, having traveled this way before. Hopefully they could. He did not want to be stuck up there at night.

Partway up the incline, Alexandria maneuvered around to ride next to him, breaking the silence of the morning. "Ren."

"Yes, My Princess?"

"It occurs to me that out of all the stories I've heard from you, I still don't know how you and General Brahms first met." She looked at him expectantly, perhaps a little too hopefully.

"It's not as entertaining as how O' Broín and I first met," Ren answered dryly. They weren't yet at the dangerous section of the road, so he could likely tell the story before he had to focus. "But if you still wish to hear it…?"

"Tell me," she encouraged.

"Our first introduction was all very official. He came in with an army courier, introduced himself, and gave me a copy of his official orders. We didn't do more than exchange a few words to each other, as he was busy getting his men settled in the camp, and I had to make sure that my own men made room for the additional troops." Ren looked back on the memory with fondness, shaking his head. "My first impression was of a very taciturn man uncomfortable with my language, so he stuck with the phrases he knew. More fool me, I didn't realize it was all words he hated."

"But when did you really get to know him?" Alexandria pressed. "Every account I've heard suggests that you became close friends very quickly."

"We did, which startled everyone, myself included. The first week, nothing drastic happened, really. I started learning Aartish, thinking that he'd feel more comfortable speaking to me if I did so." Ren rolled his eyes at her giggle. "I know, wishful thinking. And I made a few friendly overtures, like inviting him to dinner or drinks, and we learned a little more about each other that way. I didn't find his silence awkward, as I could read him somewhat, and he never turned me down or tried to avoid me, which warmed my heart. My orientation was an open secret in the army, and quite a few avoided being in close quarters with me because of it. I was inclined to like him for his open acceptance of me. But I think the turning point for us came at the end of that first week."

Proving that once again, he was listening, Arman pitched in, "The tent."

Ren shot him a warm smile over his shoulder. "Indeed. The tent. You see, we had no space on the front lines, although every man had the ability to pitch their tents, perhaps share them with a buddy. But a meeting was called back behind the lines, in one of the few standing towns, and that place had no space at all. Even generals had to share their tents, but no one was quite comfortable doing so with me, so I was more or less resigned to sleeping out in the open somewhere when Arman came up, put a hand in the center of my back, and openly guided me to his own tent."

"Caused quite the fuss," Arman recalled, amused at the memory.

"Everyone was convinced I'd seduced him," Ren explained, entertained at Alexandria's open amusement. Apparently she could picture this very well. "I thought to deny it, try to rescue Arman's reputation, but the man patently did things to stir people up even further. Oh yes, don't let that straight face fool you, he's a terrible prankster. He kept slinging an arm around my shoulders, or leaning in to whisper against my ear, perfectly ridiculous things meant to give people the wrong impression."

Alexandria regarded Arman with some astonishment. "I had no idea you possessed such a wicked sense of humor, General."

Shrugging, Arman gave her a sly smile. "It's why Ren and I get along so well."

"Our senses of humor are unfortunately akin to two peas in a pod," Ren acknowledged with a cackle. "I say unfortunately because the rest of the world suffers from it. Anyway, after that first night, it became routine. The rest of the war, we shared a tent."

"Which naturally fanned the flames even higher," O'Broín called back. "You won't believe how many bets were riding on the two of them."

"If I'd only known back then," Ren mourned. "I would have placed a bet on us too and then convinced Arman to kiss me out in the open. I could have made a pretty penny off it."

Alexandria choked on a laugh. "Somehow, I can picture him

doing it, too."

"Of course he would have, after placing his own bet." Ren shot his husband a look, not at all surprised at the lack of denial coming from that corner. "We weren't lovers then, but he would have found the idea funny enough to go along with it."

"And lucrative," Arman added with a regretful sigh. "Oh well."

Ren considered this, based off what O' Broín had mentioned before, and couldn't help but wonder, "How much do you think we could have ma—"

They heard it before they saw it, the whistle of multiple arrows launched into the air at once. Ren immediately went flat on his horse, lowering his profile, then reached for Alexandria, only to find her no longer on her horse at all. Frantically, he looked about, but Galvath had her, the bodyguard shielding her with his own body. Charles, what about Charles? Robert? Robert was in the cart, good, but what about Charles?

The prince had the sense to also go flat on his horse, calling out in worry, "ALEXANDRIA?"

"I'm fine!" the princess assured him.

"Left flank and ahead!" O' Broín boomed out, sword already out as he firmly planted himself at Charles' side.

Ren took that direction as a command and put heels to flanks, spurring his horse forward, the mane whipping at his face as he rode low. They weren't at the dangerous spot yet—they still had some visibility of the road—so where was the attack coming from exactly? O' Broín's directions aside, he couldn't quite see any—no, wait, there. The enemy was literally hugging the side of the road, balancing on the steep, rocky side of it and firing blind. No wonder they hadn't hit anyone. But why attack now, why here? Another twenty paces, they'd have much better cover and the ambush would have worked with little effort on their part. Unless—

Swearing, the obvious hit and Ren pulled hard on the reins, making his stallion's back hooves skid on the rocky road. "Arman, back!"

Not questioning, his husband immediately stopped chasing his tail and turned, his horse screaming out a protest at the abrupt change in direction.

Even though Ren saw through it, they were almost too late. Multiple enemies climbed up the side of the mountain and onto the road, coming in from behind, while still others poured out of the craggy mountain face from up ahead. If Ren had gone even three paces further along, he would have been cut off from the rest of his party and surrounded on both sides.

Divide and conquer, that was the plan, eh? Not on his watch. Ren turned again and cut a swath through two of the men trying to blindside him. He'd never been one to fight well on horseback—it restricted his movements severely—so he pulled up to the cart and tossed Robert his reins, not surprised when Arman copied him a second later. Then he positioned himself to protect Robert and Alexandria, finding himself back to back with Arman. Multiple screams rent the air, arrows still whistling as they were released, and Ren could only pray the loud thuds he heard of bodies hitting the ground did not belong to any of his. Teeth bared in a feral expression, he lifted the katana in his hands and attacked every person within range of him, careful to not leave Arman's back exposed while moving, but staying out of range of his husband's broadsword. It was an old dance, one they both knew well, after having fought side by side for so many years.

A man locked hilts with him, breathing hard, a black cloth covering his head except for the eyes. Those almond-shaped eyes gave him away and Ren's fury at the situation doubled.

Mongs.

Ren snarled as he kicked the man in the stomach, then flipped the sword in his hand in a smooth arc, neatly cutting his opponent's throat. Like a dancer, he spun in place, aiming for the next enemy, then the next, not showing any mercy. As he moved, he caught sight of Alexandria with a bow in her hand, neatly taking out enemies with sure aim, her back still guarded by Galvath.

He knew he liked that woman for a reason.

Ren felt the familiar surge of adrenaline through his veins, the heavy thud of his heart like a war drum in his ears. He kept his focus through iron will, not allowing himself to become so focused on the enemy that he lost track of his allies. This was no time to charge recklessly forward. With both hands on the hilt, he ran an enemy through and whirled, looking for the next opponent, only to find none standing. Was it already over?

Only one man in black remained alive, kneeling at Charles' feet with a blade hovering at his throat. Never before had Ren seen Charles so enraged, the normally-cheerful prince replaced by a man who looked ready to rend his enemy limb from limb then spit on the corpse.

Not trusting the area, Ren kept a weather eye on the road ahead, even as he maneuvered backwards so that he could stand near Charles. "My Prince. Any injuries?"

"A cut on my thigh, but we'll ignore it for a moment. Is everyone else alright?"

"We're all fine," Alexandria answered from behind him, the bow still in her hands although it wasn't nocked. "Galvath needs tending to."

"Not life threatening," Galvath assured everyone, although Robert ignored him, already heading for the medical kit in the cart. "I want answers first."

Charles glared down at the kneeling man. "I can agree with you there. I can see that you're Mong. On whose orders are you here?"

The Mong soldier glared back, not saying a word.

Ren shook his head. "My Prince, you'll never get an answer from him by just asking questions. May I take lead on this?"

With a wave of the hand, Charles gestured for him to go ahead.

"Something you must learn about Mongs is this," Ren tilted the blade of his katana to rest just so between the Mong's spread thighs. "They believe that a man who isn't intact cannot ascend to heaven. Isn't that right?"

The Mong's eyes went wide in his face, the white of his eyes showing clearly. He swallowed audibly and managed hoarsely in his native tongue, "You Shiirein pig."

"Yes, yes," Ren dismissed, not bothered by the insult. "Speak in trader's tongue, please. I promise to kill you cleanly and not make you an eunuch first if you answer just three questions. What was your goal in ambushing us here? Who gave you the order? And how did you know to expect us on this route, on this day?"

Glaring up at him, he hesitated a long moment, testing Ren's resolve. Ren smiled at him genteelly, the blade in his hands pressing upwards with increasing strength until the man hissed in pain. "Alright, alright! My commander ordered it. We can't afford for Scovia and Aart to become united by marriage."

"There's been talk about us forming trade monopolies because of the marriage alliance," Alexandria stated with a resigned sigh, "but we don't intend to do any such thing."

"Unfortunately, evil men are quick to suspect their enemy of what they, themselves, would do," O' Broín rumbled darkly. "He likely couldn't imagine you not abusing the alliance once you had it finalized. So your goal was Princess Alexandria's death?"

"Capture," the Mong corrected, looking away from them all. "She was to be our king's new wife."

"To that seventy-year-old man?" Alexandria exclaimed in disgust. "Eww. I just got goosebumps."

Ren did too, just thinking about it. Swallowing down his bile, he prompted, "You were awfully violent for capture."

"Not everyone wanted her alive," he admitted sourly. "We had two orders. One from Aart said kill everyone but the prince. The one from Scovia said kill everyone but the princess. We decided to let the heavens decide who got to live."

Ren's blood ran cold at the implications. That was the missing piece, the part that none of them had been able to put reason to. Traitors in Aart *and* Scovia, of course, because the intelligence of Princess Alexandria's movements had to come from both countries. Otherwise how did the enemy track her? How did they sneak a poisoner into her entourage? "Who gave the orders?"

The Mong smirked, for the first time acting as if he had the upper hand in the interrogation. "You have enemies in each court. One of them said he'd give us the information if we promised to kill the Shiirein as well as the princess. What did you do, spread your legs for the wrong man?"

A horrible, sick feeling overcame Ren and he had to work to keep it from showing on his face. He had a terrible premonition that he wouldn't like what would be said next. "Their names, Mong."

Shrugging, as it was no skin off his nose, the Mong spat out, "Eanraig Cuyler and Simeon Vilhjalmsson."

27

Not trusting the path ahead, O' Broín used the signal flare to call in for reinforcements. They kept the Mong alive, wanting a witness who could still speak, and handed him over to the local lord to detain. Ren kept himself steady as they dealt with the messy aftermath of the skirmish, knowing he couldn't do anything about the way things had turned out, but still with that sick knot forming a pit in his stomach.

Lord Ahearn led them to his own manor house at the base of the mountain late that night, giving them his best rooms and apologizing profusely for letting Mongs get anywhere near his lands. With the knowledge of their route and the plans they'd made to thwart ambushes, it was no wonder they'd attacked in an unexpected place. The Mongs clearly hoped to catch them off-guard by attacking where they had. O' Broín no doubt would investigate how they got this far into Bhodhsa territory, but Ren suspected they'd come cross-country and avoided the roads altogether to manage it. Either way, it wasn't his job to figure it out, nor to mete out punishments for this debacle.

They sent four courier pigeons, splitting up the report among the birds. Even boiled down to bare bones, the report of what happened took more than a page to explain. Two birds went ahead to Scovia, the other two winging towards Aart. Ren felt relieved he wouldn't have to investigate yet another traitor. By the time they reached their destination, saw Charles and Alexandria safely to Scovia, and returned, he had no doubt that former General Eanraig Cuyler would be either executed or exiled.

He crawled into the guest bed that night, wanting nothing more than the oblivion of sleep, but he had a sinking feeling he wouldn't manage it. No fault could be laid on the room, as it was very nice indeed, and the bed had that wonderful semi-softness to it that offered the perfect support for a man's back. The blame for his restlessness lay solely on his own door. His mind whirled without letting him even try for slumber.

Arman, ignoring the room set aside for him, climbed into bed behind Ren and drew him into his arms, Ren's back against his chest. Placing a kiss against the top of his shoulder, Arman whispered, "Don't blame yourself for this."

"I'm not," Ren responded wearily. "No, truly, I'm not, wipe that worry off your face. I refuse to bear the stupidity and crimes that other men commit. It's just…it's just that a part of me wonders what part I had to play in all of this. Why was the order given for my death as well as Alexandria's?"

"I admit I'm confused as well," Arman acknowledged. "Our families have never been close. Why would they care about you?"

"We're still missing a piece," Ren groaned. "I can only hope that by the time we reach Scovia, someone will have an answer for us."

"Alexandria won't take it well if they don't." Arman sounded far too cheerful stating that.

Ren knew why. Alexandria already threatened to send heads rolling and she hadn't even reached her country's borders yet. His mind turned back to the Cuyler family and grimaced. "You know that our monarchs aren't going to forgive either him or his family when they learn of this."

"True. Nor should they."

"Nor should they," Ren agreed. "First their daughter, now the head of the family. I keep thinking, did I do something to offend them? Something bad enough to drive them to *this*?"

Turning Ren onto his back, Arman propped himself up on one elbow so he could look down at Ren's face. "I know you, Renjimantoro Brahms. You are the kindest of men, and you have to be thoroughly provoked to cut anyone down. You really think anything you did could prompt someone to outright treason and conspiracy to commit murder?"

He really had worried Arman to get that speech out of him. Lifting a hand, Ren stroked his cheek gently, taking comfort in those blue eyes gazing so steadily at him. Nothing about Arman's expression indicated impatience or disgruntlement. "I have no answer for you."

"Their faults are not yours to carry. Let it go, love."

Ren buried his face against a warm shoulder, snuggling in. "What did I do to deserve you?"

"Something terrible," his husband intoned, then chuckled when that earned him a poke in the ribs. Leaning in, he put a kiss on Ren's head. "We're almost there. Soon, we'll be able to go home again."

"It's not going to be fun, reporting all of this and seeing the Cuyler family taken down a few pegs," Ren sighed, burrowing in a little further. "But I must admit that I'm anxious to be home again. Although I'm a little worried about what Mother has been up to, aren't you? The last I heard, her plans for our wedding were rather… elaborate."

"You're the one who said I couldn't argue with her," Arman pointed out dryly.

"I might regret that." Still, the thought of claiming this man in a public ceremony made him smile. There would likely be far too many flowers and lacey things for his peace of mind, but Ren determined he wouldn't fuss. He had the best wedding present already right here.

After another long week of riding, they reached Westerberg. Ren had never seen the palace of Scovia before, and he had to admit, it wasn't quite what he envisioned. Rather than purposefully designed, the palace gave every indication of having haphazardly grown. It was blocky, jutting out in different directions, each section three stories high and rectangular in shape. Some parts were in completely different colors of stone than the rest, with only two standing a story higher than the others. It looked…homey instead of regal.

Alexandria hit the main courtyard of the palace, calling as she moved. "Adolvsson! Tell me he's in chains!"

An elderly woman with the mark of the Palace Chamberlain on her jacket moved to intercept Ren and Arman before they could do much more than dismount off their horses. Ren followed her lead, allowing himself to be comfortably ensconced in a guest room and asked no questions. How Scovia dealt with traitors was none of his business and in Alexandria's outraged mood, she'd take care of it just fine on her own. Instead, he took advantage of the indoor plumbing to draw a hot bath, soak out the soreness of the journey, and leisurely eat a light lunch of fish, braised cauliflower, and an apple tart.

Three hours after their arrival, Alexandria knocked on their door. Arman opened it to allow her entry, and she beamed at them with open satisfaction. Somehow, despite having to follow up on a hundred things, she'd still managed to find time to bathe and change herself, as she was now in a royal blue dress that did magnificent things to her eyes. "Good, you're both dressed."

Arman quirked an eyebrow at her that asked how else she expected them to be.

"You're still in the honeymoon stage, and it has been a solid week since you had a proper bed," she answered that look bluntly. "I expected you naked and twined around each other."

"We didn't dare," Ren answered dryly. "I had a feeling you'd come for us at some point. So. Simeon Vilhjalmsson. Who is he?"

"Former Chamberlain," she answered with a pinched look to her face. "He retired some five years ago; his health just didn't permit him to keep the job. I thought of him as an uncle. He partially raised me. When I sent the report in, he was immediately questioned by my father, and the answer…well. You'll doubtless feel the answer stupid. I certainly do."

Ren invited her to take a seat in the small sitting area near the fire, but she couldn't seem to settle, instead coming to stand near the hearth. Arman sat, drawing Ren down with him, which was wise. Ren didn't think he wanted to stand for this conversation. "Alright, I'm braced."

"There is a certain body of people—and I think we have most of them; my brother was very thorough—that believes in the purity of bloodlines." Alexandria spat the last word as if it personally insulted her mother. "Specifically, they do not believe that countries should intermarry. By marrying Charles, I was doing something unnatural and taboo. Simeon Vilhjalmsson didn't say as much, but my brother got the distinct impression he felt he did the world a favor by ordering you two killed as well. Not only for marrying someone outside of your culture, but also…well, also marrying another man."

Lifting a hand to his head, Ren rubbed at his forehead, feeling a headache coming on. "Of course that factored in. You have proof of all of this, enough to prosecute him?"

"No need," she sighed. "He took his own life this morning when he heard I would arrive today. Apparently it was too much, having to face me."

As angry as she felt about all of this, Ren could see the sadness in her expression. Rising, he went and drew her into a hug, which she readily leaned into. "I'm sorry, Alexandria."

"Me too," she sighed against his chest. "It's all so senseless and stupid. I don't understand it at all. Was it really worth it? Cooperating with our enemies just to prevent my marriage? I can't see how it would be."

Ren didn't either. He could offer her no answers in that regard.

"I think," Arman offered quietly, "that the moment we understand how evil men think, we become like them. Don't wish for understanding, Princess."

Drawing back, Alexandria stared at Arman for a long moment. "And now I understand why he married you."

Snorting a laugh, Ren drew back and grinned at her. "He's not just a pretty face, you know."

"I do now." Alexandria gave Arman a wink, drawing a rare smile out of him. "Well, we received a report from my soon to be in-laws that they got your report, they're investigating, and little else. I do wish courier pigeons could carry more than a small scrap of paper."

"We all do," Ren groaned. "Trust me. It's even worse during a war. As much as I hate to say it, I feel like we should return home soon. They'll likely need us to straighten all of this out, and they might need Arman and me as formal witnesses against General Cuyler."

"You're likely right, but…" She bit her lip, trailing off as she gave Ren a measuring look. "Ren. Something unpleasant has come to my attention. The people here are not very happy about you and Arman. I know, I know, I was just like them not even a year ago. But if we're to avoid situations like this repeating, where bigotry wins out, then I think I need to show my people how wrong their prejudices are. At the very least, I want to introduce you to the warden and master of spies here. I want the three of you to start swapping information regularly."

Ren could see where she went with this. If they'd communicated better with each other, then odds were, they would have figured all of this out much sooner. It would have saved them a great deal of grief and danger. "I'm certainly game, but are you sure it will work?"

"Trust me," she assured him with that gleam of stubbornness he knew well. "I'm not going to give them much choice in the matter."

"Warden Adolvsson, Master Rundstrom," Alexandria greeted as

she swept into the room. Both men automatically rose and gave her a bow, giving Ren a moment to study them properly. Like most men of Scovia, they were fair of hair and skin, their jawlines blocky, builds massive. One of them wore the red jacket normally associated with a palace warden, the other in plain and nondescript clothes that would blend in instantly with a crowd. Ren hardly needed the introduction with them dressed like that. "Please let me introduce you. This is the Warden of Zonhoven Palace, Renjimantoro Sho—"

"Brahms," he corrected her in amusement.

With an exasperated eye-roll, Alexandria sighed. "I keep forgetting. Renjimantoro Brahms. Ren, this is Warden Adolvsson, he's been our warden here in the palace for the past fifteen years and I'm convinced the place will fall apart when he retires. With him is Master Rundstrom, our Master of Spies, and he's never allowed to retire. I forbid it."

Adolvsson unbent enough to grin at his princess. "Why am I allowed to retire and he's not?"

"Because your wife will skin me," she retorted primly. "Rundstrom doesn't have anyone to threaten me with. Pray, sit, gentlemen. I only have a few minutes with you."

They all obediently sat at the small, round table. Alexandria had pulled this meeting together in a single evening, set for the next morning, as she knew that Ren wanted to leave the next day. They were in the extra meeting room off of the warden's office, an enclosed space meant for meetings of this ilk. Someone had anticipated this meeting by putting a tea tray together, and Ren automatically poured Alexandria a cup before passing it over to her, fixed the way she liked it. She accepted it with a gracious smile and nod before promptly draining half of it. He knew she was thirsty after dragging him across half the palace, talking nearly nonstop all the while. He poured himself a cup as well, studying the other two men from the corner of his eye as he did so. They put a good face on, but they clearly didn't know what to make of him. Then again, he'd be surprised if they did, as Scovians truly did not like men of his orientation.

Either Alexandria picked up on this or she'd already anticipated their reactions. Looking them straight in the eyes, she stated firmly, "You are not to allow prejudices to interfere here. Ren is one of the strongest fighters I've ever laid eyes on. He regularly spars with Galvath, and gentlemen? Galvath does not win."

That scored a palpable hit. Even the master of spies blinked in surprise.

"He has saved my life twice over," Alexandria continued in that same brisk voice, "and I won't have anyone in this country think less of him because he's married to General Brahms. In fact, I now find that a perfectly stupid reason to think less of someone, and I'm ashamed of my thought process before I went to Aart. Am I clear enough?"

Ren sat with his teacup balanced in his hand, regarding her with open amusement. "You could not be any clearer, My Princess. Just out of curiosity, do I get any say in this?"

She arched a brow at him and pointedly sipped her tea.

"Right. I'll take that as a no. Gentlemen, greetings," Ren extended a friendly half-bow to the other two. He could tell that under their politely-neutral masks, they were both miffed at their princess and privately groaning at the thought of dealing with him. Ren wondered at Alexandria's blunt approach to this problem. Surely a more delicate touch would have gotten better results? Then again, she knew these men well; he had to trust her judgment on this.

"Warden Brahms," Adolvsson managed politely. "Princess Alexandria feels that if we were in better communication with each other, we might prevent future attacks similar to the one we all recently suffered through."

"Yes, so she's said," Ren agreed in a similarly pleasant tone. "And I must agree. More intelligence and communication between our countries will surely defeat our enemies more swiftly than a sword can manage."

Rundstrom cleared his throat, tone sliding towards antagonistic. "Forgive me, but which country are you referring to? Aart or Shiirei?"

Alexandria bristled under the question, mouth opening in protest. Ren lifted a hand to forestall her, locking stares with the other man. "Is there a reason, Master Rundstrom, that I cannot refer to both?"

The Master of Spies' eyes narrowed in calculation. "I thought you renounced Shiirei when you moved to Aart?"

"Whoever reported such to you made an assumption they should not have," Ren responded bluntly. "Shiirei will always be my native homeland, I will not deny it. Aart, however, is where I choose to call home now. They both are dear to me. I will react to protect both with equal fervor." And what exactly was he being accused of, anyway? Deserting his country? Ren expected problems because he was married to another man, not *this*.

"Rundstrom, really," Alexandria chided.

Looking entirely unmoved by his princess's displeasure, Rundstrom gave her an apologetic bow but didn't say another word.

Ren had the sinking feeling that no matter what Alexandria's wishes, these men were not about to become chummy with him or share information. He'd encountered such resistance between the other countries so many times that he could see the signs clearly. Unfortunately, such resistance took sustained effort for him to overcome and he didn't have the luxury of staying around for a year or more to manage it.

He had only one path open to him. Taking in a breath, he faced both men squarely. "Whatever your opinions of me, we have three things in common. One, common enemies. Two, common friends. And three, we're in the necessary positions to defend those friends. Can you meet me on that common ground? Please. I don't want to lose them, any of the people we're sworn to protect, for they are all dear to me."

Adolvsson shared a speaking glance with Rundstrom, then unbent enough to shrug. "He makes a good argument, Rund. Just clarify something for us, Warden Brahms?"

"If I can, certainly," Ren agreed cautiously. Just what was the issue here, really? There was some undercurrent to this conversation that Ren could sense but it eluded him. He couldn't seem to pin it down.

"We've heard rumors about how you came into Aart," Rundstrom explained with a weather eye on Alexandria. "But we've not been able to confirm the truth of the matter. There are three stories: that General Brahms seduced you into leaving your country, that you seduced General Brahms and he took you back to Aart because he couldn't bear to part with you, and then the third—"

By this point, Ren groaned, as he just knew what the man would say next, and after five years, he'd thought the rumors had finally died.

"—was that you were under confidential orders by your emperor to enter Aart and become an informant and liaison between the two monarchs. Which is it?"

"Option four, none of the above," Ren responded wearily. "Alexandria, don't make that face—"

"I will too make this face," Alexandria gasped, her cheeks

sporting high color in outrage. "Rundstrom! Where did you get that fanciful nonsense!"

"Multiple sources reported multiple variations of these three tales." Rundstrom barely flicked a glance her direction, still studying Ren carefully, as if he could divine the truth if he stared hard enough. "But I haven't had any concrete evidence to back up any particular claim. Forgive me, Princess, Warden Brahms, if I'm being offensive. But I can't hand over sensitive information to a man that I know so little about. Your war record speaks for itself in terms of valor and intelligence. I'm puzzled why a man of your education and experience ended up as a warden in a foreign country."

And that was the true crux of the matter. Ren could entirely see his point and indeed, if the roles were reversed, would likely be asking the same questions. "I will set the record straight only once, as I'm heartily sick of repeating myself. After the war, Shiirei was not in a financial state that would allow men to be able to work and support themselves. Arman—General Brahms—offered me a job in his home country because he feared what would happen to me if I stayed in Shiirei. No, we were not lovers then; not for another five years did our relationship go to that level. I went with him because he offered me the most viable choice for a living. I was discharged from the army; I had no orders from anyone, much less the Emperor. In fact, I don't think the Emperor even knew I'd left until months after the fact. Does that answer your—" allegations "—questions?"

"Yes," Alexandria stated firmly, glaring at both men and visibly daring them to ask anything else. "Yes, it does. Allow me to put this in a different perspective for both of you, since apparently you need it. After my marriage, I will be living in Aart. That means my future safety rests in this man's very capable hands. Now, in the interest of keeping me alive and well, can you at least communicate threats as you see them to Warden Brahms?"

Adolvsson at least appeared abashed. "Of course, Your Highness."

Showing little emotion, Rundstrom echoed him. "Of course, Your Highness."

Alexandria didn't believe them entirely; her expression said as much, and Ren had no doubt she'd be giving them earfuls later. She let it go for now. "Excellent. Then, to start with, exchange notes on the recent occurrence. That will give you a baseline of sorts. I really must go, I'm running late, but I'll come and speak with you all later about this."

Casually, Ren picked up his cooling tea and took a sip. It was quite delightful, although it made him dearly miss green tea for a moment. Its flavor reminded him of it. When the door closed behind her, he glanced at both men, taking them in. Would they obey to the strict letter of the law or the spirit in which it was meant? "Who would like to begin?"

28

It took three very long days of meetings before Ren and Arman could return to Castel-de-Haut. Alexandria and Galvath both urged them to stay, rest, but Ren couldn't sit still for more than those three days despite the luxury offered. He wanted this whole mess over and done with. Arman gave him no arguments, nor did O' Broín, all of them repacking and heading back, although they took the shorter way of Trader's Route.

When Zonhoven Palace finally did come back into view, Ren wanted to weep with gratitude. His arse felt like it had conformed to the saddle's shape some days ago, he had a fine layer of dust in every crevice of his skin, and he would literally kill someone to soak in a hot tub for an hour. Why couldn't open-air hot springs exist in Aart? Did he need to introduce this practice into the culture?

They arrived very late in the day, so he knew dinner had to have been served already, if not finished. Still, Ren barely considered going to his apartment first to freshen up. With the news he had, King Gerhard and Queen Eloise would want it sooner rather than later, and they wouldn't care that he stank of sweaty horse.

Fillmore greeted them with a wave as they breached the main gate. "Warden, General! You're back safely, then, good. Did the trip go as planned?"

"With an enemy ambush thrown in to spice things up," Ren joked tiredly. "Don't be alarmed, man, we made it through with minimal injuries, Prince Charles and Princess Alexandria are safely in Scovia, and we know who the culprits are. Send a runner ahead requesting an audience with our good monarchs, would you? Tell them I'll be in the Second Antechamber."

"Yes, sir," Fillmore saluted smartly before sprinting for the nearest runner's station.

They barely entered the main stable yard when Ren dropped out of the saddle with a grunt, so thoroughly sick of being in the saddle that he couldn't stand another minute of it. The inside of his legs felt chafed from the leather, and he had a raspberry that developed on his right ankle because of the stirrup. He didn't even want to think about riding for another month, at least. The other men also looked relieved to be on their own legs again. Turning to Robert, he hailed the man with a tired hand. "Robert, after you get the luggage sent up to our rooms, you have the next two days off. You've been an excellent sport this entire trip, thank you."

"Thank you, Master Ren," Robert responded with a thankful smile. "I'll be in the city visiting family if you need me."

"Understood. Go, go." Ren let his head loll about on his neck for a moment, stretching out the tension in his shoulders.

Leaning in against his shoulder, Arman murmured for his ears alone, "I'll give you a massage later."

"You are my favorite husband ever," Ren responded fervently.

Arman snorted, shoulders shaking in silent laughter. "You're easy to please."

"I can't refute that." Feeling that the day might end well, at least on a personal level, Ren felt strong enough to forge through the next hour that would surely be dismal. "Alright, let's get this over with."

With O' Broín tagging along behind, they got the usual greetings and welcome-backs from the staff as they entered the palace. Ren dredged up a tired smile for them, grateful that at this time of night, most of the staff had already gone home. He did not feel up to seeing anyone just then. The Second Antechamber sat near the main doors, and he ducked into it with a sense of mixed relief and dread. Now came the hard part.

The message had reached King Gerhard and Queen Eloise quickly, as both of them burst into the room a bare minute later. Ren gave them a bow, then winced. Owww, thighs. Cramping thighs.

"Your reports said Charles was injured. How badly?" Queen Eloise demanded, coming straight to him and pulling him up physically by the shoulders.

"Charles was a little injured, but nothing that will scar. He took a hit to his left thigh," Ren assured her, feeling bad when her shoulders slumped in relief.

"It could have been worse," King Gerhard concluded grimly.

"Indeed it could have been, and we're grateful it wasn't," O'Broín answered steadily. "I have a full report from Prince Charles and myself for you, Your Majesty, if you wish to see it."

"I certainly do, but answer a few questions for me," King Gerhard requested, heading for a chair and sinking into it. He waved the three men into chairs as well, which they took. "Alexandria reported to us that they caught the people responsible in Scovia. She was necessarily brief, but I'd like a few more details. Why? Why the attack?"

Ren answered this one. "There was a faction in Scovia that deems it taboo to marry outside of their own culture. They felt it unholy, in some way, for Princess Alexandria to marry Prince Charles."

"Enough to kill our son over it?" Queen Eloise demanded in horror. "Although considering what happened here…no, it still surprises me that such madness would be shared outside our own borders."

That did not make sense. Ren cocked his head, looking between the two of them. "I'm sorry, what?"

"General Cuyler," Arman guessed shrewdly. "His reason was the same?"

The king nodded wearily, his eyes closing briefly. "Yes. We've got men even now combing through all of his previous battles, all of his orders, and that's going to take a while, as he was in command of Our forces for several decades. But he's being rather frank over his reasons. He couldn't stand that we'd welcome a foreign general into our midst and put him in a position of power. Having Alexandria and Charles set to marry nearly drove him mad. The final nail in the coffin was when you married General Brahms. He helped the poisoner reach you after that happened. I don't think you would have been a target at all—the Scovians didn't care about you—but he put his hand in and made sure a poisoned letter reached you as well."

Part of Ren felt cold at this. A warm hand wrapped around his own and he looked up into a set of blue eyes as troubled as his own. For as many people that accepted them, that celebrated their marriage, there would always be at least one set dead against it. Ren knew he should feel blessed to only have that one, but in truth, he wished he didn't have to bear up against that hatred at all.

Queen Eloise came and put her hands on both of theirs, her expression sympathetic, but jaw set in a determined manner. "Don't you worry. He won't be able to come after you again. Gerhard and I have made sure of it."

Should he be alarmed...? "Why? What did you do?"

"General Cuyler has been executed," King Gerhard informed them, still sounding as if the day had been a decade long. "His family has been investigated, found to be most rotten from the core out, and the lot of them exiled. I found two exceptions, but they're stripped of rank and turned out. I won't have that family serving mine again."

Arman made a choked sound in the back of his throat. "The Cuyler family has been serving Aart for two centuries."

"And it only took one generation to ruin all of that exemplary service," the queen responded tartly. "Really, the gall of that family, to think they could rest on those laurels and cast judgments as they wished! It makes me fume."

Ren could tell his husband struggled with this, as well he should—he knew the family. But personally, he couldn't be more relieved. If he never got attacked again on his own home ground, it would be too soon.

"But who's in charge of Corfend Castle?" Arman asked, a trifle alarmed.

Ah. That was the problem. Ren should have expected his husband would leap first to defense and logistics. Corfend Castle sat on the coastline, one of their major sea defenses against any foreign navy, and it necessarily demanded a skilled warden. The Cuyler family had been manning it since nearly the founding of Aart. Ren could understand, even share, Arman's alarm as he wanted a good warden in the place as well.

Looking entirely too pleased with herself, Eloise announced, "We promoted Konrad to warden and stationed him there."

Ren and Arman stared at her in twin amazement. If Ren hadn't already been sitting, he would have had a close encounter with the floor. After that startled blink, Ren lit up in relief. "Did you really? Excellent, he'll be amazing at that."

"We know it," Queen Eloise assured him smugly, "after seeing what a good job he did here. I am sorry to take him away from you, Arman, truly, but we needed to send someone we could properly trust."

Arman lifted a hand to stay her, nodding reassuringly. "I wouldn't send anyone else. It means promoting everyone else in my chain of command, though."

"I know; we're prepared for that, but it's a little overdue anyway."

"Well. At least the business is behind us. I'm not sure if you still need all of this." Ren took out the sealed reports and witness statements from Charles, Alexandria, Arman, and himself, and silently handed them over. "Lord Ahearn in Bhodhsa still has the Mong in custody, if you need to pull him in for trial, but here are our witness statements."

"We'll handle it from here," Queen Eloise assured Ren, a visible tic in her jaw. "General O' Broín, you have been marvelous in Our time of need, and We thank you sincerely for it. Please feel free to stay and rest before you return to your country. I wish to send a token back with you to thank not only yourself but your king for lending us your services."

O' Broín undoubtedly heard that royal 'we' as clearly as the rest of them and gave her a deep bow. "I was happy to be of service, Your Majesties, and am thankful this ended as well as it did."

"As are we," King Gerhard assured him. "Ren, Brahms, you have the next few days to rest and recover before resuming your duties. Thank you very much for safeguarding my children."

"Our pleasure as well," Ren assured the king, speaking for both of them. Taking the dismissal, he bowed once more before leaving the room, relieved it was finally over. O' Broín followed them out and he gave them a tired smile. "I want to have dinner together before I leave."

"I do as well," Ren promised. "How long will you stay?"

"Four or five days, I think. It will take that long before I can face a saddle again. I'll send word when I'm feeling hungry." With a wave goodnight, he headed off toward the guest rooms.

Ren also felt a desperate need to be horizontal. Tired, with muscles cramping, he turned for his own apartment. Arman caught up with him in one long stride, catching his hand and lacing their fingers together. "Massage now?"

"It's like you read minds." Ren took in a deep breath and released it, feeling some of the stress of the past month leave him as he did so. "I think you're due one as well. I see you're not arguing that point. Alright, after you do me, I'll do you."

Arman gave him a lecherous waggle of the eyebrows. "Promise?"

Laughing, Ren demanded, "Where did you even learn how to do that? And no, I don't have that kind of energy tonight, I'm surprised you do."

"Tomorrow?" Arman suggested hopefully.

The idea of spending the entirety of the next day in bed with his husband held a ludicrous amount of appeal. "Absolutely. Tomorrow."

epilogue

Two months later

Ren now thoroughly regretted giving Eida free reign for their wedding. She had taken the chance to throw a final wedding for a son and ran with it like an unruly kitten with a ball of yarn. Even Anthony couldn't stop her. It had taken a full day alone to decorate the main hall with flowers, bolts of pastel fabrics, and candles on every available surface. Spending two weeks preparing for a single day, just in decorations, seemed ridiculous to Ren. Did it have to be this elaborate?

When Eida learned he knew how to sew, she'd shoved his wedding outfit in his hands and ordered him to make any necessary alterations. Ren happily accepted the job, as it gave him a chance to sit down for a few hours. He ensconced himself in the Morning Room, the only place not overrun with boxes of decorations, and enjoyed the sunlight streaming through the open windows.

The door clacked open and Arman strode through, for once not carrying something wedding related in his hands, just a simple letter. He had an interesting expression on his face that Ren couldn't quite decipher but it locked his interest. Setting the pants aside, he greeted, "What is it?"

"A request passed along through King Gerhard," Arman responded, crossing the room to hand him the letter.

Ren took it and tilted the letter toward the light to read it, his eyes scanning quickly over the page.

Ren,

I just received a request from Emperor Nakamura. Apparently the temporary fortifications built on Shiirei's northern shores, spe-

cifically Mizuno Harbor, were hit by fire a month ago and burned to the ground overnight. They're now frantic to build a new, more permanent fortress, but they've been in discussions for the past two years trying to decide on a design and failing. He's requested my aid, as he needs someone with experience in fortifications to help design something, and quickly. No one wants the northern shore to be without proper defenses for long.

To be honest, the only two people qualified to advise him in this matter are you and General Brahms. Your husband is an obvious choice, of course, but you've learned a great deal from him during your time in Hart, I think. And I need someone there who understands the culture, the language, and the political players to get the job done.

I hate to send you off, as this will take several months at the very least, but I can't afford another war in Shiirei. We, the world, cannot afford another war between the Moongs and Shiireins. If sending you and General Brahms will help safeguard Shiirei, then my convenience is a small price to pay.

I know that your marriage is set in three days, but will you please consider leaving for Shiirei after that? I don't wish to order you to return to that country, as I know how difficult being in Shiirei is for you, but I ask it of you.

Regards,
Gerhard of Hart

Ren read through the letter again, mind whirling as he thought of the logistics. Ten days to get there by ship, at least six months to design a proper fortification and get the base of it built, then another ten days home again—ye gods, they'd be gone at least seven months. More than likely a year. "Arman, you read this?"

"I did," he answered, coming to sit next to him, their thighs touching. "What do you think?"

Blowing out a breath, he let his head drop back, staring

sightlessly upward at the white plastered ceiling. "I think he's right. We can't afford to give the Mongs any sort of opening into Shiirei. They'd happily take it, and that will start another war, and Shiirei has barely recovered from the last one. Financially speaking, at least; I know they're still rebuilding. For that reason alone, we can't afford to decline. And a selfish part of me likes the idea, as I want to tell Takahiro about my marriage to you in person and see my family for a little while. But I know you hate long deployments, and it will take at least most of the year before we can justify returning home, likely more than that—"

Arman cut him off with a soft kiss, lips lingering there before retreating. Patience and affection danced in his eyes as he asked, "When do we leave?"

Looking into that face, Ren was struck again with the thought that there was literally nothing Arman would refuse him. If he knew it would make Ren happy, he'd do it. What had Ren done to deserve such unswerving devotion from this amazing man? Emotions welling up into this throat, he cleared it enough to speak. "You'll go with me. No arguments?"

"No arguments." As an afterthought, he tacked on seriously, "Although I won't take it well if they scorn our marriage."

"Try not to beat the whole country to a pulp," Ren discouraged, feeling the strangest urge to laugh. He could just picture the impending bloodbath.

"Nnh," Arman grunted in disagreement.

Ren had never said the words, but he felt them now and knew them to be perfectly true in every sense. Reaching up, he framed Arman's face with his hands. "I love you."

That blinding smile came to Arman's face, the one that melted Ren like snow in the sun, although it had a smugness to it this time. "I know."

"You've always known, I suppose, even when I doubted it myself." Ren pressed in close for a not-so-chaste kiss, pulling back before they could lose all control of themselves and make love right there on the couch. Eida had already walked in on them once. He'd hate to do that to her again.

"I did," Arman agreed, smugness growing. "Fortunately."

Yes, weren't they both fortunate that Arman could always see right through him? "You needn't be that smug about it. Now, about going to Shiirei—leave in five days?"

Arman thought about it, brows furrowing a little. "You think that's enough time?"

"I think that we don't dare linger any longer in Aart. If we give the Mongs too much of an opening, they'll take it."

Grunting in agreement, Arman darted in for another quick kiss before standing. "I'll send a reply to the king, then."

"Alright." Belatedly realizing his mistake, Ren called after his retreating back, "Say more than just 'We'll go.' That was not your agreeing face, Arman Brahms; man up, he needs more information than that."

Arman paused in the doorway, considered the matter, then offered seriously, "We'll leave in five days."

Resigned, Ren put the sewing aside completely, heading for the door. "Never mind, I'll write the response. Are you ever going to tell me why you hate words so much? Were you traumatized by too many vegetables as a child? You were tricked into swallowing a frog once and now you're cursed?"

Arman refused to rise to the bait of the ridiculous theories, just followed after Ren as he hunted for paper to write the reply with, glowing with perfect happiness.

author

AJ's mind is the sort that refuses to let her write one project at a time. Or even just one book a year. She normally writes fantasy under a different pen name, but her aforementioned mind couldn't help but want to write for the LGBTQ+ genre. Fortunately, her editor is completely on board with this plan.

In her spare time, AJ loves to devour books, eat way too much chocolate, and take regular trips. She's only been outside of the United States once, to Japan, and loved the experience so much that she firmly intends to see more of the world as soon as possible. Until then, she'll just research via Google Earth and write about the worlds in her own head.

You can find AJ either on Facebook or on her website at: ajsherwood.com

Printed in Great Britain
by Amazon